ChangelingPress.com

Dingo/Outlaw Duet

Harley Wylde

Dingo/Outlaw Duet

Harley Wylde

All rights reserved.
Copyright ©2020 Harley Wylde

ISBN: 9798553626570

Publisher:
Changeling Press LLC
315 N. Centre St.
Martinsburg, WV 25404
ChangelingPress.com

Printed in the U.S.A.

Editor: Crystal Esau
Cover Artist: Bryan Keller

The individual stories in this anthology have been previously released in E-Book format.

No part of this publication may be reproduced or shared by any electronic or mechanical means, including but not limited to reprinting, photocopying, or digital reproduction, without prior written permission from Changeling Press LLC.

This book contains sexually explicit scenes and adult language which some may find offensive and which is not appropriate for a young audience. Changeling Press books are for sale to adults, only, as defined by the laws of the country in which you made your purchase.

Table of Contents

Dingo (Devil's Fury MC 1) 4
   Chapter One 5
   Chapter Two 17
   Chapter Three 31
   Chapter Four 43
   Chapter Five 56
   Chapter Six 66
   Chapter Seven 81
   Chapter Eight 89
   Chapter Nine 102
   Chapter Ten 116
   Chapter Eleven 131
   Chapter Twelve 148
   Chapter Thirteen 159
   Epilogue 168
Outlaw (Devil's Fury MC 2) 175
   Chapter One 176
   Chapter Two 188
   Chapter Three 204
   Chapter Four 216
   Chapter Five 229
   Chapter Six 240
   Chapter Seven 254
   Chapter Eight 264
   Chapter Nine 276
   Chapter Ten 285
   Chapter Eleven 297
   Chapter Twelve 309
   Chapter Thirteen 319
   Epilogue 332
The Bad Boys Multiverse 337
Harley Wylde 338
Changeling Press E-Books 339

Dingo (Devil's Fury MC 1)
Harley Wylde

Meiling -- All I've ever known is pain. My life has been far from a fairy tale. No parents. No friends. Just an endless nightmare that I can't wake from. Until the day a man offered me his hand and promised to keep me safe. I've never trusted anyone before, but there's something about him. Maybe it's insane, but I know he won't hurt me, and when he puts his arms around me, for the first time in my life I feel loved.

Dingo -- I've always had a soft spot for women and kids in trouble. One look at Meiling, and I knew I had to protect her at any cost. The beautiful girl with the wounded soul. After all she's suffered, all I want is to make her smile, make her feel secure, and give her a chance to find happiness. But first, I need to take out the men and women responsible for hurting her. It might get ugly, and messy, but they don't call me Dingo for nothing. I'm a crazy bastard, and I won't stop until she's safe. I just didn't count on falling for her along the way.

Chapter One

Meiling

Glitter covered me from head to toe, as well as oil and other fluids I'd just as soon not contemplate. My latest client zipped his pants, gave me a wink, and walked out. He threw some money on the table by the door without a backward glance. *Asshole*. Then again, all men were as far as I was concerned.

My technical job title was exotic dancer for *The Ruby Slipper*. What that actually meant was stripping on stage, then whoring myself out after, and sometimes before. If I didn't keep the customers happy, then Trotter would kick my ass out -- right after he made sure he got reimbursed in any way he could for supposedly training me. That was a good one.

I didn't even bother putting back on the tiny scraps of cloth that couldn't remotely be considered clothing. I just grabbed the cash only to draw up short when I realized Trotter was leaning against the wall across from the door. The jackass. I handed the cash over, and when he gave me a twenty back -- an entire twenty dollars for letting my customer stick his dick up my ass -- I crumpled it in my fist and stormed off down the hall.

In the dressing room, I quickly washed off all the unpleasantness of my job and dressed in something sexy. Roxy, one of the other girls, had given me an excellent idea last night. I'd been a bit down, something I rarely let happen, and she'd suggested I find a protector. When I'd pointed out all the men in town frequented this place and were slimy, dear Rox said I needed to go visit the Devil's Fury.

Word around town was that they liked easy pussy, and well... I was about as easy as a woman could get. Not by choice, but that didn't matter much now. I'd learned I could endure anything because I was a survivor. Once I'd thought I'd get out of the system and my life would change. Fucking hysterical. The only difference was I'd gone from one pimp to another. Having my face all over the damn Internet on porn sites wasn't going to help me find my happy-ever-after. What upstanding citizen wanted a whore for a wife?

Tonight, things would be different. At the very least, I'd have a place to crash if I could convince one of the bikers to keep me all night, and maybe some food. I'd do just about anything for a hot meal and had, for that matter. I knew some of the girls stayed under lock and key with Trotter, but I'd honestly rather take my chances on the streets, and since I showed up every day for work, he didn't seem to mind. Although, there were times I had to wonder if he had someone watching me. It seemed like the type of dick move he'd make. Part of me wondered why he'd let me whore myself out for a place to sleep instead of making more money off me, but then, it seemed like the type of thing he would enjoy. Trotter liked it when we suffered, and humiliating us was always enjoyable for him.

I stepped out into the darkness and started walking. Didn't have a car, or a place to live. I'd only been out on my own about five months -- although time ran together, so it could have been longer, or shorter -- and so far I wasn't rockin' the adulting thing. Not that I'd had any role models, not ones who would show me more than how to sell my body, drugs, or do other illegal shit.

The new-ish compound for the bikers wasn't too terribly far from *The Ruby Slipper*, but walking in four-inch heels made it feel like I'd hiked for miles by the time I reached the gates. I had my large bag slung over my shoulder that had everything I owned, which wasn't much, and I fully expected the jackass at the gate to dig through it. He eyed it a moment, then raked me over with his gaze from head to toe.

"You here to party?" he asked.

I winked and gave him a sexy smirk. "You know it."

The guy chuckled and waved me through. I sashayed through the gates and up to the clubhouse. Music was pounding so loud I could hear it clearly through the closed door and windows. When I pushed my way inside, the thick smoke clinging to the air made my eyes sting as I squinted and tried to take it all in.

"Meiling?"

I blinked and jerked my head to the right, my jaw dropping as Beau came toward me, shoving his way through the crowd from the bar.

"What the hell are you doing here?" he asked, his tone a little harsh as he glanced around.

And just like that, the heart I'd thought I didn't have anymore broke in two. Of course. Me being here would embarrass him. If I'd known Beau was part of the Devil's Fury, I'd have kept my distance. The fact I hadn't seen him since he ran should have spoken volumes. I didn't blame him for not coming back for me. And I didn't blame him now for the frantic way he scanned the crowd, as if he were afraid someone would link the two of us together.

"I'm sorry, Beau. I didn't know you were part of the Devil's Fury. I wouldn't have come if..." I swallowed hard.

Beau jolted forward, and a large man leered down at me. "Prospect, you know the rules. Patched members get the pussy first. Go tend the bar."

The leather vest he wore said *Scorpion* on it. I assumed that was his name. He wasn't bad-looking, not that looks had ever mattered to me. But this was Beau's territory, and I needed to leave. Looked like I'd be sleeping in my usual spot after all.

"I was just leaving," I said.

"Really?" asked Scorpion. "Because it looked to me like you just arrived. And, honey, I have plans for you."

"I didn't know that..." I glanced at Beau. His jaw was clenched tight and his eyes were flashing. Yeah. I needed to leave. Seeing me would be a painful reminder to him. Thankfully, he'd never know what happened after he left. It was a secret I intended to take to my grave.

Without another word, I turned and walked out. I knew he wouldn't follow, wouldn't stop me. I didn't know about the other guy, but he probably didn't want some woman he had to chase down. I hurried through the gate and back onto the street, then made my way to the bridge on the outskirts of town. The laughter and crude jokes reached my ears long before the men came into view. I stopped, hesitating. I could still go down there, curl up and rest for a bit... for a cost.

My stomach cramped, and I forced myself to keep going. When Joe, an older man with cruel eyes, saw me, I knew exactly how my night would go. I sighed and kept moving until I was close enough for him to reach. His fingers always felt like they would crush my wrist when he jerked me against his body.

"There's Daddy's pretty little China girl. You going to be good tonight?"

I nodded and his grip tightened. I hid my wince, but barely. "Yes, Daddy. I'll be good."

He wasn't the first pervert to get off on being called that, and I knew he wouldn't be the last. It didn't help that my curves were understated and I looked younger than my age. Men always mistook me for being in high school. Some got off on that sort of thing, but there were times that was all that saved me.

He leered at me, yanking my shirt over my head to expose me to the others.

Would it ever end? I'd learned long ago not to fight. There was no point.

I was just their toy. A whore. I was trash and would always be trash. No one would ever see me any different.

Maybe I should have given up long ago.

He stripped me, then dragged me to the old, nasty mattress on the ground. Knowing what would happen next, I went somewhere else in my mind. Anywhere but here. I'd learned that trick long ago. Joe and his friends would grunt as they slammed their cocks into me one after the other, but when they were done, I'd get something hot to eat and get to sleep for a while without anyone else bothering me. It wasn't much different from getting fucked at work, except with these men, I didn't have to pretend to like it. They didn't care if my eyes went vacant. Then again, these sick fucks thought I was sixteen. I hadn't told them any different when they'd guessed my age. Something had told me they liked their girls less than legal. At least if they were fucking me, maybe the young girls would be safe from them.

After my belly was full of the nastiest stew I'd ever tasted, and I'd managed to sleep a few hours, I made my way back to *The Ruby Slipper* where I showered and started prepping for the lunch crowd. Just another day in hell.

I tried not think about Beau, but it was hard. He'd been such a huge part of my life for the two years we'd been at the foster home together. We'd suffered together and kept each other strong. Until the night he'd vanished. I'd always envied him his freedom and hoped he'd had a good life, that he was happy. It was too late for me.

"So, how was it?" Roxy asked, smiling wide as she started setting out her makeup.

"How was what?" I asked.

"You know. The biker place. Did they rock your world?"

I shrugged. "It didn't really look like my scene so I just stopped by for a second and then left."

No one knew about Beau. Or rather, they didn't realize he was part of Devil's Fury. I knew that my boss would probably recognize him. Beau hadn't changed all that much from when he'd been fifteen. I knew for a fact that Trotter had seen the videos my foster family had forced me to make. Beau had been locked in that same hell with me, and they'd paired us together. For all I knew, he'd told those bikers some lie about his past, and I hoped they never found out the truth. He deserved every happiness.

Roxy nudged me. "Looks like you made an impression on them."

My brow furrowed as I looked at her but she was staring at the dressing room doorway. Turning my head, I couldn't help it when my heart leapt at the sight of Beau. I wasn't in love with him. It wasn't that sort of reaction. More the love a sister had for her brother -- if that brother and sister had a very fucked-up childhood.

"Can we talk?" he asked.

"I have to get ready, Beau."

His gaze darted around the room before coming back to me. "You're better than this, Meiling."

That was fucking hysterical. "No. I'm not. And it's just Mei now."

Beau moved closer, not stopping until he was close enough I could feel the heat from his body. "Why are you here? I would have never gone there last night if I'd known you were part of that crowd. If you're worried I'll go back, I won't."

He reached out and laced our fingers together. And that was the thing that almost broke me. I stared at our hands, my throat tight with emotion as I remembered all the times he'd tried to comfort me. But I was toxic for Beau. He needed to keep far from me.

"You need to leave, Beau." I hoped like hell Trotter didn't come back here. If he saw Beau... "He knows, Beau. My boss... it's why he hired me."

His gaze shuttered, and his jaw went tight like last night. Yeah, I was a bad reminder of what we'd been through. For his sake, I needed him to walk away, and never come back. There was no place for me in Beau's life anymore. I didn't want to taint him with my presence. I was dirty, more than just dirty. The things I'd done...

"Leave, Beau. Forget you ever saw me." I shoved the pain down deep. "Forget you ever knew me."

"I can't do that, Mei. You know I can't. If I'd gone back..."

"Then you'd have been caught. I never blamed you, Beau. I still don't."

Beau tightened his hand on mine. "Come with me, Mei. Let me take you out of here."

I laughed, but there was nothing humorous about this situation. He didn't know, not all of it, and if he did, then he'd go home and bathe in disinfectant.

"This is where I belong."

"You're not a whore, Mei. That's what this place is. I don't care that it looks like a regular strip joint outside. Everyone knows if you want a piece of ass, you go to *The Ruby Slipper*, and that anything goes if the price is right. Is that how you want to live?"

I lifted my gaze to his and willed him to see the truth, the words I didn't dare speak. One day this life would kill me. I knew it. He knew it. It was a miracle I hadn't contracted something already that was incurable. Or maybe not so lucky. No one deserved to live this way.

"Leave, Beau. And forget me. It's for the best."

"I can't, Mei. Don't you understand? I never forgot. I hoped you'd gotten away, had a better life. But seeing you here, knowing that you're..." He pressed his lips together. Either unable or unwilling to say the words.

"A whore. You can say it, Beau. I'm a whore. A filthy, dirty piece of trash that men fuck any way they want as often as they want, one after the other, day after day, as long as they pay Trotter for the privilege."

"Mei, don't say that." He pulled me against him, wrapping me in his arms. It felt so good. Tears burned behind my eyelids as I breathed him in and let the comfort of his embrace soothe me. It was just a moment of weakness. It meant nothing. "Come with me. I'll help you find your place in the world. And don't tell me you already have because you're so much better than this."

I felt Roxy's presence behind me. "He's right. I don't know your story, Mei, but I can tell you've been through hell. If he wants to help save you, let him."

The sound of a lock twisting made me jolt and pull away from Beau. No. If Trotter got a good look at Beau, if he knew… I didn't know what would happen, but it couldn't be good. Trotter was evil all the way to his marrow. I'd seen plenty of men like him.

"Does the Devil's Fury need some women?" Trotter asked from behind Beau.

I gripped Beau's arms tight, not letting him face Trotter. I hoped he understood, that he'd remain still.

"Just one," Beau said. "This one."

Trotter got a gleam in his eye, and I could easily picture him rubbing his hands together like a cartoon villain.

"For all of you?" Trotter asked. "If you decide to take any video, I'd be interested in viewing it, maybe even purchasing it from you."

Beau's lip curled in a snarl, and I gripped him tighter before he could do something stupid.

"I'll let your club have her for the night. For a price, of course."

"Don't," I mouthed. He didn't want to make a deal with Trotter. It never ended well for anyone involved.

"I'm sure my Pres will pay whatever you ask. Send one of your men by the club. I need to take her with me so Griz can make sure she's the one he wants for the party. Gotta keep the Pres happy. You know how it is."

Trotter moved in closer and my heart started pounding, fear pulsing through me that Beau would be recognized. He might have his club's protection for now, but what if they knew about his past? Would they still stand by him?

"Very well. Take her for your President to inspect. He can be as… thorough as he'd like. But I expect to be compensated for her absence."

Beau waited for Trotter to leave, then he grabbed my bag and hauled me out of *The Ruby Slipper*. When I saw the motorcycle parked outside, a secret thrill went through me. I'd always wanted to ride on one. Beau shoved my bag into his saddlebags, then straddled the bike. Holding out his hand, he waited. I took a breath and let him help me onto the back, then I grabbed him and held on tight as the bike shot forward.

He went straight to the compound. When we reached the driveway, the gate was opened and he rolled through, pulling to a stop in front of the clubhouse. The very place I'd fled the previous night. Beau pulled my bag out and tossed it to me, then dragged me inside. He shoved me down onto a chair at a table surrounded by bikers. Suddenly, I worried that maybe it wasn't just that Beau didn't know me anymore, but I didn't know him either. What if he really did give me up to his club for the night?

"This the girl from last night?" an older man asked.

"Pres, this is Meiling. I told you about her last night. She prefers Mei now. We were in foster care together," Beau said.

"Beau, you can't bring strays home with you. We've got no place for someone like her unless she wants to be club pussy," the Pres said. "I thought I made that clear. And since she looks younger than my damn daughter, I don't think that would be wise."

"I'm eighteen," I said. "Not a kid. I haven't been a kid in a long fucking time."

Club pussy was better than being at Trotter's beck and call. Wasn't it? Would it mean I got to at least sleep here and get regular meals? Because it sounded like a decent trade to me. His eyebrow arched and he stared so hard I started to squirm.

"So you'd be okay spreading your legs or dropping to your knees for anyone in the club?" the Pres asked.

I shrugged a shoulder. Wasn't different from any other day of my life. "Sure. Do I get a place to sleep when I'm not getting fucked? Maybe some food?"

The man glowered at me and stood up. The others at the table were eyeing me like I was a tasty little treat, except Beau. He looked ready to murder me. I had a feeling things were about to go south. Why had Beau even brought me here? Now Trotter would be pissed when I went back empty-handed and he didn't get paid whatever huge fee he'd planned to charge. Which meant I'd spend most of the night trying to make up the loss.

"What if we demanded a demonstration?" one of them asked. I looked at the patches on his leather vest. *Demon -- Sgt. at Arms*.

"What kind of demonstration?" I asked.

He slid his chair back and beckoned to me. I stood up and moved around the table, dropping to my knees between his splayed thighs. At least these men were sexy. Even the older one. Things could be worse. Far worse.

I reached for his belt and started to work it free when a shadow fell over me. I hadn't even heard the man's booted steps. Looking up, my breath stalled in my lungs. He looked at least a decade older than me, maybe more, but the intensity of his gaze held me immobile. He held his hand out, palm up. He didn't demand I go with him, didn't yank me to my feet, just... offered his hand. I slid my palm against his, and he pulled me to my feet. The patch on his vest said *Dingo*. Like the wild dogs? He didn't seem that wild to me.

I could feel the gaze of everyone in the room as he drew me away from the table, and away from Demon. I didn't know where we were going, or why no one was protesting. He led me down the hall and pushed open a door before dragging me inside. I was expecting a bed, but the man in the white lab coat took me by surprise. Blinking up at Dingo, I wondered what the hell was going on.

He must have read the confusion on my face because he winked, the corner of his lips tipping up a little. "Relax, Meiling. Nothing bad is going to happen to you."

Too late, I wanted to say. Bad things had happened to me for a very long time. "It's just Mei. Not Meiling."

"Dr. Larkin is going to draw some blood and just check you over in general, make sure you're healthy."

And just like that the lead weight was back in my stomach. They wanted to ensure I was clean so I wouldn't give them anything. For a brief moment, I'd thought maybe... maybe someone would finally care. I was such an idiot.

Chapter Two

Dingo

I could tell by the way her eyes shuttered that she didn't understand. She thought we'd use her like a whore, the same as Trotter had done and probably countless others. Hell, with Demon's demonstration out there, I couldn't blame her. I'd been told they wanted the doc to check her out, and I knew Beau wanted to save her from the life she'd fallen into, but I hadn't realized the officers were going to be complete dicks to her beforehand. I knew that Beau was hiding something about his past, and it involved the beautiful woman standing next to me. I just didn't know what it was -- yet. Outlaw was trying to figure some shit out, with help from Wire and Shade, since his hands were shit now, and he couldn't handle a keyboard the way he used to.

"Pretty girl."

She tensed and the color drained from her face. I cut my gaze to the doc and saw he'd noticed as well. Someone had mistreated her, and evidently called her that. I'd make sure not to use it again.

"I'll need to conduct an exam, Mei, but if you'd feel more comfortable doing this in an office than a bedroom, it can be arranged," Dr. Larkin said.

She shocked the shit out of me when she started stripping out of her clothes, dropping them to the floor until she was bare. I tried not to look, but I'm fucking human, and she was the most beautiful woman I'd ever seen. The checked-out look in her eyes, however, told me that Mei wasn't with us anymore. She'd gone somewhere in her mind, likely expecting the worst. I wanted to kick the ass of every man who had ever hurt her.

I gently took her arm and led her to the bed, then helped her lie down. The fact her legs spread the second her back hit the mattress made my damn heart hurt. There was a sheen of tears in Dr. Larkin's eyes, but he worked hard to get control of himself and started the exam and took some blood. Maybe I should have left, but instead I held Mei's hand. Enough people had abandoned her already. I wouldn't be one of them.

"I need you to open your mouth, Mei. I'm going to swab the inside of your cheek," Dr. Larkin said.

Her jaw dropped and the doc took his sample.

"I should have the results back within two or three days," Dr. Larkin said.

He finished his exam, then told Mei she could get dressed, but she just lay there, unmoving. I dropped to a knee next to the bed and reached out to turn her chin toward me.

"Mei. You're not here to be the club's whore."

"It's what I am," she said. "It's all I'll ever be."

Her words broke my heart, but I could tell nothing I said would change her mind. I stroked my finger down her nose. "You're beautiful."

She didn't say anything, just stared. Her eyes were a startling green and her hair a fiery red, but the rest of her coloring and facial features screamed of Asian heritage. I didn't know if it was a parent or grandparent, but she was easily the most stunning woman I'd ever seen.

"Get dressed, Mei. I bet we can get Beau to make you a nice, juicy burger. With cheese and any toppings you want." I could see the spark of interest in her eyes. "Maybe some fries or onion rings on the side?"

Mei sat up, and I handed her the clothes from the floor and made a mental note of her sizes and to pick her up something better. In fact, I'd send out one of the Prospects to get something while she ate. No way would I let her parade around this place dressed like that. I knew my brothers wouldn't take what she didn't offer, but I didn't trust Mei to understand she wasn't here to spread her legs. If she offered, some of these assholes would gladly take her up on it, not realizing she didn't necessarily want them.

I took her hand and led her from the room, but I didn't take her back to the table with Demon and the others. I couldn't believe the Sergeant-at-Arms had been about to let her suck his dick, especially in front of everyone. What the fuck had he been thinking? Beau had come to us, asking for help. And Demon had pulled that shit? With Griz watching! I was so fucking pissed at them, but as officers, they outranked me. Unless it wasn't so much about Mei and more a test for Beau? It was possible, but I still didn't like it.

"Sit right here, sugar. I'll get Beau to make you something to eat."

Once I made sure she would stay put, and the others would remain at their table, I went to the bar and spoke to Beau. He kept watching Mei, concern for her evident by the haunted look in his eyes and his jerky motions. It was like he wanted to go to her, but wasn't sure how she'd take it. I'd never seen him like this before, and I wondered if there was something more between them. My stomach churned at the thought, which was ridiculous. I'd only laid eyes on her today. It wasn't like she was mine.

"Is she... will she be all right?" Beau asked. "I didn't know she was in that place."

"She's important to you," I said, hoping he'd offer up more information. All I knew was that he'd known Mei when he was younger. He hadn't given us much more when he'd asked the club for help getting her away from *The Ruby Slipper*.

"Mei's a part of my past, but I never should have left her. Maybe if I'd found a way to go back for her, then she wouldn't have ended up..." He clamped his mouth shut, but I heard the unspoken words just the same. *She wouldn't have become a prostitute.*

"Beau, you can't blame yourself. When you came here, you were just a kid. Hell, you're still a kid. If you'd gone after her, who's to say you wouldn't be the one whoring yourself out?" I said what I thought he needed to hear, but it made me wonder if he was right. Had Mei ended up where she did because he'd left her behind? What exactly had he been running from?

He winced and looked away, but it made me wonder about his life before he found the club. Or rather, before Grizzly found *him*. The old man did have a habit of bringing home strays. It's how he'd ended up with his daughters, and I had no doubt that when he ran across another kid who needed help, he'd bring them home too. It was just his way. It was part of what pissed me off so much about how they'd handled Mei when she'd arrived today, and why I'd intervened when I did. I still didn't know what the fuck was going on. I'd have never thought Demon or Grizzly would be like that with a woman in need.

"She needs food and clothes," I said. "You handle the food, and I'll send someone after some clothing for her."

"I don't think she has money for that kind of thing."

I narrowed my gaze at him. As if I'd expected her to pay? It was obvious she'd been struggling, and had taken a trip through hell along the way. I wasn't a big enough asshole to make her pay for stuff she hadn't even asked for, and the fact Beau thought that made me want to put my fist through his face, but I refrained -- for Mei's sake. I still didn't know how close the two of them had been, and I didn't want to upset her.

"Just make the fucking food, Prospect."

He dropped his gaze and gave a nod before heading into the kitchen. I motioned over another Prospect and reached for a piece of paper and pen from behind the bar. I scribbled Mei's sizes and made a few notes of specifically what I wanted him to purchase, then pulled out a wad of cash from my wallet.

"Henry, I want you to take this and buy what's on the list. Not a damn thing that isn't on there, understood?" I asked, handing him the money and paper.

"Got it, Dingo." He shifted from foot to foot. "Where do I take it once I get back?"

I looked over at Mei and then the officers at the table. The way Demon watched her had me clenching my teeth. No fucking way I was letting her out of my sight. Well, not unless they ordered me to hand her over, and even then, I wasn't sure I'd be able to. She was young and defenseless. Some caveman piece of me demanded that I beat my chest and warn the others off, let them know she was mine. Except she wasn't.

"Bring it to my place," I said.

"You got it."

He rushed off and I returned to Mei. I slowly eased down into the chair beside her, not wanting to startle her. After all that she'd survived, I knew she had to have a steel spine, but at the same time she seemed a bit fragile. Her gaze stayed on her hands, which were twisting in her lap. I wished there was some way that I could ease her concerns, but I knew she wouldn't believe me. It was clear that no one had ever helped her without expecting something in return, if they'd bothered to help her at all.

"How old are you?" I asked, a little worried that I was fascinated with an underage girl instead of a woman. My sister, Jordan, would kick my ass if that were the case.

"How old do you want me to be?" she asked.

"No games, Mei. I'm being serious. I need to know if you're still a kid or a woman fully grown."

"Eighteen," she said.

I tried to hide my wince. I was over a decade older than her. Hell, I was nearly two decades older. Shit. She was young enough to be my kid, not that I thought of her like that. Mei might have understated curves, but she definitely looked all woman. To me anyway, but I could understand if people thought she was younger. I didn't think the club would have an issue with it, if I wanted to pursue something with Mei, but I didn't think she'd be interested. As beautiful as she was, I didn't doubt for a second any guy in this club would fall at her feet.

Movement behind the bar caught my attention and I saw Beau heading our way with a plate of food and a drink for Mei. He set both down in front of her, then took a step back. He shoved his hands into his pockets and rocked back on his heels, but he didn't leave. I didn't know if he was waiting for her to acknowledge him, or if there was something on his mind.

"I didn't know if you still disliked mayo so I left it off," he said. "And you used to complain about onion breath so I figured you'd prefer fries."

Mei stared at the food with longing, and I gave Beau a nod to get lost. He walked off, but not without casting a few glances back at Mei. She ignored him, but she also didn't reach for her food. I didn't know for certain what was holding her back, but I reached for a fry and popped it into my mouth.

"Promise it's not poisoned. You can eat, Mei."

Her hand trembled as she reached for the fries and I eyed the burger, which was monstrous. I got up to retrieve a fork and knife from the bar and came back. Sitting down, I reached over and sliced the burger in half, hoping it would be easier for her to handle. She watched my every move, but I noticed she was still shoving fries into her mouth. On the off chance she was worried about the burger, I cut off a bite and ate it, showing her it was safe.

"No one here will hurt you, Mei."

She tensed and her gaze cut toward the table with the officers and I knew she was thinking about Demon and his demand. The fucker. I reached for her hand, giving it a slight squeeze.

"Hey, not even Demon will hurt you. None of us will, Mei. You're safe."

"No such thing," she said so softly I barely heard her. "Safety is an illusion."

Not anymore. Not on my watch. I didn't bother telling her that because it was obvious she wouldn't believe me. My phone vibrated in my pocket and I pulled it out, trying to contain the growl that rose in my throat when I read the message from Dr. Larkin.

Running tests. Semen present from multiple men.

I clenched my phone so hard I worried it might crack. I didn't know if what he'd discovered was from her job or if someone had taken advantage of her. Either way, it pissed me off that those men had used her like that. Maybe the club girls weren't much different, but at least they chose to be here. Mei had been backed against a wall with nowhere else to go. If she'd had the choice, I had a feeling she'd have walked away from *The Ruby Slipper* and done just about anything else.

Anemic. Vitamin deficient. Definitely malnourished.

I read each text as they came through. The more I learned, the more determined I became to take care of Mei. She didn't quite finish her food, but the way she shoved the plate away told me she was finished. We kept some to-go boxes behind the bar in case any of the club wanted to take some food home with them. I got up to retrieve one, then boxed up Mei's food. Reaching for her hand, I helped her stand.

"I was going to ask where you wanted to stay tonight, but I'm not going to give you a choice. Maybe that makes me an asshole, but I don't trust these fuckers not to ask you for sexual favors, and you seem intent on giving them whatever they want."

She stared at the toes of her shoes.

"Mei, I'm taking you home with me, but I don't expect anything from you. Do you understand? I'm not taking you with me for sex, but to keep you safe."

Her lower lip trembled and she gave a slight nod. I led her past the other tables, stopping only long enough to grab her bag where she'd dropped it. We went past the officers, and out the door. I wasn't about to put her on the back of my bike with her spiked heels and too-short dress. One of the club trucks was parked nearby, and I knew the keys would be tucked under the visor. I helped her into the vehicle, then got behind the wheel, flipping the visor down so the keys would drop into my hand.

I had a small house toward the back of the compound, which was still an improvement over the duplexes. Most of those were used for visitors these days. When we pulled into my gravel drive, I shut off the engine and got out. Mei didn't wait for me this time and stepped out on her own. I wondered what she thought of the place. It was white clapboard with black shutters and a red door. Adalia, Badger's woman, had chosen the colors, but I rather liked them. It was just a two-bedroom, two-bath bungalow, but there was plenty of space inside.

"Come on, Mei. I'll show you to the guest room. It's nothing fancy, but my sister said the bed is comfortable."

I led the way inside and flipped on the lights when I entered the house. Unlike the bigger homes, I didn't have a front entry or hall. The door opened into the living room, which was on the small side but sufficient for my needs. There was an eat-in kitchen through an archway, and a large sunroom to the right. The bedrooms and bathrooms were off a short hallway on the left.

"Bedroom and bathroom are this way." I made sure she was following me before I went into the guest room, turning on the ceiling light. On the off chance my sister ever dropped in, I made sure the sheets were cleaned at least every other week so they didn't smell too stale. The bed was a queen-size and there was a short dresser on the opposite wall, as well as a nightstand next to the bed. It wasn't much, but Jordan insisted the room felt cozy. She'd picked out the patchwork quilt in jewel tones and blue curtains hung from the windows on either side of the bed. I even had a cot for Lanie so she could camp out in the sunroom.

Mei hovered in the hallway, eyeing the other two doors.

I pointed to the one closest to her. "That's the bathroom. I'm afraid it isn't adjoined to your room, but you'll have it all to yourself. The other door is my bedroom, and I have a private bath in there."

She shifted from foot to foot before coming closer. When she stepped into the bedroom, I moved into the hall. The way she'd stripped down at the clubhouse made it clear she expected us to take advantage of her, to use her the way others had. She was like a skittish puppy who had been kicked once too often, but I hoped that eventually she'd realize she was safe here.

"If you need something to sleep in, you can use one of my T-shirts. The water takes a second to heat up, but you're welcome to take a shower or soak in the tub. My sister always leaves a few things here so you won't have to worry about smelling like a guy." I smiled, hoping to set her at ease. "Just hope you like gingerbread or cinnamon since those are the last scents she left over here."

"Will you be joining me?" she asked.

I shook my head and backed up another step. "No, Mei. You can stay in there until the water runs cold if you'd like. I want you to be comfortable here. There's not a bunch of stuff in the kitchen, but you can have anything in there. I mostly keep beer and bottled water stocked, but there's some soda too."

Her lips turned down at the corners and her brow furrowed as she looked around the room before holding my gaze. "I don't understand. How am I supposed to pay for sleeping here?"

I rubbed a hand over my chest to fight the ache building there. Damn. If that didn't speak volumes about her interactions with men so far, I didn't know what would. Had no one ever done anything for her just to be nice? My guess was a big fat no.

"You don't have to pay to stay here, Mei. I want to help you. There's a lock on the inside of the bedroom door and same for the bathroom. You can lock them if it makes you feel safer." I wouldn't tell her that I could easily pick those locks, but I needed her to understand she had nothing to fear from me. I'd rather rip off my arm than hurt her.

She let her bag fall to the floor, but she stood unmoving in the middle of the room. I'd never seen someone look so lost before. I clenched my hands into fists so I wouldn't reach for her. If anyone had ever needed a hug, it was Mei, but I had no doubt she'd misconstrue the act as me trying to get her to drop her panties.

"You don't know who I am, do you?" she asked, her voice whisper soft. "You haven't seen them."

"Seen what?" I asked.

"The videos."

Videos? Was Trotter filming his girls now to make an extra buck? Wouldn't surprise me, but it was the first I'd heard of it. As long as they were of age and consenting, there wasn't much anyone could do about it. But if he'd crossed a line, which it seemed he'd done with Mei, then that was different. It was clear she hadn't chosen this way of life. Were the others at *The Ruby Slipper* the same? Or were they there because they wanted to be? While I couldn't understand anyone choosing that way of life, I wasn't about to look down on someone who enjoyed that sort of thing. I'd heard some women got off on the power of stripping, watching men fall at their feet. The woman in front of me wasn't one of those, though, that much was clear.

"You have no idea what I'm talking about," she said, her eyes going slightly wide.

"If you want to tell me, you can, but it's not necessary. Your past is exactly that, Mei. The past. It doesn't define who you are. I don't know if you've ever read Robert Frost, but consider this your path not taken. The way you've had to live up to now can change, if you want it to."

She gave a snort of laughter and surveyed the room again. "I've heard that before. Usually it means I'm on my back, or worse, within hours. Like Trotter told Beau, I can handle several men at once… if that's what the club needs."

Fury rolled through me. Not at her, but at everything that she'd been through, the way men had treated her to this point. No, I wasn't a saint. I'd had more than my share of women, but they'd all been willing. Then again, the men who paid for Mei's time thought she was willing too. The thought that I'd been with anyone who hadn't been completely into it made me a bit nauseated. I'd been raised to respect women, to protect them. Maybe my current way of life made it seem like I was like the others she'd known, but I'd always prided myself on making sure the women in my life knew the score up front.

"Not this time, Mei. You're free, beautiful. You don't have to stay if you don't want to. I'm not paying for services rendered, or asking you to spread your legs for me or anyone else. I only want to help, to give you a safe place to figure things out." I couldn't seem to stop myself from getting closer to her. She held perfectly still as I reached out and ran my fingers through her silky hair. "I wish that I could track down every man who had ever hurt you. Then I'd make them suffer, make them pay for everything done to you, over and over, until they were begging for mercy."

She swallowed audibly and leaned into my touch, her gaze locked on mine. I saw the moment she realized that I meant everything I said. The darkness in her eyes lifted slightly, and there was a spark of hope. Before I did something stupid, like kiss her, I backed out of the room and went back to the living room. Hopefully, her new clothes and shoes would arrive soon.

I heard her step into the hallway and pause. "Did you mean it when you said I could borrow a shirt for tonight?"

I closed my eyes and nodded, not trusting myself to go near her. "Second drawer in my dresser. You're welcome to use any of the shirts you want. I won't move from this spot until you're in the bathroom with the door locked."

"Thank you."

My heart pounded as I listened to her head into my room, heard the dresser drawer slide open and the sound of her rummaging through my shirts, then waited for the bathroom door to shut and the lock to click. Only then did I relax and remember to breathe. Shit. I hadn't told her where anything was kept. I edged closer to the hall without going too close to the bathroom and yelled out to her. "Towels are in the cabinet behind the door and Jordan's bath stuff should still be on the side of the tub. Use anything in there you want. New toothbrushes are in the drawer under the sink."

I didn't wait to listen to her response, putting more distance between us. I flipped on the TV and found a movie I usually enjoyed, but my mind was elsewhere. What had sent Mei to *The Ruby Slipper*? Beau had said that he knew her when he was in the system, so she'd been a foster kid, but there were supposed to be programs in place to help them when they aged out. Had Mei just fallen through the cracks, or had something else happened? I wanted to know, and while Outlaw had been tasked to find out the connection between Mei and Beau, I didn't know exactly how deep he would dig. Getting information on Mei would be easy enough, but it felt like taking that route would mean I was breaking her trust. If Outlaw found anything, I'd wait and hear it with everyone else, if Grizzly decided we needed to know.

If the club wanted to know more about her, I'd let them interfere without my help. Mei needed someone who was on her side, had her best interests at heart, and didn't care about what brought her here. Well, it wasn't that I didn't care, but more that I was willing to wait on her to share when she was ready. Whatever trouble came to the gates because she was here, I'd handle it. No one was taking her out of here unless she wanted to leave with them.

Trotter's men hadn't shown for payment yet, that I knew of, but Grizzly had given the order to throw some cash at them and make them leave Mei in our care. I figured we had until morning before things went to shit and Trotter demanded we return her to *The Ruby Slipper*.

Chapter Three

Meiling

I spent the first five minutes in the shower watching the bathroom door. The knob never turned, and I didn't hear footsteps near the door. It seemed too good to be true. He had to want something in return, right? All men did. Even Beau had left me behind, and clearly hadn't wanted me here when I came by last night. I didn't know why he'd changed his mind, and I was too scared to ask. Had he told them I'd be a good little whore for all of them? The Beau I'd run into last night wasn't the same one I'd known four years ago.

Picking up the shampoo, I sniffed it, then smiled. Dingo was right. It did smell like cinnamon. I lathered my hair, then rinsed and conditioned it. I couldn't remember ever having a simple luxury like conditioner before, and it felt like heaven getting to use scented products. My foster parents hadn't cared what I smelled like, as long as I performed for them. And at *The Ruby Slipper*, those men couldn't care less if I was even clean. Several had just seemed happy I had all my teeth. Since several of the girls working there had what I'd heard called meth-mouth, I could understand. Their teeth were rotting or missing from drug abuse.

There was a pink razor on the side of the tub that seemed sharp enough. I hoped his sister wouldn't mind me borrowing her stuff. I scrubbed my body and shaved everywhere important, then rinsed my hair again. It had been so long since I'd felt this clean I almost wanted to cry. After I shut off the water, I stood for a moment, just listening. Peering around the curtain, I saw the door was still closed and locked, so I stepped out onto the bathmat and dried with the thick towel I'd found in the cabinet, wrapping a smaller one around my hair.

I'd also spotted some lotion in the cabinet and used it before brushing my teeth and finger-combing my hair. There was a brush in the cabinet too, but I didn't want to use it. The long hairs wrapped around the bristles made me believe it also belonged to his sister, and I'd used enough of her stuff already. There was a brush in my bag back in the bedroom. I should have brought my stuff in here with me.

I slipped Dingo's shirt over my head, smoothing it as it fell to my knees. Even though I didn't have on panties underneath, it was still the most covered I'd been for as long as I could remember. I didn't see a hamper so I tossed the towels over the top of the shower so they would dry, then cautiously opened the bathroom door. I could hear the TV going and saw a pair of booted feet propped on the coffee table, even though I couldn't see the rest of him. Scurrying into my room, I shut the door, then stared in amazement.

Sacks. Lots of sacks. They were just from one of those twenty-four-hour stores, but as I peeked into each one, I saw clothes, shoes, and other things that had to be for me. They were all in my size, and Dingo hadn't mentioned his sister would be visiting. Since they were in the room he'd said I could use, it had to mean they were mine, right? Tears gathered in my eyes. I ripped into the package of panties and slipped on a pair, loving the way they actually covered my ass. The only two pair I owned were thongs and I hated them. The bras were a soft material that wasn't the least bit transparent, and the clothes…

A sob built in my throat, but I tried so hard to hold it in. Jeans, modest-looking shirts, and shoes that were made for comfort and not to entice men. I lost the battle and tears streaked my cheeks as I cried so hard my throat and chest hurt. Booted steps came running toward the room, and Dingo must have slid to a stop just outside. He didn't barge in, at least not right away. As my cries grew louder, he pushed the door open and rushed inside.

"Mei? Honey, what's wrong?" He dropped to his knees next to me.

"I-I-I..." I couldn't even tell him why I was crying. I just gestured to the bags, then threw my arms around him and held on.

Dingo held me, letting me soak his shirt with my tears, and he gently rubbed my back. Eventually, I got myself under control and took a few shuddering breaths. He rested his cheek on the top of my head, just holding me. Not once did his hands try to roam somewhere inappropriate. Beau was the last person to hold me like this, and I'd only been fourteen. I hadn't realized until now just how much I missed it. My foster dad's version of affection was vastly different.

"When's the last time someone bought something for you?" he asked.

"My foster parents gave me only what they were required to purchase, and the clothes were never like this. No one's ever been this nice to me."

"They aren't much, Mei, but I wanted to make sure you had enough clothes to get by for at least a few days. You're welcome to use the washer and dryer off the kitchen whenever you need to, and we can always get a few more outfits."

I fisted his shirt and lifted my head. The concern in his eyes, the gentle way he held me, it was all overwhelming. Men had taken what they wanted from me ever since I'd hit puberty. Not once had I ever kissed someone just because I wanted to, but right now, this very moment, I wanted to kiss Dingo. Before I could second-guess myself, I pressed my lips to his. He tensed and drew back, his gaze searching.

"Mei, you don't have to do that."

"I know," I said. "I did it because I wanted to."

There was a moment of hesitation in the way he held himself, the look in his eyes, and then he leaned toward me. This time *he* kissed *me*. Dingo threaded his fingers into my hair and held me as his mouth devoured mine. I melted against him, feeling desired for the first time in my life. Cherished. Men had wanted me before, but they'd wanted to take not give.

Dingo broke the kiss with a groan and pulled away. "Mei, no. We need to stop. I didn't come in for this, didn't bring you to my home so I could take advantage of you."

"You aren't."

He caressed my cheek, his gaze holding mine. "You should get some sleep. I know it's still a bit early in the day, but I'm guessing you haven't had a chance to rest much. I'll come get you when it's time to eat."

I nodded and reluctantly turned from him. Crawling under the covers, I lay with my back to the door and tried not to feel rejected. Part of me was convinced he was trying to be a nice guy and do the right thing, but the other part had to wonder if he saw me as dirty. Yes, I'd just showered, but I'd been used by countless men. I wasn't exactly the type of woman you took home to meet your mom, or the kind you kept forever. He was trying to do the right thing and offer me a safe haven, which I appreciated, but it felt like maybe I wasn't really worthy of being here with him.

I waited for him to leave, but he didn't move. I turned over to face him and the look on his face made me start crying again. I couldn't remember being this emotional since I was a kid. I'd locked all that down years ago, or so I'd thought. Dingo came closer and sat on the edge of the bed, reaching for my hand.

"I want you, Mei. I won't do you the disservice of lying to you about it. But that doesn't mean I'm going to act on those desires. That's not what you need right now. Don't think for a second that I stopped because I don't want you."

"I feel out of place," I admitted. "I don't know what to say or do, or how to act."

"Just be you, Mei. There are no expectations, at all. The only thing I want is for you to feel safe and comfortable while you're here."

"*While* I'm here." My lips twisted. "Because eventually you'll want me to go."

He laced his fingers with mine and tightened his hold on me. "No, but I don't want you to think you have no other options. Your life has barely started. I'm quite a bit older than you and kind of set in my ways. There's an entire world out there for you to explore, once you get your feet under you. I won't stand in your way of finding happiness."

Before I could say anything else, he lifted my hand and kissed it, then stood and walked out of the bedroom. My skin tingled where his lips had touched me. I didn't know what to make of Dingo. He was the first man to ever make me crave someone's touch. I just wasn't sure if that was a good thing or not. He seemed nice, but what if it was all a lie? What did I know about him, or anyone else here for that matter? Even Beau was a stranger to me now.

I tried to sleep, but my mind was leaping from one fear to another. There was a roof over my head and food in my belly, which was a vast improvement, but I still worried there was a catch. Why would he bring me here, give me all these things, if he didn't want something in return? People didn't do nice things without there being a price.

I also worried what would happen if they found out about Beau's past. The way he'd looked at me last night, the furtive glances to see if anyone noticed us, was enough to tell me that he hadn't told them what we'd been through. I wouldn't tell anyone, but someone would eventually figure out who I was, which meant they'd find out about Beau too. I didn't know what would happen to him. Would his club be angry? Kick him out? Or do something even worse to him?

My stomach knotted and I felt the burn in my throat that meant I was seconds from throwing up. I tossed the covers off me and ran for the bathroom, hitting my knees just seconds before the hamburger and fries came back up. Snot ran from my nose and my eyes watered as I heaved until there was nothing left. I heard the sink running and blinked up at Dingo. He came closer, placing a cold wet cloth on the back of my neck.

"My mom always insisted this helped," he said. "Too much food at once?"

"Maybe," I said, my voice coming out more like a croak. My throat was raw and ached now.

"I was watching a movie in the living room. You're welcome to join me."

I nodded and got to my feet. Dingo placed his hand at my waist and reached over to flush the toilet, then handed me a toothbrush. I got rid of the icky taste in my mouth, blew my nose and washed my hands, then followed him into the living room. He motioned for me to sit on the couch before he walked out. I could hear noises in the kitchen and he returned with a bottle of water for me and a beer for him.

I tried not to tense, or stare at the beer in his hand, but alcohol never proved to be a good addition. The men at *The Ruby Slipper* always became uncontrollable once they were drunk, and my foster parents had been even worse. Logically, I knew that not everyone who drank became mean or even drank to excess. That didn't stop me from feeling apprehensive, though. Over a decade of seeing alcohol change people for the worse was a hard thing to overcome. Other than my first foster home, the others were mostly tolerable, but I'd learned that the men often drank and bad things could happen. Not as bad as what I suffered at the last house, but enough to make me apprehensive when men drank.

He only took three swallows before he set the bottle down and didn't reach for it again. I kept casting furtive glances his way, but the drink was sweating and untouched even ten minutes later. Then another twenty passed and he still didn't drink more of it. When I looked again, he was staring at me, an eyebrow arched almost as if he were challenging me.

"If it bothers you, all you had to do was say something, Mei."

I stared at the bottle a moment. "Bad things happen when alcohol is involved."

"I have one or two beers a day, on average, just to unwind and relax. It's been a while since I bothered drinking until I couldn't walk straight. Even when we have parties, I drink in moderation. But I don't have to have it, Mei. If it makes you uncomfortable, then I won't drink around you."

I dropped my gaze to my lap. "It's your house, Dingo. You can drink if you want."

The silence stretched until I started to fidget, worrying if I'd angered him but too scared to look up and see his reaction. Sometimes it was better not knowing when a man was about to strike. My heart started to pound and my palms grew slick. After another few minutes, I couldn't stand it another second. I looked up and found him watching me.

"Trotter will come for you tomorrow. I'm sure he'll be at the gates once he realizes we haven't sent you back yet."

I sank my teeth into my lip to keep from whimpering like a pathetic puppy.

Dingo leaned forward, bracing his arms on his knees. "Mei, I'm not letting him take you, but I need to know what I'm up against. What kind of hold does he have on you?"

It wasn't so much a hold he had over me, other than a lack of anywhere else to go, but he knew far too much about me. I couldn't tell Dingo. Not because of the shame I would feel -- I was used to that -- but because it meant I'd have to tell him about Beau. That wasn't my secret to tell. If Trotter came and I hadn't told them about my past, would they make me leave? Despite my uncertainty over Dingo's intentions, this was the safest I'd ever felt. I didn't want to go, especially not back to *The Ruby Slipper*. What could I tell him that would appease his curiosity without giving everything away?

"My foster parents weren't the nicest people. They're friends with Trotter. When I aged out of the system, they sent me to him. He made it sound simple enough, being a stripper, and said I'd earn good money." My fingers knotted in my lap as I thought about my first day of what I'd thought would be freedom. "If you don't keep the clients happy, whatever it takes, then Trotter beats you and has been known to force drugs into your system. He has… unique ways of punishing the girls who refuse to fall in line."

"Unique how?" Dingo asked.

"He has a special room for punishments. There's a table with restraints, and he…" I took a breath. It was harder to talk about everything than I'd thought. Well, not *everything* but the parts I was willing to share. The parts that didn't concern Beau. "He and his bouncers fuck whoever is being punished, over and over, however they want while she's helpless to fight back."

Dingo growled. "You mean they rape the woman being punished."

I gave a jerky nod.

"Look at me, Mei." I lifted my gaze and held his. "Did he ever punish you that way?"

"Once. When he realized he couldn't break me, he would just beat me into compliance."

Dingo shot to his feet and paced the room. "He's a fucking dead man! I'm going to tear him apart, one piece at a time. Fucking asshole!"

I blinked and watched as he furiously stormed across the room, then back again, over and over. He was angry. On my behalf? There was an odd feeling in my chest as I listened to him threaten Trotter. I couldn't remember anyone ever standing up for me. Even Beau hadn't, but then he'd just been a kid too.

Old enough to run away, but he wouldn't have stood a chance against our foster dad.

It was strange to have someone want to protect me. It's what I'd always wanted, why I'd even come to the compound in the first place. I'd hoped they would want to keep me, feed me, and make sure Trotter kept his distance. But deep down, I'd never thought it would actually work out. Then I'd seen Beau and everything had unraveled even faster. To know that Dingo felt that way, that he wanted to defend me against someone like Trotter, it warmed my heart and gave me hope that maybe not everyone in the world was as rotten as the ones I'd met so far.

He came to a sudden stop. "I need to let the others know. The Pres will do whatever it takes to keep you away from Trotter, but he needs to know what he's fighting for. I swear to you, Mei, that you'll be avenged and Trotter will never hurt you again."

"Wait." I stood. "If you tell him, then... I don't want Beau to find out. He can't know what happened to me. Promise me, Dingo!"

"What's Beau to you, Mei? It's obvious the two of you share a connection. Is he just a friend? A brother? Something more?"

"He's nothing, not anymore."

He folded his arms over his chest. "Not anymore, but at some point he meant something to you."

I shrugged a shoulder, not knowing how to explain it. Beau and I were in hell together, and we tried to keep each other sane. Then he'd left. My mind wandered back to that day, when the foster parents had discovered he was gone and wasn't coming back. They'd been so angry. Furious. And they'd taken it out on me every day for the rest of the time I was in the system, made sure I understood my place, that I was nothing. Less than nothing. I was just something to be used and tossed away.

"Mei." I jolted and realized that Dingo was nearly toe to toe with me, his gaze concerned. "Where'd you go just now?"

"Nowhere good."

"Beau was in foster care with you, wasn't he?" Dingo asked. "And when he left, you were defenseless."

"Something like that. I mean, yes, he was in foster care with me and yes, he did leave me behind when he ran away. It wasn't like he could take me with him. He was only fifteen at the time. I understood."

"I'm glad you do." His jaw tensed. "He left you to be abused, to be raped. Maybe you're okay with that, but I sure the fuck am not. I don't give a shit if he was a fifteen-year-old kid. Once Griz found him and brought him here, he could have told us about you. Someone would have come for you, given you a safe place to live, a chance to have a happy life. Fucking hell!"

The last was a near roar and I winced. He made a lot of good points, but like he'd said before, the past was the past. It wasn't like I could go back in time and change things, and neither could Beau. I'd survived and that was all that mattered. And now I was here, with Dingo, and things were finally looking up. I just didn't know how to ask to stay... indefinitely. He seemed to think I'd want to leave in the future, but why would I? The bed he'd given me was the softest I'd ever felt. I had hot water, good food, and even more... a man who was gentle and kind toward me. He worried over me, wanted me to be happy. I'd be stupid to want to leave all that behind, to leave *him*.

Eighteen was just a number. My birth certificate might say that's how old I was, but the things I'd been through made me grow up fast. By the time I was fourteen, I'd suffered more than most people ever did in their entire lives, even if they lived to be ninety. I figured that made me a lot closer to Dingo's age than he realized.

"Stay in the house, Mei, and don't open the door for anyone. I'll be back soon, but I need to see the Pres and fill him in." Dingo reached for me, cupping my cheek. There was only a moment's hesitation before his lips brushed mine. The kiss was fleeting, but one I felt all the way to my soul. And then he was rushing out the door, but not before locking the knob.

I just hoped that all hell wouldn't break loose when he told them what I'd shared, and that Beau didn't hear any of it.

Chapter Four

Dingo

Fucking Beau! I wanted to beat the shit out of that kid. He'd left her, and the things she'd been through... I ran a hand through my hair. I knew she hadn't told me everything, but I could fill in enough of the gaps to get a rather gruesome picture of her childhood, and even her recent years. Someone here would have given Mei a home, possibly even the Pres since he liked to bring home kids in need. But no, that little shit hadn't said a word about her.

I threw open the clubhouse doors and stormed inside. I tried to convince myself to keep walking, to go find Griz, but Beau was still behind the bar. It was like a red haze had settled over me and the monster inside wouldn't be appeased until I'd spilled that fucker's blood. With a roar, I launched myself toward him, dragging his ass over the bar. He hadn't even hit the ground good before I started pounding on him.

"You. Fucking. Left. Her!" My fist connected with his jaw, then his ribs. "She was a kid! Helpless!"

Beau didn't put up much of a defense, verbal or otherwise. Someone tried to pull me off him, but I wasn't letting him go. He needed to pay! I landed four more blows before more of my brothers came forward and hauled me away from him.

"What the fuck is going on?" Demon demanded. "Why are you trying to kill Beau?"

"He left her. Just fucking ask him! He was in foster care with Mei and he ran away. When Griz brought him here, he never said a damn word to us about her. We could have saved her!"

I was shaking and felt moisture on my cheeks. The fact I was crying in front of my brothers was what finally snapped me out of it. I shrugged them off and wiped a hand down my face.

"Saved her from what?" Beau asked, his voice a little garbled from the swelling in his lip.

"From being raped." I turned and walked off, unable to even look at him another second. We might not walk on the right side of the law, but there were rules we followed. The first was to never harm a woman. Beau knew that, and had to have known that Mei would pay the price when he left. Yet he'd never sent us after her.

A hand gripped my shoulder, drawing me to a halt. I looked over at the VP, Slash. He gave a nod to the doors down the hall that led into Church. I followed his lead, then claimed my seat at the table. I studied my hands. My knuckles were bruised and ached, but I didn't regret what I'd done. Although, telling Mei I'd beat up her precious Beau wouldn't be easy. She'd asked me not to tell him what she'd been through, but I couldn't promise her that. He needed to know that his actions had consequences, ones that she'd had to pay.

Griz slammed the gavel on the table and I tried to focus. There would be plenty of time to figure out how to tell Mei what I'd done, and hope that she'd forgive me. It bothered me that she obviously still cared for Beau. I'd have never done that to her. She deserved better than the likes of him.

I caught movement in the corner and saw that Beau was standing in the shadows, holding onto his ribs. Good. I hoped the fucker hurt. I wanted him to remember what he'd done to her each and every time he drew breath. Even then it wasn't near enough.

"I asked Beau to join us since it seems Dingo has an issue with him. Now tell us what the hell is going on," the Pres said.

"When Beau came here, when you brought him to the compound, did he ever mention where he'd come from?" I asked. "We never questioned anything about his presence here. We just knew that you'd brought him home with you, so he was now a part of the family in some way."

Griz sighed. "No. I didn't ask many questions. He was just a kid and I found him scrounging in the trash in an alley. Asked if he had a home and he said no, so I brought him here."

My gaze met Beau's. "Why didn't you tell Griz about Mei? Why did you run off and leave her? Even if you couldn't both get away at the same time, we would have gone after her if we'd known she even existed."

"I was ashamed and thought if you knew what I'd done, then you wouldn't let me stay," Beau said.

"What exactly did you do?" Slash asked.

Beau glanced toward Outlaw at the opposite end of the table. "If I give you a website, can you access it in here on that laptop?"

"Yeah, as long as it doesn't require me to type fast for very long," he said.

Beau rattled off a URL and whatever Outlaw saw made him pale.

"Holy shit," Outlaw muttered. "Is that... you and Mei?"

"Yeah." Beau dropped his gaze to the table. "When I was twelve, I was taken in by a foster family here in town. Mei wasn't there yet. The foster parents were assholes, but it wasn't anything I hadn't suffered through before. But when Mei came, their little China girl, then that's when shit got worse. The moment Mei came to the house, they looked at her different. I didn't know why at first, not until later, when it was too late. I never knew what the other kids were going through. They were threatened to keep their mouths shut."

"Worse how?" Griz asked.

"When Mei was thirteen and I was fourteen, they made us… make videos." Beau swallowed hard enough his Adam's apple bobbed. "The kind that get sold under the table or listed on illegal sites."

Grizzly shoved his chair back. "Are you telling me they forced the two of you to make pornographic videos?"

Beau gave a jerky nod.

"So you knew what they were like when you left her there," I said. "And you still never said a word, too afraid that you'd be left out in the cold. What you did goes against everything we stand for. How the fuck can you expect us to patch you in when you left a young girl behind to live through that hell and so much worse?"

Outlaw bolted from the table and threw up in the trashcan by the door. Colorado was closest to Outlaw's seat and nudged the laptop until he could see what was on the screen. His eyes went wide, then his face paled, and he was joining Outlaw at the trashcan.

"That's some fucked-up shit," he said after he'd emptied the contents of his stomach. "Jesus fucking Christ! How the hell has she not lost her damn mind? I thought that video of her and Beau was bad, but that…"

"Wish I hadn't kept digging," Outlaw said.

I couldn't look. Even when the laptop was turned so everyone could see, I couldn't bring myself to watch. But the volume was turned up and I could hear it all. My stomach knotted and my eyes and throat burned as I fought not to cry like a damn baby as I listened to her suffer. The sounds of the men, and I could tell there was more than one, and her screams tore at me. It seemed that after Beau ran off the videos hadn't stopped. They'd only become more brutal.

Beau broke. He fell to his knees and sobbed. "I didn't know. I swear to God I didn't know!"

It took me a moment to get myself under control, but I finally voiced my concerns. Well, the most pressing. "Trotter will be coming for her. You know when she doesn't show up tomorrow, he'll be at the gates demanding we return her."

"Don't," Beau said. "Please. I fucked up, and I know it. Don't send her back to him. She's paid enough for my mistake."

Yeah, she had. The completely wrecked look in his eyes was enough to convince me that Beau was telling the truth. He hadn't realized things would be that bad for Mei. It didn't excuse what he'd done, and I had no doubt that Griz would hold a vote as to whether or not he was permitted to stay. I just wondered if we made Beau leave if Mei would feel like she couldn't stay here either.

I pulled up the texts on my phone that I'd received from Larkin earlier and shared the results with the club. They needed to know everything, or as much as I knew at any rate. There was no doubt that Mei had been hiding more. She hadn't told me about those videos, or what had happened to her. I could understand why, or I thought I did. She'd been protecting Beau, but I didn't know *why*. Shouldn't she be angry with him?

"Mei was trying to protect Beau," I said. "She didn't tell me about those videos when she shared part of her past with me. For whatever reason, she seems to care for him."

"It would have been kinder if you'd just killed me," Beau said. "How can I look at her knowing what she suffered and that I could have stopped it?"

"You man the fuck up," Slash said. "That's how. You go apologize to her --" I growled and glowered at Slash. He held up his hands. "Or not. It seems Dingo may disembowel you if you go anywhere near Mei."

Griz sighed and rubbed his eyes. "I have no problem with her remaining here for however long she wants or needs, but in what capacity? We don't exactly have a place for her."

"The guest quarters?" Beau asked. "She could have her own place."

"No." I slammed my fist onto the table. "If anyone breached the compound, she'd be vulnerable. She's not staying alone, and before you open your mouth again, don't even think of saying she can stay with *you*."

"I vote that we make her an official part of Devil's Fury," Demon said.

"Are you fucking crazy?" Steel asked. "We've never had a patched female before."

"We have Adalia," Hot Shot said.

"She's not a patched member," Steel pointed out. "She's Badger's ol' lady and has a property patch."

Demon pointed at him. "Exactly! All in favor of Mei becoming Dingo's ol' lady?"

It took my brain a moment to process his words but before I could catch up, every hand around the table was in the air except Steel who seemed to be waiting for me to react. My mouth opened and shut a few times, but I didn't know if I wanted to scream *hell yes* or tell them they'd all lost their fucking minds. Keep Mei? Sounded like an awesome idea, in theory, but what if she didn't *want* to be kept?

"Mei has had enough choices taken from her already. Do you think it's wise to take yet another one from her?" I asked.

Griz grinned. "And that's why you'd be perfect for her. Congratulations, Dingo. You have an ol' lady. We'll have a property cut made as quick as possible."

Jesus. They were all fucking insane. Every last one of them. And maybe I was too because the thought of Mei being mine made my chest swell with pride, and I had to fight hard not to smile like a damn fool. I only hoped she took the news well.

"As for Beau," Griz said, "if your Mei was trying to protect him, then she likely wants him to stay. But, Beau, you're on probation effective immediately. Right now, I'm not convinced you're Devil's Fury material. I'm sorely disappointed in you."

Beau hung his head, and I knew that Griz's words had caused him nearly as much pain as seeing what Mei had suffered. Well, maybe not, but having the Pres disappointed in him definitely wouldn't be easy. Beau had been his favorite of the Prospects. Judging the faces around the table, we were all angered over what had happened to Mei and Beau's part in it all.

"Best head home and give your woman the good news," Slash said.

I stood and noticed everyone else remained seated. My gaze held Slash's and he arched a brow, then tipped his chin toward the door. All right. Got it.

Dismissed. I didn't know what they planned to discuss without me, but if I needed to know, someone would eventually tell me. I had a feeling they were going to rake Beau over the coals a bit more, or figure out the best way to handle Mei when she ventured out of my house.

Demon stood. "Wait."

I paused but didn't turn around, even though I could see him in my peripheral vision.

"I'm sorry about earlier, with Mei. I never would have let her go through with it. Just wanted to make sure you knew that," Demon said. "We wanted to see how far Beau would let things go before he spoke up, but you didn't give him a chance. Before any of us could call a halt to it, you swooped in and snatched her."

I glared at him. "That's all well and good, Demon, but *she* didn't know you were testing him. Mei thought she was here to be the club's whore, passed around to whoever whenever without a say in the matter. Do you want to know what happened when I took her to Dr. Larkin?"

Demon's lips thinned, but he remained silent.

"She stripped down to nothing, crawled onto the bed, and spread her legs. Just waiting to be used yet again." I clenched my hands into fists. "That's what your little test accomplished. So no offense, but fuck you. Fuck every last one of you that was part of that shit."

Before they could stop me, I slammed the doors open and left. I'd brought the truck back when I'd come to the clubhouse, and while I might need it again for Mei, I took my bike home. I'd love to feel her pressed against my back as I rode down the highway, but I didn't know if she was quite ready for that.

Hell. I didn't have the first damn clue how to explain to her that she was now mine. I didn't think she'd been around any clubs before, and probably didn't understand how things worked around here. She was about to get a crash course, but I wouldn't make her share my bed. Just because she'd be wearing my name, it didn't mean that she was ready for everything that went with it. I'd give her time to adjust; it was the least I could do.

At the house, I shut off the engine to my bike and pocketed my keys. I went inside and found Mei stretched out on the couch watching a movie. She gave me a smile, one that quickly dropped off her face. She bolted upright, her body tense and her posture rigid.

"What's wrong? What happened?" she asked. "Are they making me leave?"

Her chest rose and fell rapidly, and I could tell she was seconds from bolting. I didn't know what expression I wore that had her panicked, but I needed to calm her down quick. Except it might be the calm before the storm once she heard my news.

"No, you don't have to leave." In fact, she *couldn't* leave. Not without someone retrieving her.

"Then why do you look so angry?"

I cracked my neck and sighed. "I'm not angry, just... something happened and I don't know how to explain it to you."

Her gaze scanned me, stopping on my hands. "You hit someone?"

Well, that definitely wasn't how I wanted to start the conversation. I still didn't know how she felt about the Prospect. If there were feelings there, this could get messy fast. Not only would she be pissed I'd hit him, but she'd be even angrier when she heard that she was now tied to me forever.

"Beau has a busted lip, and probably a half dozen or more bruises, but he's upright, breathing, and still able to talk." I crossed the room and sank into my favorite chair, then tipped my head back, staring up at the ceiling. No screaming. That was a good sign. Maybe. "He knows what happened, Mei. They all do. And so do I."

"You? But I told you…"

She trailed off as I looked over at her, letting her see exactly what I meant. Those sounds would haunt me for an eternity. The moment it clicked into place for her, her expression shuttered. Whatever light had been in her eyes was gone. The Mei I'd seen during Dr. Larkin's exam looked ready to make a reappearance, and that was the last thing I wanted.

"Oh." She gave a humorless laugh. "So you know everything, then. All the sordid details. The disgusting things they did to me, made *me* do."

The silence between us stretched until I couldn't stand it another moment. I'd never been good with words, especially when it came to women. What I wanted to say would either piss her off, make her cry, or if I was really fucking lucky, then she'd understand where I was coming from. But it was my experience that women never did what I expected or wanted.

"Do you have any idea how difficult it was not to kill Beau for leaving you to that fate? Or how hard it was for me not to ride through the gates and track down every man who ever laid a hand on you? I want to kill them all, make them bleed, to beg for their lives, and watch as the light fades from their eyes. I want to completely and utterly destroy every single one of them." I held out my hand to her and she stood on shaky legs, then I tugged her down onto my lap. "You have to be the strongest, bravest woman I've ever met.

I don't know how you're still alive, but I'm so fucking glad you're here with me, Mei."

"You... You aren't disgusted?"

I chewed the inside of my lip, measuring my words carefully. "With you? No. I'm disgusted at the men who did that to you. But never with you, sweetheart. Not ever. To me, you're a beautiful angel. No, a phoenix. You're all fiery, and resilient. Even the strongest have a weakness, though, and I need to know what words are triggers for you. Pretty girl is out, obviously." She flinched again when I said that name. "What else?"

She took a deep breath and seemed to think it over. I wasn't sure if she was trying to decide which names bothered her most, or if she wasn't sure she wanted to share that with me yet. She'd already opened up more than I'd thought she would, even if she had kept a shit ton of stuff from me.

"China doll. China girl. Sweet thing." She ran her fingers up and down the neck of my cut. "Those are the only names they ever called me that weren't... nasty."

"Then I'll make sure I don't ever use them." I reached up and gripped her hair, turning her face toward mine. "Because you're going to be here with me for a long, long time. Need to make sure I don't fuck up and call you the wrong thing."

She licked her lips, her eyes growing darker. "Wh-what does that mean? A long time?" she asked, her pulse fluttering in her throat.

"It means you're mine, Mei. The club decided that effective immediately, you're my ol' lady. Since I don't think you know much about clubs, what it boils down to is you wearing a cut like mine but yours will say *Property of Dingo* and everyone will know you're mine and *only* mine. It also means I'm responsible for your words and actions when you're around the club. Anything you say or do will reflect on me." I studied her, looking for any sign that she might bolt. "It means you'll never be with another man other than me because I'll fucking kill anyone who dares to touch you."

"Oh." She practically sighed the word. "That... actually sounds rather nice."

My lips kicked up on the corner. "Yeah?"

She nodded. "I've always wanted to be someone's, to be protected and cared for. It's part of what brought me here last night. Even when I'd thought I'd have to be available to anyone here, I'd hoped that it would mean I no longer had to strip or answer to Trotter in any other way."

"That all you want? Protection?"

"No," she said softly. "For as long as I can remember, I've dreamed of someone loving me. I know you don't, and that's okay, but maybe one day you'll come to care for me. That will still be far more than I've ever had. I think Beau cared in his own way, but we were kids who were stuck in hell. It's not nearly the same."

I tugged her closer. "One more thing. I don't want to hear about Beau anytime soon. I still want to beat the shit out of him. Understood?"

"Yes, Dingo."

I traced her nose with mine. "Call me Jameson when it's just us. Dingo is my club name, but you're mine which gives you certain rights."

"Like what?"

"The right to be respected by every member of this club, and anyone else who enters our gates. The right to use my given name." My gaze locked on hers.

"The right to ask me for anything you need. It's my honor and privilege to take care of you, Mei. In all ways."

She whimpered right before I crushed my lips to hers. I wouldn't take things too far. Not yet. But I needed her to know that I wanted her, desired her, and that when the time was right, I was going to claim every inch of her.

Chapter Five

Meiling

Dingo had kissed me breathless, making me burn for him, and then he'd set me aside. I was still reeling from that kiss and wished that he'd kept going. I didn't know if he was waiting on me to say it was okay, or if it was something else. There hadn't been time for me to ask before his phone was ringing and he'd rushed out the door again, yelling over his shoulder that he had to take care of club business. Whatever that meant. It wasn't like I expected him to entertain me, but I had to wonder if he would forever be running out the door.

Since I didn't know when he'd be back, or if anyone would drop in unexpectedly, I changed into a pair of the jeans he'd bought for me and a pale green top. They were plain, but they were also the best clothes I'd owned since I was a kid. If all he ever bought me were things like this, I'd be in heaven. In fact, I'd gladly wear long sleeves, turtlenecks, and pants year-round if it meant men wouldn't look at me the way they always had. I wanted to be invisible.

I padded barefoot into the kitchen, remembering that he'd said I could help myself to anything here. I wasn't starving anymore, but my stomach was rumbling a little. There was a package of ground beef in the fridge, some shredded cheese, a tomato, and some peppers. I decided to brown the meat, tossing in tomato chunks and peppers. I found an onion in the pantry that I added to it, and used what little seasonings he seemed to own. I'd never been that great of a cook -- well, not any sort of cook except in my imagination -- but I'd picked up a few things here and there, mostly watching cooking shows and then making my own creations in my head that I'd hoped to try one day.

The pantry was decently stocked and I grabbed some tortilla chips, then covered them in the meat mixture, and topped it all with shredded cheese. Not the best version of nachos in the world, but they looked pretty amazing -- for my first time cooking, at any rate. I poured a glass of sweet tea and carried everything into the living room. I'd discovered that Dingo didn't have cable, but he had a few subscription services and I'd been binge-watching sappy movies on Netflix during the first time he'd been gone. During the three hours since he'd left again. I picked another one and munched on my snack while I waited for Dingo to return.

If I'd had a phone, then I might have been tempted to Google the club and see what popped up. I really didn't know anything about them, other than the little bit the girls at *The Ruby Slipper* had mentioned. I'd heard the name Demon mentioned before, but hadn't realized he was part of the Devil's Fury until I'd arrived here earlier. I could see why they giggled and talked about how handsome he was, but to me, Dingo was the best-looking of the lot. Then again, he'd been the only one who was nice to me, and kindness was far better than looks.

I'd never been kissed by a man with a beard before, if you could even consider what I'd experienced before as kissing. More like them smashing their mouths against mine as they took what they wanted, and that's if they even bothered at all. I'd never had a true kiss until Dingo, and it was everything I'd ever dreamed it would be. Part of me wanted to experience everything else with him too, but I also worried that I'd either disappoint him, or everything beyond kissing would be just as painful as it had always been. I'd never even been able to make myself come, not that I'd cared much to try more than once or twice, and even then it had merely been curiosity.

The nachos were only half-eaten when I decided I couldn't handle another bite. I set them aside and curled back up to finish the movie. Every few minutes, I found myself watching the door, hoping Dingo would return. Not knowing what he was doing, it made me worry that it could be something dangerous. While I did worry about his safety, I was also concerned about my own. If something happened to Dingo, what would the club do with me? Was I only safe as long as I was with him?

There was a knock at the front door and before I could get up to answer it, the door swung open. Beau stepped into the house, his eye blackened, his lip swollen and split, and the way he walked told me he had plenty of other injuries. I also knew that Dingo would be furious to find him here with me. My heart started to race, but I was locked in place, too scared to move. I didn't think Beau would hurt me, at least the boy I'd known wouldn't have, but this man was a different story. He'd been beaten because of me. Was he here to get revenge?

"Jesus, Mei. Don't look at me like I'm some sort of monster," he mumbled.

"S-sorry." I curled into a tight ball in the corner of the couch, my gaze darting to the door before focusing on him again. He stood between me and the hall to my room, and blocked the front door too. "I told him not to tell you."

"I needed to know," he said. "And I deserved what he did to me. I only saw a few minutes. It was more than enough to tell me how badly I'd fucked up. Did... did that happen often?"

"I don't even know what you saw," I said.

"There were three men," he said.

I gave a jerky nod. "Often enough. That was one of their favorite scenarios to film. It made them the most money."

"How old..." He looked away, and I could tell this was hard on him.

"That particular... type... was filmed within a week of you leaving. The first time."

He made a sound like a wounded bear and started pacing. "Fuck! Mei, you were only fourteen when I left. I swear I didn't know what would happen. I'd thought maybe if I was gone, they would leave you alone, or at least spend enough time trying to find me that you'd get a chance to escape. I never imagined you'd be stuck there for four years or what they'd put you through."

"I never blamed you," I said. "If I could have run away, I would have. I always hoped you'd found a safe place and were happy. It never occurred to me that you were still in town, or had joined the Devil's Fury."

"I'm only a Prospect, and after I abandoned you like that, I'm now on probation."

I glanced at the door again. "You need to go. If Dingo finds you here, he's going to be furious. He told me not to even mention your name."

He stopped his pacing and faced me. "He told you? That the club gave you to him?"

I blinked and then stared. They'd *given* me to him? What exactly did that mean? He'd said that I was his, that I'd have to wear something that said I was his property, and he'd said the club made me his... ol' lady? But he'd never mentioned anything about his club giving me to him. How, exactly, could they do that if I didn't belong to any of them? Unless they'd outright bought me from Trotter. The thought sent chills down my spine.

"Gave me to him?" I asked.

"He did tell you that you belong to him, right?" Beau asked, taking a step back. "I mean, I thought he was coming here to talk to you."

"He said I was his, but nothing about me being given to him. I don't understand any of this. I'd thought maybe it meant I was finally safe, that I belonged, but... is this club no different from Trotter? Dingo said that no one was allowed to touch me but him. Did he mean only until he grew tired of me? Am I still a whore but only for one man now?"

Beau groaned and ran a hand down his face. "Fucking hell. What do you know about the Devil's Fury MC?"

I shrugged a shoulder. Nothing, in all honesty. I'd heard the men were hot and that I might find a protector here, but I'd never paid attention to the rumblings about the club other than that. Until last night, I'd never planned on paying them a visit so there hadn't been much point in learning anything else.

"They're a law unto themselves, Mei. The police don't matter around here, or any other authority. What Grizzly says, goes. He's the one in charge of it all. The President. Dingo is a patched member, which means he has status in the club, and their protection, but he's not high up enough to claim an officer's spot." He moved closer. "Then there's guys like me. I'm a Prospect, which means I get the shit jobs as a way to prove myself worthy of being a patched member. The black vests, like mine, are called cuts. Dingo's has the club name and his name on his. Mine just says Prospect. The officers will be like Dingo and have their names on theirs, but also their positions."

I opened and shut my mouth, not knowing where to even begin with the questions. For that matter, did I really want to know? If they didn't care about the police, didn't that make them just as bad as my foster family? As bad as Trotter? Had I only traded one evil for another?

Dingo's blue-gray eyes flashed in my mind. No. There was no hatred or evil in his gaze. Only kindness, and a gentleness that I craved. I didn't know about the others, but I was certain that he was a good man.

"The club gets their money by illegal means, mostly, and it's divided among the members. Officers get a bigger cut, and anyone who helps with a certain job gets a higher percentage from that particular task than someone who didn't participate at all. They'd kill to protect their own, Mei, and with you being Dingo's ol' lady, that means they'll protect you too." He folded his arms, then winced and dropped them back to his sides. "You're his, Mei. Call it a girlfriend or whatever you want."

He'd... claimed me? Made me his girlfriend just by saying I belonged to him? Or rather by his club telling him that I was now his. I didn't know how he felt about it. He'd seemed more concerned with how I'd react, but he had to have remained single all this time for a reason. Was he angry that he was now responsible for me?

"He's a decent guy, Mei. I wouldn't leave you here with him if I thought he'd ever hurt you. I can't promise he'll be faithful. The guys get plenty of pussy up at the clubhouse. You saw what it was like last night. All those women are here voluntarily, and eager to take a ride on any cock at the clubhouse. Your man included."

Could I live like that? Knowing he expected me to remain faithful, but he could be with whoever he wanted? Was that where he was now? He'd said it was club business, but what if he was really with a woman? It wasn't like he was in love with me, or me with him, but I'd hoped that this time was really different.

I heard the rumble of a motorcycle getting close and Beau tensed, moving to the window and peering outside. He cursed and ran for the front door and bolted from the house. I heard shouting and got up to look through the blinds. Dingo had Beau on the ground, beating on him again. I wanted to intervene, to tell him that Beau hadn't meant any harm, but part of me was scared that he'd turn that anger my way.

When he released Beau and started striding toward the house, I backed away from the window and watched the doorway. Dingo came in, slammed the door shut, and turned toward me. He was breathing heavily, his face was flushed, and there was still fury sparking in his eyes.

"Did he touch you?" he demanded.

"No. He didn't get close to me."

Dingo came closer, not stopping until I could feel the heat of his body. "Why was he here?"

"I don't know. He just showed up and let himself in." I wanted to back up, but I didn't. He'd called me strong, brave. I wanted to prove him right and not run away like a frightened mouse. "I think he was trying to apologize for leaving me all those years ago."

Dingo leaned closer and buried his face against my neck, breathing me in. He settled his hands on my waist and pulled me closer. I could feel his heart pounding and I realized he wasn't just angry because Beau was here with me. Alone. He was upset because he'd been worried about me. I placed my hands on his shoulders, then slid them down his back.

"I'm okay," I said. "I was scared at first, but he didn't touch me."

"If he'd laid a finger on you, I think I'd have killed him." His voice was a deep rumble, but the sound soothed me. "Only mine for a few hours and already I'm willing to commit murder if someone does anything to hurt you. Hell, I was ready to tear apart the men who abused you before you were even mine."

He drew back, but didn't release me. I looked up into his eyes and the emotions swirling in their depths made me breathless. No one had ever looked at me like that. I reached up and gently stroked his beard, surprised that it felt so soft. When he'd kissed me, it hadn't been scratchy like I'd feared. He let me explore as I petted his beard, then ran my fingers through his hair at the base of his neck.

"Or maybe I've just known from the moment I saw you that you were mine," he said. "When I saw what Demon was doing, what he'd demanded of you, it was the first time I'd ever wanted to hit him."

"Beau said your club gave me to you," I said, needing to hear the truth from him.

"In a manner of speaking."

"Dingo, if you don't really want me here, if I'm an inconvenience, then I can go."

His lips twitched, and he gave me a slight smile. "I want you here, Mei. They only said you were mine because they knew I was going to claim you -- eventually. I'd hoped to give you time, show you that I wouldn't hurt you. They just sped up the timeline. You're mine, beautiful. Always."

"And are you mine?" I asked, almost fearing his answer.

"Yeah." His gaze locked on mine. "And when the time is right, when you're ready, I have no doubt you'll make sure everyone knows it."

I tipped my head to the side, assessing his words. "Does that mean I have your permission to go off on any women who try to get in your pants?"

He chuckled. "Yeah, baby. In fact, I hope one day you'll be confident enough to show those bitches not to mess with you. The girls at the clubhouse can be a bit… territorial. None of them are claimed, but they want to be. They'll see you as a threat, and they'll likely try to get me to sleep with them. It's just part of this way of life, Mei."

I didn't know how I felt about that, but I'd have to learn to live with it. Or find a way to make those women fear me if they came anywhere near Dingo. Then again, if I wasn't keeping him satisfied, I couldn't very well expect him to turn them away. Could I? I'd never been in any sort of relationship before and had no idea what the rules were, or if there even *were* rules.

"We have time, Mei. You don't have to figure it all out right now. I can see you have questions, and I expect you to. Ask me whatever you want. If it's not something I can share, then I'll tell you."

"Am I the only one?"

"The only woman I've claimed?" he asked.

I chewed my lip. "Yes and no. I mean, yes, I want to know the answer to that, but I also meant, are there other women here who belong to just one guy?"

"You're the only one I've ever claimed, sweetheart. Only one I'll ever claim. As to the other, Badger has an ol' lady. Adalia is the Pres's daughter, and he has two other adopted daughters. Neither belong to anyone, though. In fact, one is scared of her own shadow so you probably won't see much of her. She tends to stay in Grizzly's house."

That only gave me more questions, but I decided that if I learned too much more right this moment, my head might explode. Like he'd said, we had time. I didn't have to find out everything right now. What little I'd been told so far was enough for the time being. I'd just take the rest as it came. Living life the way I had, I'd learned to roll with the punches. Sometimes literally.

"Is your business over for the day?" I asked.

He nodded.

"So you can spend some time with me?"

Dingo looked over at the TV before dropping his gaze to me, an eyebrow arched. "Do you expect me to watch that sappy shit?"

I didn't answer right away. Mostly because I *liked* watching that "sappy shit" as he'd called it. He cracked a smile, then pressed a quick kiss to my lips.

"We can watch whatever you want, Mei. I was only teasing you. I'll even sit on the couch with you."

I led him across the living room and let him sit first, then I curled up against him. He put an arm around my shoulders and held me close. It was the closest I'd ever gotten to what I imagined normal would be like. I'd never dated, never cuddled with someone. But I had feeling that the next few weeks I would experience a lot of firsts. Dingo seemed determined to make my life better, and he already had. I didn't really believe in God or Fate, but something had made me come here last night, some unseen force, and I'd be forever grateful. If I hadn't shown up, if Beau hadn't come to get me earlier, then I wouldn't be here right now.

Chapter Six

Dingo

The rest of the day had flown by and now that it was nearing midnight I was faced with a new dilemma. I'd given Mei her own room, but that was before I'd claimed her. Now that she was mine, I wanted her in my bed. I just didn't want her to feel like she *had* to be there. Not so soon anyway. We were strangers, and she'd lived through hell for years. If anyone deserved some space, it was her.

She yawned so wide that her jaw cracked and I knew she'd reached her limit for the day. I stood and pulled her up with me. She blinked at me a few times, then gave me a sleepy smile. Getting her to follow me to the hall was simple enough, but I stopped, not knowing which door to go through.

"Mei, I'm going to leave this one up to you. I gave you the guest room and you're welcome to use it until you're ready for more. Even if you do come to my room tonight, I'm not expecting anything from you. We can just share a bed and sleep. If being in the guest room with a locked door makes you feel better, then I'm okay with that too."

She chewed her lower lip as she stared at the guest room, then glanced toward my bedroom. I didn't want her to feel pressured, so I released her hand and backed toward my room. Mei took a step toward me, then paused. I could tell she felt conflicted, but I needed her to make this decision completely on her own. I might be an asshole to most people, but not with her.

I moved farther back into my room, then turned and walked off. She'd either follow or decide to sleep in her own bed. As much as I'd love to have her by my side tonight, I'd understand if she chose to lock herself away. Her entire world had turned upside down. In my opinion, it was for the better, but after knowing nothing but pain and ugliness, it would probably be difficult for her to just accept that things were different now. If our roles were reversed, I'd be skeptical as hell about all this.

My brothers would probably think I was being too soft with Mei. I'd always been a take what I want kind of guy, and they were the same way. Not that we ever forced ourselves on women, but those who came to the clubhouse were willing and ready. Or so I'd always believed. I hadn't seen Mei last night, but I'd heard about her showing up. If Beau hadn't scared her off, she'd likely have ended up on her back or against a wall with my brothers none the wiser about the hell she'd been through. Or the fact that she'd only been searching for a place to sleep, and she'd been more than ready to exchange her body for a bed and some food. It sickened me and had me second-guessing the others who came to our gates. Were any of them like Mei? Had I been with someone who was just trying to find a way off the streets for a bit?

I scrubbed my hands over my head, wishing I knew for certain I'd never taken advantage of someone. I didn't want to be like those guys, the men like Trotter who didn't care if a woman was willing or not. The thought that I could have hurt a woman sickened me. No, I didn't make a living in an honest way, but there were some lines I refused to cross. Hurting kids or women was one of them.

I hadn't even realized I was pacing until Mei pressed her hands against my chest and stopped my forward motion.

"Did you think I wasn't coming in here?" she asked. "Is that what has you so agitated?"

I shook my head, not wanting to voice my concerns. I didn't want her to fear me, or think less of me. Right now, she saw me as some sort of hero. I wasn't. Not even close, but to her... I liked being her white knight.

"Dingo." She reached up and placed her hand on my cheek. "Jameson, what's wrong?"

"Just questioning some things right now. About my past."

She brushed her fingers over my beard and stared up at me intently. I didn't think she'd say anything at first, but she surprised me. "Didn't you tell me that the past was behind us? If it's something you can't change, then let it go. Worrying over it doesn't make a difference now, does it?"

I blew out a breath. "No, it doesn't."

It didn't lessen my guilt any, though. And I had to wonder if any of my brothers had started to contemplate the same thing. We'd never had cause to question any of the women who came here. It was always assumed they wanted to be here, wanted bragging rights or the chance to be claimed. Maybe it was pure arrogance that made us feel that way, but now Mei had blown that theory to hell and back. If she'd come here as a means of escape, then others probably had at some point too. Had they needed our help?

If I kept thinking about it, I'd just drive myself crazy. She was right. I couldn't change the past, but I could try to make sure the future of the club was different. I'd have to wait and either talk to Grizzly one-on-one, or bring it up at Church next time.

"I need to shower before I get in bed. You're welcome to use another of my shirts. I didn't think to get you pajamas, but we can fix that tomorrow." I glanced at the clock by the bed. "Or rather, later today."

She took a step back. I wanted to reach for her, bring her back closer to me, but I let her go. If I didn't put some space between us, I'd be tempted to ask for more from her than I should.

"Do you sleep on a particular side?" she asked.

I glanced at the bed and wished I'd thought to at least change the sheets. It wasn't like I'd had anyone in my bed, but I didn't think I'd put fresh ones on in nearly a week. I also didn't want to stop and change them right now. With my luck, she'd think I was trying to get rid of the scent of another woman or some shit.

"The right, but it doesn't matter. You can have whichever side you'd like."

She gave me a slight smile. "Jameson, I'm just happy to sleep in a bed. I don't care what side it's on."

I tried not to wince. I hadn't really needed the reminder of the shitty life she'd had up to this point. If I dwelled on it too much, I'd go on a killing spree. Part of the business I'd had to take care of included asking a favor of Outlaw. I wanted the names of the men in any videos online of Mei. And even more than that, I wanted all those damn things taken offline. I knew it wouldn't destroy the originals and they would possibly go right back up, but I had a feeling he'd get Wire and Lavender to work a bit of magic. Maybe they could even trace where the videos originated and wipe out those systems.

Wishful thinking, maybe, but I could hope. The last thing I wanted was for Mei to have a constant reminder out there of what she'd suffered. Once the videos were handled, then I'd take care of the rest. I would make each and every one of those men pay, no matter how far I had to go, or what I had to do. I'd kill them all if given a chance, and I'd make them die very slowly. They needed to suffer before drawing their last breath.

"I'll be back in a minute," I said, stopping at the dresser long enough to pull out a change of underwear and a pair of sweatpants, then I hurried into the bathroom.

I shut the door and set my things on the counter. I could hear her on the other side of the door. It was strange having someone in my house, especially in my bedroom. It wasn't that I'd been celibate by any means, even though it had been a while since I'd fucked any of the club whores. I just hadn't ever brought someone home. The clubhouse had served my needs well enough. My bedroom had always been my sanctuary. Hell, my entire house had been a no-fly zone for the fairer sex. I'd only been a patched member for a few years and had lived at the clubhouse before that. The house had been a perk of becoming a full-fledged member of the Devil's Fury.

I started the shower and waited until steam billowed out of the stall before I stripped out of my clothes and stepped under the spray. The first thing I'd done when I moved in was remodel the bathroom. My shower didn't have a door, just an open area that was wide enough for someone to walk through. The exterior of the shower was made of glass cubes from floor to ceiling that let in the light from the main part of the bathroom. I braced my hand on the wall and let the water beat against me.

If felt like all kinds of fucked-up that I was hard right now. She'd been abused, horribly, and yet every time I looked at her my dick came to instant attention. I wanted to kick my own ass. While I hadn't been with a woman for a bit, my hand had been just fine. I looked down at my cock and contemplated jerking off, releasing some tension and getting myself under better control. If I crawled into bed with her while I had a raging hard-on, she'd probably run back to her room.

I slicked my palm with some soap and stroked from root to tip. Closing my eyes, I pictured Mei in here with me, her hand tugging on my dick. My balls drew up as I imagined her dropping to her knees and looking up at me with those beautiful eyes. Biting my lip, I stifled my groan as I moved my hand faster. It only took a few seconds before I was coming, spraying cum all over the wall. My heart pounded against my chest as I cleaned up the mess. It still hadn't been enough. My cock was still semi-hard, and I knew it wouldn't take much to be fully erect again.

Changing the water to a much cooler setting, I hoped it would be enough to make me shrink some more. Even though I'd brought underwear to put on under the sweats, it still wouldn't hide much if I got turned-on again. All Mei had to do was look at me -- hell, just be in the same room with me -- and I was ready to go. I'd never had such a strong reaction to someone before.

I wondered how long I could stay in here before Mei would worry or get curious. I wasn't avoiding her, exactly. It was more that I wanted to avoid the awkwardness of getting into bed with her the first time, knowing that sex wasn't part of the equation. I'd never just slept next to a woman before. Would she think I wanted more if I tried to hold her? Or would it freak her out and cause her to have a flashback of some sort? I didn't know enough about her past to know if she had triggers other than certain names.

Standing in the shower wouldn't solve anything. I washed my hair, then used a special cleanser on my beard. After I washed my body and rinsed, I got out and dried off. I typically put some oil in my beard after I washed it, but since I was going to bed, I decided to just leave it. I pulled on my clothes and ran a comb through my hair before I decided I'd spent enough time in the bathroom and opened the door.

The lights were off in the bedroom, but I could make out the slight lump on the left side of my bed. I shut off the bathroom light and made my way to the bed. Mei didn't move or make a sound. On the off chance she'd already fallen asleep, I tried to slip into bed as gently as possible. I hugged the edge so I wouldn't accidentally brush against her.

"Jameson," she said softly.

Not asleep, then. "Yeah, Mei?"

She sighed. "I don't bite."

I chuckled a little. Maybe not, but now that she'd said it… yep, getting hard again. The thought of her biting into my shoulder as I pounded into her sweet pussy… Fuck!

"Didn't figure you did." But I certainly hoped she was a biter, at least during sex. Not so much at any other time.

She rolled over and faced me. "Then why are you way over there?"

I wasn't sure how to answer her. If I told her that I worried I'd upset her if I got too close, would that only make things worse?

Mei reached over and tugged on me. I shifted and reached out for her. The second I placed my hand on her hip, she snuggled closer. It felt incredibly right to have her pressed against me. When I realized she wasn't going to freak out, I relaxed and just enjoyed holding her. I'd never thought I would want to share a bed with a woman if sex wasn't involved.

She shifted even closer and I knew the moment she realized I was hard as a damn rock because she tensed. *Shit.* I tried to pull my hips back, but she wouldn't let me retreat. Being stronger than she was, I could have moved anyway, but the way her hand tightened on me was enough to halt my escape.

"I want you, Mei, but it doesn't mean I'm going to act on those desires until you're ready."

"Jameson, I won't break. If I were fragile, I'd have never lasted this long."

"It's not about breaking you, Mei. Most of your life you've had men take and take. It's time someone gave you what you needed instead of worrying about what they wanted."

She grew quiet and I thought that was the end of it. Until I felt something wet against my chest and heard her sniffle. Christ! Had I made her fucking cry?

"Kiss me?" she whispered. "Like before."

It was probably the worst idea ever, but I couldn't deny her request. Even in the darkness, her green eyes practically glowed. The brilliant hue pulled me in and I felt powerless against her. Reaching up, I curled my fingers under her chin, tilting her face a little, then I leaned closer and pressed my lips to hers. I heard her breath hitch, and I flicked my tongue across her mouth. When she opened and let me in, I knew I was a goner.

I slid my hand from her chin to her hair, fisting it as I held her captive and took what she so sweetly offered. The way she kissed me back, as if she'd never kissed anyone but me, made some caveman part of my brain kick in. Before I could even think about my actions, I'd rolled us so that she lay under me, my body pressing her into the mattress, and my cock nestled against the apex of her thighs.

Mei parted her legs and I could feel the heat of her even through her panties. Despite the insistent throbbing in my dick, I managed to at least make sure to take care of her too. I slipped a hand under the T-shirt she'd taken from my dresser, gently sweeping across her ribs and up to her perky breasts. As I palmed the soft mound, I felt her nipple harden. My lips devoured hers as I played with that hard peak, rolling it between my fingers, then pinching it.

Mei cried out and bucked against me. I drew back to look down at her and saw the surprise and awe etched on her face. The sheer wonder in her eyes was enough to calm the fire licking through my veins. I lifted off her a bit so I could tug up the shirt, going slowly in case she showed the slightest hint of hesitation. Her breasts weren't overly large, but to me they were perfect. I rolled her nipple again and leaned down to lick the other one.

"Jameson!" Her fingers bit into my shoulder as she gripped me tight. "I-I-I... W-what's happening?"

I growled and took her nipple into my mouth, giving it a long, hard suck before lightly scraping it with my teeth. Her body went tight, and I heard her shocked indrawn breath right before she shuddered and let out a keening cry that I knew I'd remember for the rest of my life. My sweet Mei had just come for the first time, and I was going to make damn sure she found that same pleasure, if not more, again and again. I couldn't remember ever having a woman so responsive to just having her nipples played with, but I loved hearing Mei's cries of pleasure.

My gaze locked on hers. As much as I wanted to take things further, I wouldn't unless I was certain this was what she wanted too. I needed her to say the words.

"Do you want me to keep going, Mei? It's okay if you want to stop."

She shook her head. "Don't stop. Please, Jameson. I need this, need you. But most of all, I want to replace all those ugly memories with something beautiful. No one's ever made me feel like this before."

"You okay with me undressing you?" I asked.

Mei struggled to sit up and pulled the shirt over her head, then tossed it aside. When she lay back, I worked her panties down her thighs and threw them on top of the T-shirt. Her mound was mostly bare, but there was the faintest shadow of red hair growing back in. It seemed my woman was a true redhead. I stroked a finger down the soft lips of her pussy, fighting back a growl when I felt how wet she was. She'd easily take me, but I could wait a bit more.

I eased down the bed until my shoulders were pushing her thighs wider apart. I gripped her legs and bent them so her feet were flat on the mattress. Glancing up her body, I saw her watching me, a hungry expression in her eyes. She might not have ever experienced this, but she knew exactly what I was about to do. I blew across her pussy, making her shiver before I licked along the seam, then speared her with my tongue.

"Oh, Jesus!" Mei lifted her hips, pushing her mound closer to my lips. "Again. Please, I need you to do that again."

My lips kicked up on one corner in amusement as I licked at her again before thrusting my tongue into her wet heat. Using my fingers, I held her open and used every trick I'd ever learned to drive her wild. She screamed my name, thrashed on the bed, and soaked the sheets as she came multiple times. Mei whimpered and moaned as I rubbed her clit with my tongue, then sucked on it hard. When she came yet again, her voice hoarse as she called out my name, I knew it was time.

I wiped her juices from my lips and beard, shoved my sweats and underwear off, then settled over her. Mei gripped me with her thighs as my cock rubbed against her wet folds. It only took a shift of my hips to lodge the head of my cock into her snug entrance. Her eyes were darker, and I could see her pulse pounding in her throat. I held her gaze as I sank into her, working my cock into her pussy one inch at a time, until she'd taken all of me.

"Is this still okay?" I asked. It would fucking kill me, but I'd back off and walk away if that's what she wanted.

"Don't you dare stop, Jameson." She wrapped her legs around me and gave me a smile that lit up her face.

I took her slowly at first, wanting our first time to be special. Memorable. Even more than that, I watched her every reaction to make sure that she was here with me and hadn't gone off elsewhere in her head. When I was certain that she could handle it, handle *me*, I gave her everything I had. I took her hard. Deep. Fast. The headboard slammed into the wall with every thrust of my cock. Mei held my gaze as I pounded into her. With a twist of my hips, I brushed against her clit. Her eyes dilated and her lips parted. I did it twice more, and then she was coming, soaking me with her release, and squeezing my dick so hard I nearly saw stars.

I gripped her ass cheek with my hand, angling her so I could slide in deeper. As I drove into her, I knew that nothing would ever top our first time. I slammed into her as my balls drew up and I started filling her with my cum. My heart was racing and I could barely catch my breath. It wasn't until I pulled out and saw our mingled release spill onto the bed that I realized I'd taken her bare.

"Shit. Mei, I..."

She leaned up on her elbows and looked down her body. Her face paled and she bolted from the bed, rushing to the bathroom. The door slammed and I winced. I was such a fucking idiot. I'd sworn to myself that I wouldn't let my dick lead the way, and yet I'd done exactly that.

"Motherfucker," I muttered.

I went to the hall bathroom to clean up, then I stripped the bed and put on clean sheets. Mei still hadn't come out and I wasn't sure if I should ask if she was okay, or just give her some space. Obviously I'd fucked up royally. I decided she'd come out when she was ready and went into the kitchen. After I guzzled a glass of tea, I brewed a pot of coffee. No fucking way I'd be sleeping now.

I heard the soft tread of her feet and turned to find her leaning against the kitchen doorway, tears streaking her face and her lower lip trembling.

"Jameson, I..." She sank her teeth into her bottom lip.

"I'm sorry, Mei. I wasn't thinking."

She gave a humorless laugh that ended in a hiccup as she fought to control her emotions. When her gaze met mine, I could see that she was retreating. I knew I should have walked away earlier, should have given her a simple kiss, then taken my ass to the other room.

"We can get the morning-after pill if you want. I can go get it." I turned around, not wanting her to see how much it hurt me to say those words. The thought of her carrying my kid made me feel all warm inside. I'd never really wanted children. Until now.

"Is that why you think I'm upset?" she asked, sounding much closer than she'd been a moment ago.

I turned to find her right in front of me.

"Isn't it?" I asked.

"No, you idiot! You had your doctor do all sorts of tests on me, but I know there hasn't been time to get them back yet. What if I'm carrying something and just gave it to you?"

I honestly hadn't even thought of that. I should have, especially as careful as I'd always been, but this was Mei. She was mine, and that's all that had been on my mind. Yeah, I knew about her past, and I'd worried about her. But that was it exactly. I'd been worried about *her* and not even thinking of myself. Another first for me when it came to a woman.

"When your results come back, we'll handle anything that comes up. I got tested not that long ago, and I haven't been with anyone since. Until you. If you have something, then we'll get treatment for you and I'll have the doc run tests on me just to be safe."

"You're being too calm about this," she said. "What if I have HIV or something? Trotter didn't always make them wear condoms. If they paid enough, he'd let them do whatever they wanted to me. And I…

I sometimes had to make a trade for a place to sleep. Those men didn't bother with protection either."

"Mei, we'll handle it. Whatever it is. For all you know, you're clean and worried for no reason."

"No reason?" she asked, her voice going shrill. "What if I just doomed us both? Or a kid? Jesus, Jameson. What if you knocked me up and I have some incurable disease?"

My heart ached at the words I was about to say. "Then we'll ask for an abortion, if it means that's what's for the best."

She paled a little. "What if I'm already pregnant? What if I find out I'm going to have a kid and we don't even know if it's yours?"

I reached for her, wanting to calm her fears. I didn't like the thought of her having some other guy's baby, especially considering how it would have been conceived, but I also knew I'd never make her give up a child. The kid would be a part of her, and I'd raise it like my own. Hell, maybe the doc had used part of the blood he drew to run a pregnancy test. Maybe she was worried for no reason.

She leaned her forehead against my chest. I wrapped my arms around her, just holding her and giving her what comfort I could.

"I've had abortions before," she mumbled against me. "I may not even be able to have kids anymore."

The thought of never sharing that experience with her, never having a kid that was a little part of each of us, hurt. If that was true, if she couldn't have kids, then we'd adopt if she wanted a family. Plenty of kids out there needed a home. Might not be able to go through the legal channels, all things considered, but I'd make it happen. The babies who went into the system sometimes got there by way of a dumpster. I'd just make sure the club stepped in first and took the kid. Hell, it wasn't a bad idea to run by Grizzly anyway. Even if no one here took those kids in, I knew some of the other clubs we called family might, or they'd know of some couple who would give them a good home.

"I'm sorry, honey." I knew the words were pathetic at best. It wasn't like a simple phrase, no matter how heartfelt, could wipe out the things she'd been through. "Whatever happens, just know that I'm right here with you. If you can't have kids, then we either won't have any or we'll adopt. Let's just focus on right this moment."

She nodded and tightened her hold on me. "I don't know what I ever did to deserve having you in my life, Jameson. I'm so glad that Beau brought me here and I got to meet you."

"Me too, baby. Me too."

Meeting Mei was the best thing that had ever happened to me. Whatever the future held, we'd face it together.

But perhaps I should have said as much to Mei. If I'd known what the morning would bring, I would have.

Chapter Seven

Meiling

My stomach rolled and bile rose up my throat as I stared at Trotter. The Prospect on the gate refused to let him in, and I'd thought I was safe as long as he was out there. It seemed I was wrong. The barrel of the gun pointed at my face showed me the error of my ways. When Dingo's phone had rung this morning, he'd grumbled something and hadn't woken up, so I'd answered it. Or more accurately, I'd pressed the button to accept the call and the man on the other end just started talking. Hearing that Trotter had come for me, I'd thought maybe I could convince him to walk away without bothering Dingo. I hadn't told anyone my plan, and the Prospect on the gate had been more than a little shocked at my arrival.

"You're coming with me, Mei. You're costing me money, you stupid cunt!"

I didn't even flinch at the names he hurled at me anymore. The Prospect looked torn as to what he should do. I saw his fingers twitch and wondered if he was about to pull the gun I saw tucked at the small of his back. That would either piss off Trotter and make things a lot worse, or he'd shoot the man who had made my life a nightmare the last several months.

Either way, I had a feeling Dingo was going to be pissed at me.

"You don't own me, Trotter," I said. The Prospect was reaching for his pocket, slowly. I didn't know what he had in there, but I also didn't want

Trotter to notice. Better to keep his focus on me. "I belong here now."

He sneered and spat at me through the chain link. "You're just a stupid whore. Your pussy isn't any more special than anyone else's. The second you're gone, they'll replace you with someone else. All they care about is a place to stick their dicks."

From the corner of my eye, I saw the Prospect slide a phone from his pocket and press a few buttons before letting it fall back inside. I didn't know who he'd just called, but part of me really hoped it wasn't Dingo. If he found out how stupid I'd been, he would erupt. And I could admit that this had been the dumbest thing I'd ever done in my life.

"I'm more than that." I stood a little straighter. "I'm not just a whore to them."

I heard the sound of a motorcycle coming down the road that curved through the compound, then a second one. Before Trotter got a chance to toss out any more threats or insults, the man who'd asked me to suck him off -- Demon if I remembered right -- and the man I'd run into my first time here both pulled up on their bikes. I didn't remember his name, and I didn't much care what it was right then. I glanced their way for just a moment, but it was too long.

A gun went off and my ears rang. There was a burning pain through my neck and the world went a little fuzzy. I tried to take a step toward Demon, but my legs gave out and the ground rushed up at me. He looked like he was shouting, but I couldn't hear anything. The compound seemed to explode with life suddenly, more bikes and men showing up. Two of them knelt beside me, one pressing a hand against my chest to keep me down and the other ripped off his shirt, holding it against my neck. Their lips were moving, but I couldn't make out what they were saying.

I sucked in a breath and there was a loud *pop* in my ears. Then everything was almost too loud as I heard shouting, more bikes, and gunfire.

"Dingo," I said.

"We're getting him. Just stay still, Mei. You've been hit."

Hit? I didn't understand what he meant at first, then I felt the cool trickle of something as it dripped from my neck. Was that blood? Was I... shot? That fucker!

"I hate that man," I said.

The man holding me down smiled at my words. "You and me both, honey. Just hang on. We've got the doc heading in, and I'm sure Dingo will be here any second."

"He's going to kill me."

The guy snorted. "No, he won't kill you, but it wouldn't surprise me if he spanked your ass. Why did you come to the gates without him?"

"Thought I could send Trotter on his way."

"I don't know if she's brave, or batshit fucking crazy," the other one muttered.

A motorcycle was coming in fast, the engine roaring toward the gates. I had no doubt it was Dingo. I heard the tires skid and then booted steps racing toward me. Dingo dropped to his knees at my side, a look of horror and grief in his eyes.

"I'm fine," I assured him.

"No, Mei, you aren't fucking fine. You're bleeding." His gaze scanned the area. "Where's the asshole who shot her?"

"Full of bullets." The guy who had been holding me down let go and rocked back on his heels, giving

Dingo more room. "If he's still breathing, he won't be for long."

Dingo looked down at me again. "Why the hell didn't you wake me up? How did you even know he was here?"

"Phone."

"Prospect called you, but Mei answered instead. Idiot started talking before he realized it wasn't you who answered. It seems your woman thought Trotter would just walk off when she told him she was staying."

"Thought I was safe behind the gate," I said. It was getting harder to breathe as the pain in my neck intensified.

The others backed away, leaving me alone with Dingo. I reached for his hand. He laced our fingers together, then leaned down to press a kiss on my lips. The shift made him press harder on the shirt against my neck. I hadn't even realized he was holding it now. Tears sprang to my eyes, and I saw the panicked look on his face as he started shouting for the doc.

"Doctor Larkin is here, Mei. I'm going to let him look at your neck, and then I'll carry you into the clubhouse, or wherever he needs me to take you. Just lie still, sweetheart."

"Who helped me?" I asked. "Thank them."

"Wolf was holding you down and Dragon literally gave you the shirt off his back."

I cracked a smile, hoping his sense of humor meant things weren't that bad. If they were, I'd have died by now, right? Being shot in the neck couldn't be a good thing. Since I was able to breathe and talk, it had to mean I would be just fine. Everyone was probably worried for no reason. A bandage and I'd be good as new. And maybe some pain reliever.

The doctor came into view, giving me a kind smile, as he reached for the shirt against my neck. Dingo relinquished it to him, and Dr. Larkin pulled it away. He reached into a bag he'd brought with him and pulled out a small packet.

"This is going to sting, Mei. It's an alcohol swab. I need to clean the area so I can get a better look at what's going on."

I took a deep breath and prepared myself. Sting? *Holy hell!* That wasn't a sting. My neck felt like it was on fire. My grip tightened on Dingo's hand and I hoped I wasn't breaking his fingers. The doctor hummed and prodded the area before giving a nod.

"She'll be fine. It doesn't look deep enough for stitches, but I want to make sure I get it cleaned well. I'll put a dressing on it, but it would be best if left alone for at least twenty-four hours." Dr. Larkin stood and picked up his bag. "But I'm not treating her on the ground near the gate. She can ride with me to your house, Dingo."

Dingo helped me stand and led me over to the doctor's car. Once I was seated, he pressed a kiss to my forehead, then shut the door. The doctor drove slowly through the compound, and I could hear a motorcycle following. I figured it was Dingo. At the house, I waited for someone to help me from the car, then Dingo led me straight to our room. I'd noticed earlier that he'd changed the bed, and my stomach knotted, remembering exactly when and why he'd done that.

"Dr. Larkin, how much longer before the test results are in?" I asked. "The ones from yesterday."

"About two more days. Why? Are you not feeling well? Any pain or anything other than from your gunshot wound?"

"No, it's not that." I looked at the bed. "We, um... We had sex earlier and I'm worried I might have given something to Dingo."

"No protection?" the doctor asked with a raised eyebrow.

"I fucking forgot, okay?" Dingo asked with a hint of growl to his voice. "Would you just stop the bleeding and get her patched up?"

The doctor helped me onto the bed, but I refused to lie down and get blood everywhere. "I need a towel to put under me."

Dingo snorted. "Like I give a shit if you bleed on the damn bed. I can replace the fucking sheets, Mei. What I can't do is replace *you*. Will you just let the doc take care of you?"

I just stared and waited. Eventually, he gave in and went to the bathroom, returning with two towels, which he folded in half and laid across the pillow and top part of the bed. It made me feel all warm and fuzzy that he was so worried about me. No one had ever cared before. I'd thought Beau had, but I had to be realistic. If he'd cared about me as much as I'd believed, he wouldn't have left and never checked to see if I was okay. I wasn't angry with him. He'd done what he needed to in order to survive. Just as I had.

I lay back and let the doctor move my hair out the way. Dingo reached up to hold it in place over my head while the doctor cleaned and dressed the wound. Whatever he put on it stung a bit, but nowhere near as bad as the alcohol swab had. I was just thankful it didn't need stitches. Maybe it was just a minor wound.

The doctor pulled some pills from his bag, then hesitated. "If you had unprotected sex, I can't give you these, Mei. Not if there's even the slightest possibility you could be pregnant."

I didn't think it was likely, but there was always a chance. Between the miscarriages, which I hadn't mentioned, and the abortions my foster family and Trotter forced me to get, getting pregnant wouldn't be easy. I'd only had one abortion with Trotter, and only because the shot hadn't taken effect yet. And even if I *could* get pregnant, I wasn't exactly mother material, was I? I didn't even know how a mother was supposed to act. I couldn't remember mine at all.

"Trotter made us take birth control. I got a shot about two months ago. I think." I frowned. It had just been two months ago, hadn't it? Was I due for another one? "He said it was cheaper to prevent the pregnancy than get rid of it."

I heard Dingo mutter something that sounded like *asshole* and the doctor didn't look too pleased either. I had a feeling if Trotter wasn't already dead, he would be soon. Dingo looked ready to murder him. As much as I would hate for him to get blood on his hands for my sake, I wouldn't exactly mourn the loss of a guy like Trotter. The world would be better off if every man out there like him were wiped off the planet.

"If the pain gets too bad, I can call in something that would be safe if you're pregnant," Dr. Larkin said. "Until then, take Tylenol if you need anything. I'll call as soon as I have your test results back from the lab. At least that will be one worry off your mind. I didn't see physical signs of anything during the exam, but there are certain diseases that wouldn't be noticeable in the early stages."

Right. So, there was still a chance I'd been infected with something. Until we knew for sure, I'd keep my hands to myself. Of course, getting shot would probably put a damper on things in the bedroom. The way Dingo was eyeing me I figured he'd be handling me like I was made of glass. Until I healed at any rate.

"When can I take the bandage off and shower?" I asked.

"Leave it on until tomorrow if you can. After that, you can clean it in the shower, but try not to submerge it in water until the skin knits together a bit. Otherwise, you might start bleeding again. It should be healed enough for regular activities to resume within a week."

I translated that into we could have sex again after a week of healing. Fate must be fucking with me. After all these years I finally have an orgasm -- multiple ones -- and find a guy who treats me well, and I only get to have sex with him once before getting injured. And yes, I could admit that I was entirely at fault. If I hadn't gone to the gate to see Trotter, then this wouldn't have happened. Then again, if I'd woken Dingo, he might have been the one shot, and what if Trotter's aim had been better with a larger target?

Dingo walked out with Dr. Larkin and I closed my eyes. Now that the excitement had worn off, I was starting to feel incredibly tired. I struggled to stay awake in case Dingo came back into the room, but it was a losing battle. I could feel my body growing heavy and my thoughts turned a bit fuzzy. As I sank into sleep, I briefly thought about Dingo and hoped that he wouldn't do anything stupid, like kill Trotter, if the bullets hadn't done the job already. He seemed like the type to seek vengeance, and I much preferred him out of jail than in it.

Chapter Eight

Dingo

Grizzly had read Simon the riot act over letting Mei anywhere near the gate while Trotter was there. Even if the kid hadn't known the asshole was armed, he should have protected Mei at any cost. While his quick thinking had gotten Demon there before anything worse could happen, it wasn't enough when the entire situation could have been avoided. He never should have mentioned Trotter over the phone without knowing it was me and not Mei who answered.

Since Beau was still on my shit list, I'd asked Henry to stand guard outside my house in case Mei needed anything. Griz had put Carver on the gate for now with Beau and Simon helping in the clubhouse. We honestly needed some fresh blood. If any of these guys washed out before being patched in, then we'd be short on manpower for the shit jobs the rest of us didn't want.

Some of the clubs had a barn or warehouse where they persuaded men to talk. I knew a few with underground bunkers for that sort of thing. Thanks to some fairly recent renovations, we now had a room under the clubhouse for those types of meetings. Griz had spared no expense to have the place soundproofed, added a drain to the floor, and a fancy lock that only patched members could access with a retina scan. Maybe he was being overly cautious, but it was understandable. We'd had enough men go to prison, and Griz was trying to protect his club while letting us get the job done our way. Not that this room would have saved Badger from getting locked up. He'd beaten a man to death when he caught the asshole raping a teen girl. Any of us would have done the same.

Now that teen girl was all grown up, and married to Badger. They'd had some bad luck, though. Adalia had lost their baby and it had hit her hard. We'd all worried about her when it seemed like she'd sunk into a state of depression. No one faulted her for it, but I'd watched as Badger tore into anyone who even looked at him wrong. He was so stressed and concerned for his woman that anyone was fair game as an outlet for him.

I glanced over at him. "You couldn't have kept him breathing a little longer?"

Trotter, or what was left of him, was in a heap in the center of the room. He'd been hit by no less than six bullets. Somehow, he'd managed to stay alive long enough for my brothers to haul him down here, get him to talk a bit, and then Badger had let loose on him. If Trotter hadn't been the worst sort of man, I might have felt sorry for him.

"Fuck, Badger. What the hell did you use on his eyes?" I asked, nausea welling up at the gruesome sight.

"Blowtorch," he said matter-of-factly.

That would explain why it looked like his eyes had exploded. They'd probably popped from the heat before the flame even touched them. Badger was a sadistic fucker when it came to torturing men, but I'd also seen him treat Adalia like a damn queen. Watching the two of them, seeing how gentle he was with her, you'd never know he was capable of something like this.

"He came to get Mei because it seems she was just on loan to him," Demon said.

"On loan?" I asked. "What the fuck does that mean?"

Demon rolled his shoulders and cracked his neck. Whatever he'd learned, it had pissed off the Sergeant-at-Arms. Demon only ever did that move when he was ready to bathe in someone's blood, and since Trotter was already dead, it couldn't be him.

"What did Mei tell you of her life before working for Trotter?" he asked.

"She was in foster care. You saw the damn video in Church yesterday. You know what her foster family was like. Why are you asking me this?"

Demon rubbed at the back of his neck. "Because her foster father somehow managed to herd her toward Trotter. It was a form of payment. Trotter got to use her to earn some cash, but once the amount the foster dad owed was paid in full, then he was supposed to deliver Mei back to the guy. It seems she was due back now. Only thing I can figure is the foster parents were hoping to get in a few more videos and make more cash off her."

Wait. What? "But she aged out of the system. How the hell could Trotter give her back? It's not like she's underage and needs a guardian."

Demon looked away, and Wolf shuffled his feet, looking decidedly uncomfortable. Exactly what weren't they telling me? Shit. "She *is* legal, right?"

"Yes," Demon said. "Now she is."

That... didn't sound good. "The age of consent in Georgia is sixteen. Are you telling me that..."

Fuck. Even if it was legal to be with her, I'd never knowingly had sex with anyone under eighteen before. But no... Mei had said that she was fourteen when those videos were first taken, and that four years had passed. She said she'd aged out of the system.

"Relax," Wolf said. "The reason Trotter was here today is that he fucked up. Mei was seventeen when the foster dad told her she'd aged out of the system. He lied. Trotter was supposed to keep a tighter rein on her and return her *before* she aged out for real. But Mei *is* eighteen now. Her birthday was last week."

I was starting to get a headache from all this bullshit. "How did she not know that she hadn't aged out of the system? Does she not know when her birthday is? Is that even possible?"

"I asked Outlaw to see what he could find, but he'll probably have the others help," Demon said. "Others" most likely meaning Wire and his woman, Lavender, another hacker who went by the name Dark Labyrinth. "I think this is much bigger than just Mei, possibly way bigger. We think that Mei's social worker might be in on it. Maybe a kickback, or they might be blackmailing him or her. Either way, I don't see Mei going back to that hell willingly. If she'd thought she'd aged out, I'd imagine she'd have fought against them. Or maybe that's what they wanted, to have her struggle. Sick fucks."

I didn't know what to make of any of this shit. All I knew was that I wanted everyone who had hurt Mei, even if they contributed by not doing a damn thing and knowing she needed help, to be hauled to this room. And then I'd make them all pay. In blood.

"Go take care of Mei," Demon said. "When we find out something, we'll call or stop by. For now, she needs you there with her. Not lost in your head and plotting to murder half the men in the city."

Wolf cleared his throat. "You do know if you want to kill every guy who's touched her, the death toll is about to get a lot higher around here. The Ruby Slipper does a shit ton of business, and as far as those men know, the women chose to be there."

"Just get me names, and I want details of how they hurt Mei. I'll decide who gets marked off the list after that." I turned to leave but paused. "She needs to know she's not alone. I know Griz is overprotective of Shella and Lilian, but meeting them might help Mei."

"Not Adalia?" Badger asked.

"Not if it's going to make you want to kick my ass. If she's up for it, then send her by. Maybe not right now, but tomorrow. Mei was resting when I left."

I walked out of the room and up the stairs to the main part of the clubhouse. Not even nighttime and already the club whores were showing up. A few of my brothers were at tables or on the couches. More than one had their dick out, which wasn't something I ever cared to see. I gave them a half-hearted wave as I left the building and went out to my bike.

Before I could swing my leg over the seat, a flash of purple caught my attention at the edge of the clubhouse. The skirt was too long to belong to a club whore. If Adalia was this close to the clubhouse, Badger would lose his shit. Deciding it was better to send her on her way before he came out, I headed over and turned the corner. Except it wasn't Adalia.

"Lilian?" I asked, keeping my voice low. She always startled so easily. Getting close to her was sometimes as difficult as approaching a stray cat. "Is something wrong? Did you need Grizzly?"

She backed up a step and shook her head.

"You know he won't like you hanging out here, especially while the other girls are inside. Better get home." I eased back a step, trying to give her more space.

"I can't. Not yet," she said.

"Can't or won't?" I asked. What the fuck was going on? If Griz found out she'd been here, he'd lose it. I'd never seen someone so protective in my life. They might be his adopted daughters, but he guarded them like they were his flesh and blood.

"Maybe a bit of both. I'm supposed to meet someone. It's only for a moment, but… they're late."

I snorted. "I'm not stupid, honey. You can say he. It's obvious you're meeting a guy, and since you're still inside the gates, that means it's a brother or a Prospect. Either way, Grizzly will be pissed as hell if they touch you."

She glanced away, her lips pinched tight. Whatever was going on, it wasn't sexual. So what, exactly, was she up to?

"I just needed some advice. Dragon said he'd help," she said.

Yeah, I bet he would. He'd probably try to help her right out of her clothes. He was a decent guy, but when it came to women, he had a bit of an issue. He'd never met a woman he couldn't charm, and their panties dropped within seconds of meeting him. I'd seen him make eye contact with a woman, give her a chin nudge, then go fuck her in a bathroom. For Dragon's sake, I hoped he kept his dick in his pants or Grizzly might kill him.

"If he doesn't show in another minute, go home, Lilian."

She gave me a quick, jerky nod. Sighing, I turned and went back to my bike. As much as she needed someone to babysit her, it couldn't be me. I had my own woman to take care of. When I'd heard that Mei had been shot, I thought my world was ending. I hadn't even realized she'd gotten out of bed, much less left the house. It was tempting to handcuff to her to me when I went to sleep, but I couldn't do that to her.

At the house, Henry was still sitting out front, leaning against his bike. He was near enough if Mei cried out for help, but had kept enough distance to be respectful. The club hadn't had any issues with Henry since he'd started prospecting for us. It made me wonder if he knew anyone else trustworthy who might be interested. Even though Griz hadn't exactly been recruiting, our numbers could drop in a split second. With as much heat as we ran into time and again, it wouldn't take much to be down a few brothers. Either from bullets or jail, if not other means.

"Henry, you have any friends outside of the club?" I asked.

"A few."

"Any who might want to prospect for the Devil's Fury?" I asked.

He tipped his head back and seemed to think it over. When his gaze locked with mine again, he gave a nod. "Know of two. Military backgrounds on both. One just came home a few months ago and has been a bit lost. Club might give him a bit of direction."

Good to know. "I'll talk it over with Grizzly. Text me their names and any info you have on them, but don't mention this to them yet."

I left Henry in the driveway and went in to check on Mei. She was still asleep in the bed, but had shifted onto her side. The white bandage was stark against her red hair and I rubbed at the pain in my chest. I could have lost her. I'd barely found her and already she'd been in danger. If her foster father thought he was getting Mei back, he'd better think again. Not only would he never see her again, but I was going to ensure that he couldn't hurt anyone else either.

Fuck! He had to have other kids in that house. Was he abusing them the way he had Mei? I pulled my phone from my pocket and shot off a text to Outlaw, asking him to look into it. Knowing the club's computer guru, he was already on it. He seemed to know what we'd want or need before the rest of us did. Even if he couldn't work the same magic with a computer that he once had, Outlaw was still a big asset to the club. He was something of a hero not only to us, but to the Dixie Reapers too, after he'd nearly died to keep Lavender safe. I'd gladly have him at my back any day.

I removed my cut and set it on the dresser before pulling off my boots. Mei was lying on my side of the bed, so I slid under the blankets on her half and scooted as close to her as I dared. If I jostled her, it might cause her pain, or wake her up. I didn't want either to happen. Even though I wasn't tired, I just needed to be near her. Reaching out, I twirled a strand of her hair around my finger. There were so many shades of red. I'd be willing to bet when the morning sun hit it, it would look like living flame.

Mei kicked out and twisted. Before she could put pressure on her wound, I managed to turn her back onto her side and pull her against my chest. With my arms around her, she settled down again, not even fully waking up.

I wanted to keep her safe, to make sure the world was a better place for her. I just didn't know how to do it. Evil lurked in the shadows, and even if I took down everyone responsible for ever hurting her, there would just be more hiding somewhere. Each of the women who were now part of this club had come here as a last resort. Adalia had been raped and was adopted by Grizzly and his wife, May. Then we'd lost May and

Griz had adopted Lilian and Shella. Lilian had suffered horribly in Colombia, and had come here after a rescue mission was launched to bring Havoc home. As for Shella... she'd had to grow up fast even though she didn't seem to have been abused as badly as Lilian or Mei. Griz had taken her in when she was fourteen and had nowhere else to go.

My phone buzzed in my pocket and I pulled it out, answering as quietly as I could so I wouldn't disturb Mei. Outlaw's name flashed across the screen right before I accepted the call.

"You find something?" I asked.

"I've found a fuck ton, and we're going to have some major problems," Outlaw said.

I eased away from Mei and got out of bed, going into the living room. Sitting in my favorite chair, I braced myself for whatever I was about to hear. If Outlaw thought we were going to have some issues, then shit was seriously about to hit the fan. I'd found over the years whatever he couldn't bury in his lines of code Wire, Shade, or Surge could. Sometimes they all worked together, and that's when the truly magical things happened. I'd seen them make people or even entire companies vanish like they'd never existed -- wiping out someone's identity or creating new ones was simple enough for them. Sometimes it seemed like they were playing God in some ways.

"What's wrong?" I asked.

"Did you know that Mei's name is actually Meiling?" he asked.

"Beau called her that when he asked for our help, but she insists we call her Mei. Why? What does that matter?"

"Because her full name is Meiling Shan Young. Her name means beautiful coral, in case you wanted to know, but it's her last name that poses a big fucking problem. Like, you need to marry her right the fuck now so you don't die kind of problem," Outlaw said. "And this is just what I've found so far. Wire is working on some other stuff with Lavender's help. I've never seen anything this fucked-up before. I know you and her dad will want justice for Mei, but I'm going to put as much as I can into the Feds' hands and let them handle at least some of it. The rest we'll bury."

"What the hell does that mean? Who's her dad?"

"Does the name Robert Young ring any bells?" Outlaw asked.

It suddenly felt like all the air had been sucked out of the room. Holy. Fucking. Shit. I was so Goddamn dead it wasn't funny. How had no one in the club known who Mei was? Or for that matter, how had she ended up in foster care to begin with? The entire club was about to implode once Outlaw shared this latest bit of news.

"Are you telling me the woman in my bed, the one I just claimed, is the daughter of *Blades*?" I asked, trying to remain calm even though I felt like I might have a heart attack. I'd never personally met him, but the stories Grizzly had told over the years... Damn. That was one man I never wanted to meet in a dark alley, and I'd not only claimed his daughter but possibly knocked her up?

"The one and only. As to how we never knew about her? I'm not entirely certain. He signed the forms for her birth certificate and he's listed as her father, and since I'm looking at actual signatures on one of these, it seems legit. I think he honestly knew about her. But therein lies another issue. The birth certificate I found was buried. Like professionally buried, and another was placed in Mei's file with social services. It lists father as unknown and mother deceased, and it has her age as being off by nearly a full year -- about nine months actually -- which makes no fucking sense to me. I mean, what was the point in changing her age? And them telling her she'd aged out of the system? What the hell? Even by the fabricated birth certificate their math would be off. How did Mei buy that line of bullshit?"

I sighed and closed my eyes. This was a mess of epic proportions. "Check into the social worker. I think you'll find your clues there. Or even higher up the food chain maybe. This is such a clusterfuck of epic proportions we may never unravel all of it. Any news on her mom or how she got into the system to begin with?"

"The mother was listed as Xi-wang Chen. She was here on a student visa around the time Mei was born. Looks like she gave birth, and about a month after Blades went to prison, the mom vanished and Mei was placed in the system. It wasn't until she was older that she ended up with the foster family from fucking hell," Outlaw said. "The assholes who abused her didn't get their hands on her until she was twelve, or what her new birth certificate indicated as her twelfth birthday. She was actually thirteen at the time. Maybe they wanted her to seem younger, or needed a thirteen-year-old but wanted control over her past when she'd actually turn eighteen? Fuck if I know. I'll dig deeper into the social worker's files and find out why she was transferred. She's been in the system since she was just a toddler."

"So Blades has a daughter that he's never mentioned, hasn't seen since he was locked up, and he has no fucking clue that she went into foster care or what she's been through," I said just to sum everything up. Fucking perfect.

It was quiet on the other end and I heard some tapping on his keyboard. Much slower than what he used to do, and I knew that this was costing him. Outlaw had to be in a lot of fucking pain, but he was helping anyway. It was just who he was.

"Something else going on?" I asked.

"I've had Wire and Lavender helping me out, and Surge has been digging too. So... congratulations?"

I knew exactly what that meant. "They married us, didn't they?"

"Yep. As of two minutes ago, there was a marriage license and certificate placed on file with the county courthouse. And you know how damn good Wire and Lavender are. Everything will look one hundred percent legit. They're working on changing Mei's name legally right now on all her other documentation. She'll officially be Meiling Shan Withers."

I snorted. "If they're so handy, once we have all the details of what happened, just have them wipe out the last decade or so of her life."

"Not until everyone has paid the price," Outlaw said, his voice low and deadly. "There are things I'll never tell you or show you, and I doubt she'll bring it up either. Don't push her to open up. Dingo, those people were seriously fucked-up. The video from Church was nothing compared to the other stuff Wire found. We're taking every last one of those fuckers down, no matter what it takes."

"Tell everyone I said thanks for helping. Let me know when you have more."

"You got it," Outlaw said. "Just… maybe break the news to her about her daddy a bit gently? And definitely tell her you're married before she asks to meet him."

"Right." That was a no-brainer.

Dingo hung up.

Sure, just go talk to the most deadly member of the club and tell him all about his precious girl sleeping in my bed. Even telling him I was his son-in-law might not save my ass. If anything, it was possible that would make it worse. He hadn't seen Mei since she was a baby. I wasn't sure how that visit would go over, or if she'd even want to meet her father.

Movement caught my eye and I glanced over at the doorway just as Mei came in from the hall. The look in her eyes told me that she'd heard at least part of my conversation. I'd hoped to ease her into everything, but it seemed that wasn't going to be possible. Now I just had to hope that she'd listen calmly and not freak the fuck out when I told her about her parents and what little else I knew about her situation.

"Did my wife sleep well?" I asked.

Her mouth dropped open and snapped shut. Yeah, this would be a fun conversation.

Chapter Nine

Meiling

I reached down and pinched my arm, but no, I wasn't still asleep. Why had he asked about how his wife had slept? Was that supposed to be me? Or was I about to find out that there was another woman in his life? No, he'd been looking at me when he said it. The last time I checked, we weren't married. Didn't we have to go before a judge or priest for that to happen?

"Wife?" I asked.

Dingo sighed. "Come have a seat, Mei. It seems we need to talk."

"I don't remember marrying you. Am I about to be tossed out by some angry woman you forgot you married?" I asked, stepping farther into the room and perching on the edge of the couch.

Dingo rubbed his hands up and down his face, something I'd noticed he did when he was stressed. Which meant he probably didn't have the best of news for me. I'd heard him talking on the phone, but I hadn't made out much of the conversation. By the time I reached the hall, he was hanging up.

"I asked Outlaw to look into a few things for me," he said. "For lack of a better word, he's a hacker. With a bit of help, he was able to dig into your past and find out some information I don't think even you're aware of."

Digging into my past? Was there something worse than the videos he'd already found? I'd thought maybe it had been enough to satisfy the club's curiosity. My stomach clenched. That would be very,

very bad. I knew exactly what someone with those sorts of skills could find without much searching, and all of it would either infuriate Dingo, or disgust him so much he'd throw me out.

"Like what?" I asked, deciding to be braver than I felt and forge ahead. Better to know now than keep wondering.

"Do you know your full name?" he asked.

"Meiling Chen," I said.

Dingo got up and moved closer, sitting down next to me. "No, sweetheart. Your name is Meiling Shan Young. Do you remember anything about your parents? Anything at all before foster care?"

"No. The first memories I have are of an old woman who smelled like mothballs. I was only with her a short time before the social worker moved me elsewhere. I didn't stay in any particular home for long until the last family," I said.

He nodded, looking as if he'd expected me to say as much. "Do you know why I was moved so much? Or why I was placed with that family?" I asked.

"Your mother was from China and was here on a student visa. We don't know yet what happened to her, but it seems that she was seeing someone. Your father, obviously." Dingo blew out a breath and reached for my hand. "This isn't going to be easy to say, so I'm just going to spit it out. Your dad is Robert Young. Around here, we know him as Blades, and he's serving a life sentence for murder. As to the other, the foster bullshit, Outlaw is still working on it. We think the social worker was in on it, but I don't know how it all fits together yet, or why they'd bother to falsify your birth certificate, unless they had a plan for you from the beginning."

I wasn't sure if I wanted to cry over finding out my father's name, or because he was a murderer. Did that mean I really was just trash? Dingo had made me feel special, like everyone in my life had lied up to this point. Now I had to wonder if everyone else was right and he was wrong. How could I be good, be decent, if my father was in prison for murder?

"Blades? What kind of name is…" And then it hit me. "He's part of your club?"

Dingo nodded. "Back before my time here. I've only heard stories of him and never met the man. Mei, he signed the paperwork for your birth certificate. He knew about you and accepted you as his daughter."

I digested those words a moment. If my father had known about me, and was still alive, then shouldn't he have sent someone for me? It seemed the President, Grizzly, liked to take in stray girls. Wouldn't he have given me a place to stay?

"Then why did no one ever come for me?" I asked. Had my own father not even wanted me? Had he thrown me away like everyone else in my life up to this point?

"And that is the million-dollar question, sweetheart. I don't know and neither does Outlaw. We haven't told the rest of the club yet that you're Blades' daughter."

"I'm not sure I want to be a murderer's kid."

Dingo tipped his head and studied me. "Not everything is always black-and-white, Mei. If anyone should know that, it's you."

My cheeks warmed. He was right. To everyone else, I was just a whore. Dingo didn't see me that way, though, and he hadn't from the very beginning. Although… I still didn't fully understand the wife comment.

"While I appreciate learning more about where I came from, what does that have to do with the wife you mentioned?" I asked.

"When Outlaw realized who your dad is, he knew that I was going to have a very short life when Blades heard I'd claimed his daughter. So he asked some friends to hack into the county government and create a marriage license and certificate for us. As far as the county and state are concerned, we're officially married, which makes you Meiling Shan Withers."

"Withers?" she asked. "I didn't even know your last name."

He rolled his neck and it cracked twice. "Yeah, well. We kind of went about all this the wrong way, but time was of the essence. Not sure your daddy is going to give a shit that I tried to save you."

"You're assuming he even cares. What if he's the reason I was given up? Did you ever think maybe *he* had me put into foster care? You said it yourself. The club didn't know about me. Would he have kept me away from the club if he was proud of me? If he'd…" I swallowed the knot in my throat. "If he'd wanted me, would I have still been his dirty little secret?"

Dingo gathered me into his arms and held me as tears burned my eyes. I fought hard not to cry. I'd learned not to show weakness, and even though I knew he would never judge me for it, I still didn't like letting my emotions get the best of me. On the streets, and in the foster care system, only the strongest survived. Crying made people think you were fragile, and that only led to trouble.

"I can't tell you what to do, sweetheart. This one is entirely up to you, but the club is going to talk to Blades once they hear you're his daughter. He'll find out you're here, that you're living in my house as my ol' lady, and he'll want to speak to you. Assuming he doesn't just hire someone to have me gutted in my sleep. That's always a possibility."

I tensed and pulled away. "What? I know you said he was in prison for murder, but then you said that not everything was black-and-white. Either he's a stone-cold killer or he's not. Which is it, Jameson?"

"When it comes to his baby girl? I'm going to think all bets are off and he'll do whatever it takes to protect you. Until someone talks to him, we'll never know why he didn't mention you. Do you want to meet your father, Mei?"

"No." At least, I didn't think I did. "Or at least not right now."

"Do you know your ring size?" he asked. "Since you're my wife, you'll need a ring." I glanced at his bare hand and he snickered. "Yes, Mei. I'm getting one too. If you want, I'll even tattoo your name on me."

I thought about the artwork I'd noticed on his body. He had one for his club across his back, and countless others on his chest and abdomen. His arms were pretty bare except his biceps, but his shirt hid those. In fact, none of his tattoos could be seen unless he was partially undressed. I wondered if he'd done that on purpose.

"Do you want me to have your name tattooed on me?" I asked.

"Only if you want to. You'll have a property cut soon. Possibly by tomorrow. You'll need to wear it anytime you leave the house. Consider it a layer of protection."

I nodded and contemplated whether I wanted to get his name on my body. It seemed so permanent, as if I were agreeing to be his forever. In my world, forever could last a lifetime or until your next breath.

But he wouldn't offer to put my name on his body permanently if he didn't want a lifetime with me, would he? I was still trying to learn to trust people. So far, Dingo hadn't lied to me. "Could we get the tattoos together?" I asked.

"If that's what you want. There's a parlor over on the main strip in town. Lots of foot traffic over that way, so even if we ran into anyone from your past, they wouldn't dare cause trouble. Especially if we take a few of my brothers with us. Wolf would be a good person to ask."

"Just you and Wolf?" I asked.

"Well, no. You haven't met Steel yet, but I think you'd like him. Maybe. He's kind of reserved. Ex-military so he's never been all that chatty with any of us. I know he'd protect you with his life. Any of the club would."

"Then ask Steel and Wolf. I just need a minute to clean up."

"Don't get your bandage wet, Mei. If you get in the shower, only let the water hit you from the shoulders down."

"I'll be quick," I promised. I stopped by the guest room and gathered my things, then moved them over to Dingo's room. Since everything in his bathroom had a manly scent, I also grabbed some of the things from the other shower. While he made his calls, or whatever he needed to do, I quickly rinsed off, braided my hair, and changed into a fresh pair of jeans and a gray shirt. It was as plain and nondescript as I could get, and I loved it. There was a pair of white tennis shoes and I put those on as well. Admiring myself in the mirror, I had to admit that this look was definitely one I'd want to keep for a while. I didn't know if it would be considered what I'd heard called "soccer mom" or what, but I liked it.

By the time I got back to the living room, Dingo was dressed and ready to go. He waited for me at the front door and gave me a smile, reaching out his hand. I slipped my fingers across his palm and let him tug me out the door.

"I didn't think you should be on my bike after this morning's incident, so we'll use one of the club trucks." He opened the passenger door, then stared at me. "Can you drive?"

"No. I don't have a license either. Or any other form of ID."

"Hmm. We'll have to fix that. Not sure I'd be the best person to teach you, though. I might ask Grizzly. He taught his girls and has the patience of a saint when it comes to women."

I wasn't sure I agreed with him on that one, but he knew the man better than I did.

I'd ridden through town with the foster family plenty of times, but I'd never paid much attention to my surroundings. I'd always been too focused on just getting through the day. Now I had the chance to look at the different stores and admire some of the historic buildings. Dingo pulled up in front of a building that seemed to have been a barber shop at some point. The red-and-white pole out front still swirled, but the glass window clearly said *Inkin' It*. The glass was smoky and I couldn't see inside, but anticipation thrummed in my veins. A tattoo! I'd never thought to get one before.

Two motorcycles parked on either side of the truck and I saw Wolf and a man I hadn't yet met get off their bikes. Maybe the Steel he'd mentioned? They lounged on either side of the entrance to the tattoo shop, arms folded, looking very much like bodyguards. I supposed that's what they were, for the moment.

Dingo helped me from the truck and we walked in together, a bell jingling as the door to the shop opened. I reached up to smooth my hair, making sure it hid my bandage. I'd learned the fewer questions people asked the better.

There was a petite woman behind the counter, her pixie-cut hair spiked up in neon pink, and her piercings glittered under the bright lights. There were two black stars outlined on her upper right cheek. The look worked for her. She came off as a badass fairy. Since I didn't know if she'd appreciate that description, I kept my mouth shut.

"Hey, Dingo. What did you bring us today? New customer?" she asked, her smile going wide. "Or are you getting more ink?"

"Both," he said. "This is Meiling. My wife."

The woman's mouth formed an O of surprise and her gaze skittered over to me. I wasn't sure what she thought of Dingo's surprise, but when she held her hand out to me, I figured I'd passed inspection.

"Hi, Meiling. I'm Deidre. Everyone just calls me Dee."

"And everyone just calls me Mei." I smiled and took her hand. "It's nice to meet you."

Dee rubbed her hands together like an eager child about to get a cookie. "What are we doing for the two of you?"

"Mei wants her first tattoo, and I want to get her name inked on me."

Dee blinked a moment, glancing between the two of us. "I see. Well, you know the policy on getting someone's name put on your body. If you can convince

Teagan to do it, more power to you. Mind if I tattoo your wife?"

Dingo looked down at me. "You might prefer Dee's touch to Teagan's. He's a big bastard."

"I'd be honored to have you give me my first tattoo, Dee," I told the woman.

"Excellent!" She bounced on her toes. "Come over to my station and tell me what you want. I'll sketch something up and we can talk logistics."

I released Dingo's hand and followed Dee to a workstation just two cubes over. The half walls let me see into all the different areas, and it looked like they had at least four artists set up. Unless some of the stations weren't in use, or were intended for other purposes. This world was new to me.

"I haven't really thought this over," I admitted. "He said I could get a tattoo, and so here we are."

Dee smiled. "Well, you don't have to get the ink today. Just tell me what you're thinking and I'll come up with some ideas. I can show you a rough sketch after we talk, and then give me a few days to flesh it out and we'll set up an appointment for the actual tattoo."

"Dingo sort of saved me. I haven't had the easiest life, but he made himself my protector from the moment he saw me. He claimed me, and now we're married. I want something that shows where I came from, but also where I'm going, if that makes sense."

Dee nodded. She grabbed a sketch pad and pencil, then stared at me.

"Um. Well, he called me a phoenix. I don't know if that gives you anything. I was in foster care. A really fucked-up family had me, and when I aged out of the system, I ended up working at *The Ruby Slipper*." I sank my teeth into my lip to keep from saying anything more. Everyone in town knew about that place, so now she'd know what type of woman I was. Or rather had been. "I didn't want to be there. I never wanted any of that."

Dee gave me a sympathetic smile. "Hon, I doubt that any of the girls over there *want* to be there. There's no shame in doing whatever is necessary to survive. But I'm going to need some time to think this one over. Come back in two or three days and I'll have a few things sketched. Once I know the direction you prefer me to go, then I can add some more details and we'll get your appointment scheduled."

"Thanks, Dee." I hesitated. "And thank you for not judging me."

Her eyebrows lifted. She set her stuff aside and stood, lifting her shirt to expose her lower abdomen. There were long, angry scars that looked like deep knife wounds across her belly and in the fleshy part over her hip. "This is a reminder that I can't trust everyone I meet," she said. "We all have a past, Mei. Some are worse than others, but it's how we use the knowledge to move forward that counts."

She gave me a hug and led me over to Dingo. He hadn't been wrong when he'd said Teagan was a big bastard. The man working ink into Dingo's skin had to be the tallest, broadest guy I'd ever seen. If he were an actor, studios would be lining up to put him in roles about giants or Titans or something. I watched as he formed my name. My full name. Meiling. I narrowed my eyes at Dingo because he damn well knew I preferred Mei.

"Stop looking at me like that," he said.

"That's not what everyone calls me and you know it."

He winked. "I happen to think your name is sexy. Did you know that Meiling Shan means beautiful coral? Seems fitting."

He thought I looked like coral? I tipped my head to the side as I stared at him, trying to puzzle how I even remotely resembled that.

"You're beautiful, with a fiery color, and you can be prickly," he said.

I huffed and rolled my eyes. Should have known it wasn't completely a compliment. If he wanted *Meiling* on his wrist, then it wasn't like I could stop him. Especially at this point, since my name was already formed in a black script, but Teagan was adding some shading in a pinkish hue around it that almost made my name look like it was glowing. It was actually a bit fascinating. I'd never seen someone get a tattoo before.

After the design was finished, and the tattoo had been cleaned and covered, Dingo paid and we walked out to the truck. I'd thought we were done, but apparently I was wrong. Instead of opening the truck door for me, he led me across the street to *Dyson's Jewelry*, with the two bikers watching our every move from their spot across the street outside the tattoo shop. He'd mentioned getting wedding rings since we were legally -- illegally? -- married. I just hadn't realized he meant *right now*. Didn't something like that cost a lot of money? We hadn't discussed finances, and while his home was nice and his furniture was decent, nothing screamed *rich guy*.

We entered the store, and he went straight to the glass case of wedding rings. It was hard to miss with all the sparkling diamonds, and took up the entire center section of the store's display. Blackwood Falls wasn't anywhere near big enough for this, was it? It almost looked like they had more diamonds than residents.

"May I help you?" asked a man in a gray suit.

"I was a dumbass and married this beautiful lady before buying any rings. Thought I'd remedy that by stopping by your store," Dingo said.

The man eyed me, then Dingo, his gaze staying on the black leather covering his torso a little longer than I'd have liked. Were we about to be kicked out just because Dingo was a biker?

"Anything in particular? Perhaps a plain band?" the man asked.

I squeezed Dingo's hand. "I don't need anything."

He gazed down at me with a look that clearly said we weren't leaving without rings. I sighed and looked at all the shiny things in the case. They were beautiful, but completely unnecessary. I'd never owned jewelry before, and I'd get along just fine without having any now. It was a frivolous expense.

"I want my wife to have the prettiest ring in the store. Anything she wants."

"They're all so sparkly," I murmured.

The man eyed me. "Maybe something a little less ostentatious?"

I nodded. "I don't want anything flashy. Something plain is perfectly fine."

Dingo bumped my shoulder with his. "Meiling, I want you to have the best. You don't have to pick the cheapest thing in here."

I worried at my lip until I tasted blood, too anxious to even bother correcting his use of my full name. I didn't want to discuss this with him, not in the middle of the store, but I needed him to understand that I didn't want anything that would draw attention to myself. I liked being nondescript, blending into the background. It was safer.

"Your wife seems like the type to enjoy understated things. With her coloring and pretty eyes, she doesn't need anything ornamental to make her shine," the man said.

I glanced at him in surprise and he gave me a kind smile. The tension eased from my shoulders a bit and I hoped he could see how grateful I was. Maybe Dingo would listen to him without me having to spell it out for him.

"That it, Meiling?" Dingo asked, watching me intently.

"Yeah. I want to wear a ring that shows I'm yours, but I don't want it to draw attention."

He nodded and looked in the case again. After a moment, he pointed to a silver colored band with pink roses etched into it. "What about that?"

The salesman smiled. "Excellent choice. This band is white and rose gold. If it's not the correct size, we can re-size it or special order one."

He removed it from the case and held the black velvet box out to me. I just stared, almost afraid to touch it. Dingo slipped the ring from the box and eased it onto the ring finger on my left hand. And it fit perfectly. I had to admit, it was very pretty and delicate. I loved it.

"It's perfect, Meiling." He kissed my cheek. "We'll take it."

"Are you going to wear one?" I asked. "You said you would."

"Yeah, but I'd have to take it off at certain times, like when I'm working on the bike. Wouldn't want it to get caught up in anything."

The man cleared his throat. "If I may make a suggestion. We don't sell them here, but there are bands made of a type of rubber material that seem popular with fireman, law enforcement, and men who work with their hands. I believe you can order them online if you know your size."

He looked down at his hands. "I've never worn a ring before."

The man pulled out a ring of little circles and held one up. "Let's try this one. Once you know your size, you can order your ring. Or if you'd like, we can place an order for you to pick up at your convenience."

After a few tries, Dingo found his ring size and placed the order for his wedding band. He paid for our purchases and thanked the man. I smiled up at him as we stepped out onto the sidewalk and immediately ran into someone.

"I'm sor…" The words died on my tongue.

"Time to come home, girl," my foster father said.

Dingo put himself between us and growled like a damn bear. "My wife isn't going anywhere with you."

Chapter Ten

Dingo

The audacity of this fucker! I hoped Mei stayed behind me. Wolf and Steel were crossing the street, coming up behind the asshole. The man reeked of alcohol and sex. His bloodshot and glassy eyes made me wonder if he hadn't partaken of something other than just booze.

"She can't marry you," the guy said. "I didn't give my permission and she's my daughter."

I moved in closer, bumping him with my chest until he stumbled into Steel and Wolf. Steel had a blade pressed against the dick's side within seconds and Wolf had a grip on his shoulder so tight my brother's knuckles were stark white. Pain flashed in the man's eyes.

"Let's get one thing clear. A father doesn't whore out his daughter or make videos of her having sex with other kids or men in exchange for money. You're a child pornographer, and a pedophile. Simple as that. If you think I'm letting you anywhere near Meiling, then you have no fucking clue who you're dealing with."

The man puffed up. "I've got connections."

"Yeah? I don't think they'll do you much good in hell, until I send them there to meet you." He paled and I smiled, flashing my teeth at him. "Good. We understand each other. You're on borrowed time. The two of us will meet again, and I can promise my face will be the last thing you see before the flames start licking at you."

Steel pressed the blade harder and a trickle of blood soaked the guy's shirt. He squealed like a damn pig and tried to jerk away, but Wolf held him too tight.

"If I find out that you've put your dick into any kids, and I *will* find out, then I may just have to keep you alive for a while. Let you suffer. Did you know that in prison men who rape children don't fare so well?"

I backed away and nodded at Wolf and Steel. It seemed Steel wasn't quite satisfied yet and sank his knife deeper. Not enough to kill the bastard, but he'd need stitches and probably feel that one for a while. Maybe it would slow him down and give any kids in his house a reprieve. I knew Outlaw and the others were still working on getting everyone safely away from this douchebag and his sorry excuse of a wife. I wasn't about to tip that hand, though. Let them find out the hard way. "Until we meet again."

I reached back and took Mei's hand, noting that she trembled. Skirting around the man responsible for her pain, I led her over to the truck. Wolf followed close on our heels, but Steel remained where he was. I saw him lean in and whisper something to Mei's foster father. I hated thinking of him like that. He wasn't a father of *any* sort. No, he was a pimp and nothing more. The fact he'd used the system to find his victims sickened me. He'd known no one gave a shit about the kids he took, and someone on the inside was helping him. They were all going down. Every last fucking one of them.

I got Mei settled in the truck, then burned rubber as I tore down the street and headed back to the compound. Wolf rode my tail on his bike, and I knew Steel would catch up. Beau was on the gate and he threw it open as I pulled in. I didn't stop at the clubhouse but took Mei straight home. I knew I'd have to talk to Grizzly and the other officers, let them know about my little run-in while we were in town. First, I needed to make sure Mei was all right.

She didn't seem too steady as I helped her into the house, carrying her back to the bedroom. She stood by the bed, just staring blankly. I made her sit and pulled off her shoes, then worked her jeans down her legs. When she still didn't move or acknowledge me, I removed my boots and cut, then picked her up and laid her down. I settled next to her, putting my hand on her belly. "Meiling, talk to me."

She took a shuddering breath and let it out. "He won't stop."

"Oh, he'll stop. I'll make sure of it. In the middle of town wasn't the right place or time, but I can promise he won't be able to hurt you or anyone else again when I'm done with him."

She turned her head to face me. "Did you mean it? About sending him to prison and what would happen?"

"You mean will he get raped every day, probably multiple times a day, while he's there? Yeah, I meant it. And if no one volunteers on their own, I'll fucking pay them to make it happen. He needs to experience the pain he's inflicted on you and anyone else."

Her gaze dropped to my chin. "He'd come into my room. After Beau left. Said he had to make sure I could take someone bigger before he let those men have me."

A red haze settled over my vision as I contemplated all the things I wanted to do to that fucker. But as much as I'd love to put him in the ground, I knew that would be too quick and easy. No, he needed to suffer, to be in pain, to be humiliated. I wasn't going to let him have the easy way out, no matter how good it would feel to spill his blood. Then again, no one said I couldn't make him bleed *before* he went to prison.

"What do you need from me, Meiling? I need to know you're okay, and you look far from it right now."

She sighed and moved closer, pressing her lips to mine in a quick kiss. "First, stop calling me Meiling and just call me Mei. Second… Give me a good memory? Right now, all the ugliness from my life is crowding my mind. I don't want that darkness here in our bedroom."

"You sure, Meiling? I don't want to do anything that might make things worse. Not to mention the doc said to take it easy until you healed better."

She reached up and placed her hand on my cheek. I waited for her to get upset over the use of her full name, but she ignored it that time. "I'm sure, Jameson. I know it's you here with me. If my neck starts hurting too much, or it looks like I'm bleeding, then we can stop."

I hesitated a moment. We still hadn't heard back from Dr. Larkin, and even though there was a chance I'd already gotten her pregnant, I didn't want to double down. "If we do this right now, I'm going to use a condom. Not because I'm worried you'll give me something, but because I don't think you need me planting a kid in you right now."

Her lips twitched in a slight smile. "You may have already done that."

I nodded. "True, but until I know you're ready, I don't want to take any more chances like that."

She kissed me, her tongue sliding across my lower lip in a teasing lick. "All right."

Fuck. My dick was hard as iron after that little flick. I could just imagine what it would have felt like across the head of my cock. I wouldn't ask her for that. When she was ready, she'd let me know. Right now, I was content just giving her pleasure. Whatever she'd allow, that's what we'd do. I'd only known her a few days and already she was the center of my world.

I stripped off my clothes, never taking my eyes off her, then reached for her. I helped her out of her shirt and bra, leaving her panties on for the moment. Leaning down, I took her nipple in my mouth, giving it a slight bite. She squealed and gripped the back of my neck, pushing me tighter against her breast. I took the hint and teased the hard peak with my teeth and tongue until she was panting.

Her breasts were turning pink from whisker burn, but it didn't seem to bother Mei. If anything, she just begged for more. Her legs shifted and I could tell she was rubbing her thighs together. I slipped a hand down her body and cupped her pussy, feeling how wet she was, soaking her panties. I shoved the material to the side and thrust a finger into her.

Mei screamed and bucked. I sucked harder on her nipple as I added a second finger to her pussy, stroking in and out, hard and as deep as I could go. She shattered, soaking my hand and the bed with her release. The wet sound of my fingers driving into her only made me harder, but I wanted her to beg for my cock.

I pressed my thumb against her clit and worked her pussy faster. Switching to the other breast, I bit her nipple and felt her come so hard I worried she'd break my damn fingers with those tight pussy muscles of hers. She was panting as I pulled back to stare down at her, her eyes were barely open and her face was flushed.

"Need you," she said.

"You sure?" I asked, working my fingers in and out a few more times.

She nodded. I eased my fingers from her, sucked off her juices, then reached for the bedside table and pulled out a condom. After I'd rolled the latex down my shaft, I practically tore her panties from her, then flipped Mei onto her belly. Lifting her ass in the air, I notched my cock against her entrance and thrust, not stopping until I was balls-deep. I groaned, closing my eyes as she squeezed me. *Fuck.* I wouldn't last if she kept that up.

I gripped her hips and fucked her fast and hard. I took her like a man possessed, but the way she gripped the headboard and screamed for more, I couldn't have slowed down if I tried. I growled as I rode her pussy. The sound of our bodies slapping together was all I could hear other than her muffled "more" and "right there" that slipped from her lips every few seconds.

My balls drew up and I knew I was seconds from coming. I slipped a hand between her legs and rubbed her clit in small, tight circles until she yelled my name, her pussy clenching down so tight I couldn't hold back. I drove into her, not stopping until every spurt of my cum had filled the condom. My lower back and balls tingled from the force of my release as I eased out of her. Only to stare at the very bare head of my dick.

"Shit."

"What?" Mei asked, looking back over her shoulder.

"Condom fucking broke."

She snorted, then giggled. It wasn't long before she was laughing so hard she had tears streaking her cheeks.

"I'm so glad you find this amusing."

She wiped at her cheeks and took in a shaky breath. "I'm sorry. It's just... you refused to knock me up until I was ready, but I think this might be Fate saying a great big fuck-you to your plans."

She wasn't wrong.

"Either that, or someone in the universe knows I can't get pregnant and the condoms aren't necessary." She sobered. "Well, unless I really am going to give you something."

I removed the condom and got up to throw it away and clean myself off. Before I got back in the bed, I grabbed my phone from my discarded jeans and texted Dr. Larkin.

Put a rush on those damn test results. I'm tired of her worrying about it.

I tossed the phone onto the pile of clothes and climbed back into bed with Mei. My cum was leaking out of her, but I shifted her thigh to get a better look. I had to admit, it was rather hot. Using my fingers, I shoved it back inside her. Mei moaned and her eyes slid shut.

"Greedy wench," I muttered, but I couldn't keep the smile from my face.

"Only with you," she said.

I kissed her hungrily. "Good. Because you're my wife and I'd fucking kill anyone who touched you. This is my pussy." I curled my fingers and hit just the right spot. She came instantly. "See, it knows who its master is."

She huffed at me. "My pussy, as you put it, isn't a living creature, so you can't be its master."

I shifted so that I pressed against her, pushing her into the mattress as I settled most of my weight over her. "Maybe not. But I can be *your* master."

"If you keep making me come until I can't think, then I'll call you whatever you want."

I studied her, looking for any signs that I'd gone too far, even if I was just being playful. Her eyes were clear, and I didn't see a hint of the shadows lurking. It seemed the memories of her past had been banished for the moment. One day, I hoped they would be gone for good. So distant that she never thought of those days again.

"You know, a hard cock is a horrible thing to waste," she said, wiggling against me. "Better put it to good use, don't you think?"

"Is that your way of saying you need a good fucking?"

She ran her fingers through my beard. "No, I'm saying that I need my husband to take control of my body, give me more pleasure than I can stand, and own every inch of me."

Everything in me froze at how she'd phrased that. "Mei, what are you…"

She covered my mouth with her hand. "I'm not going to crack mentally or otherwise, Jameson, and I need to prove that to both of us. I need you to take me like you would one of those club whores. Take what you need from me, treat me like you would any other woman, and not some broken thing that needs to be rescued. I need… you. All of you. I can tell you're holding back for the most part, and while it's sweet of you, it's not necessary."

"But you're not a club whore. You're my wife, Mei. There's a difference. And your wound…" I trailed off realizing the bandage was still white and she seemed to be fine.

She arched an eyebrow. "Really? I once read that men want a lady on their arm and a whore in the bedroom. Are you trying to tell me you're any different?"

Well, no. I wasn't, but I didn't like linking her to the word "whore" either. Especially not since that's what she'd been. Not by choice, but the fact remained that she'd been a prostitute. On the other hand, I knew she was partially right. I was treating her like a victim. Some fragile thing that couldn't handle the real me, or the world I lived in. I couldn't shelter her and expect her to flourish.

"I'm not into that crap that women seem to gush over about that guy, Gray or whatever, but I do need a safe word from you. Something that I'll know means one hundred percent that you need me to back the fuck off. If I do something to trigger a bad memory, or cause you to have an anxiety attack or something, I need to know." I stared at her hard. "I'm about ninety-eight percent certain you have PTSD, Mei, and that's not something to play around with."

"Coral," she said. "My word is coral."

"Promise me you'll use it if you start to even feel like you might be slipping out of the moment."

"I promise," she said.

I couldn't believe I was about to do this. Not with Mei, but if it was what she needed, then I'd give it to her. Hell, maybe I needed this too.

I went to the closet and reached up on the top shelf. Gripping the silk corded rope, I pulled it down and carried it over to the bed. I gripped Mei's wrists and bound them, making sure it was tight enough she couldn't break free, but not enough to hurt her. My heart hammered in my chest as I looked at her, my wife, vulnerable and trusting. And that's when I knew... I was falling for her. Hell, I may have already fallen.

I backed away from the bed and pointed to the floor. "Kneel."

Mei rocked herself toward the edge of the bed and put her feet on the floor. I clenched my hands so I wouldn't reach out and help her. She managed to stand, then sank to her knees at my feet. Her hair was wild and all over the place. I pulled it back from her face and fisted it.

"Open," I demanded.

She parted her lips, and I dragged her closer to my cock. I painted her lips with the pre-cum gathered on the tip, then thrust inside. It felt as fucking amazing as I'd thought it would. She sucked as I went deep, and fuck me if she couldn't take it all. As I drew back, I felt her tongue flick the vein that ran along the underside and a chill ran down my spine. So. Fucking. Good.

"That's it, baby. Suck me. Take me deep." I tightened my hold on her hair, holding her steady as I fucked her mouth. The green of her eyes turned brighter and the complete trust she was giving me was humbling. "Gonna come, Mei. You suck me dry, then get me hard again."

I shot a load of cum down her throat, and she swallowed it down. Her tongue worked me as I stroked in and out of her mouth, not stopping until the last drop had been wrung from my balls. My dick still filled her mouth, but even after coming twice so close together, I was still pretty fucking hard.

"Such a good girl, swallowing it all," I murmured, releasing her hair and running my fingers over her cheek. My gaze shifted to her bandage, making sure I hadn't made her wound start bleeding again. It seemed fine. "You want more, don't you?"

She hummed at me, the vibration making my cock get harder.

"Want my cum in your pussy?"

She did that sweet little sound again. Fuck, but I loved the way that felt with me filling her mouth.

I dropped my voice a little lower. "Want my cum in your ass?"

She whimpered and squirmed, but I didn't see any signs of distress in her eyes.

I pulled free of her lips and pointed to the bed. "Lean over it. Feet on the floor, but together. Chest to the mattress."

Mei struggled to get to her feet but managed to follow my orders. Her pussy glistened and I fisted my cock, enjoying the view. If I were younger, I'd jerk off and come on her before I fucked her again, but at my age, if I tried that, I wouldn't last through everything else I wanted to do to her. Hell, I was surprised I was still hard after coming twice already, but Mei brought out the beast in me.

I approached Mei, grabbed her hips, and rubbed my cock against her. I adjusted my hips until I could press inside her. Taking it slow, I watched as my cock disappeared inside her pussy an inch at a time. Her cream coated me as I bottomed out, then pulled back, only to thrust into her again.

"Fuck, Mei. I wish you could see this. You look fucking beautiful taking my cock."

I worked one of my hands between her and the bed, seeking her clit. It was hard and slick. She whimpered when I started to rub it slowly. I needed her to come at least once, to know that she was enjoying this and it wasn't me just taking what she offered.

"That's it, sweetheart. Need you to come on my dick."

"I like it when you talk dirty to me," she said.

Fuck.

"Do you?" I asked. "You like hearing how hard it makes me to see your pussy taking my dick?"

She wiggled her ass.

"It seems you *do* like that." I leaned over her, pressing my cock deeper. "I'm going to fuck this sweet pussy, fill it up with my cum, then I'm going to fuck your tight little ass until you're begging."

Her breath hitched. "Jameson..."

"You like that, Mei? Like hearing that I'm going to use you? Fuck you any way I want?"

Her pussy got hotter and wetter. Shit. She really did like hearing that. My hips slammed against her ass as I pushed both of us to an orgasm. She came first, screaming out her release and thrashing under me. I didn't even finish coming before I pulled out. Spreading her ass cheeks, my cum splashed onto her tight little hole. I used it to ease the way as I worked my finger inside her.

She took me so easily it gave me pause, reminding me of what she'd suffered.

"Don't," she said. "Don't go there, Jameson."

"Mei, what am I..." *What am I doing?* I was treating her like all those other men had done. Using her.

"You're doing what I asked you to do," she said softly. "Now fuck me." She looked at me over her shoulder, her eyes blazing brightly with heat and passion. "I know it's you. I'm right here with you. Now put your cock in me and make me come."

I worked her some more, getting out the lube and making sure she could take at least three fingers. When I didn't think I would hurt her, I lined up my cock and pushed through the tight ring of muscle. Once I'd breached her, I slid in easily, her body accepting the intrusion.

"Fuck, Mei." I held her open, watching as I fucked her. Despite the number of women in my past, this was a first for me. "Never done this before. You tell me if I hurt you."

"You've never…" She snorted, then giggled. "All right, then. I'll be sure to use my word if it gets to be too much."

I went deep and held still, my cock twitching inside her. Reaching up, I unknotted the ropes and removed them. "Play with yourself, Mei. I need you to come."

I spread her wide again, and started stroking in and out. Her ass was tighter than her pussy and felt like fucking heaven. Her hand was between her legs and I hoped she worked her clit like I'd said.

"I've never been able to make myself come," she said.

"Keep going, baby. Imagine it's my fingers rubbing you. Focus on how it feels to have me fucking you right now."

Her breathing got heavier and a flush crept down her neck. I knew she was close.

"That's it, beautiful. Come for me. Come right the fuck now."

"Jameson!"

Her ass clenched down as she came, and I drove into her hard and fast, taking what I wanted. What I needed. I roared out as my cum filled her ass, my hips slamming against her as I kept thrusting, not stopping until I had nothing left to give. I panted, still buried inside her.

"Jesus fucking Christ, woman. I think you almost killed me."

Mei giggled and tightened her muscles. My overly sensitive cock gave a jerk and I pulled free, wincing a little. I was still holding her open and watched my cum leak out of her.

"Well, sweetheart. I think you can now say that I've claimed all of you. Is that what you wanted?"

I helped her stand up and she turned to face me. "It's exactly what I wanted, and what I think we both needed."

"Good." I sighed and kissed her softly. "Because I think I want to do that again sometime. Not every time. Just… every now and then."

"I'm good with that," she said, then smirked a little. "So, if you don't know anything about *that* book, how did you know the man's name and to tell me you needed a safe word?"

I felt my cheeks warm and couldn't believe I was fucking blushing. "I didn't read the fucking book."

"Right. Of course. You just… tripped in a bookstore and it fell open to that exact part of the story?"

"Shut it," I muttered. I wasn't going to have my wife giving me shit just because I'd been curious. Besides, the guy had seemed like an ass. I still didn't understand why women sighed his name. "I'm way better than him."

"Yes, you are." She grabbed my beard between her teeth and tugged.

"Did you just billy goat me?"

"Yep."

Life with Mei was going to be interesting. And I couldn't have been happier to see her this way. She was smiling and looked genuinely content. So I probably shouldn't bring up her father again. I'd just sneak off to go visit the man without telling her. I nearly snorted at myself. Yeah, even I wasn't stupid enough to think she wouldn't be pissed over that one.

"Not to ruin the mood, but I think I need to shower and dress, then head over to the prison."

"Why?" she asked, taking a step back.

"I need to talk to Blades, Mei. He needs to know about you, and that you're mine. And I need him to tell what he remembers so we can unravel this whole fucking mess."

She sighed and nodded. "Fine. We'll shower and head over there."

"I didn't say you had to go with me."

"No, you didn't. I honestly don't know if I want to meet him. I'm just worried if I don't go, he might find a way to have you murdered before you make it home, and I've grown rather attached to you." She glanced down. "Especially certain parts of you."

I smiled and pulled her into my arms again. "I like this side of you, Meiling. Don't ever change."

Chapter Eleven

Meiling

I'd never been to a prison before, and I wasn't too thrilled over the experience. Thankfully, I hadn't set off the metal detector, or whatever the hell that thing was I had to walk through. Dingo wasn't so lucky. He'd had to strip down to his underwear in another room so the guards could make sure he wasn't sneaking anything in. I wasn't sure if I wanted to laugh at the expression on his face, or go kick their asses for putting him through that.

We'd been shown to a room with nothing more than a table and two chairs inside. Dingo had insisted that I sit and he stood behind me. A tall man with broad shoulders and white hair came into the room. The prison orange didn't do much for him, but I was grateful for the shackles around his wrists and ankles. The guard fastened the chain between his wrists to a ring on the table, then stepped out of the room.

Blades eyed Dingo, his gaze resting on the cut. "So, one of you finally came to see me. Been a while. No one's ever brought a pretty woman with them, though."

Dingo put his hand on my shoulder and squeezed.

"You're Robert Young?" I asked.

"Don't go by that name anymore. I'm Blades. Who's looking for Young?"

I took a breath and knew that I needed to do this. I could let Dingo lead, but if this man was truly my father, then I wanted to hear it from him.

"I'm Meiling Shan Young." I paused. "Your daughter if my birth certificate is correct."

Blades fell back against the metal rails on his chair. "Fucking hell."

"So you do know who I am?" I asked.

"Yeah. Told your mother not to bring you here. Why did she let you come now?" Blades asked.

"She didn't. I don't even remember her," I said.

His gaze shot to Dingo. "Are you responsible for her being here? How she'd get mixed up with the club? I told Xi-wang to keep away from the Devil's Fury."

"We don't know yet what happened to Xi-wang. Shortly after you were locked up, your daughter went into foster care and her mother vanished without a trace," Dingo said. "As to why she's with me... she's my wife."

Blades shot to his feet. "Like fuck she is!"

"Sit down, old man," Dingo said. "She's been accepted by the club as my ol' lady, and we're legally married. Besides, she could be carrying your grandchild."

Blades looked ready to explode, but he sat. Slowly.

"Why the fuck are you here?" he asked, his attention focused on Dingo.

"We need some answers. Mei doesn't remember her mother, and never knew about you. In fact, her birth certificate was buried and a false one put in its place. You tried to keep her a secret, but it's time to talk."

Blades looked away, then gave a jerky nod. "Fine. I'll tell you what I know, then you explain what's really going on."

"I can live with that," Dingo said.

"I met Meiling's mother when she was on spring break. Prettiest woman I'd ever seen. And far too damn young for me. She was only nineteen to my forty-four." He got a far-off look in his eyes and smiled faintly. "I kept an eye on her, but didn't approach her until she needed me."

"Needed you?" I asked.

"Some guys were hassling her. I stepped in and sent them on their way, with a few broken ribs for their trouble. She looked at me like I was some kind of hero. After that, we spent every second of that week together. When it was time for her to return to school, she promised to keep in touch." His gaze scanned my face. "You look a bit like her, except you got my red hair and green eyes."

I glanced at his hair and he chuckled.

"I'm sixty-two, darlin'. The red faded long ago."

"If my mother left, how is it you signed paperwork acknowledging I was your daughter?" I asked.

"She came back. Dropped out of school and came running straight back to me. When she told me she was pregnant, and the baby was mine, I knew I'd stay by her side. Well, as much as I could. Club life would have chewed her up and spit her out. I kept her in an apartment in town and saw her as much as I could while keeping up appearances."

I narrowed my eyes at him. "You mean you fucked around on her. Typical."

"Now don't go getting your feathers ruffled. Only woman I ever loved was your mother, but the Devil's Fury was a rough place back then. I'd imagine it still is. She wouldn't have survived there, and if I'd stopped fooling around with club pussy, my brothers would have been suspicious."

I wasn't sure I bought that excuse, but whatever. I motioned for him to keep talking.

"The day you were born was the happiest of my life. But one look at you and I knew I couldn't let you anywhere near the Devil's Fury. That wasn't the life I wanted for you. Your mom was smart. Really fucking smart. If you were anything like her, I knew you'd do well in college and make something of your life. Better than being a biker's woman or a club whore."

Dingo's hand tightened on my shoulder, but I patted his fingers, letting him know I was fine. And I was.

"What happened after that?" I asked.

"I did the best I could, but like I said, different type of club back then. Or so I hope if you're mixed up with them. I went on a job that went south. People died and the finger was pointed my way. A witness saw me covered in blood fleeing the scene. I got hauled in and sent to prison. Saw your mom once after that and told her to never come here again."

I slumped in my seat. "So you don't know what happened to her, or how I ended up in foster care?"

"Nope. I never even heard that she was missing. No one ever came and asked about you, but you were mine legally. If someone finds out what happened, I sure the fuck want to know."

"Outlaw is working on it," Dingo said. "He's a hacker for the club, and has some friends who are even better at it than him. What we've gathered so far is that the social worker in charge of Mei's case was dirty. I don't know yet if it was a blackmail issue or what, but the files on Mei were falsified and she was placed in a..." Dingo's words dried up at that moment, and I knew why.

I looked up at him before meeting my father's gaze. "He doesn't want to tell you."

"Did they hurt you?" Blades asked.

"They made her into a whore by the age of fourteen," Dingo said, his voice deep and husky. He couldn't hide the pain it caused him to say that.

Blades' hands fisted on the table, and his face turned a startling shade of purple. He roared out his rage and stood so fast his chair kicked over. The man must have been strong as an ox because he ripped the chain free of the table and proceeded to put a dent in the metal surface as he pounded his fists against it. The guards rushed in, but Dingo held up a hand, cautioning them to stay back.

"Give him a minute," Dingo said.

"No. Fuck that shit." Blades looked at me before lifting his gaze to Dingo. "I didn't fucking kill those people. You find out who did, get me out of here, and I'll handle the men who hurt my daughter."

"I didn't hear that," one of the guards muttered. "Did. Not. Fucking. Hear. It." He walked out, dragging the other one with him.

"Are you trying to say you're innocent?" I asked.

Blades gave a bark of laughter. "No, daughter. I'm far from innocent, but I didn't commit the murders I was accused of. If Outlaw can find out what happened with your situation, then maybe he can help with mine. When I got locked up, there wasn't someone capable of digging up that kind of dirt, not within the club, and certainly no one who gave a shit about me. You get me out of here, and I'll make sure they all fucking pay."

"On one condition," Dingo said.

"What's that, boy?" Blades asked.

"You give your blessing for me and Mei to be together." He cleared his throat. "I love her, and I will love and protect any children we have together. If we're ever blessed with any."

He loved me? My eyes went wide and I looked up at him. He loved me, and he decided *now* was the time to say something?

"You're an idiot," I said to my husband. "But I love you too."

He grinned down at me.

"Fine. You have my blessing, as long as you make her happy. Fuck up, and I'll God damn bury you where they'll never find your body," Blades said.

"If I fuck up, you have my permission to feed me to the pigs."

Blades hesitated. "We have fucking pigs?"

Dingo burst out laughing. I hadn't seen a single pig at the compound and I had a feeling it was just a turn of phrase. It was, right? People didn't actually... No, I didn't want to know. This was one of those "ignorance is bliss" moments.

Blades eyed me. "I know I'm a stranger to you, girl, but I'm your dad. I get out of here, and I'll make things right for you. I don't expect you to call me anything other than Blades, until I've earned the right to be called anything else."

I didn't know what to make of him. He certainly wasn't anything like the father I'd always dreamed of, but he wanted to protect me, and wasn't that what a dad was supposed to do? Protect his kids?

"We'll have to agree to disagree," I said. "Daddy."

The old man cracked a smile, and I could have sworn I saw a bit of moisture in his eyes, but he sobered quickly and focused on my husband again.

Some sort of silent communication passed between them. Next thing I knew, Dingo was leading me out of the room, but I broke free. It was against the rules to get anywhere near the prisoner, or so we'd been told, but since we seemed to be bucking the authority anyway, I ran to my father and threw my arms around him. He hesitated only a moment before hugging me back.

"Love you, Meiling. Always have," he said, his voice gruff. "Even if I can't get out of here, remember that. You were wanted, and you were loved. Never doubt it for a moment."

"Thank you, Daddy."

I broke free and returned to Dingo's side. He gave me a slight smile before leading me from the room. After giving the guards a nod, we walked down the corridor and made our way out of the prison. We'd taken the club truck again. Dingo insisted, feeling that it wasn't safe for me to be on his bike, and maybe he was right. He'd pointed out that I'd be an easy target out in the open. I'd get to ride with him soon enough, I hoped.

"Can Outlaw really get him out of there?" I asked.

Dingo sighed and pulled out his phone. He called the man in question and put it on speaker.

"Before you say anything, know that Mei is right here and can hear you," Dingo said when Outlaw had picked up.

"Good to know. I'm assuming this isn't a social call, then?" Outlaw asked.

"We just saw Blades. He claims he didn't murder those people and wants to know if you can dig anything up that might clear his name. If we can get him out, he said he'll handle whoever is responsible for hurting Mei. He was fucking pissed when he heard what she'd been through, and I just gave him a broad generalization without the details," Dingo said. "If he knew about those videos, or exactly what they'd done to her, I think he might kill everyone inside those walls just to get out and make things right for her."

Outlaw whistled. "That's a tall order. I mean, we're talking about something that happened what? Eighteen years ago? Even if there was camera footage from back then, which is not a guarantee, then it probably would have been erased or vanished in other ways by now. They didn't upload that shit to the precinct digital files so I could access online. It would be in a box, probably gathering dust in some evidence locker."

I didn't like hearing that. At all. "Please, Outlaw? I know we haven't officially met or anything, but I just met my dad for the first time in my life. I want to get to know him, to get to hug him whenever I want. Will you at least try to find something to clear his name?"

I heard a muttered "dammit" on the other end of the line and he heaved a sigh. "You don't play fair. I never could say no to a woman in need."

"Does that mean you'll help?" I asked.

"Not me, but hang on. I'm going to conference in the others," Outlaw said.

"Others?" I asked Dingo.

"He means the other hackers. He's the one for our club, but a few others we're friendly with have their own version of Outlaw. The Dixie Reapers actually have a husband and wife team who are supposed to be the best in the country if not the entire world."

Well, that sounded promising. Assuming they would actually help. I didn't know if they'd care about an old man locked up in prison for murder. But that old guy was my dad, and until I'd seen the way he reacted, heard how much he'd wanted me, I hadn't realized that I wanted, and needed him, in my life. And not behind bars. Maybe he wasn't the nicest guy, and maybe he really was a killer, but I deserved the chance to get to know him and make those decisions for myself. Like Dingo had said. Not everything was always black-and-white. Maybe Blades fell into the shades of gray category.

"Dingo. Mei. I've got Wire, Lavender, Shade, and Surge on the line," Outlaw said.

"Hey, guys. And lady," Dingo said with a smile. "We need your help. Meiling's dad is none other than Blades. He said he was set up eighteen years ago and has been serving time in prison for some murders he didn't commit. He asked us to clear his name so he can..."

"So he can kill everyone who ever hurt me," I said. I looked over at Dingo and shrugged a shoulder. It was true. Why sugarcoat it? "While I don't condone murder, I'm thinking this time it might be okay. We're talking about rapists and anyone involved in putting me into their hands."

I heard a round of cussing that sounded like it came from every single one of them. Even the woman. Lavender? I waited to see what they'd say. If they didn't agree to help, then I didn't see how Blades would ever get out of prison. Murder was kind of a lifetime thing, right? No parole?

"Outlaw, send us what you have," Lavender said. At least, I assumed it was Lavender since she'd been the only woman introduced. Unless someone else was listening.

"You know there's no way to access anything that will exonerate him," said another voice.

"I already told them that, Wire. But they want some help and I figured if all of us worked together maybe we could find a solution."

"You know, we might not be able to find evidence to clear his name," said Lavender, "but that doesn't mean we can't *clear* his name."

Um, what did that mean? Dingo seemed as puzzled as me, as he stared at the phone with his brow furrowed. There was some whispering that sounded like it might be Wire and Lavender. The others remained pretty quiet.

"So, we're going to go do a thing," Wire said. "And that's as much as you need to know about it. Just forget you ever said anything about Blades. Work on that other shit."

I heard a click and stared at the phone. Did he just hang up? And what the hell was that about?

"Um, so it seems Wire and Lavender are going to handle your dad," Outlaw said. "Once the two of you hang up, I'll talk to Surge and Shade, and we'll see what else we can find on Mei's issue. It sounds like we might need to work fast. And don't even ask what that was about because I'm not telling you. The less you know the better."

"I'm starting to think the 'ignorance is bliss' is going to be my mantra from now on," I said, earning laughter from the men on the phone. "How do the club women cope?"

"You'd have to ask them," Outlaw said. "And I'd get home quick. I saw Badger chasing after Adalia. Looked like she was heading your direction. On foot."

"Shit," Dingo muttered before hanging up and starting the truck.

"Why is she on foot? And why is it a problem she's coming to our house?" I asked. "I'd love to meet someone else in the club, who doesn't have a penis."

He snorted. "Cute. The problem is that Adalia could have driven to the house, or asked Badger to bring her by. If she's walking and he's going after her, then he told her to keep her ass at home and she didn't listen."

Well, all righty, then. It seemed the men of the Devil's Fury were all a bit overbearing when it came to their women. Dingo was nice, and I knew he was trying to keep me safe, but I could tell that once he realized I wasn't a porcelain doll he'd probably pull the caveman routine on a regular basis. Not that I'd minded the way he exerted his dominance over me earlier. I'd never been so turned on.

I knew he'd been worried I'd freak the hell out, or just check out completely. Honestly, I'd been a bit concerned myself, but I knew if I didn't at least try, then I'd never feel whole again. I needed to know that I could handle him, handle being... normal. Or whatever the fuck normal was. I just knew it wasn't *me*. But then, anyone who'd lived through the hell I'd survived would have some scars, either physical, emotional, mental, or some combination of the three. All things considered, I thought I was doing amazingly well. Or maybe I was just suppressing everything and pretending that it was all fine.

I held on tight as Dingo skidded around a corner, approaching the compound gates at a speed that was a bit concerning. The gate flew open as he got closer and he pulled through, not stopping or even slowing down. If anything, he floored it and sped toward the house. When he came to a stop in the driveway, there was a woman in our front yard, yelling at who I thought must be Badger. I seriously needed a meet and greet or something. Regular names were hard enough to remember, but this was getting ridiculous. I'd end up calling someone Coyote or something and their name would really be some other animal. Like Wolf. Although, I'd already met him so I figured I was safe remembering his name. Maybe.

I got out and slowly approached the couple. "Hi. Are you Adalia and Badger?"

They stopped mid-argument and faced me. I didn't understand why he didn't want her here. Was it because of my past? Adalia smiled and started to move closer, but Badger grabbed her arm. Everything in me tensed at the move, but she didn't seem to be in any pain. But she was plenty pissed if the narrowing of her eyes and flash of teeth was any indication. She snarled at him like a feral animal.

"Badger, so help me God, if you don't let go right now, I'm going to rip off your balls." He growled and pulled her closer to him. Adalia only slapped at his hand. "Let go!"

"Y'all aren't inspiring confidence in Mei right now," Dingo said. "She's going to think we abuse our women."

Badger released his woman and folded his arms over his chest. "She fucking walked here after throwing a fit like a damn child."

"Well, you were being unreasonable," she said.

"You're still recovering, Adalia."

Recovering? I didn't know what was going on, but she looked fine to me. Had something happened? Had she been sick? I was glad he hadn't tried to stop her from visiting because of the life I'd led, and his worry for her was kind of touching.

Her shoulders drooped and she gave him the most pathetic look I've ever seen. "I lost our baby, Badger. I didn't die. I'm not *going* to die. We'll just… either give up or try again when the doctor says we can. You can't keep me locked up in the house, watching my every move. You're doing the overprotective thing and it's making me lose my mind a little."

Oh. Oh! I approached them again, this time I didn't stop. I knew a little of what she was feeling. Maybe I hadn't exactly wanted my baby -- any of them -- and the decision had been taken from me either by Fate, my foster family, or Trotter, but it didn't mean I couldn't offer her some comfort. From one almost-a-mom to another. Or in her case, she'd probably already thought of herself as a mom. And she had been. Even if that little one hadn't lived, he or she had been wanted and would have been loved. That much was plain to see.

"Would you like to come in and have some coffee?" I asked. "I'd offer some hot herbal tea, but I don't think we have any."

"You drink tea?" Dingo asked. "Why didn't you say something?"

"Peppermint. The hot kind," I said, "and I didn't say something because it wasn't important. We have other stuff going on. Tea is the least of my worries."

Adalia heaved a shuddering breath, obviously trying to pull herself back together, and gave a nod. "I'd love to come in for some coffee. And Badger is going to stay right the fuck here and give me some space before I decide to smother him with a pillow."

Her husband, or whatever he was, rolled his eyes but didn't move. I could see how much he loved her, and he was just worried about her. It was understandable after they'd suffered a loss like that.

"Come on. I'll brew a pot, and we can get to know each other," I said. "I've never had a friend before, but if you're taking requests, I'd like to sign up."

Adalia smiled and looped her arm through mine. "I think I'm going to like you."

"Same here." I glanced at Dingo. "Keep Badger company. Outside the house."

My husband winked at me as I led Adalia inside. She sat at the kitchen table while I started the coffee, then I claimed the seat across from her. I'd never really done the girl talk thing before, but it could be fun. Assuming I didn't fuck it up.

"I know why you're here," Adalia said. "So you don't have to feel like you need to go over what happened to you. We can just talk, or just sit. Whatever you want."

"Thanks. I guess news of what I've been through has spread through the club."

"Yep. If it makes any difference, every woman here has been through hell before getting saved by the Devil's Fury. Their names sound so ominous, so... angry. Threatening maybe? But really, they're a bunch of teddy bears when it comes to women and kids." She smiled. "And the clubs they hang out with are the same way. I know there are some really bad ones out there. Your foster family would fit right in with those. But Devils' Fury, Devil's Boneyard, Hades Abyss, Reckless Kings, and Dixie Reapers are all solid guys. They may do dirty shit to make a living, but they protect their own, and they won't stand by and let a woman or kid get hurt."

I'd kind of already figured that out about Dingo, but it was nice to know the entire club was that way. I was still not certain how I felt about Demon and Grizzly, but letting go of that first impression wasn't going to be easy. Maybe with time I could get past it. After all, Demon had come to help when I'd been shot.

"You said women. How many of us live here?" I asked.

"I have two adopted sisters," Adalia said. "My adopted father is Grizzly."

My mouth opened and shut a few times. "I'm sorry, I know it's been mentioned before, about him adopting kids, but he just doesn't seem the type. It's a little hard for me to picture."

"He did more than that," she said. "When he brought me home, he was still married. May was the best mom I could have ever had. Cancer took her from us. But Grizzly and May tracked me down after Badger saved me and went to prison."

"Wait. Badger was in prison?" I asked.

She nodded. "I was a teenager when I was raped. Badger happened to walk by and hear me. He pulled the guy off me and killed him with his bare hands. Went to prison. When he got out, I'd been living at the compound for a while with Grizzly and May. Well, just Grizzly by then. I'd been in love with him since that night, so I got my happy-ever-after in the end. Sort of."

I reached for her hand, giving it a squeeze. "I'm so sorry about your baby. I know that must have been hard."

"It was." She sighed. "And it's not the first time we've lost one. Maybe I'm just not supposed to have children. I have endometriosis, so I knew there was a chance I'd never have any, but I'd hoped that we could."

I wished I had some words of wisdom, or even comfort, for her, but I was out of my depth. The coffee finished brewing and I got up to fix us two cups. I placed them on the table, then got the milk and sugar, but Adalia waved me off. I put a little in my cup, then put the items away before sitting down again.

"Who are the other women?" I asked, hoping to distract her from her melancholy thoughts.

"My adopted sisters are Shella and Lilian. Grizzly brought Lilian home when she was fifteen. She's twenty-one now, but she kind of keeps to herself. Like you, she was a prostitute not by choice but by force. My dad took her in and has tried to help her heal." She sipped her coffee. "And Shella is nineteen now. Her baby sister, half-sister, is part of another club. Shella didn't share the same dad so mine took her in when she needed a home, and gave her a place to have a fresh start."

"Is she... was she..." I didn't know how to ask.

"She was abused and neglected but not like you or Lilian. She's stronger than Lilian by far, and more outgoing. At least, when she's outside the compound she is. Around here, she's the quiet one." She smiled. "They just haven't seen her when she's in town with her friends from school. Totally different girl then. Not a wild child, exactly, but she lets loose more."

"I hope I get to meet them sometime soon. It would be nice to have some friends. A family." I traced the woodgrain pattern on the table. "I met my father for the first time today. I'd thought I didn't want to know him, but I was wrong."

Adalia tapped the table with her finger. "You know what we need?"

I raised my eyebrows and waited for her to continue.

"We need a girls' night. I seriously don't see Badger letting me leave the compound without him, but my dad set up a room for us girls. It has a huge TV, two arcade games, and an entire bookcase full of sappy movies. You in?"

I wanted to say yes, but going into Grizzly's home? I still didn't know how he felt about me. There was this voice at the back of my mind saying he didn't really want me here, and I *had* brought a lot of trouble with me.

"My dad won't bite," Adalia said. "He just needs a chance to see that you fit in here, that you're part of us. Dingo claimed you, so you're not going anywhere. Might as well tame the big bear now."

"Fine. I'm in. But if your dad is pissed that I'm at his house, then I'm leaving."

"Fair enough." Adalia smiled. "Now, let's go tell the men they aren't allowed to come with us. Watch. Badger's head might explode. It'll be fun."

Her idea of fun and mine didn't seem to mesh, but I'd go with it for now. I only hoped she was right about Grizzly. He didn't look like the kind of man you wanted to piss off. Then again, maybe he didn't know that my dad was Blades. Would that make a difference? I wasn't just tied to the club through Dingo, but through my dad too. That meant I really did belong here, right?

If this all went wrong, I hoped Dingo wouldn't mourn my loss when Grizzly ripped off my head for daring to enter his house and speak to his kids.

Shit. Why had I agreed to this?

Chapter Twelve

Dingo

Knowing that Mei was safely hidden away at Grizzly's house gave me the freedom to handle a few things. Namely, the social worker in charge of Mei's case. I was saving the foster parents for Blades, unless we couldn't get him out of prison. Then I'd handle those fuckers too. But first, I needed to have a conversation with Miss Demoira Humes. I double-checked the information Outlaw had given me before knocking on the door. The kids' toys in the front yard didn't bode well. I'd never been the kind of man to take a kids' parent away from them, not knowingly at any rate. I didn't doubt that some of the men I'd help bury had left behind women and kids. Then again, their families were probably better off without them. This time was different, though.

A woman who appeared to be in her forties answered the door, a flour-dusted apron tied around her neck and waist. She smiled before her gaze landed on my cut, then I watched as the blood drained from her face. Yeah, bitch. Time to pay the piper.

"You can either let me in, or I can come back at a more convenient time. Like, maybe when you're sleeping?" I asked.

She stepped back and let me into the house. More signs of children were scattered around the living room, and I heard giggling from down the hallway. So there were kids in the house. Hers? Or was she fostering? Even more important, were they safe with a woman who sold out countless young girls?

"What do you want?" she asked, fisting her apron. "I've never done anything to your club."

"Now that's where you're wrong." I pulled out a photocopy of Mei's original birth certificate and held it up for her to see. "Recognize this?"

She whimpered and her lower lip trembled. Good. Bitch needed to be scared right now. She pointed to it with a shaking hand. "Where did you get that? Judge Proctor got rid of it."

"So, you have seen it before. We'll get to the judge in a moment because that's a story I need to hear. For right now, I want you to understand that there's no escape from what you've done. The man listed on this birth certificate is none other than Robert Young, or as we call him, Blades."

She slumped against the wall at her back. "I didn't know he was part of your club. I didn't... I..." She audibly swallowed. "The judge said the father wouldn't be a problem."

"And the mother? Did he say anything about Xi-wang Chen?" I asked. We still hadn't determined what happened to her, and that bothered me a fucking lot. I wanted to tell Mei that her mother was fine, or at least give her some sort of closure. The more Outlaw discovered about this fucked-up mess, I knew it wasn't likely that Xi-wang was still alive. "What did he do to her?"

"You have to understand. I was fresh out of school, and Meiling was one of my first cases. Judge Proctor was a powerful man. Still is. He made it clear that I'd pay the price if I didn't follow along."

"I need to know everything. Start at the beginning and work up to the point where Beau Stevens found her being whored out at *The Ruby Slipper*." Her eyes went wide. "Yeah. I'm guessing

Beau was one of yours too. He's been far out of your reach for a while, though, hasn't he?"

She tugged up the sleeve of her shirt and showed me some deep burn marks. The kind that looked like they came from a blowtorch, or something equally hot. "This is what happened when Beau ran off and I couldn't find him."

"And you didn't call the police? Report the judge and anyone else involved? Why? Because you were in too deep by then?" I asked.

"The judge owns this town and everyone in it. Well, anyone on the legal side of things. The District Attorney is his golfing partner. The Chief of Police has dinner with him every Sunday night. There isn't a single place I could have gone." She sighed and motioned to the living room. "Have a seat. I'll tell you what I know, but I need a promise from you."

"Do you really think you're in a position to make ultimatums?"

"I have some kids here who will need homes. Part of my silence was paid for by the right to keep them safe in my home. They're different. I don't like the word disabled or retarded, even though some would call them that, but my children are special. I needed to ensure they didn't fall into the wrong hands."

I hated it when the bad guys decided they had a heart. It fucked with my head. "Fine. I'll make sure the kids are taken care of if the need should arise."

"Meiling wasn't the first, nor was she the last. I was paid to look the other way and make sure she ended up in a certain home. Same for Beau Stevens." She twisted her hands in her lap. "I've been haunted every night of my life by what might be happening to those kids."

I pulled out my phone and accessed the video Outlaw had sent me. I still couldn't watch the damn thing, but I started it and made sure the bitch watched every second. She was sobbing by the time it ended, and I was back to wanting to murder every fucker who'd ever hurt my wife. Not that the need for bloodshed had ever truly died down.

"That's just a small taste of what Mei suffered because of you and every other fucking asshole who put her with that family. I'm not here to ease your conscience, *Miss* Humes. I'm here to make you pay." I hope she could tell I'd rather spit on her than show her any respect. I put my phone away. "It was your fucking job to protect her, protect Beau, and all the other kids you fucked over because you were scared. Be thankful I'm the one on your doorstep. If Blades were here, you'd be begging for your life, and he wouldn't give a shit there were children nearby."

"He's in prison," she whispered.

I just smiled because I knew it wouldn't be long now before that wasn't the case. Outlaw had assured me that several pieces were already falling into place. Either by tonight or tomorrow morning, Blades would be back home where he belonged. And this town, this fucked-up shithole, might very well burn to the Goddamn ground before he was done getting vengeance for his daughter, and I had a feeling for the woman he'd loved.

"Xi-wang. What happened to her?" I asked.

"I was told not to ask, and I didn't. Not exactly." She looked at me with haunted eyes. "She was young. Beautiful. And Chinese. It's the non-white girls that are in the highest demand for the prostitution and pornography. He has a special clientele."

"So she ended up having the same fate as her daughter?" I asked, needing her to be as clear as possible. If there was a chance Xi-wang was still alive, we would find her and bring her home.

"She was sold. To a brothel."

I waited, knowing she would give me more, if she knew it. And something told me if she'd learned that much, she'd have kept going.

"She's not the same Xi-wang Mr. Young knew, and she never will be."

"But she's alive."

Humes -- because I refused to even think of her as Miss Humes - nodded. "If you can call it living. They stole her soul, wiped out every trace of who she once was, and now she's just a shell. I've been to see her a few times. Not that I ever approached, but I observed from a distance."

"She's a bit old to be a whore, isn't she?" I asked, not meaning in a cruel way, but I knew the younger they were the better in that type of work. If men wanted to fuck a forty- or fifty-year-old woman, they'd just stick with their wives. It was the thrill of being with someone younger that they couldn't land on their own, without having to pay for the privilege. The younger the girls, the more they were willing to spend.

"She trains the new girls. She's a den mother of sorts, I suppose. Can't think of what else to call her. They used her up, but kept her for whatever reason. Usually, when the girls are done, they're shipped off elsewhere or just tossed in a shallow grave."

"And knowing this you could still be a part of all that nastiness? If Mei hadn't come to us, that would have been her fate."

"I felt like I didn't have a choice," she whispered. "What are you going to do now?"

"I want the names and locations of every kid you fucked over. If they aren't alive anymore, you still give me what you have. Then you have twenty-four hours to make things right."

"The kids..." She glanced toward the hall. "They can't go into foster care. Not here."

"I'll make a call. Have them packed and ready. Someone will take them to a safe location and see that they're placed with people who will give a shit about them. Raise them as their own, and keep the fucked-up people like you far away from them."

"What happens if I come to your gates?" she asked. "After the kids are... gone."

"If Blades is back, then I'd say I hope you have a high threshold for pain and can withstand days of torture. And if he's not... I won't be much kinder, Humes. I don't give a fuck why you did what you did. The fact remains that Mei and countless others paid the price."

She nodded and stood. "Then I guess I have some things to get in order. And for whatever it's worth, I'm sorry."

It wasn't worth shit, and she damn well knew it. If she showed at the gates, I had no doubt she'd receive the type of welcome she deserved. But if she were smart, she'd turn herself in to the police. Not that it would keep her out of our reach. I stepped out of her house and called Outlaw. I didn't think Grizzly would take on any more kids, but that didn't mean some of the other clubs wouldn't be willing. I didn't know how many were here, but it didn't matter. We'd make sure they were safe one way or another.

After I ended my call, I got on my bike and drove to the end of the street. I could go back, check on Mei, and let someone else handle the rest. I could, but I wouldn't. I also knew that I wasn't getting my hands on Proctor without some help. I shot off a text to Steel, knowing he'd respond.

Meet me on Holly Grove Lane. Judge Proctor is neck deep in this shit.

It didn't take long for an answer. *I'm coming. So are the others.*

I didn't know which others were coming with him, and I didn't care. As long as we got to Proctor, and managed to get him into our special room, that's all that mattered. The how didn't mean shit to me. I rode over to the affluent part of town and stopped at the end of the judge's street. The homes were large and beautiful. It looked like the perfect place to raise a family. Little did they know that a monster was on their street. Their kids weren't safe. None of them were. If a man could sell out children he was sworn to protect, what else would he be willing to do for the right amount of money?

I heard the pipes of my brothers' bikes long before they arrived. Steel, Wolf, Demon, and Dragon looked every bit as pissed as I felt. I gave them a nod and we approached the judge's home. I didn't think for a moment we'd have the element of surprise. The moment I walked into Demoira Humes' house, someone would have alerted the judge. It was clear she hadn't liked her part in things, and a man like Judge Proctor would have kept eyes on her, made sure she toed the line.

We coasted into the long driveway and stopped near the front steps of the opulent mansion. It seemed kiddie porn and prostitution paid well. Not surprising considering how many fucked-up individuals there were in the world. Hell, even what they called horror movies these days raked in the cash, the more grisly the better. To me, a scary movie should be like the old eighties slasher flicks, or a good haunting. Not that hacking up people crap that seemed so popular now.

Although, I'd seen enough of them to have a few ideas for the dear judge.

He opened the door before we even made it up the steps. He sneered as his gaze swept over our cuts, but the fact he wore a suit probably worth a grand or more didn't make him better than us. What he did behind his closed doors made him far worse than any man in our club. Even Blades was a fucking saint compared to this asshole.

"Time to pay up, Judge," I said as I went toe to toe with him.

"You honestly think your pathetic little club can take me down? Do you know how many people I have in my pocket in this town?"

My phone chimed and I checked it, smiling when I saw Outlaw's message. "Well, Your Honor, as of about thirty seconds ago, I'd say none."

I turned my phone so he could see the screen.

Chief of Police, half the officers, the District Attorney, and anyone else aside from Mei's foster family and the judge are done. The Feds were just leaked videos of every last one of them in compromising situations with minors.

"Sorry, Judge Proctor, but your days of running this place are over. And all those kids are going to have a chance at a decent life."

"You think you know it all?" He laughed. "You know nothing!"

His words made me pause, and I had to wonder if he was bluffing, or if there was something more going on. Did this go even deeper than the judge and his friends? Did it expand beyond our town and county? He might think he wouldn't talk, but he would. They always did. Anything to have the hope they'd escape the fate that awaited them.

"Take him," I said. "We'll make him talk at the compound."

Steel and Demon grabbed him, hauling him away as he screamed like a little bitch. A few housewives peeked out their front windows, but they disappeared just as fast. One look at us and they decided maybe their neighbor wasn't worth the trouble. If they knew what sort of man he was, they wouldn't care what happened to him.

Wolf hung back. "So you're married to Blades' daughter."

"Yep. It would seem that way." I cracked my neck. "Badger's with Adalia. Guess we're keeping it all in the family, so to speak. But if I have any daughters, none of you fuckers get any ideas."

Wolf burst out laughing and walked off. Yeah, the fucker might find it funny right now, but since we all seemed to fall for younger women, it was possible someone I considered a brother would end up with my kid. Wasn't too sure how I felt about that, but Blades and Grizzly seemed okay with it. Sort of. Might be one of those "keep your enemies close" situations. They knew exactly where to find us if we fucked up.

I got on my bike and hauled ass back to the compound. I had every intention of pulling whatever I could from the judge before ending his life. It just didn't occur to me that someone else would step in. Should have known when we put out the call for help that a bunch of nosy fuckers would show up.

I eyed Havoc. "Where's my sister?"

The Sergeant-at-Arms for the Devil's Boneyard just smiled, which made my stomach drop. He brought her here? My psycho fucking sister? Shit. If she'd met

Mei already, I hoped she decided to play nice. My sweet wife still had a ways to go before she was even half the spitfire Jordan was. My gaze strayed from Havoc to the others. He'd brought Magnus and Phantom with him. And the Dixie Reapers had sent Wraith, Tempest, and Grimm.

"Is this a fucking party or something?" I asked. "Anyone else coming to join us? You act like we're taking down the entire damn state."

"Maybe you are," said a voice behind me. I turned and groaned.

"Kraken. And who came with you?" I asked.

"Ratchet and Stone."

I hoped Havoc and Jordan didn't plan on staying at my place. Shit. Had they brought my niece with them? No fucking way I could deal with that hellion right now. I loved Lanie, but that kid was something else.

"Relax," said Havoc. "We were originally coming to meet your wife and see if you needed anything, but now we're here for another reason."

What the hell other reason could there be? My sister stepped out of the clubhouse and ran for me, throwing herself into my arms. It would serve her right if I dropped her on her ass.

"Hey, Jordan. This is an unexpected surprise."

She hugged me tighter. "Where are the kids?"

What... Oh. "You want to adopt one of the kids the social worker had?"

"Well, one of those or one from the home your wife lived at. We aren't picky," said Jordan.

"Any of them would be lucky to have you as their mom, Sis. I'm sure the kids will be rounded up and brought here soon. For now, why don't I introduce you to Mei?" I asked.

"She already met her," Havoc said. "Your wife looked a little overwhelmed, so she went home, and I made Jordan leave her in peace."

"Well, if you'll excuse me, I have someone to gut." I tried to step around them, but Havoc placed a hand in the middle of my chest.

"Not to tell you what to do on your own turf, but you're not going down there."

"Why the fuck not?" I asked.

"Because Blades is home." Grizzly stepped out of the shadows. "He needs this one, Dingo. She's his little girl. I need you to step back. Take care of Mei, help with the kids, whatever. But you leave Blades to handle the cleanup."

I stared at him, then the clubhouse. I didn't like it, but he had a point. If Blades was home, then he had a right to take care of his daughter in whatever way he saw fit. I gave a nod and got on my bike, going straight home. If that's where Mei was, then that's where I wanted to be.

Chapter Thirteen

Meiling

The moment Dingo entered the house I ran for him. Seeing my dad, knowing he was free, and what he planned to do, was more than I could handle right now. I didn't question how my dad had been freed. I knew that Wire and Lavender had something to do with it, but I didn't know exactly what. Either they had really high-up connections somewhere, or they were just fucking awesome at what they did.

And meeting Dingo's sister! That woman was something else. I looked forward to getting to know her better, but I needed a moment. Or several.

"Everything okay?" I asked. "You seem stressed."

"Just saw that we had a bunch of company, including my family."

"Jordan said they'd stay somewhere else. She thought we might like our privacy since we're newlyweds. I didn't disagree with her. I'd have had sex with you even if they were down the hall, but I'm not ready to entertain someone twenty-four-seven just yet. Was that okay?" I asked.

Dingo pulled me against his chest and kissed me. "Perfectly fine, Meiling."

I glowered at him. "Mei. Not Meiling."

"Your daddy may say otherwise. Shall we let him decide?" he asked.

"That was a low blow and you know it." I sighed. "Fine. Everyone can call me Meiling if they so desire. But I'm still going to introduce myself as Mei when I meet new people."

He rubbed his beard along my neck, then licked the shell of my ear. A shiver ran down my spine and I tightened my hold on him. How could one man have so much power over me? I just had to be near him and my panties got wet.

"How about you decide which name you like better after I yell it out while I'm coming inside you?" he asked.

Damn. He didn't play fair. I let him lead me into the bedroom, and smiled as he shut and locked the door. It seemed he didn't trust everyone to keep out of the house, but I knew I was safer here than anywhere else.

"Get naked," he said.

I pulled my shirt over my head, then stopped. "Are you going to do the bossy thing again?"

Dingo prowled closer, tugging on the waist of my pants until I was pressed against him. "Depends. Did you like it?"

I nodded. Maybe it would seem wrong to some people, after what I'd been through, but in some way it had been cathartic. I'd had men boss me around during sex for so long, but not a single one had ever cared if they were hurting me. Some had gotten off on my pain. When I gave myself over to Dingo, I knew that no matter what he demanded, he'd make sure I was safe and that I enjoyed it.

Maybe sex with him was my version of therapy. I didn't see myself ever sitting in an office with some shrink telling them my life history and answering "and how did that make you feel" until I wanted to vomit. I may have never actually been to one, but I'd watched enough TV that at least some of that had to be accurate.

If being in therapy was as frustrating as it appeared, then I'd give it a hard pass.

His lips brushed mine in a barely there kiss. "Strip, woman. I want you completely bare, middle of the bed, ass in the air. Let me see that pussy. I bet you're soaked, aren't you?"

My cheeks warmed. Yeah, I was soaked. That deep growly voice going low like that? It was almost enough to make me come without him doing anything else. When he stepped back and started to remove his clothes, I finished pulling off mine and scrambled to the center of the bed. I pressed my chest to the mattress and put my ass in the air like he'd demanded.

"Such a good, obedient wife. I might have to reward you," he said.

Reward? Oh, yes, please! I knew exactly what that meant. He was going to make me come so much and so hard that I'd forget my name. I was more than eager for whatever he wanted to do to me.

He spread me open and I felt the heat of his breath right before he licked my pussy. He moaned before lapping at me again.

"You taste so damn good, Mei."

"Jameson, please."

"Need to come?" he asked.

"Yes!"

The mattress shifted under me and I felt his cock brush against me. He positioned himself, but then didn't move. I felt his hand slip around my hip and he started to rub my clit.

"Going to do this a little different," he said.

"Wh-what's that mean?"

"It means, my wife, that I'm going to tease the hell out of you, but I'm just going to sit here. You want this dick? You're going to have to fuck yourself with it."

I was going to... I blinked. Well, that really was different. I couldn't recall ever doing something like that. As he worked the hard bud between my legs, I could feel myself getting wetter. I wanted him so fucking much. I rocked back, testing things a bit. His cock slid inside and I moaned, my eyes closing at the pleasure. He hadn't been kidding, though. He wasn't moving.

He pinched and teased my clit, making the ache build inside me. Soon was I rocking back and forth on his cock, taking him faster and deeper. It still wasn't enough.

"Need more," I whined. "Please, Jameson."

He wrapped an arm around my waist and sat back, taking me with him. My breath left me in a *whoosh* as he impaled me on his cock. Oh! Now *this* was much better. He started working my clit again and I rode him. Tossing back my head, I let the sensations wash over me. It wasn't long before I was coming. I could feel my release coating him and covering us. I'd never come so hard before.

"That's it. Don't stop now, Meiling. Keep coming."

He rubbed my clit faster and reached up with his other hand to twist my nipple between his fingers. I kept rising and falling, taking him as far as I could, at a pace that was leaving me breathless. It wasn't until I'd come twice more that he knocked me forward onto my hands and knees.

He fisted my hair, holding me in place as he fucked me. It wasn't gentle, and he wasn't trying to get me off. He was taking.

"That's it. My good little wife." He growled and slammed into me harder. "Take it all. Squeeze my dick with that pussy and make me come. You want that, don't you?"

I tried to nod, but I couldn't move. He not only had my hair gripped too tight, but the way he entered me, with his body half over mine, I was pinned in place.

"Beg me," he said. "Tell me you want it."

My heart thumped wildly in my chest. "I need it, Jameson. Need you to fuck me. Need you to come inside me."

I heard the headboard, or maybe the wall, crack as he doubled his efforts. He came with a roar, *Meiling* on his lips, and then fell atop me. I could barely breathe, but I didn't care right now. I could feel his cock twitching inside me, and everything felt right in my world. Especially since Dr. Larkin had called while he was gone. I'd only known because he'd spoken to Grizzly.

"Something I should tell you," I said. "Seeing as protection doesn't seem to work for us. When you remember it."

"What's that?" he asked, his voice muffled by my hair.

"Tests came back. I'm clean, which means you should be too. Unless of course you lied and fucked someone since you were last tested."

He pulled his hips back and slammed his dick into me again, making me moan and giggle at the same time. Yeah, he was still rock-hard. I was starting to think he was a superhero when it came to sex.

He rolled off me but cuddled me close to his chest. "Know what this means?"

"Um, that we don't have to even attempt to use a condom again? That didn't exactly work so well anyway."

"Right." He brushed my hair out of my eyes. "Because I want a family with you, Mei. If you don't want one right away, that's fine. We'll discuss birth control options with Dr. Larkin. But someday, when you're ready, I want a family with you."

I chewed on my lip. I'd heard where he was and what he was doing. I also knew about all those kids who would need homes. Maybe not the ones I'd lived with because that would be all kinds of awkward for all of us, but Humes had several she'd tried to protect.

"I want to adopt one of Miss Humes' kids," I blurted.

He went tense and lifted up on an elbow to stare down at me. "Are you sure?"

"Yes. I know it's asking a lot, Jameson. Those kids are special needs and maybe I'm not the right person to be a mother to anyone, much less someone who needs extra care, but I really want to do this."

He caressed my cheek, then pressed his lips to mine. "Meiling, all you ever have to do is ask. I'll give you anything I can. If you want to adopt one of those kids, then that's what we'll do."

"Will they let us?" I didn't want to bring it up, but my past *was* an issue for something like that. "I'm known around town as being a whore. And this club isn't exactly all sunshine and roses to the people outside the gates. What if they don't think we'd be fit parents?"

He cracked a smile. "Honey, do you think we do anything the legal way around here?"

"Well. No?"

"Right. No. We won't be the only ones adopting some of those kids. Let Outlaw and the others handle it. They'll make it all look legit, and trust me when I say no one in this town will question it. Especially once half the police department is rounded up by the Feds, along with some other big fish in town."

I'd heard about the judge and Chief of Police. I ran my fingers down Jameson's chest. I could feel the steady beat of his heart, and it calmed me. Gave me the courage to ask the question burning in my mind.

"My dad. He's going to kill all those people, isn't he?"

"Most of them. Probably not *all* of them," he said. "We have to leave some for the Feds, and I'm sure it won't take much to make it look like the others fled the country. You okay with that?"

Was I okay with my dad murdering people? I shouldn't be. A good person wouldn't cheer him on, would they? Either I wasn't all that good, or maybe I just didn't see rapists and pedophiles as people. They were monsters, and as far as I was concerned, the world would be better off without them. If they went to jail, they'd eventually be released. If I let my dad handle it, then no child would ever suffer at their hands again. "I'm good," I said.

"So, now that I've used both your names during sex, which one do you prefer?"

"Really? We just talked about getting a kid and my dad offing a bunch of people and you want to ask about my name?" I probably shouldn't expect anything remotely normal from my life, and certainly not from my husband.

"Which is it?" he asked.

"Fine. I like the way you say Meiling, especially when you're coming."

He grinned, then rolled to his back, taking me with him. I sprawled across his chest and snuggled closer. His cock was still knocking against me, wanting back inside, which almost made me laugh.

"I'm happy," I said. "I don't remember ever being happy before. Not until you."

"I'm glad, Meiling. You make me happy too," he said, running his fingers through my hair.

His phone started ringing and he groaned, but I scrambled off him and tugged it from his pants. Grizzly's name was on the screen so I quickly handed it to him.

"Better answer it," I said. "I really don't want your President beating down our door while I'm naked and have your cum leaking out of me."

He smacked my ass as he took the phone from me. When he answered, he put the call on speaker.

"Meiling is here with me," he said. "And she's listening."

"Her daddy pulled some information from the judge. This thing was even bigger than we thought. Outlaw is going to have everything delivered to the Feds. To everyone, including his family, it's going to look like the good judge took a little trip to a non-extradition country. But this is far from over. I'm sending out as many men as I can, even those that aren't mine, to round up any kids involved. Each club is going to make arrangements to take some home with them. I've placed a few calls to see if some others will volunteer to house a few. Wire, Lavender, Outlaw, and the others are making sure there's no trace of those kids in the system. No one will come looking for them."

"How many kids are there?" I asked.

"Twenty at last count," Grizzly said. "But we're finding more. Meiling, there's something else. I don't know if Dingo told you but your mom is alive."

I turned an accusing gaze toward my husband. He'd known my mother was alive and hadn't said anything? Shouldn't he have opened with that when he saw me? What the hell?

"She's not in a good place, Meiling. Better let your dad handle it. I'm arranging lodging for him as we speak so he won't have to stay with you or at the clubhouse. But he's going to need you, Meiling. They both will, if he brings her here."

"Thanks, Pres," Dingo said. "And thanks for selling me out. I hadn't told her yet."

Grizzly laughed. "Lesson learned, boy. Don't hide important shit from your woman unless it's club business. Now get back to trying to make grandbabies for Blades, and don't tell me you weren't."

The call ended and I stared at my husband. "Were you going to tell me at all?"

He cleared his throat and set his phone aside. "I was. I just didn't know how. Humes has kept up with Xi-wang and said that your mom isn't the same woman as before. She's empty. Meiling, they used her up. I'm not sure she can be saved, baby."

Tears burned my eyes. "We have to try."

"I'm sure your dad will do his best."

His best had better be good enough. I'd gone from no family to having everything I'd ever wanted -- or I would as soon as my mom was here. If he didn't bring her home, I would.

Epilogue

Blades - One Month Later

It was interesting, being on the other side of the table at the prison. The man who had raped my daughter and sold her again and again was chained down. He wasn't looking so great, either. Every time he moved and winced, I wanted to smile and scream a big "fuck you" in his face. I'd found him easily enough. He hadn't even tried to hide from me. After working him over for a few hours, I personally delivered him to the prison gates, along with copies of the videos of him and several minors. With most of the local police force gone, it hadn't been likely the local jail would have housed him. Besides, I'd made a few friends inside and knew they'd take good care of him while he waited for his trial. Something that the judge had wanted to expedite, but I'd asked for a little help slowing things down. No way this asshole was being released on bail, so he'd have to remain in prison while he waited. And he'd be waiting a long time.

"Something wrong, Simpson?" I asked.

He didn't answer, but he didn't have to.

"Don't like having multiple dicks shoved up your ass? Or are you not even worthy of a fuck? Bet they just use whatever's handy." I couldn't contain my smile another moment. "I have some excellent news for you."

"What?"

"Your wife? The bitch who stood by and let you and others like you rape and torture all those kids? Found the perfect place for her. She'll be fucked as much as you will for the foreseeable future. Seemed fitting. You thought it was good enough for those kids, so it must be an amazing thing you want to experience yourself, right?"

His jaw tightened, but he didn't say a word.

"You'll be especially happy to learn that your paperwork seems to have been misfiled." Now that had his attention. "You're not ever leaving here, unless it's through the morgue. Congratulations. You've just secured yourself a permanent seat in hell, even if I have to pay off anyone who knows your name to forget you exist. Or maybe sitting isn't your favorite thing these days."

The little bastard started to cry. "You can't do this to me!"

"Oh, I can, and I did." I stood and made my way to the door. The two guards I'd gotten to know the best during my stay came in to take the prisoner away. But I stopped them, holding up a hundred to each of them. "See that he gets extra special treatment tonight."

"You got it." One of them flashed me a smile as he pocketed the money. "We don't like baby rapers around here. He'll get all the special care he could ever need. For however long he's breathing."

I patted him on the shoulder and left as Simpson screamed and begged to be released. I could have killed him. Had actually thought about it. In the end, I'd thought this might be a more fitting punishment. I'd made a lot of friends inside over the last eighteen years, and some were very appreciative. I'd saved more than a few of their asses during fights. Yeah, good ol' Simpson was going to have a very difficult time behind bars.

Most of the other men involved had been dealt with, by me. Outlaw had helped cover my tracks, and as far as anyone was concerned, those men had gone into hiding. A few were delivered to the Feds, or left in plain sight for them to find. But each of those men and women would get special treatment in prison, including Humes, even though she'd turned herself over to the police voluntarily. Too little, too late.

The Harley Fat Boy outside the gates gleamed in the sunlight. My old ride was long gone, but the club had bought this one for me as a coming home present. Not that getting to be part of my daughter's life wasn't present enough. I'd taken care of her demons, laid them all to rest. Simpson had been the last, him and his wife. Now it was time to give Meiling the one gift she wanted more than anything. I'd had Outlaw looking into a few things, making sure Xi-wang was where we'd thought. I also had to make sure all the bad guys were dealt with, in my own way.

I rode my bike through town and hit the highway. *The Silk Purse*, a specialty brothel, was just across the state line. I hated that she'd been so close all this time and no one had even known. My fault. Shouldn't have kept her to myself. It was too late to change the past, but I was determined to give Xi-wang and Meiling a good future. One with a family.

I pulled into the parking lot and stared at the building that had housed my woman for too fucking long. If I'd ever heard a word of what she'd been through, I'd have dug my fucking way out of prison to go get her. I'd have done anything to save Xi-wang. She'd been my entire world from day one. I'd imagine I looked at her the way Dingo looked at my daughter. He was a good sort, and she was crazy about him. If I'd ever thought she wasn't happy, I'd have gutted the bastard.

I got off the bike and headed inside. The moment I saw her my fucking heart broke. My beautiful girl was just as stunning now as she'd before, even with the scars clearly visible on her face and arms, and a few silver threads in her hair. She gave me a slight bow as I drew closer, but her eyes never met mine.

"Welcome to *The Silk Purse*. What will be your pleasure tonight?" she asked, her voice still holding the accent I'd so loved all those years ago.

"My pleasure?" I asked. She still didn't look up. "I came to take my woman home. Our daughter needs her."

She went still, completely frozen. Slowly, she lifted her head and her gaze locked with mine. The Xi-wang I'd known was there, but just barely. I could see her, but I could also see the road of pain she'd traveled while we'd been apart.

"Xi-wang."

"Robert?" she asked softly. "You went to prison for murder."

"Didn't do it." I reached for her, tugging her against me. "But I did kill a few people since then. They all deserved it."

I stroked her cheek and wished I could turn back the clock. She'd had my heart the moment we locked eyes that first time. I'd have given anything to keep her safe, and I'd failed. I'd failed both her and our daughter.

"The people who put you here have been dealt with," I said. "They also were responsible for turning our daughter into a whore. I still don't know the entire story, but it seems the family she was with last has been part of a child pornography ring for decades. The family business of all the fucked-up things. Any kids in the area who weren't white or fully white were flagged. When the pedophile making the videos got requests for certain types of girls and boys of certain ages, then they'd be sent to him. Our daughter could have been sent to him much sooner, so there's a small blessing in all this fucked-up mess."

She flinched and looked away, but I turned her face back to mine.

"Xi-wang, never do that again. I know what you've been through, and it doesn't matter."

"It does," she said. "I'm dirty."

"No, you're beautiful. My stunning woman, the mother of my child, the only woman to ever have my heart."

Her eyes misted with tears and one slipped down her cheek. I brushed it away before kissing her softly. She resisted at first, then I felt her arms come around my neck as she kissed me back.

"I love you, Robert," she said. "I fought, so hard. I was yours, only ever yours."

"It's time to go home, China." She smiled at the name I'd always called her. But the smile slipped from her face as she touched her scars and looked at her surroundings. I could tell she was retreating, that she would refuse to come with me, and I couldn't let that happen. She belonged with me. If I'd not kept her from the club all those years ago, maybe none of this would have happened. Or maybe they'd have chewed her up and spit her out. Too late to second-guess myself now. "You're mine. Do you hear me?" I asked.

"I want to be yours. In my heart, I always was."

My hold on her tightened. "You always have been and always will be my China. The love of my life."

She was still withdrawn, more than I'd have liked, but what I was seeing was more than I'd expected. I'd been led to believe that she was empty, dead inside. But my China was still there. "Our daughter is married," I said. "To a member of my club."

Her gaze jerked to mine. "You said they were dangerous."

I snorted and looked around. "China, do you see where you are? Did you hear what I said happened to our daughter? Trust me. The club is the safest place for both of you. Things have changed since I went away. It's a good place to raise a family. *Our* family."

"They hurt her?" she asked.

"Yeah, honey. They hurt her bad, but she's healing. Dingo is good to her, worships her."

"She might need to talk, about what happened." Xi-wang locked her gaze with mine. "You think she'll accept me? That your club will?"

"They'll love you, just the way I do. There's a house. It's ours, but we'll have to make it a home. Think you're up for the task?"

She gave me a smile, a real one that gave me hope. "Okay. They won't like me leaving."

I pulled a knife and smiled. "They don't call me Blades for nothing, China. You let me handle the people who run this place. Go out and wait by my bike."

She nodded and paused only long enough to kiss my cheek. It looked like I would get a little bit bloody before I got to take my woman home, but she was worth the effort I'd have to put into finding a clean shirt.

"All right, you fuckers," I yelled out. "Who wants to die first?"

I heard movement to my right and laughed. They could run, but they'd never make it. I was going to take down every last one of them, set the women free, then burn this bitch to the ground. *The Silk Purse* was officially closed for business.

Outlaw (Devil's Fury MC 2)

Harley Wylde

Elena -- I lost my parents as a kid, but a reverend and his wife took me in. They were good to me, even if there had never been many hugs. Then they started pushing me to marry a man I didn't want, so I ran. I should have known the moment I walked through the clubhouse doors of the Devil's Fury my life would never be the same. I just didn't count on a bad boy biker being the one to finally make me feel wanted.

Outlaw -- The Devil's Fury are my family, my brothers, but I'm not the same man I was years ago. I'm scarred and broken, or so I'd thought. The little Latina who came to the clubhouse, then pulled out a damn book to read had my attention right away. When someone tries to hurt her, I know that I'll keep her safe. In fact, I'll just keep her. She's awakened a part of me I'd thought I'd lost. Didn't count on her bringing trouble with her, or nearly losing her, but she's mine and I will fight for her to the very end.

Chapter One

Elena

The man I'd been ordered to call Father had been droning on for what felt like hours. The tent was stifling hot thanks to the bodies crammed inside, and I'd honestly rather have been anywhere else. I'd heard horror stories about being in foster care, but when my case worker had told me a preacher and his wife wanted me, I'd thought I'd been lucky. It wasn't so much that they abused me, but they expected perfection, and I was far from perfect. Things could have been worse. I'd been out of the system for a few years now, and I still had a place to live. Most kids would have been kicked out.

The only job I'd been permitted was at the library. My "parents" had thought it was a safe enough place to be, and respectable. That last part counted the most with them. My necklines had to be high enough to never show even a hint of cleavage. I wasn't permitted to wear anything that hugged my curves, and had a closet full of baggy pants, tops, and ankle-length skirts. What my parents hadn't realized was that I'd been saving since I got my job. They thought I spent my money on clothes or going out with my friends. Not that I had many of those. None, actually. Not genuine ones.

Two weeks ago, I'd purchased a phone at the grocery store a few towns over and added a month of service, then purchased an additional phone card for when that plan ran out. In the tire well of my trunk, I'd stashed a duffle bag with clothing and shoes of my choosing, along with that phone and card. Using a bank my parents hadn't had access to had worked in my favor. I'd already withdrawn every penny I had and closed out the account. All I needed now was the perfect moment. The way my mother kept pushing Garrison West at me, I knew that moment was *now*. The subtle hints from the past year were now more of a demand.

There was no way I would marry the deacon of our church. He was fifteen years older than me, but it wasn't his age that was the problem. Honestly, my celebrity crush was old enough to be my dad. The difference was my crush was hot, and Garrison wasn't. Not even a little. But even that wasn't the deal breaker. No, it was the fact he expected me to remain barefoot and pregnant in the kitchen that rubbed me the wrong way. I had no problem being a mom, but Garrison didn't want a wife. He wanted a broodmare.

My mother had told him more than once, in front of me, that I was still a virgin and would be an excellent wife for him. She even commented on my "birthing hips." Seriously, who said that anymore? The only reason I hadn't tossed my V-card was because I didn't want a one-night stand with some drunk guy in a neighboring town, and no one in Ridgemont would touch me. Our sleepy town boasted a population of seven thousand, and anything that happened around here got back to my parents. As to the other... I didn't care to find out if what she said was true until I was having those babies with a man who loved me.

The woman next to me leaned in close to whisper. "Such a good sermon! You're so lucky to have such an upstanding man as your dad."

I gave her a weak smile and nodded.

"And to have Garrison West interested in you! My, you must be so thrilled!" The woman tittered before sitting all the way back in her seat.

I tried to keep the smile on my face, but it was difficult to do.

My father stepped away from the makeshift pulpit and started mingling with his congregation. Now that he was finished telling everyone about the wages of sin, I knew people would head toward the tables of food. While it was somewhat chaotic, I decided that now was my one and only chance. I stood from my seat, making sure my mother was preoccupied, and I made my escape. The moment I was free of the tent, I breathed a little easier. The small purse hanging from my shoulder had my wallet and keys inside. I pulled out my keyring and popped the locks on my car.

"Please don't see me," I muttered as I started to run for the vehicle.

The little hatchback beeped and the lights flashed, but no one seemed to notice. I stopped and looked behind me just to be sure, then hastened my pace and opened the door. I slid behind the wheel, my hands shaking as I tried to calm my racing heart. Tossing my purse onto the passenger seat, I started the car and headed for the highway. I didn't care where I went, as long as it wasn't here! With some luck, it would take them at least an hour or two to figure out I wasn't at the revival, or at home. I'd already disabled the GPS on my car -- *Thank you, YouTube!* -- and hoped they didn't have another way to track me. Since I'd never been permitted to have a phone, I didn't have to worry about ditching one.

Not once in all the years I'd been with the Tolberts had I ever given them a reason to doubt me.

I'd followed the rules, toed the line, and made sure I kept them happy. I knew that neither of them would have ever thought I'd run away, but at twenty-one that's exactly what I was doing! I debated going through Atlanta, but I worried I'd get stuck in the god-awful traffic and someone would catch up to me. Instead, I skirted around the city. Well, more than skirted. I headed for Carrollton and took Highway 27 south. I didn't have a destination in mind, but I'd have loved to see Florida.

"All right. I may not know where I'm going, but I do believe in fate and I know I'll end up where I'm supposed to be." At least, I hoped that was true. My life might have been far from perfect, but at least it hadn't been entirely awful. Things could have been much worse after my family died, or at least that's what I'd been told happened. I didn't actually remember the details. That part of my life was a bit fuzzy, either because of how long it had been or maybe it had been too traumatic.

I made it as far as Cuthbert, Georgia before my back and neck started aching. I hadn't driven farther than a half hour since I'd had my license. As much fun as a college town might have been, I wasn't ready to stop just yet. The more distance between me and my family the better. I'd been on the road for roughly five hours, but I didn't think that was enough. Between Cuthbert and the Florida state line, I had no choice but to pull over. I would just have to hope that the reach of Reverend Tolbert didn't come quite this far.

The exit had a small sign posted. *Blackwood Falls.* I hadn't ever heard of it, and since the population was under ten thousand, I had to hope that no one else had either. It seemed like a good enough place to get lost for a day or two. A motel with blinking cherries beckoned, and I pulled into the lot near the front office. I couldn't stifle my groan as I got out and walked inside. It felt entirely too good to stand up and stretch. Ringing the bell on the counter, I twisted one way, then the other as I waited.

A frail woman, who looked like a stiff wind would knock her over, used a walker to approach from behind the counter. She gave me a gummy smile, and I couldn't help but hope she had someone helping her run the place. She pushed a book toward me and I realized the motel was still old-school and I had to write my information down to get a room. When I was done, she told me the price per night and I handed over some cash to cover two nights.

"Diner is down the street," she said. "But young thing like you probably wants the Devil's Fury. Seems like all the girls want to go there. I might be an old woman, but I wasn't always. I understand wanting to kick up your heels. Go to the edge of town and you can't miss it. Just look for all the cars and bikes."

"Thank you," I said.

Cars and bikes? Just what kind of place was Devil's Fury? After having religion crammed down my throat for so long, I had to admit the name alone intrigued me. I took my room key -- which was an actual key! -- and drove down to room six. After I put my things in the room, I knew I needed a hot bath, then I'd decide where I wanted to go, or if I just wanted to nap. The trip had been rougher than I'd imagined, but then I'd never been anywhere this far from home before.

I filled the tub with steamy water, then sank as far as I could. A whirlpool tub would have been amazing, but this would do. I could feel my back cracking and popping as my tension slowly eased. The stress of the last few weeks, then my fear of getting caught, had wound me up tight. The water must have felt a little too good because the next thing I knew I was opening my eyes and the bath had become ice-cold. Draining the water, I shivered and stood. After drying off, I pulled on a knit dress that hugged my upper body and flared out to my knees. The peep-toe shoes I'd picked up looked adorable with it. I changed out my purse to a slightly larger one, tossed in a sexy romance I'd hidden in my car, and decided it was time to get out of the motel room for a while.

The thought of checking out the Devil's Fury still lurked in the back of my mind, and after I started the car, I found myself heading to the opposite side of town.

"It can't hurt to just check it out, right?" Not that I expected an answer since it was just me in the car.

The last thing I anticipated was a club of some sort, or the line of motorcycles out front. A man stood at the gate and waved me through. Sure, the lady at the motel had said bikes, but I'd thought maybe she meant the kind you pedaled. Then again, the name Devil's Fury should have clued me in. I might not have experienced anything like this before, but I wasn't stupid. I didn't think so anyway. After I found a spot to park, I grabbed my purse and got out, smoothing my dress before locking the car.

Inside, smoke and music filled the air. I coughed and waved a hand in front of my face as my eyes adjusted to the dim lighting. My mouth dropped open at the sight of nearly naked, and fully naked, women. The men wearing leather vests -- cuts? Hadn't that been what they were called in books and shows? -- were openly touching them, and a few... my cheeks burned! Were those women giving blowjobs? Out in the open? Exactly what kind of place had I come to? The words *Devil's Fury MC* were stitched on the back of each cut, and I now realized I'd entered the den of a motorcycle club. I'd heard of places like this, but no details. Now I understood why.

Knowing I should leave, I went to take a step back, except my feet seemed to have a mind of their own and carried me farther into the room. What was I doing? This was insanity! Good girls like me didn't belong in places like this. Or was I really a good girl? Just because it had been demanded of me, maybe there was a wild child hidden deep inside, some part of me that craved this type of setting. I had to admit that the freedom these women seemed to have, the courage to display themselves so openly, made me wish I was a little more like them.

I tried to skirt around the outer edge of the room, clinging to the wall, as I found a table in the corner. I sat down and observed the room, wondering if I should get up and leave. Part of me was fascinated. I'd read romances, when no one was looking, but I'd never seen anything like this in person before. Honestly, the books I'd read seemed almost tame in comparison. A few had talked about bondage, but I hadn't been brave enough to try and sneak something racier for fear my parents would find out.

The women didn't seem to care who looked at them, touched them, or what else was demanded. One of the men pushed one of the women over a table and unzipped his pants. I knew I shouldn't look, and yet I couldn't turn away. The look of bliss on her face as he rammed himself inside her made me squeeze my thighs together. An ache started to build, and I shifted in my seat. He kept thrusting, and when his hand cracked down on her ass, I couldn't contain my gasp. I couldn't see his *thing* from this angle, but my cheeks burned just the same. I should get up and leave. I really should.

A cold bottle of beer was placed in front of me and my gaze jerked up to a young man standing by the table. He winked and walked off, not saying a word to me. Hesitantly, I reached for it, wondering if I was supposed to pay. I'd never had a beer before. Or been to a place like this. For that matter, I'd never been to a bar or a dance club either. What was the protocol for accepting a beer from someone I didn't know? Was I supposed to pay for it? Surely if he'd wanted payment, he'd have stayed longer. Or was the repayment meant to be a different sort? My gaze scanned the room again. Could I do that? Let these men use me if that's what they demanded?

The first taste of the brew had my nose wrinkling and my lips pursing. Why did people drink this stuff? It was so bitter! The last thing I wanted to do was draw attention to myself, more so than I already had, so I kept drinking. By the time I'd finished the bottle, I was feeling a bit more at ease. Maybe more than a bit. My skin was warming and if I moved my head too fast the room spun. When the second bottle arrived, I pulled out my book and decided to read and enjoy my drink. So far, no one had bothered me.

And if I did glance at the women around the room, and the men using them as they wanted, maybe no one noticed. It was wrong, and yet I couldn't help but envy them. They didn't care what people thought or said, or so it seemed. What would it be like to experience that sort of… freedom?

The words seemed to blur and dance, so I blinked a few times, trying to bring the page into focus. Was I drunk? Off one beer? I didn't remember taking more than a swallow of the second one. I hadn't realized there was enough alcohol in those to do that to me. I tried to turn the page and my fingers fumbled, slipping off before I tried to grab hold again. My stomach churned a little and I hoped I wasn't going to be sick. Wasn't that supposed to be a morning-after type of thing if you drank too much?

I cut my gaze to where the women and men were openly engaging in various sex acts, and I wondered again if I would be required to do that too. Was that why I'd been given a drink? I gasped and put my hand to my throat. Had they drugged me? The bottle had already been open when it was delivered. I'd heard stories of girls getting drugged at college parties, but... It couldn't happen to me, right? And if they did demand that I drop to my knees, would I want to? I'd always thought I didn't want a one-night stand, but the idea of some guy forcing me to the floor or over a table, of everyone here watching... it made my blood heat and I throbbed between my legs.

Maybe I was a slut. Wasn't that what my foster parents had called women like these? Sluts and whores? The yearning I felt, the desire to be used like they were, to be exposed to anyone who wanted to watch... it was unlike anything I'd ever felt before, or wanted. Or maybe I'd always wanted something like this and just hadn't known how to ask for it, or where to even begin.

Turning back to my book, I decided I'd try to read just one page, and then I'd head back to the motel. This wasn't the place for me. I was a good girl. A sweet girl. I... I still couldn't seem to focus on the words, or hold the book right. My thoughts were swirling around my mind like a tornado.

The hair on my nape stood up and I could tell someone was watching me. I tried to covertly glance around the room, but it didn't seem as if anyone was paying me attention. I looked over at the bar, but the young guy who had been supplying my drinks was busy. Scanning the crowd, I still couldn't figure out who was watching me, but the feeling persisted. Trying to shrug it off, I went back to my book. Or tried.

Everything got worse. The entire place was swimming and spinning. I felt like I was swaying. My body slid sideways and I couldn't seem to stop it from happening. Two strong arms wrapped around me. A hard body pressed against mine and an earthy smell filled my nose. I tried to get my legs under me, but they felt like noodles. Before I could utter a word, the man lifted me into his arms, carrying me like a bride, and someone else snatched my purse and book from the table.

The fresh scent of the outside air hit me, but my eyes were closed to help keep the nausea at bay.

"I'll find out who drugged her," a deep grumbly voice said. "Take her to your place, Outlaw. Keep an eye on her. I want to know who she is and why she's here. Girl like that doesn't belong in a place like this."

Outlaw? What a strange name. And yet the sheer strength of the man holding me made me feel as if an ordinary name would never do for someone like him. I didn't know how he'd earned that name, but the man speaking seemed to trust him with me. Not that I knew either of them. For all I knew, they would kill me and hide the body. That didn't seem to be what they wanted of women, though. I thought back to the woman bent over the table, and I wondered if this man would do the same with me.

For whatever reason, the idea didn't trouble me. If anything, it turned me on even more.

"I'll keep her safe." I felt the vibration of his words and realized it was the man holding me. Outlaw is what the other one had called him. It made me giggle the more I thought about his name. Was he like Billy the Kid? Or Jesse James?

"Careful with that one." The other man's voice was laced with humor. "Looks like she'll be a happy drunk, but she might come out of it like a pissed-off honey badger. I'll check in after I have this shit sorted."

I heard the door open and loud music pour out before things got quieter again. The man holding me started moving, going down the steps, then I heard the crunch of his boots on gravel. He muttered a curse and something I didn't quite catch about trucks, but otherwise remained silent. I didn't have any sense of time but eventually I heard another door open and shut. Where was he taking me? I could open my eyes and find out, yet I didn't know if my stomach could handle it. I knew I should be terrified, but I couldn't seem to muster a hint of fear. I just felt... good. Was this what it felt like to be buzzed? I'd heard the girls in church whispering, but I'd never experienced anything like it myself.

Of course, they'd also giggled and whispered about other things too.

"Can you open your eyes, sweet girl?" the man asked.

I fought my eyelids and won the battle, opening them a little. Things were still not quite in focus but I tried to look up at the man holding me. I could see that his hair was a reddish brown, and he had a beard. Nothing else was clear enough at the moment. My eyes slid shut again and I groaned, my head starting to pound.

"Can you tell me your name?" he asked.

"Elena," I whispered, or tried to. My tongue felt heavy and like it was tied into knots. Even to my ears it didn't sound right. What was wrong with me?

"I'm Outlaw and you're safe. No one will touch you or hurt you. Do you want the couch or my bed?" My breath caught and I must have tensed or something. I could almost feel his urgency to reassure me. "Alone. I meant you could have my bed all to yourself."

I tried to answer, but everything started to feel heavier, like I was being weighed down and pulled under by thick sludge. My mind went blank, and then I was out. Only one thought hit me right before I sunk completely under. *I hope he really is nice and won't hurt me. Or maybe he'll hurt me in a good way.*

Chapter Two

Outlaw

Jesus Christ. The curvy body pressed against me was starting to get a rise from my cock, which was startling enough I nearly dropped her. It had been over four years since I'd had the shit beat out of me and had nearly died. And during that time, I hadn't gotten hard once. Didn't matter if one of the club sluts had her tits pressed against me or in my face. A few had even rubbed all over me, and still nothing. The doctors hadn't found any reason my dick wouldn't work, but like my hands, it seemed to have been damaged during the attack. Or maybe it was something just fucked up in my head.

Not that I would have done anything differently. Even if I couldn't hold the simplest of items without a shit ton of pain going through my fingers, or type, for that matter. My days of hacking were pretty much over. I could do some basic digging, but the hardcore stuff I had to hand off to someone else. It was a bit humiliating. I'd never been the level of Wire and Lavender, but I'd held my own. Until now.

The important thing is that I'd distracted the assholes long enough that Wire's woman was safe. That's all that had mattered.

I carried Elena to my room and eased her down onto the bed. I flexed my hands a few times, wincing as sharp pain shot through them. Carrying her hadn't been easy. Not because she was heavy, but because my fingers had been broken in multiple places. Three had even been shattered. They hadn't healed quite right, but I wasn't about to have surgery now to try and fix anything. I could still use them, but certain things caused me a good deal of agony. I'd also noticed that after more than a few minutes, my grip would weaken if I was holding something. Holding small objects made my fingers cramp and hurt, and riding a bike was sometimes more difficult, but I wasn't about to admit that shit to anyone. It made me feel far older than my thirty-six years.

The little Latina in my bed was a pretty thing. Her long, dark hair hung in glossy waves and I itched to touch it. I'd felt it brush against my arm when I'd carried her from the clubhouse. She had curves in all the right places, even if she did look a bit young. I hoped like fuck she wasn't underage. Not only because I'd gotten hard holding her, but the club could be in some serious shit if we'd let someone not-quite-legal in the gates. I wondered if the shithead on duty had even checked her ID when he let her inside, or if he'd just seen a pretty face and waved her through. We'd had some issues with that in the last several weeks.

I just didn't know what the hell to do with her right now. It was obvious someone had laced her drink with something, but I didn't know what, or who. We had some new Prospects, but I'd thought they were vetted. I couldn't do the job anymore, but I'd asked for some help from Surge and Wizard. Now I was wishing I'd gone to Wire instead. I tried to keep my distance from him and Lavender. Every time that woman looked at me, I could see that she felt responsible for what happened. I didn't want her feeling guilty over something she couldn't control.

"I don't know where you've come from, or why you're here, but I won't let anyone hurt you," I murmured to the sexy woman in my bed. She seemed innocent. Sweet. And too damn young for me, not that my body cared.

Heading back to the front of the house, I checked my phone for any messages, then decided to make some coffee. I didn't know how long it would take Grizzly to sort shit out, but I wanted to stay alert in case anyone came for Elena. She was the fourth woman who had been drugged, and so far, the slippery fucker had evaded us. My money was on a Prospect doing this shit, but it could have easily been anyone at the clubhouse. There were plenty of women up there who were regulars, pretty much all club whores, and those women didn't like competition.

My front door opened, and I heard the heavy tread of the Pres's steps. He had a gait that was slightly off and easily discernable. Grizzly shoved young Simon into the kitchen just as I was pouring a cup of coffee. I handed it off to Griz and pulled down a second mug for me. Then I sat and waited. Simon was jittery, his hands twitching, his eyes darting around the room. He knew something was up, but I wasn't certain if he was necessarily guilty. I heard the door again and this time the Sergeant-at-Arms, Demon, entered.

"Start talking," Demon said.

"I-I don't know what you w-want," Simon said, his Adam's apple bobbing as he swallowed hard.

"The girl. Who drugged her?" Demon asked.

His eyes went wide and flew to me, then both club officers. "I didn't drug anyone!"

"Didn't say you did," said Grizzly. "But I think you know who did. Or suspect at any rate."

"I took her two beers, but I didn't put anything in them. I delivered them myself." He shifted in his seat. "I'd never do that to a woman."

"Anyone have access to them before you took them to Elena?" I asked.

Simon's brow furrowed and I could tell he was seriously thinking it over. "I'm not sure. I had just opened the first one before I set it down on the bar when someone called my name. I only turned away for a minute, maybe two, and then I carried the drink over to the woman in the corner. The clubhouse was packed tonight. I didn't pay attention to who was at the bar. Colorado said that all women got free beer. I'd noticed the woman at the corner table didn't have anything, so I was just trying to follow orders."

Grizzly folded his arms and looked up at the ceiling a moment before directing his gaze at Demon. "Pull the clubhouse tapes and see if you can spot anything unusual. Maybe we'll get lucky this time. In the meantime, Outlaw, she's your responsibility. Do whatever is necessary to keep her safe, and make sure she isn't going to complain to the law about this. *Whatever* it takes. We'll handle this shit storm in our own way."

I nodded but my gut cramped. I didn't like the idea of bending her to my will. Not like that anyway. I wouldn't mind commanding her in the bedroom. *Shit.* My dick was getting hard again. One thing was for sure, I should thank her for curing me. It had been so long since I'd gotten laid, or been able to come, that I was tempted to shoo these fuckers from my house and go jerk one off in the shower. Elena was passed the fuck out and wouldn't know the difference. I'd be in and out before she even woke up.

"I didn't mean to hurt anyone," Simon said. "You know I'd never drug a woman, right? I'm not into that shit. Any asshole who rapes a woman needs to die a painful death, and I can't think of another reason to drug them."

Couldn't exactly disagree with him on that one. I knew all my brothers felt the same. Especially since Grizzly had a tendency to adopt teens who'd been abused in some way or another. His eldest, Adalia, was with Badger now, but the other two were younger. Lilian was all grown up and old enough to have a man of her own, but she was still reserved and jumped at shadows. Silva had done a number on her, and I wasn't sure if she'd ever fully recover. The Pres had assured her she had a home as long as she wanted, and so far, she hadn't moved out of his home.

Lilian was actually the second woman the Pres had adopted, and not too long after her, he'd taken in yet another teen, Shella. While Shella had never said anything about being sexually abused, she'd obviously been neglected and had to fend for herself. She was stronger than Lilian, but Griz kept her on lockdown as much as he could.

"Am I in trouble?" Simon asked. "I swear I didn't know there was anything in her drink."

"You're free to go, kid. Keep this quiet for now," Demon said.

Simon practically ran from my house with Demon following. Grizzly sighed and paced for a moment. I knew he was pissed this happened on his turf. Even worse, it wasn't the first time. So far, whoever was responsible had been smart enough not to get caught, which just irritated Griz even more.

"When I find out who's doing this..." He grumbled some more under his breath before coming to a stop. "It's obviously not Simon. Henry is on the gate tonight. That leaves Beau, Carver, and the four new guys. With Beau's history, I seriously doubt he'd pull this shit."

"If it's even a Prospect, Pres. You know as well as I do it could just be someone who's here at every damn party. Who would gain anything from this? So far, we caught on before anything bad happened. Those girls ended up with patched members who could tell something wasn't right."

He nodded.

"Maybe we're looking at this wrong. What if it's not happening because someone wants the girls to agree to anything? What if it's someone jealous of those women?" I asked.

"You mean another female?" he asked. "Like a club whore?"

"Wouldn't surprise me. Look at the trouble some have caused for other clubs, and even here a few years back. Tasha poked holes in the all the condoms in the community bowl, hoping she'd get knocked up and land herself the title of old lady."

Griz snorted. "Like any of us would have claimed her. The baby, sure, but not her. Good thing one of the other girls noticed and reported it. That would have gone sideways fast."

No shit. A lot of us could have been daddies from that fiasco. Although, after my dick stopped working, I'd often thought that it would have been nice to have a kid. Then I'd lost hope. Until Elena. If my dick was getting hard again, then maybe it would work well enough to make a baby, assuming my little swimmers were up for the challenge. Only one way to find out, but I had to get myself a woman first.

Griz's phone started ringing, and I recognized the tone. It was Shella. He stiffened as he answered and I tried to tune him out. I could hear the urgency in her voice even if I couldn't understand the words. Then Grizzly roared like a fucking bear before screaming out, "*I'll kill him.*" He ended the call and started stomping toward my front door.

"Problem, Pres?" I called out. "You need backup?"

I heard more growling before he answered.

"No, but Dragon better fucking run."

What the hell? I stood up and went to the front entry. Dragon? He'd nearly died not that long ago, caught up with some shit that impacted a lot of clubs in the south. I couldn't imagine him fucking shit up. Although, it seemed the club officers hadn't seen fit to send anyone after him. He'd been tortured because Griz made a call that had gone sideways.

"Why?" I asked.

"Because he knocked up my daughter." Grizzly snarled. "Fucker got Lilian pregnant."

I tried to take that in for a moment. Little Lilian? Pregnant? She jumped every time one of us got too close. How the hell had Dragon gotten near enough to get a baby in her? Not that it seemed to matter right now. The way Grizzly was huffing and puffing, there wouldn't be much left of the baby daddy once the Pres was done with him. Part of me wondered if I should call and give the guy a heads-up, but if he'd been messing around with the Pres's daughter, then maybe he deserved his fate. Yeah, it had worked out for Badger when he'd knocked up Adalia, but Griz knew his eldest daughter was head over heels for Badger. With Lilian... well, that was a different story. He sheltered her even more than he had Adalia. And Shella -- I shuddered to think what would happen if anyone even thought of asking her out on a date, much less getting near enough for anything else.

After I was certain no one else was going to wander into my house, I headed back to my bedroom and checked on Elena. She still slept soundly, but depending on what she was given, she could be out for a while. Her chest rose and fell steadily. I moved closer and reached for her, pressing my fingers to the pulse point in her wrist. Her heartrate seemed a little fast to me, but I wasn't a doctor by any means. Until Griz gave the okay, I didn't want to bring in anyone to check on her. Since he was already on the warpath thanks to Dragon, I didn't really want to piss him off more.

I hoped that whatever was in her system wouldn't have lasting effects. I trailed my fingers down her arm, feeling how soft she was, and my dick started to get hard again. With a groan, I made myself turn away and went straight to the bathroom. I shut the door and started the shower before stripping out of my clothes. I hung my cut off a hook on the back of the door and left everything else in a pile on the floor. Steam started to billow out of the shower stall and I stepped inside, shutting the glass door behind me.

The water pounded my shoulders and back, and I had to admit it felt fucking awesome. I'd been carrying more tension around since I hadn't been able to jack off or get laid. I eyed my cock, still hard and upright, and hoped it really did still work. Using the shower gel in the corner, I soaped my hands, then grabbed my dick and gave it a tug. I'd pay for it soon when it felt like my hands were on fire and hurt like hell, but it would be worth it. A groan spilled out of me at how damn good it felt. I gripped a little harder and twisted my hand on the downstroke.

I leaned back against the shower wall, spread my legs a little, and used my free hand to cup my balls, rolling them a little on the next stroke of my cock. It wasn't long before my hand was flying up and down my shaft, and I could feel my orgasm getting closer. I bit my lip to keep from crying out as I came, cum coating the glass of the shower door.

My heart hammered in my chest and as I tried to catch my breath, my gaze lifted and I froze. The pretty Latina I'd left in my bed was now in my bathroom with her jaw practically on the floor as she gaped at me. *Shit*. Even worse, just seeing her there was enough to make me hard again. Her gaze drifted to the cum splattered on the shower door and her jaw snapped shut. She looked up at me again, but there wasn't fear in her eyes. No, it was worse -- curiosity. I was wishing I had one of those frosted-glass doors instead of one you could clearly see through.

"I didn't think you'd be awake anytime soon," I said.

She just stared, not moving, not talking. She barely even blinked.

I gripped the shower head, detached it from the holder, and rinsed the shower door. Locking it back into place, I debated washing off or just getting out. The gorgeous woman was still watching me, and I had to wonder if she was frozen in place or if she just liked the view. Maybe it made me an asshole, but I shampooed my hair and washed my beard, letting her look her fill. After I rinsed, she was not only still there, but she'd inched a little closer.

Part of me wanted to extend an invitation, but even I knew that was a dick move. She'd been drugged, and whatever she'd been dosed with could be making her act this way. I grabbed the shower gel and started to wash, trying not to linger anywhere for long, even though my cock was throbbing. I felt it twitch, but I didn't dare try to rub another one out, not with her in the room.

"Elena."

She focused on me and licked her lips. Jesus. That one small move was enough to make me picture her on her knees, my cock in her mouth.

"You're not making this easy. I'm trying to be a good guy and do the right thing. Do you even know where you are?" I asked, rinsing the soap from my body.

"Devil's Fury," she said. "And you're… Outlaw?"

I nodded. It seemed she'd been alert enough to at least pick up my name. "So you weren't completely out of it when I brought you here."

"I feel fine," she said. Her gaze scanned me again, lingering a little too long on a certain part that would like to get intimately acquainted with her. "Maybe a little fuzzy headed, and I ache in places I shouldn't, but that's it. Not like before when I couldn't stand or grip anything. Everything was spinning."

She ached in places… Shit. My gaze scanned her and I noticed her nipples were poking through her dress, and it made me wonder if her panties were wet. It seemed my shower was turning her on, as much as I was getting hot knowing that she was watching. I'd never been an exhibitionist before, always taking my women off the clubhouse main floor and into a private room, but the way she devoured me with her gaze, I'd happily take her in a room full of strangers.

"Darlin', I need to get out of this shower and I'm not sure you want me doing that while you're in the bathroom. There's a difference in seeing me naked through the damn glass and me being right there in front of you."

Her gaze caressed what she could see of me, and fuck me if she didn't lick her lips again. It was almost like she wondered how I'd taste. Maybe she fucking knew I was wondering if her pussy was nice and sweet or sharp and tangy. "I've never seen a naked man before."

Christ! And now I was hard as a fucking steel post. A virgin? I'd known she was too good for this place, but shit. I smacked the back of my head against the shower wall, trying to knock some sense into myself. It was so fucking tempting to step out and see what she'd do.

"Elena, I have more control than most men, or I usually do, but you're proving to be one hell of a temptation."

She took another step toward the shower. "Does that hurt?"

"What?" I asked.

Her gaze dropped to my cock. "When it's hard like that, does it hurt?"

Fuck me.

"Is it comfortable? Not exactly. And if I stay hard without any relief, then yeah, I guess you could say it hurts, just not like… it's not the same type of pain you'd feel with an injury or anything. More of an intense discomfort, unless I'm wearing pants, then it can fucking hurt after a while. It's hard to explain to someone who doesn't have a dick."

This had to be the weirdest moment of my life. My cock kept jerking in time with my heartbeat, and a woman who had never seen a naked man kept staring at me, and asking questions. I wasn't quite sure what to make of it all. I shut off the water and decided to see if she'd flee when I opened the shower door. If I'd put the damn towel closer, then I could have reached out and snatched it without having to leave the shower all the way.

I pushed open the shower door and stepped out onto the mat. Elena didn't back up, she didn't scream. If anything, she swayed toward me, like she might come closer. I knew it had to be the drugs she'd consumed. Snatching the towel off the counter, I briskly dried myself, then wrapped it around my waist and brushed past her to get into the bedroom. Yanking open the dresser drawer, I pulled out a pair of underwear and stepped into them. Once they were in place, I used the towel to dry the stray water droplets from my chest and back. I wasn't a prude or embarrassed over being naked, but it was a little strange having her stare at me like that. Normally if a woman was eyeing me, it meant we were about to fuck. Or it had in the past, when my dick had worked.

"Can you tell me more about how the drug made you feel?" I asked. I needed to get her mind off my cock, and mine too for that matter. And if we could find out more, then maybe we'd have a shot at figuring out what it was. It was obviously being administered through the drinks, but that didn't narrow it down much. So far, none of the woman had remembered anything except feeling drunk. Something told me Elena had never been drunk before, which meant her description might help a bit more.

"I tried to flip the pages in my book, but I couldn't seem to grab them. The words just swam across the page, and when I looked around the room everything blurred. My body felt heavy and I started to fall. Even my tongue felt heavy, and I had trouble speaking."

I nodded. I'd been the one to catch her. She'd seemed out of place and I'd been making my way over to her table when I realized something wasn't quite right. But if the person drugging the women was another woman, I didn't understand how they could have seen Elena as a threat. She'd hidden in the corner, keeping to herself. I'd nearly laughed when I saw her pull out her book. That had definitely been a first. Women came here to party, not read. It had been obvious she didn't belong at the Devil's Fury clubhouse. Unless... unless this wasn't about jealousy. What if someone was trying to get the club in trouble by drugging these women?

In which case, we had way more trouble on our hands than we realized.

"Was I really drugged?" she asked, worrying at her lower lip.

"Yeah, I think you were, but I'm not sure who did it. Until we figure some things out, you're staying here."

Her eyes went wide. "S-stay h-here?"

"Yep. You need to call someone? Parents? Sister?" I eyed her up and down. "Boyfriend?"

She folded her arms under her breasts, making them plump up even more. Damn. If she pushed them up even higher, they'd spill out of her dress, not that I'd complain. Ever since I'd noticed her, I'd been imagining her naked. I'd had a certain type most of my life, and Elena fit it to a T. Curves for days, long, glossy hair, and pouty lips. And the sweet, innocent look was really doing it for me. I'd never been with a woman who wasn't experienced, but the thought of being someone's first brought out my inner barbarian.

"If you must know, I left home and I'm striking out on my own." She tipped her chin up at a defiant angle that was cute as fuck.

"Yeah? How old are you, Elena?" *Please say you're at least eighteen so I don't have to kick my own ass.*

"Twenty-one."

Huh. Well, that made her older than I'd thought, but younger than I usually liked. And it made me wonder why the hell she was just now leaving home. Unless maybe she'd been living with her parents while she went to college.

She licked her lips and her posture relaxed a little. "I was in a foster home until I aged out of the system. I guess technically, I was still in a foster home, but they weren't getting paid after I turned eighteen. My family was nice so I stayed. They could have told me I had to leave, but they didn't. I'd thought things were going well, and maybe I'd have time to save some money and get a place of my own. Except, lately they keep pushing this man in my direction, wanting me to marry him and pop out a bunch of babies."

I didn't even pretend to know what was wrong with that scenario. Maybe it made me a sexist asshole, but I rather liked the idea of her having a bunch of kids -- mine. Maybe she didn't want to be a mom? Or was there something wrong with the guy they wanted her to marry? Had he given her the creeps? Maybe he'd been a horrible kisser. Whatever the case, she'd decided to leave everything and everyone she knew to escape a marriage to him.

"Is he ugly?" I asked.

Her gaze scanned me again, and I could have sworn she whimpered a little. "Not exactly, but he doesn't look like you either."

I bit the inside of my cheek so I wouldn't laugh. Her honesty was a bit refreshing, especially since she wasn't doing it in a way meant to entice me. I had a feeling she was just being her. Or at least her on drugs and alcohol. Who knew if she was this chatty completely sober. Honestly, the fact she could still be impaired was the only thing holding me back from trying to seduce her.

"Yeah? So what's so horrible about him?" I asked, trying to distract myself and find out more about Elena.

"Nothing. He seems perfectly nice. He's older than me, but he's the type that looks down on women. You know, the ones who only want their wife barefoot and in the kitchen?"

I nodded. Yep I knew that type well, since that was me. Then again, with my way of life, having a woman with a job outside of the club could be dangerous. I'd want her here where I could protect her, or at least working at one of our businesses. I had to admit, the idea of her barefoot in my kitchen was rather appealing. Didn't sound like the type of thing she'd go for, though. As for her comment about him being older, I wondered if she'd gotten a good look at me from the neck up yet. She'd definitely gotten an eyeful of my cock. I was fifteen years older than her. While I'd been told I looked younger, I knew I didn't look anywhere near her age.

"He didn't look like the kind of man who knows how to make a woman orgasm," she blurted, then her cheeks flared a bright red.

Huh. I wasn't quite sure what to say to that one. The obvious choice was, *I can*! Well, obvious if I wanted to be a dick. She needed a safe place while Grizzly figured out who was drugging the women, and here I was thinking with my cock. In my defense, I was just so thrilled the damn thing worked, it was a little hard to control myself at the moment. I almost felt like a thirteen-year-old boy again. Yeah, I'd been the kid who jacked off at every opportunity even back then.

I'd expected her to freak out when she woke up at my place. Instead, she'd come to stare at me as I showered and asked a million questions. It was cute the way she kept saying whatever popped into her head. I didn't know if it was the drugs still in her system, or if she was always like this. I liked it.

"I only have one bedroom set up," I said. "Like I said before, you can either sleep in here and I'll take the couch, or you can have the couch. Whatever makes you the most comfortable."

She hesitated a moment, and I wondered what she was thinking. If she weren't so... pure, then I'd have offered a third option -- we both take the bed. Then again, the way she eyed me like I was her favorite dessert, she just might accept my offer. Then if she woke tomorrow and I discovered she'd still been flying high on the drugs in her system, I'd have felt like a fucking asshole. Yeah, I needed to try and remember to keep my distance.

"I have a motel room. All my things are there."

She wasn't arguing about staying so that was a plus. Maybe she understood exactly how much danger she could have been in. It was a good thing I'd noticed what was going on. If I hadn't seen her, known the exact moment the drugs took effect, then any of my brothers would have just thought she was tipsy and willing. Whoever was behind this shit, we needed to find them and stop it. Preferably before something really fucking bad happened.

Chapter Three

Elena

I was crazy. That was the only explanation. Completely and utterly insane. What normal person woke up in a strange man's home, watched him masturbate, then asked a million questions while eyeing him like a piece of candy? Me, that's who. Apparently, I wasn't as normal as I'd always thought. And then he'd demanded that I stay here. I should have refused, or at least put up a fight, but I had to admit I was captivated by Outlaw. Maybe I was still tipsy from the beer, or whatever I'd been given. I wasn't ready to admit that I'd been drugged. Yes, I'd briefly wondered if that had happened, but I'd never drunk alcohol before. It was possible that having two beers could do that, right? The thought that someone had done that to me was too scary for me to think on it too long.

No, I couldn't completely lie to myself. I'd been intrigued by the things happening at the clubhouse from the moment I'd stepped through the door. The way I was feeling, the urgent need to reach out and touch him, to beg him to touch *me*, none of that could be blamed on the drinks I'd had. It was all me. And now I was going to stay here, with temptation within reach. If he asked me to share a bed with him, I didn't think I'd have the strength to say no. I was far too curious about how it would feel to experience the things I'd seen earlier tonight, or the scenes I'd read in books.

There was only one motel in town, so Outlaw hadn't needed the name, but I'd given him my key so he could have someone get my things. I still hadn't answered his question about where I wanted to sleep. It hadn't escaped my notice that this would be the perfect opportunity. I'd always been interested in learning about sex -- in a more personal way than reading -- but I'd never dared sleep with anyone. Even if I'd gone to another town, somehow my foster parents would have found out, and then I had no doubt there would have been hell to pay. Or they might have just kicked me out. I'd wondered more than once if they'd have pushed so hard for me to marry Garrison West if I hadn't been a virgin anymore. I didn't know if he'd have cared either way. All he wanted was a broodmare.

Being here with Outlaw, a man who definitely made my body come alive, was the perfect chance to lose my virginity. Guys like him had probably slept with hundreds of women, if not thousands. He looked like the type who would take what he wanted, and his name alone gave off that vibe. Not that I thought that was his real name. I'd read a book last year about a woman who fell for a guy in club like this one. Well, maybe not quite like this one. These guys made me think they didn't care about the law much, but the ones in my book had kept everything legal. Still, they'd all had... what were they called? Road names. Yes, they'd had road names. I figured Outlaw was the sexy guy's road name.

He was making dinner at the stove while I sat at the kitchen table, trying not to stare too long, or drool for that matter. He hadn't put on a shirt and was only in a pair of well-worn jeans. The women I'd known most of my life all sighed and got giddy over a man in a suit. I'd thought men were handsome before, but Outlaw... Yeah, it seemed I had a type, and it definitely wasn't a straitlaced businessman.

"Where were you going?" Outlaw asked without turning around.

I couldn't help but admire his ink. His back was covered in tattoos, but I'd noticed none of them would show if he had on a shirt. His arms were bare of any designs, and while his chest didn't have any either, I had seen something in script across his ribs. I wondered if the lack of ink in other spots was on purpose. Did he not like just anyone being able to see them? I'd also seen a lot of scars, some red and angry-looking, and I wondered where they came from. It looked like he'd been through hell.

"I didn't have a particular spot in mind. I just needed to get away." I still wasn't sure I'd run quite far enough.

He hmm'd but didn't remark other than that. I felt like I needed to explain myself to him, but I didn't know why. What did it matter why I was leaving or where I was going? I'd told him about Garrison before I'd even really thought about it. Maybe it seemed like a ridiculous thing to him. Running off to avoid a man. It wasn't like I'd been beaten or worse. I'd just felt stifled.

"Guess I seem kinda silly to you." I twisted my fingers together in my lap. "The type of women who come here probably don't run away just because their family wants them to marry someone they don't like."

"Wouldn't know," he said. "I don't really have conversations with them."

Oh. Well, that said plenty. I guess you didn't really need to talk to someone to have sex with them, but it seemed a bit cold to me. It was another reason why I was still a virgin. Even if I'd been tempted to just get rid of my V-card, I'd wanted the moment to be special. While I didn't think Outlaw thought I was the least bit unique, I did think he seemed like the type of man who knew what he was doing in the bedroom. Even if we didn't have a lasting relationship, or any type of relationship, I'd be willing to bet I'd enjoy sex with him. A one-night stand with some random stranger wouldn't ensure that I'd like the experience. But this particular man seemed sure of himself, like he knew exactly what he was doing.

"I haven't been with a woman in a long time," he said. "Not much use talking to one if I didn't plan to sleep with her. I'm not exactly the type to give a shit about things like hair products, the best nail salon, or whatever the fuck else y'all talk about."

I chewed on my lip, certain I should be offended, but I found him rather funny. It would be like a woman assuming all men thought about were car engines, sports, and beer -- and while all that could very well be true for *this* man, I couldn't see Garrison West knowing the first thing about cars or drinking beer.

"Not all of us care about that stuff," I said.

"No? Then what do you like to talk about?" he asked, finally turning to face me. He folded his arms over his chest, and my cheeks warmed as I felt my panties grow damp.

"Books. I love to read."

He smirked. "I noticed. Don't believe I've ever seen a woman come to the clubhouse and pull out a book. You seemed completely out of place."

He wasn't wrong. I wasn't anything like those women. Or rather, I'd never been permitted to be like them. I couldn't deny that I'd wanted to join their ranks tonight. Maybe not as a free for all with any and all of the men there, but if Outlaw was the one claiming my virginity? I'd be completely on board with that.

"Yeah. The lady at the motel suggested I stop by. Guess she thought that was why I'd come to town or something. You get a lot of women who drive here just to come to your clubhouse?" I asked.

He shrugged a shoulder. "Guess so. Plenty of local girls stop by too."

It felt like my heart was racing, and I could barely breathe. There was so much I wanted to know, but wasn't sure if I should ask. It would be rude to ask why he hadn't been with anyone, wouldn't it? If I made him mad, would he make me go stay with someone else? I didn't know if they were as nice as he was. Of course, I could only go off the little interaction I'd had with Outlaw so far, but he hadn't tried to take advantage of me when I'd been watching him shower. I'd never been so brazen in my life! I didn't know what had gotten into me.

I squeezed my thighs together. Didn't help. An ache was building again and I didn't know what to do about it. Outlaw seemed to watch my every move. His gaze darkened and he couldn't hide the fact his cock had gotten hard again, assuming it had ever gone down. The girls at church sometimes had whispered about the guys they'd been with and how it took them some time to recover after having sex. Even though Outlaw had only gotten himself off, he didn't seem to have an issue getting hard again. As I thought about how sexy he'd looked stroking himself, I felt my nipples get hard and I got even wetter between my legs.

"Poor angel," he murmured. "All worked up and you don't know what to do about it, do you?"

I shook my head. No, I didn't. I didn't doubt for a second that he knew how to make it stop, make me feel better. Maybe make me come. I thought about him jerking his cock in the shower, the way he'd stroked fast and hard. My breath got choppier and I squeezed my thighs even tighter together. Didn't help.

"Just how naughty do you want to be, Elena?" he asked.

"Make it stop," I said. "Please. I know you can."

He came closer and dropped to his knees in front of me. He shifted the chair and spread my legs so that he was kneeling between them. The rough touch of his fingers sliding up my legs made me shiver.

"I can make you come," he said. "But I need to know this is what you want. You still feeling a little drunk or impaired in any way? And don't fucking lie to me."

"No, I'm fine. I told you I didn't feel like I was drugged anymore." He stared and I knew what he wanted me to say. "I want this."

He pushed my dress farther up until my panties were exposed. He tapped my hip and I lifted a little so he could work the material up more. The cool chair kissed the backs of my thighs and my cheeks warmed again. I was half-naked in his kitchen. The hungry look on his face as he stared at my panties made me even wetter.

Outlaw groaned. "Jesus, you're fucking killing me. I can see you soaking your damn panties. Can I take them off, pretty girl?"

"Y-yes. You don't have to ask before you do every little thing. I already told you I want this." My breath caught at the look in his eyes.

He arched an eyebrow. "Did you just give me the green light to do whatever I want with you?"

I gave him a jerky nod. Probably a stupid idea, but I really did want him. He slid his hand farther up my legs, up my thighs, then his thumbs brushed over my panties, right across the wet fabric between my legs. I whimpered and spread myself open more. *You're such a hussy!*

"Lift up," he said.

I pulled my butt up off the chair and he tugged my panties down. He tossed them to the side and licked his lips as he stared at me. Even though I'd despaired of ever being with a guy, I'd always trimmed down there. I didn't shave it bare, but the hair I did keep was so short it was hardly there. Outlaw spread the lips of my pussy and swiped his thumb across my clit.

I cried out from the sparks of pleasure that shot through me. He did it again, then rubbed in small circles until a keening sound escaped my lips. My hips bucked as I came. I felt him slip a finger inside me, pumping in and out, as he kept working my clit. It made my orgasm seem never-ending. I briefly wondered if I should be embarrassed that I'd come so fast. Other women probably held out longer.

"Tight. Hot. Wet. I bet this pretty pussy tastes good too."

My breath caught. He wasn't going to put his mouth there, right? I'd read about men doing that, but I hadn't realized it was something they actually did. I'd thought it was just fiction, made up for books and movies.

He pulled his finger free and then slipped it into his mouth, sucking off the wetness left behind from my pussy. If anything, it just made me want more from him.

"You done?" he asked.

Done? Was he asking if I wanted to stop? Because now that I'd had a taste, I wanted more. A lot more. I wanted... everything. "N-no."

He grinned and stood up, then pulled me to my feet. Outlaw made quick work of getting the rest of my clothes off, giving a low growl as he released my breasts from my bra. He cupped them, stroking my nipples and squeezing the mounds.

"Are we going to have sex?" I asked, blurting out the words.

"No, baby, but I'm going to make you feel good."

Disappointment hit me, then embarrassment. I probably wasn't as thin or pretty as the women he dated. Even the ones at the clubhouse tonight had been a lot thinner than me. I'd always had a little extra padding. Outlaw cupped my cheek and I focused on him again.

"None of that," he said. "I'm not rejecting you, Elena. Trust me. I want you more than my next breath."

"Then why are you saying no?" I asked.

He lifted me onto the edge of the table, pushing my legs apart, then he plunged a finger inside of me. He thrust it in and out several times before adding another one. It burned a little but still felt incredible. When he rubbed my clit again, I nearly saw stars.

"Because if I take this virgin pussy with anything other than my fingers or mouth, then I'll want to keep you. I'll go in bare, fill you up with my cum, and I'll keep you with me forever."

My heart took off, slamming against my chest with every beat. No one had ever spoken to me like that before. I kind of liked it. He moved in closer, his beard scraping my jaw and he placed his lips near my ear. He kept fucking me with his hand, but it was his words that had the biggest impact.

"I'll fuck you again and again, coming inside this tight little pussy, marking you with my cum. I want to see it slide out of you, slip down your thighs, and then I want to shove it back inside you where it belongs. I want you to take my cock in your mouth, suck me off, then get me hard again. Then I want to bend you over and take you hard and deep, pounding into you until you're screaming my name. When your pussy can't take any more, I'll claim your ass." I whimpered, and rocked against his hand. I felt him smile against my ear. "Oh, my angel likes that idea, huh? Have you dreamed of a good ass fucking? My naughty girl. Want my cock to stretch you, fill you, and claim every inch of you?"

I nodded. Yes! Yes, I wanted that so much. When I'd read about it, it had seemed so taboo, so... dirty. His fingers drove into me harder and faster and I screamed out as I came. "Outlaw!"

He growled again, backing away. He sucked his fingers clean, and I could see the outline of his cock. I got off the table and dropped to my knees in front of him. Reaching up, I unfastened his pants and shoved them down his hips. When his cock sprang free of his underwear, I noticed how red and angry it seemed. I had zero experience, but I wanted to at least try to suck him off.

"You don't have to do this, Elena."

"I want to," I assured him.

"I'm clean. In case you were wondering. I wouldn't let you do this otherwise," he said.

I wrapped my hand around his shaft and leaned forward, licking the head. His taste exploded on my tongue, and I moaned as I licked up more of the pre-cum. I hadn't expected to actually like the way he tasted. Fitting my lips around the head, I swallowed as much of him as I could, using my hand at the base like I'd read about.

"Jesus! You're going to make me come already," he said, his fingers sliding into my hair and gripping the strands tight. It felt like his hand spasmed for a moment, but I couldn't be sure. He used his grip to control my movements and soon he was fucking my mouth with hard thrusts. "Gonna come, Elena. If you don't want a mouthful, you'd better pull off."

I didn't stop and soon I felt the warmth of his release, trying to swallow it all, but I felt some dribble from the corner of my mouth. When he was finished, I tried to pull away, but he locked his fingers in my hair again.

"Uh-uh. You've started something now, pretty girl. Get me hard again."

Get him hard again? My eyes went wide. Did that mean he was going to... No, he'd said that if I gave him my virginity that he'd own me, that I'd be his and he wouldn't let me go. People didn't do stuff like that, right? We didn't even know one another. So why did the thought of him doing what he wanted, making me his and never letting me go, make me all wet and needy again?

I sucked and licked until he was hard as granite.

Outlaw pulled me free of his cock and helped me stand. His gaze took me in from head to toe, then back again. He lingered on my breasts a moment before leaning forward and taking a nipple into his mouth. As his teeth scraped the sensitive peak, I gasped and arched against him.

"Dinner," I said, noticing the smoke from the pot.

"Dammit," he muttered backing away from me. He tucked himself back into his pants, pulling them up, and he went over to the stove. "Looks like I'm ordering pizza."

I couldn't decide if I was disappointed that we'd had to stop, or if I was relieved. He'd given me more than I'd ever thought possible, more pleasure than I could stand, but I didn't know that I was ready for things to go further. Yes, the little demon on my shoulder was begging for more, for *everything*, but deep down I had to wonder if I'd regret making that kind of decision right now. I'd only gotten my freedom this morning. Was I ready to give it up and hand myself over to someone else?

His turned and his gaze honed in on my breasts, then dipped lower. The heat in his eyes, the way he watched me, made me want to throw caution to the wind. Would giving up my newfound freedom be all that difficult if he made me come like that all the time? *No, bad Elena! Stop thinking about sex!*

"Pizza?" I asked, trying to keep both of us off the topic of sex.

"Right. Any particular kind?"

"No anchovies. Or olives. Or mushrooms."

He smirked. "Is that all? Are you sure you don't want just plain cheese?"

"Well." Now that he mentioned it. I rather liked the five-cheese pizza we usually ordered at home, on the rare occasions my foster father had permitted us to spend money on something like that. "I'm actually okay with that."

He snorted. "Right. So one cheese for you, and one with everything for me. I'll place the order and have a Prospect bring it over when it arrives. I think it's best I keep you away from the clubhouse right now."

"I did okay before," I said, then tried not to wince. No, I really hadn't. I'd been drugged, and if Outlaw hadn't brought me here, who knew what would have happened to me.

"Right. Let me explain something to you. In that clubhouse, if you aren't claimed as property by a brother, then you're free game for anyone there. Someone wearing a cut like mine walks up and tells you to suck their cock, you do it. Is that what you want? Want your first time to be in that dirty clubhouse?" He prowled closer, not stopping until the heat of his body pressed against me. "You want to be used, pretty girl? Become a club whore?"

"N-No. Not a club whore."

He grinned. "Not a club whore, but you *do* want to be used. Maybe just by one man?"

"Maybe," I said. "And the clubhouse wasn't so bad. I kind of liked it."

It felt like my entire face was on fire, but from the flare of interest in his eyes, I knew I'd only decreased my chances of ever leaving this place. I was almost certain he'd been close to taking my virginity, and by his own admission he'd own me then. I was playing a game that I was destined to lose, especially since I didn't quite grasp all the rules. But a part of me thought maybe losing wouldn't be so bad. Maybe in losing my freedom, I'd gain something better.

Chapter Four

Outlaw

The way she'd lit up when I'd talked about her being fucked in front of everyone had me wondering just how dirty my little innocent Elena was. It seemed she had a wild side just begging to be set free. I'd never liked sharing, and even now I knew I'd never let anyone else have her. But if she wanted them to watch, then maybe I could handle that. Every now and then. Maybe. Or maybe not. I really didn't like the thought of anyone else seeing those beautiful breasts on display.

I'd placed our order and made sure the dipshit knew not to enter the house without knocking. Too many fuckers were used to just barging in here, but with Elena under my roof, I didn't much care for my brothers or the Prospects coming in and seeing all of her. At least, not without my permission. She was sexy as fuck, and the way she'd sucked my cock… Shit!

Instead of letting her get dressed again, I'd snatched her clothes off the floor and put them in the laundry room. She'd eyed me, but hadn't protested. The way her nipples beaded, I could tell she liked me being all bossy and dominant with her. I wasn't into putting labels on things. I just knew what I liked, and a woman who was willing to obey was hot as fuck. Didn't mean I wanted a doormat for an ol' lady, though. No, I liked a little sass in my women, just not in front of my brothers.

I went to my room and pulled a shirt from my dresser. Elena was still standing in the kitchen, looking a little lost at the moment. She shifted from foot to foot as she glanced around the room. Her hands were fisted at her sides, and she worried at her lower lip. I stopped in front of her, pulling the shirt over her head. As much as I'd love to see her beautiful body on full display, I didn't think she'd want to lounge around the house without anything covering her. She'd been completely innocent until I'd corrupted her tonight. For that matter, she was still technically a virgin.

I should feel disgusted with myself. Grizzly had asked me to take care of her, protect her. Instead, I'd nearly claimed her. If he knew I'd already stripped her naked and made her come, he'd probably kick my ass, and I'd deserve it. Maybe it was the inability to come for over four years, or maybe there was just something about her that made me want to hold on. Either way, I knew I wasn't doing her any favors. She wanted to leave, start a new life somewhere, and I should let her do that. Didn't mean I was going to.

"Come on, angel. We can put something on TV while we wait for the pizza to arrive. Your things should be delivered by then too."

She hesitated, tugging on my hand so I wouldn't walk off. "Were you really going to have sex with me, and then not let me leave?"

The right thing to do would be to tell her the truth. The easier thing would be to lie my ass off and deny the hell out of it. Something told me she'd been lied to enough in her life already. That family who took her in might not have abused her in the physical sense, but I had to wonder if they weren't so strict that they damaged her psychologically or emotionally.

"Look, things work different around here than what you're used to. We don't follow the law set by other people. We make up our own rules, and answer to the club officers. Maybe popping your cherry and keeping you, making you mine forever, is all kinds of fucked-up to someone not used to this way of life, but around here, it's just how things are done. Some of the time anyway." Dingo would have taken his sweet time with Meiling if the club hadn't pushed things along a bit. Same for Badger and Adalia. But I'd talked to Wire enough to know that the instant attraction I felt for Elena was exactly how he'd felt about Lavender, and everything turned out okay for them.

"So you really wouldn't have let me leave?" she asked. "Ever?"

"What do you think it means for me to claim you?"

She shrugged a shoulder, and I could tell she really didn't have a clue. I wasn't sure how to explain it without making her run screaming into the night. Most of the women who came here had some idea of how things worked with Devil's Fury, and other clubs, but Elena was a different story. It was like she'd lived her life with blinders on, never pulling her nose out of a book long enough to actually live her life and experience things for herself. It wasn't just that she didn't know about club life, but it was almost like she'd lived in a bubble and hadn't had any fun at all. Her naivety was a little cute, and I loved her innocence. Perhaps her foster family was to blame for her lack of life experiences. They sounded like a bunch of tight-asses.

I scratched at my beard. "You said you want to start your life over, be independent and all that shit. This way of life, what you'd get if you were mine, is the exact opposite of what you want. As my woman, it wouldn't be safe for you to be out there working a job unless it was a business the club owned. I wouldn't put you on lockdown to be an asshole, but to keep you safe. I have enemies and so does the club. They wouldn't hesitate to snatch you up and use you to make me do what they wanted."

The look in her eyes said she was both appalled and intrigued. There was more to the little Latina than I'd first thought. Yeah, she was all prim and proper on the outside, but it was becoming more and more clear that she was a naughty little vixen on the inside. I was only too happy to help her bring that side out to play. And I was willing to bet that she'd let me.

"Come on. I'm not laying claim to you right here and now."

If I wasn't mistaken, she looked a little disappointed by the news, but she followed me into the living room. I sat in my favorite chair and propped my feet on the ottoman, then held out my hand to her. She eagerly came forward and I pulled her down onto my lap. Elena snuggled in closer, and I had to admit it felt really fucking right to have her in my arms. I turned on the TV and put on a comedy. I didn't think she was a blow-up-the-bad-guy type of TV watcher, but then again, she'd surprised me plenty of times already tonight.

Like right now. I'd almost expected her to balk when I'd wanted her in my lap. With everything else she'd let me do tonight, perhaps I shouldn't have been all that surprised. Elena was curious if nothing else, but I didn't think she realized I was serious about not letting her go. I knew the world she'd come from was nothing like mine. Although, the way her foster parents were trying to marry her off to that guy, maybe it wasn't so different after all. A little more legal, but no less political. Our politics just typically didn't involve marrying off women.

There was something bothering me about Elena's situation. If this guy was so amazing that her foster parents wanted her to marry him, why was he still single? For that matter, why had they put so much pressure on her that she'd felt the need to run? I had a feeling there was more going on than she'd admitted, or possibly it was more than she knew. It made me want to dig a little and see what would come up.

"Tell me about your foster family," I said.

"My foster dad is a reverend. He and his wife insisted I call them Father and Mother. I always thought it was because they couldn't have kids and really wanted children, but the longer I was with them, the more I had to wonder about it all. They didn't act the way I thought parents did."

"What happened to yours?" I asked.

"I don't really remember, but I was told they died. We lived in a small two-bedroom apartment in a not so great part of town, but I do know they loved me. My mom would always give the best hugs, and my dad seemed to constantly be working, but he was always nice to us. One day, they didn't come pick me up from school. But… it's been so long, I don't remember what they looked like. I remember loving it when Mom hugged me, but not what she smelled like, or what the hugs felt like."

"You didn't ask questions?"

Elena snuggled closer. "I was in elementary school. Old enough to know something bad happened, but not brave enough to ask. When the social worker said my parents would no longer be taking care of me, I was scared. Then the preacher and his wife took me in. They seemed nice, and I'd heard horrible stories while I was waiting to be placed. They had a group home type of place where everyone waited to be assigned a foster family. Some of the kids had been in and out of foster homes dozens of times."

"What's the name of the preacher and his wife?" I asked.

"Martin and Suzy Tolbert. Her name is actually SuAnne, but everyone calls her Suzy."

I filed that bit away for later. "And your parents?"

"Sara and Diego Vargas."

"So you're Elena Vargas? Or did you take the preacher's name?"

She stiffened. "No, I didn't take his name! They never offered to adopt me, even though they let me live with them even after I was out of the system. They treated me well, but it never truly felt like home."

I rubbed my hand up and down her arm. "All right, angel. Just a question. Didn't mean anything by it. Why don't you tell me more about this guy they wanted you to marry?"

She tipped her head so she could look me in the eye. "Why are you asking so many questions about me? Isn't it a little late? You've already seen me naked. The mystery is gone."

I snorted. "Sweetheart, the mystery is far from gone. And I'm just trying to figure out who you are, where you come from, and whether or not that family of yours might come looking for you."

She chewed on her lower lip. A hint of worry flashed in her eyes. "I don't know if they will or not, but I did think they might. It's why I wanted to keep moving. They were so insistent that I marry Garrison West, and it seemed… strange."

If she thought it was odd, then something was likely wrong with the situation. She knew those people, had lived with them. So it made me wonder, what did this Garrison West have over them that they'd try to foist her off on him? And why did he want Elena in particular? Oh, I got it on some level. She was gorgeous and any man would want to keep her, but something seemed off.

I patted her thigh. "Hop up a minute."

She stood and I got up, then motioned for her to take my chair. I walked out and down the hall. While I could use my laptop to just scratch the surface of Elena's issues, I had a feeling I'd need to do more than that. And thanks to my busted hands, it would require a phone call to Wire and Lavender, or at least one of the others. I winced at the thought of hearing Lavender's voice. I was moving on as best I could from what had happened, and she needed to as well. Telling her that didn't seem to do anything.

I closed my bedroom door, opened the closet and shoved my clothes to the side. Placing my hand on the palm reader, the secret door slid open and I went into what I considered my cave. The door closed behind me and I sat down in the most comfortable chair ever created. The three large screens were ready and waiting, and I reached out to caress the keyboard. I fucking missed this. Most of what I was capable of doing these days only required my laptop. It was like I'd lost part of myself that day, but I tried not to let it get to me. Some days I succeeded, and others... Well, there was a reason my drinking had increased.

I ran a quick search for Garrison West, just checking out any social media profiles, or any mentions of him available to the public. I needed to figure out who he was, where he came from, and then I could dig some more. The guy looked like a douche. All teeth and fake smiles. His hair looked like it wouldn't dare blow in a breeze, and his suit didn't have so much as a wrinkle anywhere. The shine on his shoes was enough to blind someone if the sun hit the surface just right.

Deacon at the church. Owned his own company. One wife, deceased. No kids.

"Who are you, Garrison West?" I muttered.

It didn't take much to find the donations to the Church of the Holy Light, run by Reverend Martin Tolbert. It was the amounts that made me pause. What the fuck kind of business was he running that he could donate fifty grand a month, and more importantly, what the fuck was the reverend doing with all that money? My fingers ached as I kept searching, but I found the other church records, including all the expenses. It seemed the good reverend was pocketing ten thousand a month from those donations, but the rest was going to... Bryson Corners Customs? What the absolute fuck?

Why was a small church in Georgia sending that kind of cash to a bike shop out in Oklahoma? I knew of the place, had seen some of their awesome work, but it was starting to look like they were shady as fuck. When I couldn't break into their systems, I knew I had to call in reinforcements. I stared at the phone, a stupid landline, but it couldn't be traced or cloned like a damn cell phone. I'd made sure nothing left this room unless I wanted it to.

I dialed Surge and put the phone on speaker. The room was soundproofed and I knew that even if Elena wandered back this way, she wouldn't hear a damn thing I said. It rang a half dozen times before rolling over to voicemail. I hung up and tried again. And again. After the fourth attempt, I gave up and called Wizard. He picked up after two rings.

"Please don't tell me you've found trouble again," Wizard said.

"You make it sound like I go looking for it."

"Maybe not, but it sure does find you easily enough. What's up?"

I stared at the screen and all the shit I'd gathered so far on Garrison West. "I'm going to encrypt some files and send them your way. Need you to look into Garrison West and his connection with Bryson Corners Customs. He's using a church to send money their way and I want to know why. I also want to know how else the church is involved."

"Since when do you give a shit about churches?"

I scratched at my beard. "Since the reverend's foster daughter showed up here. She said they were pushing her to marry the guy. Found a marriage license for his deceased wife. No kids. I want to know if he's a threat to Elena."

It was quiet on the other end. I encrypted the files and sent them to Wizard. If I hadn't heard him breathing, I'd have wondered if he hung up. It didn't take long before I heard a string of cussing, though. He must have opened the files, but I was curious about his reaction.

"That's not Garrison West. Or maybe that's what he's going by these days, but that's not his real name," Wizard said. "He's a motherfucking traitor, and I can promise you that Attila is going to shit a damn brick."

What the hell was he talking about? And how did he know this guy? I'd have remembered if I'd seen him at any functions I'd attended where Hades Abyss was present. He couldn't have been one of their brothers, could he?

"Attila?" I asked. The name was familiar, but I couldn't place where I'd heard it. He definitely wasn't Hades Abyss.

"Pres of the Savage Raptors MC over in Bryson Corners. That custom shop is owned by the club. The man claiming to be Garrison West is none other than Grady Hampton, aka Bastard. His colors were stripped in every way possible, and his ass was left for dead on the side of the road about fifteen years ago. I have to wonder if Attila knows where that money is coming from, and now I really want to fucking know why that asshole is sending it."

He brought up a good point. Why send money to a club that left you for dead? Unless he hadn't been the only traitor. It was bad enough that the clubs had to deal with shit from Prospects or the club girls, but when your own brother turned on you, then it was all kinds of fucked up. With all the shit we dealt with on a regular basis, we had to be able to trust the men at our backs. If they'd stripped his colors and nearly killed him, then this guy had seriously fucked up.

And I really didn't like that he had his eye on Elena. What did he want with her? It made me curious about his previous wife too. Had he done something to her and covered it up?

"Can you let me know what you find out? Also, look into Martin and Suzy Tolbert. It's the reverend of the church and his wife. I need to know their connection to all this and what West has over them."

"On it." There was a pause, but I knew he hadn't hung up. "This woman... she mean something to you?"

"I'm claiming her, assuming Grizzly doesn't kick my ass for it."

Wizard whistled long and slow. "Wow. Okay. I thought, um... you know..."

I winced. Yeah, there were a few people outside my club who knew about my issue. Except it wasn't a problem where Elena was concerned. Still, a bit embarrassing to have Wizard remind me.

"Everything works just fine," I said.

"Good. That's really damn good to hear."

My brow furrowed as I stared at the phone. "Why the hell do you care if my dick works?"

"I don't, but Lavender does. No, wait. That came out wrong. Don't tell Wire I said that because he'll kick my ass, and I don't just mean the type that leaves bruises. He'll fuck up all my shit and close out my accounts, maybe even make me vanish."

He wasn't wrong.

"Look, I've spoken to her a few times and she's expressed some concern over you. She feels terrible about what happened, and when she thought you'd never get a chance to settle down and be as happy as she is, it kind of tore her up inside."

That's exactly what I hadn't wanted to hear. I saw the way she looked at me, and could hear it in her voice when we spoke on the phone. It's why I'd avoided her as much as possible. I didn't hold Lavender responsible for what happened, didn't blame her even a little. She'd been a victim and couldn't have stopped them if she tried. Giving in to their demands wouldn't have changed anything, except she'd have suffered greatly before Wire arrived. I'd bought him time, and I didn't regret it for a moment.

"Tell her that I found someone and that everything is fine."

"It's not, though, is it?" Wizard asked. "You may have found a woman, and maybe you'll be happy enough, but you'll never be a hacker like before. You may not have been on the same level as Wire and Lavender, but you were pretty badass. Now you're having to ask the rest of us for help."

I ground my teeth together so I wouldn't unleash my building temper on him. To be fair, the guy was being a dick. It wasn't like I needed this shit pointed out to me. I lived it every fucking day.

"Thanks, asshole," I muttered. "Just give her the damn message and get back to me when you have something."

I hung up the phone before I was tempted to drive all the way to Mississippi to strangle the fucker. Who needed enemies with friends like Wizard? I made sure everything was locked down and exited my secret space, only to step out of the closet and come face-to-face with Elena. She looked around me as the wall slid shut, closing off my cave.

"Do I even want to know why you have a hidden room? Or what you were doing in there?" she asked.

"Maybe I'm a superhero and that's my lair," I said.

She eyed me from head to toe, then back again. "You don't look the part of a superhero, but you don't act like a villain. I'm not sure where you'd fit into that universe. Maybe you're more of a Robin Hood?"

"Let's just go with that for now."

I grabbed her hand and led her back to the front of the house, only to hear an insistent banging on the door.

"That's why I was trying to find you. I think our food is here," she said.

"Pick a spot. Table or living room. I'll bring the pizza to you."

She wandered off in the direction of the kitchen and I made sure she was out of sight before opening the door. The Prospect on the other side shoved the pizzas at me and took off running. Either he thought I was pissed, had been warned away by Grizzly, or he had a job to do. Whatever the case, I was alone again with the hot little Latina in my house. And there was food… didn't get much better than that.

Top three things a man needed to survive were all available now. Pizza, beer, and sex. While I wouldn't take what Elena didn't offer, I had no doubt that I would have her screaming my name again. She was mine, even if she didn't realize it yet.

Chapter Five

Elena

What was it about the sexy biker that made me feel so at ease? We'd talked and laughed over pizza. While he'd had a few beers, I'd stuck with water. The two drinks I'd had at the clubhouse were going to be my first and only. After that experience, I didn't see myself ever wanting another drink. Granted, I may not have met Outlaw if someone hadn't spiked my drink. They were convinced that had happened, but I didn't want to believe it. Why would someone do that to another person? What if I'd tried to drive back to the motel and I'd died, or hit someone else?

The club seemed to one hundred percent believe drugs had been put into at least one of my beers. Although, Outlaw seemed more interested in my foster family and Garrison West than in me being drugged. I didn't understand why. Was I concerned they might come looking for me? Sure, but it wasn't like they could force me to go with them. I was over eighteen and they didn't control my actions. If I wanted to leave, then I could. Simple as that. I'd only wanted to sneak away to avoid confrontation.

"It's getting late," Outlaw said. "I'll check outside before I lock up. Your bag should be here by now."

"Is that secret code for you want sex? Or do you actually want to go to sleep?"

He smirked at me. "Baby girl, I'm always up for sex, but you've had one hell of a day. Probably should get some rest."

He wasn't wrong about that. Between driving all the way here, then the incident at the clubhouse, the mind-blowing orgasms he'd given me, and all the time we'd spent talking, I had no doubt that dawn would be here soon. Not that it seemed I'd be leaving anytime soon. Was it wrong that I'd gotten a bit of a thrill when he'd said if he took my virginity that he'd keep me? Did that mean there was something wrong with me? Women didn't really like the caveman routine, did they? I had to admit it kind of turned me on when he got all bossy.

"And where am I sleeping?" I asked, remembering he'd mentioned only having one bed.

"With me," he said. "Safest place for you is right by my side."

I couldn't tell if that was a line or if he really meant it. Yes, he was a badass biker, but wasn't I just as safe on the couch? We were behind a fence. A guarded one at that. I didn't think they let people through unless they wanted them here. Of course, the guy who had let me in didn't exactly check my car or anything. I could have easily brought a gun inside and he wouldn't have known it. Maybe Outlaw was right to be cautious.

He stood and reached for my hand, tugging me in his wake. "Come on. I won't bite. Unless you want me to."

A shiver skated down my spine. The good kind. It would be so easy to just give myself to him, let him call the shots. Staying with Outlaw wouldn't be a hardship. He was sexy as hell, and I didn't doubt for a second that I'd enjoy every moment of my time with him. I'd always wanted my freedom, to have a life that was of my own choosing. That was the keyword. Choice. Did I want a job and a place of my own? Sure.

But I also wanted Outlaw. If having him meant that I couldn't have those other things, it was a trade I was willing to make. I'd felt more alive tonight than I ever had before.

He held onto me as he got my bag from outside and locked up the house, then led me down the hall to the bedroom. My bag was tossed near the dresser. Then he pulled the covers down and I slid into the bed, scooting over to give him room. I was still wearing his shirt, and *only* his shirt, but it made me feel a little bit naughty. I'd never gone to bed without panties on before, or pajamas for that matter. Outlaw stripped all the way down and my jaw dropped. He was going to sleep naked? Like, completely, totally naked? I may have not ever shared a bed with a guy before, but that wasn't normal, was it? Did all men just crawl into bed without any clothes on?

"Um." My mouth opened and shut a few times, but I couldn't seem to string two words together. Should I demand he put something on? He'd probably just laugh at me if I did. Outlaw didn't seem like the type to follow directions, especially from a woman. Maybe I should be offended by that, but I wasn't.

He winked at me. "Sorry, babe. Don't own pajamas."

Outlaw turned off the lights and got into bed, immediately reaching for me. I went willingly enough, curling against him. The fact his cock was starting to get hard and push against me was more than a bit distracting, but if he could ignore it, then I could certainly try to do the same. I'd never shared a bed with someone before and I felt a little awkward. I placed my hand on his side as I cuddled closer, my head tucked under his chin. It was rather nice, and I felt my body start to relax.

The strength of him surrounding me, his scent teasing my nose, the warmth of his body pressed against mine... I'd never felt so wanted in my entire life. So... protected. No one had ever been that affectionate with me, not that I remembered. My memories of my parents had faded over the years. I remembered my mother giving me hugs, but I didn't remember how it had felt, or how she smelled. Sometimes her face was even a little hazy in my mind.

My foster parents had only shown affection when people were looking, and even then they were on the reserved side. It was strange that some man I'd never met before, one who admitted to not walking on the right side of the law -- as if his name weren't enough of a clue -- could make me feel cherished when those in my life who were supposed to take care of me didn't have that same effect.

"You're thinking too hard," he murmured. "Sleep, Elena. You'll need it."

He pressed his cock against me and I got the message loud and clear. I needed sleep because he wanted to keep awake doing other things. My cheeks warmed as I thought about him taking my V-card. Then I remembered what he'd said earlier. Was he even going to give me a choice? For that matter, did I want him to? I'd never felt so confused, and yet certain, at the same time. He left me reeling, but I knew that I wanted what he was offering.

"You said you weren't going to have sex with me because then you'd keep me."

He chuckled, but it was a harsh sound. "That's because I *am* keeping you. You're right where you're supposed to be."

No asking. Just telling. I should have been angry. Yelled, screamed, told him that he had no say over what I did. I was a grown-ass woman in charge of my own life. And yet... all I felt was this warmth, like I'd finally found the place where I belonged. I'd read countless romance novels, and I'd always sighed when the heroine found her prince. Outlaw was far from Prince Charming, but maybe he was just what I needed. I had to wonder if he was the piece that had been missing from my life. I'd always thought it was loving parents, but now I wasn't so sure.

"Not going to argue?" he asked.

"Am I supposed to?"

He kissed the top of my head. "No, but I expected at least a little bit of a fight. Wouldn't have changed the outcome. If you'd have tried to leave, I'd have just gone after you."

I tried to still my mind, to blank everything and just sleep, but I couldn't. As much as everything he said was turning me on, I had to wonder if he'd said those same words to another woman some other time. I wasn't stupid. He wasn't a virgin like me. The women I'd seen at the clubhouse had probably volunteered to keep his bed warm on many occasions. It was a disturbing thought. I didn't have any idea if the men I'd seen last night were with someone or single. If they did have a woman at home, did she know they were with other women? Would I be expected to just look the other way?

Outlaw sighed. "Baby girl, what's going through your mind?"

"If you claim me, what does that mean? I know you wouldn't let me leave, but what exactly would I be to you?"

He rolled to his back and pulled me tight against his side. I felt his fingers tugging on my hair as he played with the strands. For the longest time, he didn't say a word, and I worried he wouldn't answer my question. Then he finally spoke.

"This club, they're my family. I consider the men here my brothers. Right now, only two of them have women in their lives they've claimed. Badger has Adalia as his ol' lady, and Dingo claimed Meiling. When someone like me claims you, it's forever, Elena. I won't let you go. Ever. Once you're mine, that's it. Anyone else touches you, I'll hand their ass to them. They fuck you, I'll kill them."

My breath hitched and my eyes went wide. He'd just admitted that he would murder someone. The first frisson of fear settled in me. I really didn't know anything about this man. What if I made him so angry he decided to kill *me*? Suddenly, all the warm fuzzies were fleeing. My heart slammed against my ribs and I tensed a little. I tried not to, but I couldn't help it.

He stroked his fingers down my arm. "Calm down, angel. I'd never do anything to hurt you."

"Just other people?"

"There's something you need to understand. I think you've lived your life with blinders on, and it's part of what I like about you. The sweetness and innocence. You don't find that around here. A few years ago a friend of mine was dragged from her home. Those men took me too, thinking I was her husband. I let them beat the shit out of me to keep them distracted. If I hadn't, they'd have raped and tortured her. It cost me, a lot, but I'd do it again in a second. Those men were dealt with."

I tried to digest what he was saying, but it was hard. It was one thing to read about stuff like that in paper or see it in a movie. I'd never actually known anyone who faced that kind of thing. He was right. I *had* been living life with blinders on. Not once had it ever occurred to me that the ugliness in the world could ever touch me. It was naïve, and I realized that now, but that didn't make murder right. Did it?

"I will protect you with my last breath, Elena. If that means I kill someone to do it, then so be it. There are monsters in the world who deserve to die. If they don't, then countless others will be hurt or worse. If I can stop just one of those men from taking a life or ruining an innocent, then I'll do it." He took a deep breath and let it out. "The room I came from earlier, it's where I keep my computers and other tech. I used to be a hacker. A damn good one."

"Used to be?" I asked.

He held up a hand and flexed his fingers. "The beating I took resulted in most of the bones in my hands being broken or crushed. They don't function the way they used to. Some of it is nerve damage, some of it just the bones not healing quite right. I'm not quick enough on a keyboard anymore to be of much use. I can dig a little, but I can't risk going too deep and getting caught because of my fucked-up hands."

I didn't know anything about hackers, or computers for that matter.

"I'm not a good guy, Elena. Not like other men you've met. And I'm not counting Garrison West in that scenario, or even your foster father. I think they're neck deep in some shady shit. The point is that yes, I will kill to protect my family, to protect *you*, and I'll do whatever else is necessary to keep you safe and give you all the things you want or need."

I traced the tattoo over his ribs with my finger while I thought about everything he'd said. He'd been honest even though he didn't have to be. At least, I assumed he was being honest. I couldn't think of a single person who would admit to being capable of killing someone unless they would actually do it. This wasn't the type of conversation where such a thing could be a boast. If he'd said as much to another man, then maybe I could have passed it off as bragging or trying to seem tougher than he was, but I knew that wasn't the case. He truly meant that he'd hurt someone to keep me safe, even kill them.

"I should let you go. I know it's wrong to keep you, lock you up here at the compound, and keep you with me. It's selfish. Probably the most selfish thing I've ever done, but I can't let you go, angel. I've never met anyone like you before, and I somehow doubt there's another like you out there."

"Do I have to share you with those other women?" I asked.

I saw his faint smile in the dim light that was starting to stream through the windows. His gaze locked with mine, and the humor I saw there made me wonder what he found so funny.

"Angel, none of those women can hold a candle to you. I don't want them. Only you." He grabbed a fistful of my hair and tugged lightly. "You're it for me, baby girl. So no, you don't have to share me. Any of those bitches puts her hands on me, you have my permission to put her on her ass."

I wasn't the violent type. I'd never so much as yelled at someone before, much less gotten physical. Did he want me to do that? To shove someone, or get into a fight over him? Just what sort of rabbit hole had I fallen down? Then again, if this was Wonderland, it was a really fucked-up version.

"So we'd be exclusive," I said, hoping he wasn't going to disagree. "A couple?"

"More like you'd be my wife, except not necessarily with all the paperwork involved. But if you want a wedding, I'm happy to marry you. You being my ol' lady, wearing a cut that says you're my property, that holds far more weight around here than a marriage ceremony."

Married. He wanted to marry me. My head was starting to hurt, and I didn't think it was from a lack of sleep. It was all too much to take in at one time. We hadn't even known each other for a full day.

"Sleep. I'll answer any other questions you have when the time is right." He stroked my arm again, the movement slow and gentle. It was hard to imagine the tough guy having such a soft side.

"Outlaw," I said, my voice heavy with sleep as my eyes started to close.

"Call me Noah," he said. "But only when we're alone like this."

"Noah." I smiled. The name didn't seem hardcore enough for a biker, but I liked it. "Don't let me sleep too long."

"You've had one hell of a day, angel. You sleep until your body says it's time to get up. There's nothing going on that can't wait a little while." He ran his fingers through my hair. "We can talk about whatever you want later."

"Thank you," I murmured.

He hugged me tighter. "For what?"

"Taking care of me."

Sleep pulled me under. My dreams were full of monsters, dragons, and knights in shining armor on motorcycles. When I woke, the bed was empty and the sun was shining brightly. I didn't know how much time had passed, or where Outlaw had gone. But I did know one thing… my subconscious had tried to tell me that Outlaw was my hero, and I thought perhaps it would be a good idea to listen to that little voice.

It had made me run when Garrison West was pushing to marry me, and from what Outlaw had said, it was a good thing I'd left. If an upstanding member of the community, someone who was a church deacon, wasn't who he seemed to be, then maybe a biker really was the good guy in this scenario. One thing was for certain. I had to trust someone, and my gut was telling me to trust Outlaw.

I got out of bed and went to find him. Seeing another woman in his arms made my stomach drop. The way she clung to him, the look on her face... My throat tightened and I took a step back, but movement caught my attention on the other side of the room. An imposing man with red hair and a beard stood watching me, a boy who looked to be about three or four clutched in his arms. The man's gaze pinned me to the spot, then a slight smile curled his lips.

"No worries, little one. That's my wife. She's not going to take him from you," the man said.

I jerked my gaze back over to the couple, to find Outlaw staring at me. He pulled away from the woman and held his hand out to me. Against my better judgment, I went to him, letting him pull me against his side. My brain felt scrambled and I wasn't sure which way was up.

"Elena, I'd like you to meet Lavender and Wire. They came to help."

Tears misted the woman's eyes. "I'm so glad he found you. I've been so worried. I thought I'd ruined his life."

Ruined his life? How would she... and then it all became clear. *This* was the woman he'd protected. It wasn't until that moment I noticed the small swell of her stomach. He hadn't only saved her, but he'd given their child a shot at living. If she'd died, that baby would have never existed. I didn't know how long ago he'd helped her, but it was possible the little boy wouldn't have existed either.

I'd never felt prouder of someone than I did in that moment with Outlaw. Because of him, three lives had been saved. That was also the moment I realized all those scars, or at least a lot of them, had come from the beating he'd taken to keep Lavender safe.

I felt like such a bitch for thinking the worst when I'd walked in.

"It's nice to meet you," I said.

Outlaw gave a soft growl. "Angel, what the fuck are you wearing?"

I glanced down. "The same shirt you gave me last night. It wasn't like I knew you had company."

"Go change. Now." He gave me a nudge toward the door, and I saw Lavender roll her eyes. It seemed like she was used to the caveman behavior and I figured her husband must be the same way.

I gave her a little wave and scurried off. I hoped he didn't plan on me returning right away because I seriously needed a shower, and I wasn't going back out there until I'd had one.

Chapter Six

Outlaw

"Stop looking at me like that," I told Lavender. She was giving me puppy eyes and it was annoying the fuck out of me. "I told you I was fine. I repeatedly have told you that none of it was your fault."

"Good luck," Wire muttered. "Been telling her that for four damn years."

She reached out like she was going to touch me, then thought better of it. Probably a good idea considering how well Elena had handled seeing me with another woman. If she'd have fucked things up, I'd have been pissed. Thankfully, Wire noticed Elena before I had and said something before she could disappear.

"You grew your beard back," she said.

"Yeah. Took a while for some of the scars to heal, and even now there are spots that don't grow hair very well. It's long enough you can't tell." I ran my hand over it. "Figured the scars would scare any kids I ran across when I'm in town. They tend to shy away from most of us already. Don't need to give them nightmares."

Wire sat, settling his son in his lap, and Lavender took the chair next to him. I leaned against the counter, waiting on Elena to come back. She'd been gone at least twenty minutes and I was starting to think she wasn't coming back. Atlas banged his hands on the kitchen table and I smiled. The kid was cute, and if he was anything like his parents, he was fucking smart as hell too. I wondered how long before they had him at a computer, or did they already? I really should have kept in touch better, but Lavender's guilt had weighed on me.

"Is this one a girl or a boy?" I asked, pointing to Lavender's belly.

"We don't know yet," she said. "I'm kind of hoping for a girl, but we have another two months before we find out."

She looked around the room and I wondered if she was nervous about being here. I'd been surprised as hell when they'd shown up. Should have known that Wizard would run his damn mouth about the shit going on with Elena. Something told me Wire knew more than I did at this point.

"Where are y'all staying?" I asked. "Because I don't have a guest room set up."

"Grizzly wasn't around when we got here, but Slash said he had a room we could use. What's up with the Pres?" Wire asked.

Shit. I'd forgotten all about that clusterfuck yesterday. I hadn't gotten so much as a text from Grizzly, or anyone else, about the situation with Lilian and Dragon. If we were down a brother, I'd have surely heard about it, which meant Dragon was still breathing. For now.

"He tore out of here last night saying Dragon knocked up Lilian. That was the last I heard from him."

Wire whistled. "Damn. I hope that boy can run fast."

"Boy?" I asked. "You're in your forties, not pushing sixty. Dragon is maybe a decade younger than you."

"Yeah, well, I wasn't dumb enough to knock up the Pres's daughter," Wire said.

"And that would be a good thing," said Lavender, "since Torch's oldest daughter is thirteen. The club wouldn't even bother hiding the body because there wouldn't be enough of you left to bury."

Wire made a face. "It was hard enough for me to handle our age difference. That's just sick."

I couldn't help but laugh. "Hey, man, you brought it up."

Lavender looked around again. She seemed almost jittery, and I couldn't figure out why. I was about to ask if she had ants in her pants when Elena came back in, dressed in jeans and a modest teal shirt. Her hair was still wet, but she'd braided it. Before I could say anything, Lavender leaned closer to Elena and whispered something. My woman smiled and nodded for Lavender to follow her.

"What the fuck was that about?" I asked.

"She probably has to pee. Again," Wire said. "I swear when she's pregnant she goes about every half hour. And when she's closer to her delivery date, it will seem like she goes closer to every ten minutes."

"I didn't need to know that."

He shrugged a shoulder, then smirked. "You brought it up."

Fucker. I flipped him off and he only laughed. I'd have worried about corrupting Atlas, but if that kid hung around the Reapers, he'd likely heard and seen far worse.

"Do you want to talk about your situation with or without Elena present?" Wire asked.

"Probably better if I hear it first and then figure out how to break it down for her. She's led a very sheltered life."

He nodded. "All right. Anyone else need to know about this?"

I sighed and rubbed the back of my neck. I hadn't told anyone what was going on, and I knew Griz would be fucking pissed at me. Or rather, he would be if he weren't worried about his daughter. If there was ever a time to fuck up, this was it. At least the fallout would be minimal. "We'd better tell everyone. They don't know shit about this yet."

"When the girls get back in here, I'll leave Atlas with Lavender and we can head over to the clubhouse. Better text your crew and let them know to get their asses to Church. It would be nice if just once we could find a woman who didn't have hell riding on her heels. But then, I guess our lives would be too fucking dull," Wire said.

That was the damn truth. Every single ol' lady at every single club we called friend or family had arrived with a shit ton of trouble following, except maybe Isabella. Then again, she'd been part of a deal brokered between Torch and her dad, Casper VanHorne. Yep, we definitely didn't do anything the normal way when it came to our women. Why bother starting now?

I sent a text to Demon, Grizzly, and Slash. I figured they could chew my ass out now, but still get everyone gathered at the clubhouse. Even though Wire hadn't told me what he'd discovered, I knew it had to be bad if he'd come all this way with his family in tow. Any other time, he'd have just picked up the phone. Of course, there was always the possibility that Lavender had used it as an excuse just to come visit. She might not have been convinced I really had found someone and needed to see for herself.

The only one to respond was Demon. *The Pres and VP are dealing with an issue. Church in 10.*

I showed Wire the message and he gave a nod, then yelled out for Lavender to hurry the fuck up. If I didn't know he worshiped the ground she walked on, I'd have thought he was being an asshole to her. Lavender was just as crazy about him, for whatever reason. It was clear the two were meant for each other, both badasses in their own right, but I didn't know how she put up with him. I had no doubt if they'd have been at home and he'd done that, she likely would have smacked him on the back of the head, but she wouldn't disrespect him like that in front of others.

They worked together, even if at first glance they seemed like an odd pair. Even pregnant, Lavender was wearing her jeans, mint-colored Converse, and a *Dark Crystal* shirt. With her plastic-framed glasses perched on her nose, and her hair pulled back in some sort of messy knot, she looked every inch the geek. Wire was just as bad as her, except he kept that side hidden. He looked like any other biker, and I knew he was a force to be reckoned with both behind a keyboard and in person. Anyone who went after his brothers or his family was going to be fucked-up when he was finished.

Elena and Lavender came back into the room and Wire handed Atlas to his wife. I crooked a finger at Elena and she came close enough that I could pull her against me. Reaching up, I smoothed her hair back from her face and gave her a quick kiss.

"I have something to take care of and Wire is going with me. Think you can keep Lavender and Atlas company?"

She tipped her head to the side. "Are you in trouble? Or am I?"

"Wire looked into a few things for me, but we need to discuss it with the club. Not sure how long we'll be over at the clubhouse, but I'll send a Prospect this way. He'll stay outside, but you can let him know if you need anything."

She ran her fingers over my beard. "I'll be fine."

I winked at her, gave her one last kiss, then headed out with Wire on my heels. I stared at the large SUV in my driveway, knowing it had to be Lavender's because Wire wouldn't have let her walk from the front of the compound, and realized that Elena's car wasn't here and must still be at the clubhouse. I'd have to make sure it was moved at some point, but right now, I kind of liked knowing she didn't have easy access to make an escape. She seemed content enough to stay where she was, but I hadn't officially claimed her yet. Until I had, I wasn't taking any chances.

I led the way to the clubhouse on my bike and parked right out front near the steps. There was a small car toward the end of the building and I knew it had to be Elena's. I'd never seen it before and she certainly hadn't walked here. Wire pulled up next to me and we headed inside. One of the newer prospects, Dax, was behind the bar. I motioned him over and he jumped the bar to rush over. Sometimes these guys were more like eager puppies, which amused the shit out of me.

"I need you to go to my house, but stay outside. Wire's woman and kid are there, and my woman is there too."

His eyes went wide, but he gave a jerky nod. "I'll go right now."

He took off at a run out of the clubhouse and I just shook my head before heading to the back. Almost everyone was already in Church, so I took my usual seat and Wire leaned against the wall. Even though we had guests often enough, there were only enough chairs for the patched members. When we added to our ranks, we'd bring in more seats as needed. While guests were honored in some ways, having a seat at the table during Church was a respect thing. If you weren't patched in, you weren't sitting at our table.

Demon banged the gavel on the table and I realized Griz and Slash wouldn't be joining us, nor would several members it seemed. It seemed Slash was helping track down Lilian. I hoped he'd already gotten everything situated for Wire and Lavender. I didn't know where they were, and it wasn't my place to ask. I scanned the room and realized Dragon was one of the guys missing. I hoped Grizzly wasn't working the poor guy over. There was no fucking way he'd forced himself on Lilian, which meant she had to have consented. I still didn't see how he'd gotten that damn close to her, but she must have liked him more than the rest of us. The woman still jumped whenever I got too close.

"As you can see, Grizzly, Slash, and several others aren't here today," Demon said. "Dragon got Lilian pregnant, but before Griz could talk to her, she packed her shit and left."

Whoa. I hadn't seen that one coming. No wonder we were a little light on brothers today. I'd be willing to bet the Pres had them all out searching for his daughter. This was seriously fucked-up.

"So that's who she was waiting for," Dingo said.

"What?" Demon narrowed his eyes. "What the fuck do you know about it?"

Dingo lifted a hand to calm the Sergeant-at-Arms. "Nothing really. One of the nights I was at the clubhouse I saw her lurking in the shadows outside. Told her to get home, but she said she was waiting for someone. She mentioned Dragon, but said she just needed some advice. Didn't think it was my place to do anything more than warn her away from the clubhouse, and it seemed harmless enough."

Demon cursed. "You'll need to tell the Pres that you saw her here. Maybe he'll go easier on Dragon. He was fucking pissed as hell."

"Dragon's not in the basement, right?" Wolf asked. The thought had crossed my mind too. "Because there's no damn way he took her against her will. That's just not the kind of guy he is."

"No. He's off searching for Lilian. It seems he about lost his shit when he heard she was pregnant and missing." Demon shook his head. "Not sure what's going to happen there, but for right now, I'm in charge. Outlaw has been sitting on some information that he'd like to share with us. Griz is pissed about that too, by the way, so expect an ass-chewing later."

I hadn't expected anything less. I glanced at Wire, not really knowing yet what he'd discovered, but he wasn't volunteering info. I told them what I knew so far about Elena, why she'd come to our gates, and the people she'd left behind. When I got to the part about Garrison West really being Bastard from the Savage Raptors, the temp in the room dropped about ten degrees. Demon went so still that I worried he'd turned to stone.

"Bastard is still alive?" he asked quietly.

"It looks that way. I honestly have no idea who he is. I sent everything I had to Wizard and he identified him, then he conferred with Wire. I haven't heard what's been discovered since then," I said.

Demon ran a hand through his hair. "Bastard wasn't just a patched member of Savage Raptors. He was related to the Sergeant-at-Arms. When General stripped the colors off Bastard's skin, he was doing it to his brother. Not just a brother through the club, but one he shared a father with. It gutted the club when they found out he'd betrayed them. And now this..."

Wire pushed off from the wall and moved closer to the table, but he didn't sit. He hadn't brought a laptop in with him, or any files. I didn't know if he had anything concrete, or if he'd just stored everything in his head.

"Wizard hit a wall and asked me to look into this shit. And what I found is disturbing. Bastard isn't just sending money through the church back to his brother's club. He's laundering funds that are going through his business. It didn't take much for me to follow the trail right back to the Savage Raptors, and since I know Attila would never own a fucking brothel, much less multiple ones, then I think he has another rat in his house," Wire said. "I also peeked into the Raptor accounts and the funds coming from guns and drugs don't match what's been sent from the church. Whatever funds are being deposited into the Raptor's main account is all legit business. So someone is running a side scheme for that too. That money isn't going into the club funds. It's being routed in a way that makes it look like the club is in on it, which is clever considering how fucking stupid Bastard was back in the day. Makes me curious who his partner is."

"What brothels?" Demon asked.

"They cater to certain needs. From what I found, there are five, and they're easily pulling in a few hundred grand a month. Whoever is getting the funds to Bastard, they're also sending money out through several other contacts. The biggest red flag is that the money never enters the Savage Raptors' accounts. Not from the brothels, guns, or drugs. Even worse, they aren't dealing in marijuana like the club typically does. We're talking cocaine and meth. The money is being sent into offshore accounts under a false name. Terry Simpson," Wire said. "I haven't been able to figure out who he is yet, but I do know how he's operating."

Dingo whistled. "Damn. That's a lot of cash to keep out of the club's hands, and I know that crew would never own a brothel, not even if the women volunteered to work there. They would personally tear them down if they knew they existed."

"Worse than that," Steel said. "I'm older than a lot of you, and I was around when that shit went down with Bastard. He didn't ask to leave, he was thrown out. They didn't label him a traitor lightly. He was caught with underage girls, pimping them out like what Trotter was doing here, except not a single member of his stable was over the age of sixteen. Sick fucker."

Something about all this was bothering me. It was that skin-crawling sensation I got when the pieces of the puzzle didn't quite fit but I knew they should, if the puzzle was a life and death matter anyway. Bad enough that I had no idea how those two managed to run something like this without the Raptors figuring it out, but maybe they'd had help. It had saved my ass more than once. Brothels. Bastard. The dead wife... I looked at Wire. "What did you find on Bastard's wife?"

"He faked her death. She's definitely dead now, but she wasn't then. Even worse, she wasn't the first. He's legally, and illegally, married a dozen women in the last twelve years. He fakes their deaths and sends them to his accomplice at the Savage Raptors, who then puts them to work in the brothels or uses them as drug mules. Best part is that as the grieving widower, he gets any life insurance money. He's been clever and seems to have multiple identities, addresses, and never uses the same insurance company. I didn't think he had it in him, but he's gotten smarter since he had his colors stripped."

"Why the fuck couldn't it just be something easy?" Dagger asked. "Anyone else sick of this shit? Why do people have to be so fucking awful? Anyone who preys on women and kids should be neutered, then tossed into general population at the worst prisons in the country."

I didn't think any of us would disagree with that.

"He wanted to marry Elena," I said. "Do you think he'd have sent her to his accomplice too? Or did he actually want her for a wife?"

Wire ran a hand through his hair. "She was going to be a mule. I'm pretty sure anyway. With her being a Latina, they may have hoped she could get across the border and back without raising too many eyebrows, especially if she maintained her connection to the church and her foster parents."

"She'd have never gone for it," I said. I didn't have any doubt about that. If she'd balked, she might have ended up dead or worse. Whatever had told her to run, I was glad she'd listened to that inner voice. It may have very well saved her damn life.

I wasn't sure how much of this I should tell her, or what Demon would allow me to say. This was a club matter now, and club business didn't get discussed with the women. Sometimes I had to wonder if they were really safer not knowing, or if we were just fooling ourselves. If we got involved in this shit right now, and Lilian was still out there on her own, it could end badly if the wrong people found her. I didn't know who we'd piss off if we did more than just hand off information.

Since Elena was here and had brought it to our attention, it was possible that Demon would want to stay hands on. I hoped I was wrong, though. The last thing I wanted was to bring trouble to our doorstep now that I had a woman to think about. Assuming no one denied my claim on her. With Griz gone, I didn't know if I could get a vote or not.

"She's mine," I said. "Elena. I'm claiming her."

Demon eased back in his chair and stared me down. I didn't blink, didn't flinch. Finally, he cracked a smile and gave a nod. "All right. I don't think anyone in this club would deny you the woman you want. No vote needed."

"You don't need to run it by Griz? He was going to look into who drugged her. If she hadn't come home with me, we would have never known about all this other stuff. And I still don't know who roofied her drink."

"You mean no one told him?" Dagger asked.

"Told me what?"

"We found out who's drugging the girls," Demon said. "They got sloppy. We don't have her on camera, but one of the regulars from town bragged to her friends that she was taking out the competition. Thought she'd snag herself a spot as an ol' lady. Not sure how she figured that would work, unless she thought docile was a turnoff."

"And is *she* in the basement?" Wolf asked.

"What is your fascination with the basement?" Wire asked. "If you're so fixated on it, go down there."

Demon, Dagger, and Steel all burst out laughing. I realized Wire hadn't seen that addition to the clubhouse and had no idea that's where we interrogated people, but it still earned him a glare from Wolf. Couldn't blame him for wondering where the woman was because I wanted to know the same thing.

She could have gotten Elena hurt. What if we hadn't noticed and she'd tried to drive herself out of here?

"She'll be handled," Demon said. "And since it seems she harmed the property of a brother, her punishment will be severe. I'll take care of it."

"I'll need a property cut," I said.

"I'll have Magda make one. Give her a few days. She's getting up there and her hands don't work as well as they used to. Until then, I'll make sure everyone knows that Elena is yours. No one will fuck with her, and she'll be protected." Demon slammed the gavel on the table. "Now everyone get the fuck out of here. I have shit to do."

I stood and Wire followed me from the room, but he hesitated outside the door. When Demon came out, he went to speak with him. I kept my distance. If Demon wanted me to hear what they were discussing, he'd let me know. After a few minutes, it didn't seem like Wire was going to wrap it up anytime soon so I decided to leave him to his discussion. It wasn't like he didn't know how to get to my damn house. I took my bike through the compound and pulled up in front of the small home I'd be sharing with Elena from now on. The Prospect was standing near the front door and I dismissed him before going inside.

The sound of laughter drew me to the living room and I smiled at the sight of Elena holding Atlas. Maybe one day we'd have a kid of our own. Even if my dick worked, I'd been told I had a low sperm count during one of my many tests after the incident years ago. Probably something I needed to discuss with her. If she wanted kids, I'd try my damnedest to give them to her, but it probably wouldn't happen overnight. Not unless we were really fucking lucky.

"You're home," Elena said, smiling widely.

"Yeah." I glanced at Lavender. "Your man hung back to talk to Demon."

Lavender took Atlas from Elena. "It's nice enough outside I think the little man would probably like some playtime. We'll be out front if you need us, but I have a feeling the two of you need to discuss a few things."

She leaned against me as she went past and I gave her a brief hug. Elena twirled her hair around her fingers, her expressive eyes belying her nervousness. I wasn't sure how much to tell her, but I needed to make sure she knew she was mine without question. The rest... I'd tell her what I could.

Chapter Seven

Elena

Wire, Lavender, and the adorable Atlas had left to rest, saying it was time for the little boy's nap, which left me alone with Outlaw. I was still processing what he'd told me, but it was so hard to believe. I didn't know how the Garrison West who had charmed everyone at church, and even around town, could be the same man he called Bastard, a traitor from another club. It was just... baffling.

"Why would my foster parents help him?" I asked.

"That's the million-dollar question. If Wire knows, he didn't share it with me. I'm glad you left when you did. If you'd stayed and ended up with that guy, he'd have made you disappear and turned you into a drug mule or worse."

I'd talked a bit with Lavender while he'd been gone. She'd explained the way the club worked a bit better than Outlaw had, or maybe it was more that she'd been able to tell me how it worked from a woman's perspective. Anyone could see that she was happy with Wire, and their son was adorable. I could also tell she thought the world of Outlaw, and she swore that he was one of the best guys she knew.

I'd already come to terms with him claiming me, but hearing all the good things she had to say about him made me feel better about my decision. No, I didn't know her, and she could have been lying, but I didn't know why she'd bother. The affection she held for Outlaw was clear, and didn't seem faked or forced.

I did have to wonder if I was so wrong about Garrison, couldn't I be wrong about Outlaw too? I'd thought the church deacon was just after a babymaker, but if he had something far worse planned, and I'd never once felt like I was in serious danger, then what if I was making a mistake to stay with Outlaw? In my gut, it felt like the right thing to do, but I didn't think I could trust my instincts right now. He was praising me for running the way I had, but I hadn't escaped because I felt like Garrison was evil, I'd only run because I didn't want to be badgered into a marriage I didn't want.

"Demon said they found the woman who drugged you," he said. "It was a regular. He assured me that she'll be handled. Not sure what he plans to do, but I have no doubt he'll scare the hell out of her so she keeps her distance."

"Any more surprises?" I asked.

He sighed and tugged on his beard, seeming troubled as he stared at a blank spot on the wall. What else could he possibly need to tell me? It couldn't be worse than all the rest, could it? Was I still in danger? Had the club told him that I couldn't stay?

"You're scaring me, Outlaw. Just tell me."

His gaze jerked to mine. "Told you when it's just us you can call me Noah."

"Fine. Please tell me what's wrong, Noah."

He held out his hand and I went to him. His arms came around me, and it almost felt like he was scared I'd run if he let me go.

"Demon gave the approval for me to claim you, so as of now, you're officially my ol' lady. But there's something I haven't told you about me." He chewed the inside of his mouth, his gaze locked on mine. Whatever it was, I wished he'd just say it. "When I came home four years ago, after I kept Lavender alive, the doc ran all sorts of tests trying to figure out what all was wrong with me. One of those tests was for fertility."

His cheeks warmed and I tried not to smile. It was cute that he'd get all bashful talking about something like making a baby. Then the words really registered. If he was concerned about how I'd handle the news, then did that mean he was sterile? Would we never have kids if I stayed with him? While I hadn't wanted to be barefoot and pregnant all the time, I'd always wanted a baby or two at some point.

"I told you that I knew I was clean. The reason I know is that ever since I came back, I haven't been with a woman. I couldn't get hard. At all. Not even with those little blue pills. Nothing worked." He reached up and smoothed my hair back. "Until you. Just holding you in my arms was enough. It's why you caught me jerking off in the shower. It was the first time in four years, and I wasn't even sure my dick would work right."

"What does that have to do with anything? It's obvious that it works. I mean, you came in my mouth, and you got hard again after." Now it was my turn for my face to feel like it was on fire.

"Yeah, getting hard doesn't seem to be an issue when it comes to being with you, but there might be a little problem with getting you pregnant. I'm not sterile, but I do have a low sperm count. The doc said it would be difficult to knock someone up, but not impossible. Just might take a while."

I reached up and placed my hand on his cheek. "Is that what had you worried? I'm okay with waiting a while. I already told you I don't want to be pregnant all the time, or even right away. If it's a few years before we have a baby, I'm all right with that."

He pressed his forehead to mine. "You know, can't knock you up if we haven't had sex. Not sure now is necessarily the time, but definitely soon."

I pressed my lips to his, just a brief kiss, but I appreciated that he wasn't being pushy about it. It wasn't that I didn't want to have sex with him, because I really, really did, but after everything I'd dealt with the last twenty-four hours and learned today my mind was spinning. Not to mention my stomach was growling. Loudly. I felt my cheeks warm, and Outlaw chuckled.

"Seems I need to feed you, then maybe I can introduce you to a few other people around here. I don't want you to feel isolated or alone."

"I'd love to meet some of the other women here. I'm sure the other club members are great, but there will be times that having another woman nearby would be nice."

He nodded. "All right. I'll see what I can do. Probably won't get a chance to meet Shella since her sister ran off, but I'll see if Meiling is free and maybe Adalia. Griz is going to have Shella on lockdown, or so I would guess. If I'd had a kid run off, I'd put the other one on house arrest. But first let's see what's in the kitchen. We might have to go out. Now that I know the threat to you, at least here, has been handled, I'm not so worried about leaving the compound with you. Or the house for that matter."

"You don't think Garrison, or Bastard, whatever his name really is will come after me?"

Outlaw sighed. "Honestly, I don't know the guy, hadn't even heard of him before this, so I have no idea what he'll do. I would think that trying to chase you down would take up too much time and it would be easier for him to focus on someone else."

That didn't make me feel much better. I might have wanted to escape the life I had, but it didn't mean that I wanted any of the single ladies at the church to fall into his trap either. I also didn't like that I had no idea how my foster parents were involved. They'd seemed so nice, if a bit strict at times, that I had a hard time picturing them working with a guy like that to launder money. What if they'd somehow gotten caught up in whatever illegal thing he was doing and didn't have a way out?

I might not love the Tolberts, but they had clothed me, fed me, and treated me well. Bad language, R-rated movies, and rock music hadn't been permitted, and I'd had to dress a certain way, but they hadn't hurt me. I'd just felt suffocated by them. It didn't mean they deserved to have bad things happen to them if they weren't willing participants in whatever Garrison was doing.

Outlaw ran a finger down my nose. "I'll see if I can figure out what's going on with your foster parents, but no promises. I think Demon wants the club to steer clear of this as much as possible."

"I understand, I just don't want them hurt if it can be helped. If they're as rotten as Garrison is, then they deserve whatever happens, but what if they're being forced to help him?"

He nodded. "I wondered the same thing. Not much I can do if the club officers tell me to stay out of it. I know you're worried, and I'll try to help if I can, but you may have to let this one go, angel."

I didn't like that answer, not even a little. I also felt really bad about leaving them. If I'd stayed, I'd have been in trouble from the sound of things, but had

I endangered them by ruining his plans? Garrison didn't sound like the kind of man who would take kindly to me running off.

Outlaw rubbed between my eyebrows and I realized I was frowning. "Tell you what. I'll text a few friends, see if anyone has contacts up near your foster family. Maybe they can just check on them, discreetly, to give you peace of mind."

"Thank you." I hugged him tight. "I know it seems silly. I was running away from them and now I'm worried they might be hurt."

"Not silly, angel. They took care of you when you needed someone."

He tugged his phone from his pocket and tapped on the screen for a few minutes. When he was done, he slid it back into his jeans and led me to the kitchen. I helped him search the cabinets, pantry, and fridge to get an idea of what we might eat, but it was apparent that he needed to make a grocery run. I had to wonder how he managed it when he had a motorcycle. It was a good thing I had a...

"Crap!"

"What?" he asked.

"My car! I forgot all about it."

He folded his arms over his chest. "What do you need your car for?"

Wait. Was he trying to tell me I couldn't have it? I mimicked his pose and narrowed my eyes, which only seemed to amuse him since his lips tipped up on one corner. "Why can't I have my car?"

"If you need to go somewhere, I can take you."

Oh good grief. I knew he could be controlling and all dominant, but this was ridiculous. I rolled my eyes and huffed at him. "Are you serious right now?

How are you going to take me to the grocery? Where are we going to put everything?"

His eyebrows shot up and he outright smiled. "Are you sassing me right now?"

I shifted from foot to foot, not sure if I should admit it or not. He prowled closer, sat down on the nearest kitchen chair, then before I time to move, he grabbed my wrist and yanked me across his lap. His hand cracked down my ass three times in rapid succession.

"Ow! What the hell, Noah?" *Smack. Smack.* "Stop it!"

"Sassy girls get spankings." His hand cracked against my ass again. "And if you weren't a virgin, I'd already have your pants down and be balls-deep inside you just to remind you who's the boss in this relationship."

I gasped in outrage, but he rubbed his hand across my aching backside, then slipped his fingers between my legs, rubbing the seam of my jeans against my clit, and it quickly turned to a moan. It wasn't fair that he could make me feel like this. I should be furious with him. I was a grown adult, not some wayward kid who needed to be punished. He rubbed a little harder and I nearly came. Maybe being punished wasn't exactly horrible.

"Noah." I nearly sighed his name. "Don't stop."

He laughed softly. "A moment ago you were yelling at me to stop."

"You're not playing fair and you know it."

He shifted me so that I was sitting on his lap, his arms around me. The way he looked at me, I could feel it all the way deep down. No one ever had seen me as anyone important, but when Outlaw's gaze held mine, it was like I was the only person in his world. I reached up and ran my finger along some of his scars. He didn't flinch away, just let me touch him.

"I'm glad it was you who brought me home last night."

"I was heading your way before you started to fall out of the chair at the clubhouse. You looked cute sitting in the corner trying to read. And completely out of place. Then I noticed something didn't seem right."

"My white knight." I smiled. "You're unlike anyone I've ever met before."

He placed his hand at the back of my neck and tugged me closer until his lips pressed to mine. He kissed me slow and soft. I'd have never imagined someone who looked so tough could be this gentle. When he licked at my bottom lip, I opened and let him in. He tasted like coffee, and his beard tickled a little. All too soon, he was pulling away.

"Food, Elena, or I'll take you to the bedroom. You need to eat, and I need time to cool down."

I kissed him again, then stood up. Even though I'd dressed earlier, I hadn't put on shoes yet. Rushing to the bedroom, I grabbed a pair of tennis shoes and socks, and slipped them on. He was waiting by the front door when I was finished. I reached for his hand and when he led me outside, I stopped and stared at the shiny gray truck parked in the driveway.

"That wasn't there before," I said.

"Had a Prospect drop it off. We'll take this to get groceries, but I'll have someone bring your car over by tomorrow night. I don't want to keep you under lock and key, but I do want to keep you safe."

"How many girlfriends have you had?" I asked.

"Are you really asking me that?"

I shrugged. "Yeah. I've never dated anyone before. I just didn't know how many..." I stopped.

Maybe I really didn't want to know. If he'd been with twenty women, fifty, did I really want to think about that? He'd picked me. That should be enough.

"Get in the truck, angel." He gave me a stern glare. "No discussing past women. I told you there hasn't been anyone for four years. It's just you and me in this relationship, and it's staying that way. Anyone else is such a distant memory I don't even remember their names or faces."

Good answer. Didn't know if it was true or not, but it did make me feel a little better. From what I'd witnessed at the clubhouse, it was obvious the guys were complete whores and slept with anyone who'd bend over and offer. I didn't think all men were like that, but it wasn't like I had the experience to know for sure.

I climbed into the truck and Outlaw reached in, fastening my seatbelt for me. To some, it might have made him seem high-handed, but I liked that he was trying to take care of me. I'd never felt special in my entire life, until now. His bossiness didn't make me feel like he looked down on me. I could imagine it would turn off some women, but I liked it. I couldn't say for sure if I only liked it when Outlaw did it, or if I was just more submissive than some. I'd met women who were loud, brash, and charged after whatever they wanted. I'd never been like that and probably never would be, and that was fine. My one attempt to take control of my life had landed me here.

Outlaw got in the truck and started it, then backed down the driveway and headed to the front of the compound. Now that it was daylight, I could see everything more clearly. A lot of the homes were really cute, and something you'd find in any blue-collar subdivision. Although a few were larger, and I wondered if those belonged to the men he mentioned were officers. Sounded important, even if I didn't quite grasp the difference in whatever part Outlaw played with the Devil's Fury.

I'd just have to learn things along the way, and hope I didn't screw up so hugely that I would embarrass him, or get him into trouble. If I did get to meet the other women, I hoped they could help me out. Lavender had explained how things worked with the Dixie Reapers, but that didn't mean the Devil's Fury handled stuff the same way.

He reached across the console and took my hand, threading our fingers together. It felt right, being here with him. I knew I had to be crazy. No one met someone and just decided to live with them forever. Life didn't work that way. Or I'd never thought it did. Maybe all those sappy romances I liked weren't so fictional after all.

Chapter Eight

Outlaw

I ended up taking Elena to my favorite restaurant in town, a steak place that had baked potatoes so big they almost needed a separate plate. Her eyes had gotten so wide when she saw the food that I'd nearly laughed. It had been nice going out with her. I hadn't been on a date for so long, not even before the incident. Dating and the club didn't really go hand in hand. If I wanted to get laid, all I had to do was head over to the clubhouse any night of the week. No bullshit drama. It had been fun for a while, then I'd started getting tired of the easy pussy.

After dinner, I'd stopped by one of the twenty-four-hour stores and grabbed a few groceries. Elena helped fill the cart, then I made sure she had everything she needed to be comfortable at the house. It hadn't looked like she'd packed much. Getting her to spend money hadn't been easy. I'd always thought women loved to shop, especially with someone else's account, but not my angel. She'd worried that it would cost too much.

I wasn't exactly hurting for money. There weren't millions in my account, but I did all right. I didn't have to pay for my house so my bills were minimal. At any given time, there was at least ten grand in the bank. Not buying a lot of computer shit had helped, even if the reason I didn't sucked. I'd watched more TV the last few years than I ever had before. The basic shit I was able to do didn't require much of an upgrade to my system. I didn't have to stay on top of it like I had before. In fact, tech gadgets just didn't appeal as much these days.

Never thought my sixty-five-inch TV would be used for romantic comedies, but Elena seemed to enjoy them. She giggled at something one of the characters said, but I'd tuned it out about ten minutes in. As long as she was happy, that's all that mattered to me. I could watch action movies, horror, or anything that wasn't this sappy shit when she was otherwise occupied. I got the feeling even her TV time had been limited by her foster family.

Just watching Elena was entertaining enough. I loved the way her face lit up when she laughed. She had a beautiful smile. Beautiful everything really. I knew I was a lucky bastard that I'd found her last night. If any of my brothers had reached her first, I might have lost my chance to make her mine. Even though we didn't really know much about each other, I got the feeling that she was the one woman meant for me. Why else wouldn't I have had a reaction to a woman in four years? Nothing else made sense. The doctor had said there was no medical reason I hadn't had an erection. Looked like I'd just needed the right woman.

"You're staring," she said, her gaze swinging my way.

"Just admiring the scenery."

She rolled her eyes and went back to her movie. It was cute. I might have spanked her earlier, but I liked her sass. It meant she was getting comfortable around me. Of course, she hadn't exactly been timid from the moment she'd woken in my bed. I found her curiosity and honesty refreshing. No games with my angel. She said what she meant, and if she had a question, she asked.

I hadn't told her yet, but Dingo was bringing Meiling over soon. I wanted her relaxed when they got here. It wouldn't surprise me if the visit was short. With Meiling expecting their first child, Dingo was even more protective than usual. He watched Mei like a damn hawk, and stayed glued to her as much as possible. When he wasn't by her side, her mother was.

I hadn't even thought about Mei's mom when Elena had asked about the women at the club. Everyone called her China, the nickname Blades had given her, but she was still reclusive. It was rare to see her outside of their home, except for when she went to Dingo's place. She and Mei had become close. As far as I knew, China didn't even speak much to Adalia, Shella, and Lilian.

Fuck. Lilian.

I checked my phone, but still no update on the Pres's daughter. I didn't know if she'd been found, or if she'd managed to leave the entire state before they realized she was missing. If anything happened to her, Griz would lose his shit, and it seemed like Dragon might as well. I'd have never pictured the two of them together. Lilian jumped at shadows and Dragon had always been front and center with everything. Although, I could admit he'd changed some since the day several members of nearly every club across the southern states had been taken. He'd almost died during the altercation, and only Grizzly's reluctant acceptance to let drugs come through our territory had saved the guy.

I also hadn't heard back from anyone about Elena's foster family. Either no one had friends in the area, or they had bad news they didn't want to share. If anything happened to the Tolberts, I had a feeling Elena would blame herself. It wasn't her fault, none of it was, but she seemed like the type to try and shoulder that responsibility anyway.

The doorbell rang and I got up to answer it. Elena cast a quick glance my way before going back to her movie. I hoped that she and Meiling got along. There weren't a lot of women around the club, except the club whores. I'd prefer that she not hang out with them, but if that's what she wanted, I wouldn't exactly stop her. Not unless I thought they might hurt her. The bitch drugging people hadn't targeted ol' ladies, but she hadn't had access to them either.

"Hey, Mei. Dingo. Come on in," I said after opening the door.

Elena bolted upright when I walked into the living room with our guests. I made the introductions, then wondered if I should have told Elena about Mei's rough past. It wasn't a secret around here what she'd been through, but I wasn't sure how my angel would react when she heard about it.

"Ladies, we'll be in the kitchen if you need anything," I said, then jerked my chin at Dingo for him to follow me. I knew if I didn't prod him along, he'd just stay glued to his wife's side. "How's she doing? Baby okay?"

Dingo ran his hands through his hair, looking tense as hell. "So far everything seems fine, but I keep waiting for something bad to happen. Between her previous miscarriages and the abortions forced on her, I'm scared shitless that she won't carry to term, and I know it will destroy Meiling. I told her we could adopt, even seriously thought about bringing home one of the kids we rescued when all that went down. She wanted to, but there were so many others ready to jump in, couples who had been together for a while and older widowers like Griz. We decided that we'd try to have a kid first and adopt later if it didn't work out."

"She's in good hands."

"Yeah, I know. So, how are things with the new woman?" He smiled a little. "I can see why you like her. She has that sweet and innocent look to her."

"That's because she was raised by a reverend and his wife. She *is* sweet and innocent."

Dingo stared a moment. "Are you telling me she's a virgin?"

"Yep. As tempted as I've been to toss her over my shoulder and go properly claim her, I don't want to fuck it all up either. Her first time should be special. Isn't that what all those damn romantic movies are about?"

He snorted. "Do I look like I would fucking know?"

"Really? You want to play that card? Do you really think I had no idea what you were reading all those times you thought you were being sneaky?"

"Shut up," he muttered. "Meiling already gives me shit about it."

"Learn anything?"

He flipped me off and I laughed. "Listen, I know that you want your girl to get to know everyone, but until Meiling is further along and we're certain the baby has a good chance of making it, I'd really prefer that she stay home as much as she can. If Elena wants to come over, that's fine."

"I'd introduce her to Adalia, but I never know how Badger will react. His woman is in the same boat as yours, but I really don't know if Adalia will survive losing another baby. I worried she'd hurt herself after the last one."

"Yeah." Dingo sat heavily on one of the kitchen chairs. "I think we all worried about that. She seemed so fragile for those first few weeks. I don't think the doc wanted her to get pregnant so soon. I'm hoping nothing bad happens to the baby."

Damn. I'd just realized three of the Devil's Fury women were pregnant all at the same time. Meiling, Adalia, and Lilian. At least the kids would all be close in age and have playmates. Pretty soon this place might start looking like the Reapers' compound. Another few years, we might be installing a playground like they did. I'd never thought I'd see the day that would happen. For so long we'd all remained single. Once Grizzly's wife died, there hadn't been any ol' ladies left except Magda and she was ancient. Then Badger had gotten out of prison and claimed Adalia. Just six months ago, Dingo had claimed Meiling. Now I had Elena. If Griz didn't kill Dragon for knocking up Lilian, I'd be willing to bet those two would pair up.

"We're all getting domesticated and shit," Dingo said. "Blades hasn't officially claimed China, but I think it has more to do with all she's been through than anything else. He doesn't want her to feel like he owns her. You should see them together when he thinks no one is looking. The man is completely in love with her."

"I'm sure that makes Mei happy. She finally has her parents."

"Yeah, the three of them just had to go through hell to find each other. So what are you going to do about your girl's situation?"

I didn't have a fucking clue what he was talking about. The look on my face must have conveyed that because he winced, and I could see him trying to backpedal, which meant he knew something I didn't.

"Start talking," I said. "What the fuck is going on?"

"Shit," he muttered. "I thought Demon messaged everyone about it. The Tolberts are missing. Disappeared along with Garrison West. No one has seen them or has any clue where they went. I don't know if he took them hostage or if they went willingly. I don't know if Wire is looking into it or not. He wanted to take the family out somewhere and has been gone the last hour."

"And since you don't know where West and the Tolberts went, they could be trying to track Elena."

I got up and ran to my room, yanked open the closet door and slammed my hand on the pad to open my secret space. My heart was hammering at the mere thought of someone trying to take her from me. Not after I'd just found her. I darted inside and threw myself into the chair. My fingers were flying over the keys faster than they had in ages as I hacked into the cameras near the church where the dear reverend presided over his flock. I didn't know how much time had passed before I saw them getting into an SUV with Garrison West. He didn't seem to have a gun on them, and the reverend looked pissed. The woman, though, she looked scared shitless.

I flexed my fingers and winced as they cracked and popped. Pain shot through them and up into my wrists going as far up as my elbows. As much as I wanted to keep going, I knew I was done. If I pushed it, the ache would reach my shoulders and I wouldn't be able to hold so much as a fucking pen for the next few days. I took note of the time stamp on the cameras, the location, and shot off an email to Wizard, Surge, and Shade. They'd have to track them from there.

"You going to tell her?" Dingo asked from behind me.

I spun my chair to face him. He leaned casually against the doorframe, but I noticed the way he was taking everything in. No one in the club had seen this space before. "Not until I know more. I don't want her to worry if they went willingly."

"I didn't know you had all this. Figured you did everything on your laptop."

"I use it when I need to bring stuff to Church. Most of my work was always done in here first. I have a secure link I use to share files between the two machines when needed, or I can save shit on a flash drive."

Dingo's gaze fastened on my hands, which I was still flexing. They hurt like a fucking bitch. He backed out of the room and I stood to follow, making sure the door slid shut and locked behind me. I didn't hear any sounds coming from the front of the house except the movie Elena had been watching. I crept that way and peered around the corner, smiling when I saw that both she and Mei were watching it. Mei had claimed my chair and propped up her feet, but the two seemed content.

"Is she okay?" Dingo whispered.

I walked off with him following. When I got to the kitchen, I started a fresh pot of coffee and just shook my head at him. I understood his worry, but I was surprised Mei hadn't beat him over the head with a skillet by now. He had to be driving her crazy.

"Your wife is fine. She's watching a movie with Elena, and they both seem comfortable and entertained." I pressed the button to start the machine and turned to face him. "Look, I get it. I really do, but eventually you're going to make your woman crazy by hovering."

"Meiling likes it when I hover," he muttered.

"No, I don't," Meiling yelled from the other room. "And I'm pregnant, not deaf. You're driving me crazy just like he said. Go work on your bike or something and let me breathe."

Dingo glanced that way with a narrowed gaze, but he stayed put. I knew the chances of him leaving her here were slim to none. Not unless I opened up my house to all the ladies. It wouldn't really bother me, and Elena might enjoy all that company. Pulling out my phone, I shot off a message to Badger, Griz, and Blades.

Elena and Mei are watching a movie at my place. Adalia, Shella, and China are welcome to come join.

I didn't know if Griz would see the message or not, but hopefully he'd get word to Shella. Might do her some good to be distracted right about now. I knew she had to be worried about her sister. Adalia, Shella, and Lilian were all adopted, but Shella and Lilian were particularly close. Or had been. Since Shella spilled the beans about Lilian's pregnancy, there might be a bit of a grudge right now, which would explain why she'd run before Grizzly could get to his house. Something told me she hadn't planned on telling him until she couldn't hide the pregnancy anymore.

I got a message from Badger first, or rather from his phone. I had to laugh when I read it. *I'm coming whether he lets me or not.*

"Think Adalia is heading this way. I'm sure Badger will be right on her heels."

"You still got a grill out back?" Dingo asked.

"Yeah. There's a table and four chairs back there too. Wolf put in a deck for me a few months back and it looked a little bare. Grabbed the table set on clearance. Why?" I asked.

"I'm going to have a Prospect bring some steaks and beer over. If Badger is coming with Adalia, I have no doubt that Blades will come with China. If she agrees to leave the house at all."

"Right. So the girls get the house and we'll hang out back so everyone can hover over their women but stay out of sight."

Dingo flipped me off, but I knew that's exactly what he was thinking. It wasn't long before Shella showed up with Dagger in tow. I didn't even ask. I'd have thought Griz told him to watch over his youngest, except the look in Dagger's eyes said it was more personal than that. What was that saying? Not my circus, not my monkeys. I wasn't getting involved. At all.

"Hey, Shella. They're watching a movie in the living room. Go make yourself comfortable." She gave me a little wave and disappeared, leaving a disgruntled-looking Dagger in the kitchen with us. When Blades and China showed up, I was shocked as fucking hell. The timid woman didn't even look at any of us, just gave Blades a kiss on the cheek and wandered off.

After China left, Blades eyed Dingo. "My girl doing okay?"

"So far. I try to keep her as still as possible, but sometimes it's like wrangling a tornado." He glanced in the direction of the living room and lowered his voice. "Maybe you or China could talk to her. She might listen to her parents better than me."

Blades snorted. "Boy, if you're scared she'll hear you, then you're already screwed. That girl has you by the balls."

I coughed to cover my laugh, but Dagger was grinning as well. Everyone knew that Meiling had Dingo wrapped around her little finger. Anything she wanted, he'd give her if he could. I also knew that if anyone fucked with her, he'd take them down and make them bleed. Same went for Blades and China.

The front door slammed and Badger appeared a moment later, looking pissed as hell. Looked like Adalia got her wish and really was coming with or without him. I knew she was giving him hell, but it was clear to everyone how much he adored her. They'd been destined for one another. Even Griz hadn't stood in the way.

"Steaks and beer are on the way here by way of Prospect. Let's head out back so the ladies can breathe a little easier," I said. "We'll hear them if they need anything."

"Popcorn!" Shella yelled from the living room.

I heard the soft tread coming toward us and Elena came into view. She smiled my way, then went straight to the cabinet where I'd shown her I kept all the snack type stuff. She pulled out a few bags of popcorn and while she worked on fixing them, she grabbed soda, bottled water, and juice from the fridge.

"You need help, angel?" I asked.

"I've got it. I think y'all are making the others upset, though. Something about overbearing, suffocating men."

I reached out and tugged her closer, kissing her softly. "We're heading out back. Just yell if you need anything."

She gave my beard a quick yank, then went back to what she was doing. I herded the guys out back and quickly realized I didn't have enough chairs. A quick text to the Prospect bringing the supplies fixed the issue. I only hoped he brought enough beer. I had a feeling these guys would need it. Especially Badger and Dingo.

Chapter Nine

Elena

"They're gone," I said as I carried two bowls of popcorn to the living room. "Can someone help me grab the drinks? Outlaw offered, but I thought it would be better to get the men out of here faster."

"Thank God," Meiling muttered. "I love Dingo, but he's driving me crazy with all the hovering."

"If you think he's bad, you should see Badger," Adalia said.

"Your men worry for you," China said in her heavily accented voice. "It's a good thing. They love you. Why would you complain about that?"

Meiling reached over and took her mom's hand. I hadn't learned much about any of these women, but Mei had immediately introduced China as her mother. Shella was the youngest of the group, and so far the most talkative. With her sister missing, I'd expected her to be reserved. I had to wonder if she was just trying not to think about it, and talking was her way of keeping her mind off things.

"I'll help," Shella said, jumping up from her seat. I eyed the living room and realized we were all crammed on the couch with no space to spare. I wasn't about to ask any of the pregnant ladies to lift anything, though. After Shella helped with the drinks, I'd grab two of the kitchen chairs and bring them in.

She followed me to the kitchen and we grabbed as many bottles and cans as we could, then took it all to the living room. While Shella handed out the drinks, I went back for the two chairs. Meiling had claimed

Outlaw's chair when she'd arrived, but now Adalia and China had more space on the couch. I didn't think there were more women who would pop in, but we'd have an extra spot if there was. I knew Lavender and Wire were still here somewhere, even though I hadn't seen them since earlier.

"Does Outlaw do the alpha male thing where he tells you what to do and when to do it?" Adalia asked. "Badger's worse about it when we aren't at home."

"Um, maybe a little. He'd probably be worse if I were pregnant, though."

She laughed. "Oh, don't even doubt it. To be fair, the club doesn't have kids running around yet. I've had two miscarriages and Meiling hasn't had much luck either. It's her first with Dingo, though, so we're all hoping this one makes it."

I wasn't sure what to say to that. I didn't know anything about these ladies. How had they met their men? Why had they decided to stay? Or were their guys like Outlaw and just decided they were keeping them? It wouldn't have surprised me.

Meiling shared a look with Adalia and her mother before turning her gaze toward me. "We all have some pretty horrific pasts, except Shella. She was more sheltered, even though she didn't have it easy either. Our guys can be a bit much to handle, but at least we know they care. For me, it was the first time I'd ever felt wanted."

My gaze shot over to China to see if she was offended, but she offered a soft smile.

"My daughter was taken from me when she was very little. I was sold to a brothel and she was placed in a very bad foster home. Blades was in prison at the time. It was only six months ago that we all found each other again." China glanced at her daughter. "I was worried my Meiling wouldn't want me in her life after the life I'd led, but my baby needed me so I came home with Blades."

My heart ached for what they'd suffered. Adalia didn't share her story, but I had to wonder if something equally as bad had happened. She'd said she had a horrific past, but I didn't know what that meant. While I'd been in foster care, the reverend and his wife had never hurt me or abused me.

"What do you think of the club so far?" Shella asked. "When I first found out my half-sister had a daddy in the Devil's Boneyard MC, I wasn't sure what to think. My mom started fucking up her life even more and I ended up taking Payson to Irish. To say he was shocked was an understatement, and his woman was less than pleased."

My jaw dropped a little. "He had a kid with your mom while he was with someone else?"

"No! No, Irish and my mom had a fling before he'd claimed Janessa. But she's great with Payson. They offered to let me stay, but I didn't want to be in the way. Grizzly took me in and I've loved living here. He's been the best dad."

"I haven't really been around the club yet. I came to a party and someone drugged my drink. It's how I ended up at Outlaw's house," I said.

"I heard Demon gave that bitch a lesson she won't soon forget," Meiling said. "I'm just glad they figured out who was behind it, and why she was doing it. That could have ended badly for the club."

It got quiet and no one seemed to know what to say. I didn't either for that matter. I wanted friends, though, and if these ladies were attached to guys in the club, then I'd be seeing them a lot. Or so I thought. I rubbed my hands up and down my thighs, a bit nervous. What if they didn't like me?

"I don't normally do stuff like go to a biker club. I was passing through and the lady at the motel said I should check this place out. She left out exactly what the Devil's Fury was when she gave me directions."

Adalia laughed. "I bet that was a surprise. You seem a little…"

I rolled my eyes. "Yeah. I know. Outlaw says I look all sweet and innocent."

"Are you?" Meiling asked.

My cheeks warmed. "Not as much now as I was that's for sure. I don't know what it is about that man, but I seem to lose all sense when he's around."

The snickers told me that I wasn't the only one who suffered from that affliction when it came to the Devil's Fury men. Even Shella was blushing a bit and cast a glance toward the back of the house. I'd noticed when she arrived that the man at her heels had seemed extremely interested in what she was doing. Now I wondered if she felt the same about him. He'd been quite a bit older than her, but Outlaw was over a decade older than me. Age didn't seem to matter much around here.

"So what trouble followed you here?" Adalia asked. "It seems to be a common theme. Meiling was trying to escape the owner of the strip club, among others. China was brought here by Blades when he found her in a brothel. Grizzly and May checked up on me after Badger found me in an alley. He killed the man who was raping me and went to prison. Shella's mom was an addict who didn't give a shit about her kids, only her next fix. And Lilian…"

Shella sighed. "It's my fault she's gone. She didn't want Grizzly to know about the baby. I thought someone had hurt her. I didn't know she'd wanted to be with Dragon. After all she went through in Colombia, I didn't see how she could stand to be touched."

My mouth opened and shut a few times. My life hadn't been anything like theirs. Sure, I'd lost my parents when I was younger and went into the system, but I'd lucked out. Escaping a marriage to Garrison West had been lucky, but I hadn't even realized I was in danger. I'd just known I didn't want to marry him, so I'd left. My story was so… tame compared to theirs.

"A man I knew as Garrison West, but the club knows him as Bastard, wanted to marry me. My foster parents were pushing me to accept so I left when no one would take no for an answer," I said. "But until then, my life hadn't been bad. Strict, and a bit suffocating at times, but no one had ever hurt me."

"I heard Badger grumbling about Bastard," Adalia said. "He's bad news and I'm so glad you didn't end up in his hands. I overheard part of his conversation on the phone. Something about the marriages not always being legal and he made the women whores or drug mules."

I nodded, that's what Outlaw had shared with me. I didn't know if he was supposed to tell me or not, but I was glad that he had. It made me feel a little less silly for running when I did. I only wished I knew if my foster parents were in on it, if they'd known who he was and what he'd wanted with me, or if they were in danger. If he'd heard anything since we'd talked, he hadn't brought it up.

I didn't know how these women lived like this, with only being told certain things, even when it pertained to them. Didn't it bother them? I knew that Outlaw thought he was keeping me safe, but wouldn't it be better if I knew that danger was coming? Of course, he'd said he wasn't an officer, so I assumed that meant he didn't make the rules and just followed them.

"I know that look," Adalia said. "That look spells trouble. What are you thinking?"

I chewed my lower lip. "Well, wouldn't it be better if we knew when we were in danger? I mean, it's great the guys want to protect us and all, but if trouble is coming I would think we'd be less likely to have something bad happen if we knew to watch for it. Right?"

Meiling sat forward a little. "Go on."

"What if we demanded that they tell us when bad things are coming down on the club, or if one of us has garnered the attention of someone who wants to hurt one or all of us?" I asked. "That's stupid, right? They'd never go for that."

China smiled faintly. "You'd be surprised what men will be willing to do with the proper motivation."

Shella folded her arms over her chest. "Great. I have nothing to withhold since none of the guys here will touch me."

Adalia arched an eyebrow at her. "None *here*, but you're hooking up with someone somewhere, aren't you?"

Shella blushed and nodded. "A few guys at the college. Nothing serious. It's just some fun."

Something told me that none of the guys knew about it, especially the one who had followed her. I could see him using any of those poor college guys as target practice. No doubt she was going to be trouble for whatever guy who tried to wrangle her.

The back door slamming into a wall startled me and I shot up out of my chair. I whirled to face the rear of the house and Outlaw, along with the others, came charging through. He stopped in front of me, placing his hands at my waist, and I could tell by the look in his eyes that something was really wrong.

"We just got word from Grizzly," he said.

Shella shot up out of her chair. "What? Is something wrong with Lilian?"

"He lost her trail, but Dragon was still searching for her," Outlaw said. "That's not the news. Attila contacted him once he reviewed the files that were sent over about the rat infestation, and the trouble Bastard is trying to cause. He thinks it's Shepherd, who is conveniently missing."

"And my foster family? Are they involved? Was anyone able to find out?" I asked.

Pain flashed in his eyes. "Angel, your foster mom is gone. Her body was found on the side of the road. They shot her and dumped her."

My heart slammed against my ribs and I felt tears well in my eyes. "They?" My voice cracked, but I didn't care. The woman hadn't been the warmest, but she'd taken me in when I didn't have anywhere else to go.

"We think the reverend is part of the scam," Outlaw said.

"It's worse," Badger said. "Don't hide this shit from her. You see any officers here? You think any of us are keeping this from our women?"

"What's going on?" I asked.

"Your foster father, the good Reverend Tolbert, is the brother to Shepherd at the Savage Raptors. It's not a coincidence that Bastard ended up as a deacon of that church. We think your foster dad went and got him the night he was left for dead, and they've probably been working together this entire time," Outlaw said.

"And if your foster dad is related to a traitor, and helped Bastard all this time, it's possible he's partly responsible for the women who were put into brothels or used as drug mules. Don't shed any tears for that asshole," Badger said.

China was clinging to Blades and I had to wonder if this was all too much for her. Meiling looked a little pale too.

"Grizzly wants a handful of us to go help the Savage Raptors track down the three men. I'm volunteering," Blades said. "I couldn't keep you safe, but maybe I can prevent them sending any other women into a situation like yours. I'll return soon, my China."

I looked away as he leaned down to kiss her. My heart was breaking. Not just because a man I'd thought was good ended up being evil, and not just for the loss of Suzy Tolbert, but for these women with traumatic pasts who were having to face all this again. I felt like I'd brought this to their door. If I hadn't shown up, if Outlaw hadn't brought me to his house and asked me all those questions, would this ugliness have ever touched the Devil's Fury?

"Angel, whatever dark thoughts just went through your head, forget them," Outlaw said.

"If I hadn't come here --" He pressed a finger to my lips, silencing me.

"Without you, we may not have ever known what was happening, which means that Attila may not have found out for several more years. If ever. Think of all the women you could be saving, all the ones they won't be able to hurt once we catch them," Outlaw said.

"He's right." Meiling pulled away from Dingo and came closer, placing her hand on my shoulder.

"No one deserves to live that kind of hell. It's a painful reminder of my past, and same for my mother, but we'd rather our guys go off and stop those monsters before others are hurt."

"Thanks," I said. "I needed to hear that."

Outlaw cupped my cheek, drawing my focus back to him. The worry in his eyes made my stomach clench. He glanced at the others and seemed to do some sort of silent communication that cleared not only the room but the house. Everyone left, and we were alone once more.

"We're leaving in a few hours," he said.

"Guess that means you need to pack."

He pulled me tighter against him. "No, it means I need to officially claim my woman. Then I need to pack."

I gave him a faint smile and pushed up on my toes so I could kiss him. "Only you would think of sex at a time like this."

"Baby, with you around, I'm *always* thinking about sex."

Chapter Ten

Outlaw

I locked up the house to make sure we wouldn't be interrupted, then I led Elena to the bedroom. If she'd thought I was kidding about claiming her, she was wrong. No fucking way I was going off without making sure she was mine in every way possible. In fact… *Work your magic and make Elena my wife.*

It only took Wire a second to respond. *Did that earlier. You've been married for the last few hours.*

That fucker. He must have done that after Church. I smiled and tossed the phone aside, pulling Elena against me. She placed her hands on my chest, but she didn't push me away. She fisted the material of my shirt and held on.

"When I get back, we'll go ring shopping," I said. "Unless you want to tell me your size now and I'll surprise you."

"Ring size? I don't need a ring, Noah."

"My wife certainly does need a ring."

Her eyes widened slightly. "Wife?"

"Let's just say if anyone goes looking, they'll find all the proper papers saying we're married. If you want an actual wedding, then we can talk about it when I get back, but as far as the world is concerned you're now Elena Borden."

Her brow furrowed. "Like that girl that murdered her family?"

"Lizzie Borden?" I asked. When she nodded, I debated admitting the truth. I'd seen the look in people's eyes when I'd answered that question in the past, but decided not to keep it from her. "Distant cousins. Her direct line ended with her and her sister, but I'm related through her father's side several generations back. We share a great-great-whatever grandfather. Like I said, distant. Very, very distant."

"Elena Borden," she said, as if she were trying out the name. She smiled up at me. "I like it."

"Good, because I wasn't giving you a choice. You're mine, angel, and I'm never letting you go."

Her grip on my shirt tightened. "I didn't want you to."

I kissed her, taking possession of her mouth like a starving man. Her lips parted and I deepened the kiss, wrapping my arms around her. I didn't know why fate had picked her for me, but I wouldn't argue. There was no one like Elena in all the world, and she was mine. Only mine. Forever.

I made quick work of removing my clothes. Her hungry gaze watched my every move, and I could see her nipples harden under her shirt. When I reached for her, she came willingly, let me strip her until I could hold her naked body against mine. I ached for her and worried that this would be over far too fast.

"We don't have a lot of time," I said, glancing at my phone display from where I'd tossed it on the floor. "I need to know we're on the same page, Elena. No condoms. I want kids with you, if it's at all possible. I know I'd said that I would give you time, but I don't want to. I want a family with you more than I've ever wanted anything."

She ran her fingers through my beard. "I ran from a man who wanted to keep me pregnant, or so I'd thought. But he wasn't you, Noah. I want a family with you too, and I don't care when it happens. If you want to try now, I'm okay with that."

I cupped her cheek and kissed her softly. "I don't know what I ever did to deserve you."

"You're a bad boy biker." She smiled. "It's probably the other way around. You're *my* reward for being so good all these years."

"I can live with that." I lifted her into my arms and walked over to the bed, then eased her down onto the mattress. She looked so beautiful spread across my bed. I stretched out beside her, trailing my fingers over her soft skin. Her nipples hardened more, and I lightly brushed my thumb across one.

Elena gasped and arched into my touch. I gave the peak a little pinch before leaning over to take it into my mouth. I flicked the bud with my tongue before scraping my teeth over it. I felt her fingers grip the back of my neck as she tried to hold me in place. Smiling, I pulled away just to show her I could. She growled in frustration, which was cute as hell, but it quickly turned to a moan when I focused on her other nipple.

I loved how responsive she was. I stroked my hand across her belly, then a little lower. My fingers brushed the top of her slit and I could already tell she was wet. I rubbed my beard across her breasts as I slid a finger into her tight pussy. She felt so fucking incredible that I worried I'd blow the second I got inside her.

My phone started ringing on the floor, but I ignored it. Those fuckers could give me enough time to be with Elena at least once. She reached up and grabbed my beard, forcing me to look at her for fear she'd yank it out.

"What, angel?"

"They need you. We're out of time."

"They can fucking wait," I said. "I'm only sorry this isn't the most romantic setting for your first time."

"Noah, I don't need flowers or anything. I just need you." She kissed me. "Now shut up and make me yours."

"I don't want to hurt you." It wasn't that I'd been with a virgin before, but I'd heard that it could sometimes hurt a woman the first time. The last thing I wanted to do was cause her pain right before I left.

Elena tugged on me so I covered her body with mine. Her legs parted and I settled between them. My heart was pounding and I didn't remember feeling this way even my first time with a girl. My cock nudged against her slick folds. I reached between us to get the right position, then slowly sank into her. She paled, but otherwise she didn't show any signs of discomfort.

With one hard thrust, I buried myself inside her. She gasped and tensed a moment, but gradually, she began to relax. My dick pulsed and twitched inside her. She was so fucking tight, and felt so damn right. I was nearly shaking from the effort to not take what I wanted. If we'd had more time, I'd have jerked off first so I'd have had more control.

"I'm fine," she said. "Really. It pinched a moment and there was a bit of a burn as you stretched me open, but it's not painful."

"I can move without hurting you?"

She nodded.

I gave her a few short, slow thrusts, just to test if she was telling the truth or what she thought I wanted to hear. When she didn't seem to be in any pain, I took her harder and faster. Our bodies slapped together, but I knew I couldn't hold out long. Not this first time. It had been over four years since I'd been inside a woman, and even if it had just been yesterday, Elena felt like perfection and would have still tested my limits.

Using my thumb, I circled her clit. It took a few tries to get just the right amount of pressure and speed, but soon she was gasping and arching, trying to get even closer to me. I shifted my hips on the next thrust and must have hit the right spot because she came, crying out my name. The heat of her release made my balls sizzle, and it only took another three strokes before I was filling her with my cum.

I kissed her as my cock jerked and the last few spurts shot from the tip into her. I savored her taste and wished the moment could last forever, but the damn phone was ringing again. Reluctantly, I drew back and stared down at her. Her cheeks were rosy and her eyes were shining brightly. I wanted to remember her like this forever, all happy and content, sated.

"My perfect angel," I said, toying with her hair. "I wish we had more time."

"I understand, Noah. Just go and hurry home. But be safe. If anything happens to you…" She drew in a sharp breath. "I can't lose you. I know we're still new, but I think it would break my heart if you didn't come home."

I traced her nose with mine. "I'll come home to you. Whatever it takes."

Kissing her one last time, I withdrew from her body. It killed me to rush through a shower instead of getting to spend a few more hours with Elena. It was one thing to fuck and run with some club whore or one-night stand, but my angel was my one and only. It felt wrong on so many levels. Waiting would have been better, but despite my reassurance to her that I'd return, part of me knew there was always a chance I wouldn't make it. Being part of the club meant there were always risks. I'd accepted that when I'd asked to prospect.

She was curled up in the bed, the covers pulled up to her chin as I quickly pulled on my clothes and shoved a few things into a bag. I hoped we wouldn't be gone too long, but it was a good twelve to thirteen hours from here to Bryson Corners. And since I was going, it would take even longer unless I took one of the club trucks. As much as I loved riding my bike, with my fucked-up hands, I couldn't handle long trips. Even holding the steering wheel of a car was difficult after a half hour, but it was still easier than handling a bike that long of a distance.

When I was packed up, made sure I had the weapons I might need and enough ammo, then sent a quick *I'm fucking coming* to Dingo so they'd leave me the fuck alone, I knelt on the bed next to Elena and leaned over her. She tipped her face up and I kissed her, trying to show her everything I was feeling and didn't have time to say. I backed away, grabbed my bag, and walked out after one last lingering look at my woman. I knew if I didn't get the hell out of the house, I'd never leave her.

There was already a truck in the driveway with the engine running, so I knew one of my brothers had realized I wouldn't be able to take my bike. I wasn't sure if I wanted to thank them, or start cussing because I felt like a damn cripple. I tossed the bag into the backseat, then removed the gun from the back of my jeans. I put it in the compartment in the armrest for easy access, but hoped like hell I wouldn't need it. Technically, you weren't supposed to store a firearm in the car that was loaded, but it wasn't like we gave a shit about the law. We broke it a hundred different ways all the damn time.

I pulled away and went straight to the gates where Dingo, Blades, Badger, Slash, and Hot Shot were already waiting. Slash took the lead with the others following and I started to pull forward and take the rear position when someone pounded on the passenger side. I stopped and Beau jumped in. He held up his hands and I knew it wasn't his idea to babysit me, but I could understand. If my hands got too bad, it made sense to have someone else who could drive for a while.

"Fine. But don't speak to me," I said as I pulled forward again, catching up to my brothers and taking the rear spot.

"For the record, I volunteered when they said they needed someone in the truck with you," Beau said. "I have a lot of shit to make up for."

I snorted. That was a fucking understatement. After the hell he'd left Meiling in, I was surprised Dingo hadn't just fucking outright killed him. If it had been my woman, Beau would be in pieces buried in multiple graves by now. I might have even left him alive while I hacked him up.

"You don't have to even acknowledge I'm here, but if you need me to drive at some point just let me know. Slash said they were driving straight through with minimal stops."

Great. Just fucking great. I sighed, knowing I'd have to ask him to drive at least once, maybe more. Nothing could make me feel more like shit than admitting I couldn't do something as well as a damn Prospect. I knew it wasn't my fault and couldn't be helped, but it didn't make it any easier to swallow.

If we made it back home safe and sound, I'd have to talk to Grizzly and Slash. As much as I wanted to give the club everything I could, trips like these just weren't going to be possible. I'd only tried this once since the incident, and it hadn't gone too well. Probably why they'd stuck me with Beau.

There were times I wasn't sure if I was any damn good to them anymore. I couldn't work a keyboard as well as before. Yeah, I could get shit started and do basic stuff a ten-year-old could figure out, but any heavy lifting had to come from outside the club. Couldn't drive long distance without help. Couldn't lift heavy shit, or grip things for too long. What fucking good was I?

My phone started ringing and I tried to pull it from my pocket. I fumbled it a few times, trying to answer the fucking thing before I threw it at Beau.

"Take care of that."

He cleared his throat and showed me the screen. *Elena*. I didn't remember putting her number in my phone, but I didn't keep it locked and she'd had plenty of chances to do something like that. Beau handed the phone back and I answered the call, putting the phone to my ear.

"Everything okay, angel?" I asked.

"How far away are you?" she asked, her voice so soft I barely heard her. My stomach knotted and I jerked the truck over to the side of the highway, stopping.

"Elena, what's wrong?"

"I'm not sure. There was a loud bang and a lot of popping sounds. I heard a lot of shouting and now everything is quiet. Too quiet." She let out a breath that sounded shaky even over the phone. "I'm scared, Noah."

"I'm coming. Find a place to hide and stay there. Make sure your phone is on silent so it won't make any noises and give away your location."

"Hurry."

The line went dead and I tossed the phone on the seat, then yanked the steering wheel, and headed back the way we'd come. Beau didn't say anything, but as I pressed the pedal harder, he reached up to grab onto the oh-shit handle. A glance in the rearview showed that one of my brothers had turned around as well, but the others kept going. I didn't know if he was coming to find out what was going on, or if someone had called him too.

Beau glanced in the sideview mirror, then turned to look out the back. "I think it's Blades."

"Whoever it is, I hope they were warned there's trouble ahead. Elena said she heard a loud bang and a lot of pops, some shouts, and then it all went quiet. I think the compound is under attack, or was. I have no idea who the winning side was, but I'm not taking any chances."

Beau grabbed his phone and started texting. I didn't know who he was trying to reach and I didn't much care right then. All I could think about was getting to Elena. We'd only been gone about thirty minutes, if that. Since I was driving a lot faster than before, I hoped we'd get there in about fifteen or less. As we neared the clubhouse, I saw the black plumes of smoke and my heart nearly seized.

What the fuck?

I didn't even slow down as I hit the town limits and I flew through the open gates of the compound. The clubhouse looked like it had been in a warzone. Most of the building was gone and the other half was falling down. The two houses closest to it were also in shambles. Bodies lay across the parking lot, and I saw two that said *Prospect* across the back. The other bodies weren't wearing colors.

A woman stood in the center of it all, her hair looking a little fried, and her clothes were covered in grime. She was screaming and waving a gun around. The truck either hadn't caught her attention, or she'd decided we weren't a threat. It was in that moment I realized who she was yelling at.

I jumped out of the truck. "Elena!"

My woman turned a startled gaze my way before focusing on the idiot with the gun. She kept ranting, and I couldn't make sense of it at first.

"You couldn't just marry him? You ruined everything! We had a plan. It was all a done deal, then you went and fucked it up," the woman screamed.

I caught movement from the side of the clubhouse that was still mostly standing. I couldn't make out who it was, but he was wearing Devil's Fury colors. When he turned back around and I saw the rifle, I knew exactly who was there. Only Steel had a 12 gauge like that one. The crack of the rifle echoed around us as the woman fell to the ground. I didn't even stop to see if she was dead, just went running straight for Elena.

"I told you to fucking hide," I yelled as I jerked her into my arms. My heart was about to beat out of my chest.

"I didn't have a choice," she said. "Shella was out there. One of your guys got her away when I distracted Martha."

"Martha?" I asked.

"Martha Simms. She went to our church. I didn't even realize she was that close to Garrison, but if any of her ramblings were to be believed, she was in on it with him. How many people are involved in this? Is the entire church in on it?" she asked.

"I don't know, angel. I'm just thankful as fuck that you're all right. I nearly had a heart attack when I realized you were in trouble." I hesitated a second, not wanting to scare her further. "Any idea how she knew where to find you?"

"She didn't say. I didn't have a phone she could track. I thought I turned off the GPS thing in my car. How else could she have done it?" she asked.

I didn't know, but I'd love to find out. Although, if we settled this issue, then it wouldn't matter if anyone knew where she was because she'd be safe from these assholes.

"Is anyone else concerned that Blades was right behind us but didn't come through the gates?" Beau asked as he walked over. "Or the fact Wire and Lavender could have been in the clubhouse?"

Steel joined us, slinging his rifle over his shoulder. "Bike flew past right as you came barreling through the gate. Guessing it was Blades, in which case, he saw something you missed. We'll probably get a call for a clean-up soon. Wire and Lavender took their kid home already. Left about ten minutes after y'all drove off. As for you two, Slash said he still needs you. Reinforcements are heading our way, and part of the Hades Abyss are joining you in Oklahoma."

I held Elena tighter, knowing there was no damn way I could leave her here. Not with the gates wide open and the clubhouse blown apart. I still wasn't sure what had happened, but it seemed I didn't have time to ask questions right now.

"Take her with you," Steel said. "The Boneyard crew is offering spots to the women for now, but I know you won't sleep easy with her so far away. Not with all the shit circling her. Havoc, Jackal, and Stripes are coming to get Meiling and the others."

Beau started back for the truck. "I'll take you to your house so Elena can pack a bag. I'll drive to Bryson Corners. She needs you right now."

Normally, I'd smack the shit out of him for giving orders, but he was right about my woman needing me. I kept an arm around her as I led her over to the still-running vehicle. I opened the back door and helped her in, then got in right next to her. It didn't take long to pack a week's worth of clothes for her, and any other essentials she needed, then we were back on the road. I remained in the back so I could keep her calm.

This shit was getting ridiculous. Whatever it took, we had to put a stop to Bastard and Shepherd.

Chapter Eleven

Elena

I didn't know what I'd expected of the trip to Bryson Corners, but the Savage Raptors' compound wasn't like anything I'd seen before. Sure, they had a clubhouse like the Devil's Fury, and I had no doubt there were wild parties there too. They also had a garage where they worked on their bikes, enough homes for their members, a group of three duplexes that seemed to be used for guests, and a small building that I'd been told had studio apartments for the Prospects and a few of the club girls. They'd spared my delicate sensibilities by not calling them whores or sluts. I'd barely refrained from rolling my eyes when they tried to put a different spin on exactly why those women were here.

Their club was bigger than I'd thought it would be. Since the Devil's Fury felt like they needed to help, I was expecting small numbers. I'd never remember all the people I'd met so far. I lost count after about the fifteenth patched member, and I knew they had at least another twenty, plus all the Prospects. Outlaw had refused to leave my side, and kept muttering something about me not having a property cut yet. Not that I thought he had to worry. He'd done just about everything except pee on me to make sure everyone knew I was off-limits. It would have been cute if hadn't been so damn annoying.

My stomach was in knots already because I knew that Garrison was somewhere nearby, and my foster father too, most likely. Since Martha had come for me, I had to wonder if they knew their operation had been blown apart. She'd said I messed everything up. I wasn't quite sure what that meant. It could have been something as simple as they needed another woman to replace me, or it could have meant they knew the club was on to them.

"Outlaw, you're the one who first discovered this mess. We need you to go into Church and tell them how it all started," Slash said.

Outlaw's hand tightened on mine and I knew he was about to refuse. I wasn't sure what was and wasn't allowed. I tried to make eye contact with Dingo, hoping he would understand Outlaw's fear of releasing me and find a solution. He finally noticed what must have been a panicked expression on my face and he hustled over from where he'd been talking to two Raptors.

"What's going on?" Dingo asked as he stopped in front of us.

"I need Outlaw to head into Church with the Raptors," Slash said.

Dingo's gaze dropped to where Outlaw was gripping my hand. I was starting to worry I'd lose feeling in my fingers. For someone who said their hands didn't work that great, he sure did have strength when he needed it.

"Elena can hang with me while you go take care of that," Dingo said. "I'll keep an eye on her."

Outlaw reluctantly released me. I leaned up to kiss his cheek and watched him walk off with Slash. Flexing my hand, I stared at my fingers and wondered when the tingling sensation would go away. Dingo laughed softly and slung his arm around my shoulders, leading me back over to the men he'd been talking to.

"Elena, this is Stinger and Truth. Guys, this is Outlaw's woman," Dingo said, motioning to each as he introduced them.

Truth eyed me up and down. "She's not marked."

Marked? Did he mean the property thing? Or was I supposed to wear a damn sign that said I belonged to someone?

"We don't necessarily ink our women," Dingo said. "They can get a property stamp if they want one, but we only make them wear a cut. Hers just hasn't been finished yet."

"And he let her come here?" Stinger asked.

"Someone tried to kill me and blew apart the gates at the compound," I said. I felt Dingo tense next to me and I looked up, realizing that perhaps he hadn't known that. "Meiling and China were fine. They were being sent to the Devil's Boneyard with the other women. Slash apparently set it up so I thought you knew."

"This related to what's going on here?" Truth asked.

"The guy you know as Bastard was part of my foster father's church. He wanted to marry me, but I ran off when everyone was getting too pushy about it. One of the ladies from church attacked the compound with some other men," I said.

"What men?" Dingo asked.

"They weren't wearing any identifying marks. Steel was there. He may know more," I said.

"You boys always have this much drama over there?" Stinger asked.

I tipped my head to the side and studied the men. "Wasn't Bastard one of yours? Seems to me the drama started here."

Dingo coughed, but I felt him shaking with laughter. The look he cast my way told me I should probably shut up, even if he did find me amusing. Truth's narrowed gaze said the Raptors didn't appreciate it so much.

"Mouthy wench," Stinger said. "Might want to watch that around here. It seems the Devil's Fury is a little more lax with their women."

I glanced around, almost expecting to see women with leashes the way he was talking. I'd known that bikers were different and I needed to watch what I said or did. The last thing I wanted was for Outlaw to get in trouble because of me, or for these guys to look down on him.

"She's just shook up from what happened," Dingo said. "Besides, she's only been around the club a short while. It will take her some time to adjust."

"Didn't start out as a club girl?" Truth asked.

My back stiffened. Not that I looked down on those women, but no, I most certainly hadn't been one of them. Until Outlaw had claimed me, I'd still been a virgin. No man had ever seen me naked except him. For that matter, I'd never seen a naked man until him either.

"This one is the reverend's foster daughter," Dingo said. "She was sweet and innocent before Outlaw corrupted her."

Truth came closer, his eyes going dark. "Are you telling me this bitch lived with that man? And you think she's not been a part of it? I bet she's been feeding them information. That it? You a rat?"

"N-No," I stammered. "I'd never do anything to hurt Outlaw or his club."

He snarled like an angry beast. "Bullshit. I bet I can make you talk."

Before I could process what was happening, he'd yanked me away from Dingo and was dragging me to a back hall. I heard Dingo struggling to reach me, but when I looked over my shoulder I saw that three of the Raptors had him pinned. My heart was slamming against my ribs, and I barely kept my footing as Truth pulled me down the dark hallway and shoved me into a room.

I stumbled and caught myself against a metal table. He took advantage and cuffed me to it. Yanking hard, I tried to break free, but I couldn't. I cried out as he slammed me down on the table, my cheek pressed to the cold surface.

"They may trust you, but I don't."

"Please," I begged. "I'm not part of what's happening. I didn't even know about the Devil's Fury before I ran away."

He leaned over me, caging me in and pushing me harder into the unforgiving metal table. "Did they send you down there? Make you pretend to be a virgin so you could snag the club's attention? Because you screwed up. Should have fucked an officer instead of Outlaw."

Tears burned my eyes, but I couldn't even try to fight back. The way he'd pinned me, I couldn't move, could barely even breathe. I heard a crash from somewhere nearby and a roar of outrage. The door to the room slammed into the wall and Outlaw threw himself at Truth. They fell to the floor and Outlaw immediately started hitting the other man.

"Jesus." My gaze shot to the doorway as I tried to stand up. An older man stood there, horror in his eyes as he looked from the men on the floor to me. He quickly came into the room and unfastened the cuffs. "Sorry, girly. Not sure what came over Truth."

I turned to face the men and saw Truth slam Outlaw's head into the wall. As he staggered and slumped to the floor, I screamed and tried to run to him, but the man who had freed me held me back.

"Truth, get the fuck out and go straight to my damn office," the man yelled.

"But, Pres…"

The man holding onto me growled. "I said right the fuck now. You've fucked up royally this time. She's protected by the Devil's Fury, one of their ol' ladies. What the hell is wrong with you?"

Truth spat blood on the floor. "She's the reverend's daughter. You don't find that a little too convenient?"

"You're a fucking idiot. If it weren't for her, we wouldn't have known we have a damn rat, or that Bastard was still alive." The man released me and I ran to Outlaw, kneeling beside him as Truth was shoved from the room. "I'll have some men come in and get him up. The club doctor can look him over."

"No," I said. "Not your men. I don't trust them."

The guy sighed. "Fair enough. My name's Attila, and I'm the club president. I apologize for the idiot who accosted you. He'll be dealt with. I don't tolerate that kind of shit around here."

He stepped out and I heard him shouting. Dingo and Slash came into the room. Both of them started cussing when they saw the shape Outlaw was in. He had a busted lip, his knuckles were bleeding on both hands, and a bruise was already forming on his right cheek. That was just what I could see, but I had a feeling he had bruises elsewhere too.

"I'm so fucking sorry," Dingo said. "I tried to stop him, tried to come after you, but they held me back."

"I'm fine, but I'm not so sure about Outlaw," I said.

"Let's get him up, and we'll take him to the place you'll be staying tonight. I'll make sure you have the place to yourselves. If you need anything, one of us will be next door. They were going to have us pile into one of the duplexes, but fuck that shit," Slash said.

They lifted Outlaw and half-carried him between them. He was awake, but he stumbled the first few steps. I could tell he was hurting, and I was so angry I wanted to scream. We went out into the hall and I heard Attila yelling at his men. By the time we made it to the common area, half the Raptors wouldn't hold eye contact with us, but two of them came forward. I glared and they froze.

"We just want to help. I'm Maui and this is Ravager. I'm sorry for what Truth did. It was uncalled for."

"At least tell us what you need and we'll personally see to it," Ravager said. "Anything."

"Outlaw and Elena will be taking one half of the duplex and we'll need the other side for the rest of us," Slash said. "I want to be close in case they need me, but I think they should have some space."

"Not a problem," Attila said. "Elena, please make a list of anything you need while you're here. The club will take care of it at no cost to you or the Devil's Fury." Slash growled and Attila held up a hand. "I know it doesn't make up for what Truth did, but I'll make sure Outlaw is compensated not just for bringing attention to Bastard and Shepherd's dealings, but also for the trouble he and his woman encountered from my club."

Outlaw mumbled something that I didn't quite catch. I leaned in closer and he said it again, his gaze holding mine. *Should have bought you a ring.*

"A ring?" I asked. "You're worried about me having a wedding ring right now? Are you kidding me?"

He gave a half-smile, then winced when it made his lip bleed more.

"Wedding ring?" Attila asked.

"She's not just his ol' lady," Badger said. "She's his wife."

Attila closed his eyes, muttered under his breath, then gazed at his crew with pure hostility. I had a feeling they were in for a major ass-chewing once we were out of the clubhouse. Slash and Dingo helped Outlaw outside and then into the truck. Beau drove us to the duplex with the others following on their bikes. I could tell that Outlaw hated them seeing him like this, so once he was in the bedroom and seated on the edge of the mattress, I shooed everyone away.

I knelt at his feet and helped remove his boots, then carefully pulled his shirt over his head. I couldn't contain my gasp as I saw the damage that asshole had done to him. Bruises were forming across the ribs on his right side. I pressed on them, trying to figure out if they were broken, but I was far from a doctor and didn't have a clue what I was looking for.

"I'm sorry," he said.

"What? Noah, you have nothing to be sorry for."

He shook his head. "I didn't protect you. First that bitch got to you at the compound, and then I left you in a room full of men I've never met. I came out of Church and saw them pinning Dingo to the wall and you nowhere in sight. He yelled out that Truth had taken you down the hall."

"I'm fine." I rubbed my hands up and down his thighs. "Really. I was scared, and I didn't know what he'd do to me, but he didn't hurt me."

Outlaw lifted his hand to my face and I grasped it, then pressed it to my cheek. "Couldn't fight him off. After the first few blows, it was hard to maintain a fist."

I kissed him. "Noah, you charged in there and protected me. That's all that matters. I hate that your hands hurt you so much, but if you're worried I'll think less of you, then you're wrong."

"None of us do," Badger said from the doorway.

I gasped and turned to face him. "Where did you come from? All of you left."

"Came back to make sure you didn't need anything." He stayed where he was, but I could see he was assessing Outlaw's injuries. "The club doc is a good one. Wouldn't hurt to let him check you out. Attila has his crew under control, and no one will even think of hurting Elena. Your wife is safe."

"Please let him look at you," I said. "I'll worry about you all night if you don't."

Outlaw gave me a half-smile. "Fine. He can come check me over."

"There's one more thing. One of the Raptors is outside. Rebel is a silversmith and wants to talk to the two of you about wedding rings," Badger said.

Outlaw seemed conflicted, but I told Badger to let the guy in. It wouldn't hurt just to hear what he had to say. The guy who came in was carrying a wooden box. He barely stepped inside the bedroom before stopping. His gaze was on Outlaw and he never once looked my way.

"My name's Rebel, and to help make amends for the dumbassery of my brothers, I brought some rings for your wife to check out."

Outlaw snorted. "Dumbassery?"

Rebel shrugged. "Seemed like the best way to describe it. In Truth's defense, once we received the files about Bastard and the scheme he was running, we did some digging. Turns out a girl Truth had been seeing hadn't just left him like he'd thought. She'd been taken and put to work in one of Bastard's brothels. She couldn't handle it and killed herself."

My heart hurt for him, and that poor woman, but it didn't excuse his behavior. I'd told him the truth, then he'd forced me into some sort of interrogation room and cuffed me to a table. I still didn't know what he'd planned to do to me.

"I don't know if anything I have is your wife's size, but when I'm not filling custom orders, I tend to tinker a bit and make random things. May I show the two of you some of the rings in this case?" he asked.

Outlaw gave a nod and Rebel came farther into the room. He set the box on the bed next to Outlaw and lifted the lid. The inside was lined in velvet and the rings were truly breathtaking, but there was one in particular that held Outlaw's attention. I watched as he reached into the box and lifted out the silver band that looked like it was made of angel wings. The detail was incredible and I could see every feather.

I held my hand out to him and he slipped the ring onto my finger. It was a perfect fit, as if it had been made for me. He held my hand and rubbed his thumb over the band. "Angel wings for my angel."

"If you'll let me measure your finger, I'd be honored to custom make a wedding band for you," Rebel said. "I can ship it to your house when it's done."

I could tell he was about to say no, so I gave him puppy eyes in hopes he'd agree. I got another of those half-smiles, and then he told Rebel to go ahead. The guy measured Outlaw's finger, made a note of the size, then packed up his stuff and left. Badger followed him out, leaving me alone with Outlaw. I hoped the doctor wouldn't be long. The bruising was darkening so fast that I was worried he might have broken bones.

I lifted one of his hands and kissed his fingers. I wished I could take his pain away. He audibly swallowed and I could have sworn I saw his eyes tear up as he tugged me closer. Outlaw wrapped his arms around my waist, just holding on. He pressed his head against my chest and I ran my fingers through his hair.

"Thank you for agreeing to the ring," I said. "And I love mine."

"Anything for you, angel. I'd pull the moon from the sky if it was what you wanted."

I rested my cheek against the top of his head. "I think I'm falling for you, and it's so fast that I'm scared. You just keep saying and doing all the right things, and I'm afraid I'll wake up tomorrow and it will have all been a dream."

He laughed. "I'm no dream, angel. If anything, I'm a nightmare. But I'm real, I'm here, and I'm yours, just like you're mine."

"Good because I don't want anyone else. I think you've ruined me for all other men."

He kissed my collarbone. "That's the plan."

We stayed like that, with him holding me, and me playing with his hair until the doctor arrived. Thankfully the news wasn't as horrible as I'd feared, but he did advise Outlaw to refrain from more fights and said to take it easy a day or two. After leaving some painkillers, the doc left and Badger made himself scarce. It was just the two of us, and in that moment, I realized that there was no one I'd rather face the future with than him. Maybe I wasn't just falling for Outlaw. Maybe I'd already fallen.

Chapter Twelve

Outlaw

My club decided I'd helped enough, but I wasn't so sure. It had been two days and the Raptors and my brothers weren't getting results. There was one last card that I could play, if I dared. On a trip through Texas about two decades ago, I'd run into a guy at a rodeo. Like, literally ran into him, and we'd started chatting. Last I'd heard, he was a cop in this area. As much as I knew the Raptors didn't want the law involved, I knew putting a bug in the right ear could be beneficial.

While Elena had slept last night, I'd done a little digging and found Carson's number. It wasn't like he'd been hiding since it was listed in the damn directory for Bryson Corners. I just hadn't called him yet. Something told me it would be a good move, but I didn't want to piss off Attila, or Slash for that matter. They said they had this shit handled, but I had this gut feeling it was all going sideways if I didn't reach out to Carson.

"You've been fiddling with your phone for twenty minutes," Elena said. "Whoever you're going to call, just do it already."

"Not that simple, angel. It could land me a ton of trouble. The club too."

She sat next to me and placed her hand on my arm. "Noah, if you think whoever this person is can help, then call them. If you're wrong, then just give the guys a heads-up that you fucked up and trouble is coming, but I don't think you'd ask for help if you weren't sure you'd get it."

She was right. I was about ninety percent certain that Carson would want to help. Mostly because he was a good guy and believed in doing the right thing. Back then he'd been riding the circuit, but now he was a cop. From the commendations I'd found for him on the Bryson Corners PD website, it seemed he was doing a good job of protecting this town. He had to know about the shit Shepherd and Bastard were doing, even if he didn't know who was behind it.

I dialed his number and waited for him to answer. He picked up after a few rings.

"Office Benson, do you remember a guy named Outlaw from a really fucking long time ago?" I asked.

"You mean the out-of-place biker at the rodeo?" I could hear the smile in his voice. "Why the hell are you callin' me after all these years?"

"I'm in Bryson Corners, and there's trouble brewing in your little town. Thought you'd want to know about it." I cracked my neck. "Look, some of my crew is here at the Savage Raptors' compound. It's too much to discuss over the phone. Can we meet somewhere?"

It was quiet, then I heard him sigh. "Yeah. If you swear this shit won't touch my family, you can meet me at the house. Just don't be scarin' my wife and kids."

"Text me the address. Mind if I bring my wife with me?"

"Go ahead. Peaches would like the company."

I hung up and flexed my aching hands. "Think you can get ready pretty quick? We're going to Officer Benson's house. He's got a wife and kids there, so you can talk to her if you don't want to hear all the shit I need to tell him. It's nothing you don't already know."

"Just give me ten minutes and I'll be ready." She kissed my cheek, then walked out.

I was as dressed as I was getting. I'd take my cut with me, but I'd leave it in the truck. There were people who saw a club's colors and panicked a bit. Didn't want that happening. Back home, everyone was aware of the club and either gave us their support or a wide berth. I didn't know shit about Bryson Corners, though. Even though they had a custom bike shop, it didn't mean they liked non-AMA sanctioned clubs in their town. The Savage Raptors lived here, but I didn't want to go borrowing trouble when it wasn't necessary.

Elena came back in a pair of jeans and a modest shirt. It hugged her curves, but the neckline wasn't overly low. I'd noticed that even what she considered her sexy clothes tended to be on the more conservative side. Probably her upbringing with the reverend and his wife. Didn't matter to me what she wore, as long as she was comfortable and hadn't chosen the outfit because she thought it was what I wanted her to wear. I could be a controlling asshole at times, but I tried to save that for the bedroom.

"Come on, beautiful. We'll take the truck. If anyone asks, we're just going out to meet up with some friends in the area," I said.

"I doubt they'll ask me anyway."

She wasn't wrong. I'd heard about the sass she'd given the Raptors while I was in Church with their officers. It might have brought some heat down on us, especially me, if Truth hadn't fucked up and lost his shit so spectacularly. By running off to interrogate my wife, he'd pretty much given Elena a free pass. I didn't see Attila or anyone else saying a damn word if she opened her mouth again.

In fact, one of the Prospects had dropped off some papers last night. To make amends for what Elena had suffered, and my own wounds, which my ego was honestly bruised worse than the rest of me, Attila had not only punished Truth, but he was offering me a hundred grand in reparations. I wasn't going to say no since we could use that money as a nest egg. Now that I had a wife, and hoped to have at least one kid someday, it would be smart to start saving.

I helped her into the truck, then got in on the driver's side. When I reached the front gate, they waved us through and didn't even stop us to ask where we were going. I couldn't decide if I was insulted that they saw me as such a weak link, or glad they didn't give a shit where I went. The fact I wasn't needed was going to make this a lot easier.

Elena pulled up the address from the text Carson had sent and got directions. The neighborhood was cute with modest homes. A lot were on the smaller side, but well-maintained. Carson's house had toys in the front yard and a bicycle turned over sideways in the driveway. I stopped on the street along the curb, and hoped this wasn't an area that ticketed anyone parked on the street. I hadn't seen another car in this area that wasn't being driven or in a driveway.

I hadn't even cleared the truck before Carson stepped out. He'd aged since I'd last seen him, but then so had I. He gave me a smile as he came closer, his gaze scanning me from head to toe, probably determining if I was a threat to his family. I'd left my gun in the truck since he said he had kids. I hadn't wanted to upset his wife. While he was a cop, and I knew he was armed, he likely kept his weapon locked up when he was off-duty. Unless he had to go back to work, but that didn't seem likely since I didn't see a badge on his belt.

"Long time no see," he said, slapping me on the back. "Damn. Is it me or did ya get uglier?"

I flipped him off, but he just laughed. Elena got out of the truck and gave him a little wave.

"I'm Elena, his wife."

"Nice to meet ya. I'm Carson and my wife Peaches is inside. So are the kids, so watch where ya step. They have crap everywhere."

We followed him inside, where he made the introductions to his wife and three kids. Elena went off with Peaches and Carson led me out back. They had a nice deck with a table and chairs. He already had two cold bottles of beer set out, and I noticed he'd left the top on mine.

"Figured ya might be like me and not trust anyone," Carson said, taking a sip of his drink. "Bottle opener's attached to the house."

I glanced back at the house and saw a metal opening screwed into the side of the house, like those old-fashioned ones they used to have when sodas all came in glass bottles. I popped the top off my beer, then settled back into my chair.

"Trouble come with ya, or did ya follow it?" he asked.

"Followed it. The Savage Raptors have a rat that's causing some problems, but it's the kind that might be affecting your town. The kind that causes an increase in illegal guns and drugs, or missing women around town."

He nodded. "Yep. Seen a lot of that for a while now. Figured it was tied to that club, but ain't been able to prove it."

"It's not the club. Savage Raptors have some legit businesses around town. But one of their men is a rat and is dealing this shit on the side, along with a guy who got his colors stripped about fifteen years ago. We think Elena's foster dad is on it, and from a recent incident at our clubhouse, possibly some of the congregation of his church."

Carson held up a hand. "What the hell? A preacher doin' this shit?"

"So it seems. I'd thought maybe Bastard was holding something over the reverend, but once the wife was shot and dumped, it became apparent that wasn't the case. The good reverend seemed a little too comfortable with Bastard. The wife, though, she was scared."

Carson whistled. "What do ya want me to do? Ya know I can't take this shit to my chief unless you want cops all over this. I'm thinkin' that ain't why ya came to me, so what am I supposed to do?"

I'd thought about this, and I hoped I was making the right call. There was a chance my club was going to have a fucking fit and I'd be in a world of trouble when we got home. But if I was right and this was just the distraction needed, then it might help the Raptors and my brothers get a handle on the problem and find both Bastard and Shepherd before it was too late. And where those two were, the reverend was probably nearby.

"If I give you some locations of brothels that Shepherd was running with funding from Bastard and Reverend Martin Tolbert, could your department raid those facilities and save the women? None of them are there voluntarily."

He leaned back. "And just maybe flush out the rats for the Savage Raptors?"

"Yeah. That's my hope. Look, there's no way the Raptors are going to let you have Bastard or Shepherd. They'll be handled in a way that you don't want to know about. Trust me on that. But if the police were to get an anonymous tip about women forced into prostitution not just in your town, but in this county and several others, that might shine a favorable light on law enforcement for a while."

He gave a bark of laughter. "Yep and these are sure enough dark times when it comes to wearin' a badge. All right. Ya get me those addresses and I'll see what I can do."

I'd come prepared, expecting him to offer to help. Reaching into my pocket, I withdrew a folded piece of paper. I'd written out the locations first thing this morning when I'd toyed with the idea of calling Carson. I seriously hoped this didn't backfire, but I needed a distraction to help out the Raptors and my brothers, and those women needed help. I couldn't think of a better solution.

Elena stepped outside with a little girl in her arms. The kid was cute with light mocha skin and blonde curly hair. The bright blue eyes told me she'd be a knockout when she was older. Right now, she was just all chubby and adorable. And damn but did my woman look good holding a kid.

"I see my Charlie girl found ya," Carson said, grinning and holding out a hand to the little girl. She latched onto her daddy's hand and babbled at him.

"She's so sweet," Elena said. "Peaches sent me out to see if the two of you wanted anything. She said she'd made some Rotel dip and if you wanted any, you needed to speak up now or Daisy would eat it all."

Carson snorted. "True enough. My little Daisy does love her some chips and dip. How 'bout it? The two of ya stayin' for a bit?"

"We can hang out a while," I said.

"Good." He flashed a grin at me. "Least this ways I'll know ya ain't out there causin' trouble. I'll get that info to my chief, but I'm off duty for the rest of the day. We can have us a nice visit, and maybe that woman of yours can teach my Peaches a new recipe or two. God do I love her, but my stomach would like some variety."

"I heard that," Peaches yelled from inside. The cute blonde was heavily pregnant and glaring at her husband as she stepped outside. "Carson Benson, don't you go telling these nice people that I don't cook good enough. You have no complaints if your pants are any indication, and don't even try to say you need more room for anything other than your waist."

He winced. "Damn, woman. That was harsh."

Elena laughed and paused before following Peaches back into the house. "You've been married long enough to have three kids with another on the way and you still haven't learned not to piss off a pregnant lady?"

"I adopted Daisy," he admitted. "But those others… Yep, that woman of mine is hell on wheels when she's expectin'."

"Angel, would you bring us some chips and Rotel?" I asked Elena. "Daisy sounds fierce. Not sure I want to fight her for some later."

She smiled and headed inside, but I knew she'd bring something out soon. It was quiet in Carson's neighborhood. Almost too quiet. If his kids were home, where were all the others? Shouldn't they be out playing? Even his school-aged kids were home, so I'd assumed that classes weren't in session right now. Unless they homeschooled, which was always a possibility. I didn't see how that woman managed it while pregnant. She had her hands full.

"Ya got a good one," he said, motioning toward the house. "Seems sweet."

"She is. I'm lucky to have her," I said.

"Ya gonna be okay here for a sec? I'll go call the chief and tell him about that tip I got."

I waved him off and took another swallow of my beer. If this all went to shit, at least I'd done something to try and help. It was better than sitting at the Raptors' compound and not doing a damn thing. They may not see it that way since I involved the police, but it was too late to second-guess myself now. I'd just have to ride this out and hope everything went well.

Elena and I spent the next three hours visiting with Carson and his family. She seemed to get along really well with Peaches, and their kids were all just too damn cute. It was partway through the strawberry shortcake that Peaches had made when Carson's phone went off. He excused himself only to come back several minutes later and give me a nod. It seemed the issue had been handled and the brothels were raided. I didn't know what that meant for the Raptors or my brothers, but I shot off a quick text to Dingo.

Created a diversion. Might flush out Bastard and Shepherd.

He didn't respond for a while and I started to worry. Then my phone chimed with an incoming message. *Fucking brilliant. Got Shepherd and closing in on Bastard.*

I smiled, thankful that it seemed to have worked out. I only hoped that Slash and Attila felt the same way. Pissing either of them off wasn't in my best interest, especially Attila since I was on his turf right now. Until all the players in the game were apprehended, I decided the safest place I could keep my woman was at a cop's house, so we settled in for the rest of the day, and I hoped that when the dust settled, all my brothers would still be standing. I also looked forward to heading home. I'd had my fill of Oklahoma for the time being, but now that Elena and Peaches had hit it off, I had a feeling we'd be making another trip in the future.

Chapter Thirteen

Elena

Outlaw was smart, but he wasn't very sneaky. When we'd stayed to visit with Peaches and Carson for so long, I'd known that he was waiting out the mess with Bastard and my foster father. What I hadn't counted on was Badger showing up to tell us it was time to go. Carson hadn't batted an eye at having a biker other than Outlaw on his doorstep, but I'd noticed he'd kept his kids and wife in the house. I liked that he was so protective of them. He seemed like a good man, and I knew that Peaches adored him. It was in her eyes when she looked at him, and the way she spoke about him.

I wondered if I looked at Outlaw that way. Even though we hadn't been together for very long, he already meant so much to me. I may not have planned to stop in Blackwood Falls, but it seemed that someone had been guiding me that day. My foster mother would have said it was God, but after all I'd seen and heard about since I ran away, I wasn't sure if I still believed in God. Then again, evil hadn't prevailed. Not only had Bastard been caught, but so had the reverend.

"I don't understand," I said. "How could they have kept that hidden from me?"

Beau was driving and Outlaw was in the backseat with me. He'd been holding my hand or touching me in some way ever since we'd left the Savage Raptors' compound. I didn't mind it, and even though there was an audience, I'd have been happy if he'd wanted to do more than just touch me. I ached for him, but since he'd been healing, I'd tried to keep my hands to myself.

"Don't look at me," Beau said. "No one tells me shit."

Outlaw snorted. "Because you're a punk-ass Prospect, and on probation at that. But to answer your question, angel, I'm not really sure. Maybe you didn't see it because you didn't want to, or perhaps it's because you didn't expect to find that sort of behavior at your church."

"But everyone was in on it?" I asked. "All the adults? Except my foster mom, right? She wasn't the most loving person, but I can't see her doing something like this."

He nodded. "That's what Slash said. Apparently the reverend started running off at the mouth, confessing all his sins and everyone else's too. It was Bastard who would marry the women and then make them disappear, but the ladies at the church helped lure them in. We found quite a few legit marriages between him and the women he'd sent to Shepherd, and according to the reverend, he pretended to perform marriage ceremonies for Bastard on many other occasions."

"Why?" I asked. "I just don't understand why."

"Money," Outlaw said. "It makes men do stupid shit. For what it's worth, your foster mom didn't know what was going on. He kept her in the dark. She honestly thought you were going to marry an upstanding man if she paired you with Garrison West. Doubt she ever knew he'd been part of the Savage Raptors, or that he went by Bastard for so long. The woman either followed her husband blindly, or she wasn't the brightest crayon in the box."

"I didn't love her, and I don't think she ever loved me, but I hate that she died. They murdered her! What's going to happen to them?"

"Didn't ask, and I won't. The Raptors will take care of Shepherd, the reverend, and Bastard. I can promise that none of them will ever be heard from again. They'll make the three of them vanish one way or another," he said.

It didn't really matter what happened to them, as long they couldn't hurt anyone else. But that still left the rest of the church congregation who had been in on it. It didn't seem right they wouldn't be punished. I must have been frowning because Outlaw rubbed his finger between my eyebrows.

"Everything will be fine, angel."

"I was just thinking of all the others involved."

He smiled. "The Savage Raptors will make sure they're rounded up. All the shit that Bastard and Shepherd were running was set up in a way that incriminated the club. Attila won't stand for that. He'll make sure every last person responsible pays the price."

I cuddled closer to him. "Is it bad that I want them all to disappear too?"

"No, honey. Just makes you human, and tells me you have a soft heart. You want to protect the innocent, and that's commendable. There are evil people in the world, and most of the time the only way to handle the problem permanently is to make them vanish. Some are resting in shallow graves, and others will never be discovered no matter how hard people look."

I yawned and closed my eyes. "How much longer until we're home?"

"About six hours," Beau said. "So if the two of you want to nap or whatever, I'm just going to stare out the windshield until I see the compound. Just pretend I'm not even here."

Even though I'd gotten hot thinking about being at the clubhouse, taken in front of everyone, I could tell that Outlaw hadn't been into it. He was too possessive, which I kind of liked. I wasn't going to ask him for something that made him uncomfortable. I didn't know if it was because of his scars and he didn't want to expose himself in front of everyone, or because he just didn't want to share me. Either way, I was fine with it. As long as I had him, I didn't need anyone or anything else.

He toyed with the ends of my hair while his other hand stroked my arm where I'd thrown it across his abdomen. I was content, like a happy cat dozing in the sun. It was crazy, all that had happened in the past few days. Even the last week for that matter. It had been about that long since I'd arrived at the Devil's Fury compound. The fact I was married to a guy I didn't really know wasn't something most people would ever understand, but for me it was like I'd finally come home. With Outlaw, I'd found the place where I belonged.

"If the women were going to stay at that other place, Devil's Boneyard or whatever, is that where we're going too?" I asked. It hadn't occurred to me until just then, but with the extensive repairs the compound probably needed, I wasn't sure if Outlaw would think it was safe for me to be there.

"The gate is already repaired and same for the two houses that caught part of the blast. It's going to be a little while before the clubhouse is back in order. Not sure what Grizzly will decide to do," Outlaw said. "Nothing wrong with our house, right?"

"No, it was fine."

"Then we'll go home. I may not be able to do much, but I'll help where I can. Even if I can't swing a hammer, I can at least supervise."

"Did you ever find out exactly what happened?" I asked. "I know Martha was threatening me and shooting at people, but I got there after the clubhouse had been destroyed."

Outlaw sighed. "The men she hired were muscle for hire, but they came prepared. Or so they thought. Tossed a homemade bomb through the window. Unfortunately, Martha hadn't informed them of how well-armed we were so most of them were killed. The few who lived were all too happy to talk."

I shook my head. It just baffled me how Martha could have done something like that. She'd always seemed so sweet, more like the type to bake you an apple pie than plan your death. It made me wonder if I'd ever truly known anyone in my life. I felt safer with Outlaw than I did with anyone else. As far as I knew, he hadn't lied to me. What little I did know about him, I'd be willing to bet if he'd lied it was to protect me. But those people, the ones I'd trusted and thought were good, they were lying to me as a way to use me.

Being around the Devil's Fury was removing the blinders I'd lived with for so long. I no longer just assumed that people were good, or were who they said they were. I'd seen too much ugliness, and heard about even more. It wasn't that I'd never watched the news or read about current events, it just hadn't seemed possible for that stuff to ever touch me. I knew now I'd been incredibly naïve, and I'd even go so far as to say stupid. I didn't know that it was necessarily a good thing that I would now assume that people I met weren't as they first appeared. On the one hand, I'd possibly be safer. On the other, I hated that there was so much evil in the world that it had come to that.

I knew that Outlaw didn't do things the legal way, and I knew he was capable of hurting people, but he also protected those weaker than him. The entire club seemed to have a soft spot for women in trouble, and from what little I'd heard from Meiling that extended to kids too. They looked all tough and badass, and I had no doubt they really were, but they also had a soft mushy center when it was needed. Despite the things they did or had done, they'd kept their souls and maintained a certain level of integrity. I could respect that. Even Badger and Blades who had both been to prison weren't stone-cold hardened criminals with no capability of expressing emotions. It was clear they loved their women, and Blades definitely loved his daughter.

"What are you thinking about?" Outlaw asked.

"Just how much my life has changed, and while a lot of it is for the better, it's kind of sad that there are so many bad people in the world. If we have kids, I'll be worried every time they're out of my sight."

"Trust me, angel, no one is getting near our kids. If they do, I'll find them and make sure they never hurt another person ever again."

I smiled, knowing he spoke the truth. It wouldn't surprise me at all if he ran a thorough background check on anyone our kids wanted to date when they were old enough. Assuming we ever had any. He'd said he might not be able to have a baby with me, but I looked forward to trying.

The rest of the trip was quiet and I dozed off and on, until I saw the compound come into view. I winced at the clubhouse, which was already in the process of being torn down. Outlaw was right and the two nearest houses were already repaired, but it looked like they were going to have to completely remove the clubhouse and start over. I didn't have any idea how much time something like that would take, but I knew it would mean they were hampered a bit when it came to their meetings, or Church as they called it. Not to mention the parties.

Beau took us straight home, and Outlaw helped me out of the truck. Beau put our bags inside the door, then started walking down the road. I glanced at Outlaw, but he wasn't paying attention.

"Why didn't Beau just take the truck?" I asked.

"The club had four vehicles. Out of those, only the truck we were using and an SUV survived. I'm afraid your car was also destroyed. They never got around to moving it. So for now, we get to use the truck while I find you a new vehicle, but I'm thinking you need a small SUV at the very least. I'd prefer something bulletproof, but I figured you'd balk at that one."

I folded my arms and stared at him. "Bulletproof? Really?"

He shrugged. "What can I say? I want to make sure my woman is safe."

"Fine. We can look at an SUV. I had insurance on the car although I'm not sure homemade bombs are covered."

Outlaw came closer and pulled me against his chest, kissing my forehead. "We'll get it handled. We can always use part of what Attila gave us. I'd planned to use it as a nest egg, but I'm sure we can find you a new or close-to-new SUV for around twenty grand, maybe less. Just depends on how loaded you want it and how big."

"Just need enough room for the two of us and maybe a baby at some point. Something smaller is fine."

He kissed me and while it started out sweet and slow, it wasn't long before he was backing me down the hall toward the bedroom. I heard the door slam shut, but I didn't much care right then. His hands felt like they were everywhere, and he soon had both of us naked.

"Been too fucking long, angel. I know why you kept your distance, but I'm not waiting another second."

"Good. I didn't want you to."

He tackled me and we both tumbled to the bed. I giggled as he rubbed his beard against my breasts, then he took my nipple between his teeth and I almost begged him for more. I slid my fingers through his hair and wrapped my legs around him. That wicked tongue of his! He flicked it against the hardened tip before sucking hard and slow.

"Noah!"

"That's right, angel. Let me hear how much you love what I do to you."

"Don't stop." I pressed my hips closer to him. "I need you."

He teased the other side before sliding farther down my body. He broke the hold I had on him and shoved my thighs wide, settling between them. At the first stroke of his fingers along my slit, I moaned and parted my legs even more. Then he held me open and went after my clit with his tongue, flicking, circling, and driving me crazy. I squirmed and bucked, wanting more yet also wanting to pull away from the intense sensation. He banded an arm across my waist, holding me in place as he worked my pussy, not relenting until I'd come twice.

He placed a kiss on my inner thigh before covering my body with his. I felt his cock brush against me, and then he thrust hard and deep. I cried out, my eyes closing. He didn't even give me a second to adjust, just drove into me again and again. I clung to him, holding on, as the bed slammed into the wall with every thrust.

"Noah! Oh, God. More. Harder!"

He growled and gave me what I wanted. Our bodies slapped together and sweat coated our skin. I came so hard I felt my release soak the bed under me. It felt like I was flying. I screamed so loud and long my throat was sore. He grunted as he pounded into me, the warmth of his cum filling me up. I felt his cock jerk inside me and wished we could stay like this a while. I liked feeling this way, like we were joined in both body and soul. "I love you, angel."

His intense gaze nearly took my breath away, and so did his words. "You love me?"

"Yeah, I love you, angel. I know it's too soon, and maybe it's crazy that I feel this way already, but I think I knew from the moment you pulled out your book in the clubhouse that you were meant to be mine. I don't ever want to imagine my life without you."

I reached up and stroked his cheek, then ran my fingers through his beard. "I love you too, Noah. So very much."

He kissed me soft and slow, but I felt other parts of him getting hard again. He didn't even break the kiss before he started thrusting. It seemed that we were starting Operation Baby Making right now, and I was perfectly fine with that. The thought of a little Outlaw running around filled me with warmth and happiness.

He kept me in bed for at least three hours, until we both needed a break. My stomach was growling and I seriously needed a drink. I sat at the table while he made pancakes and bacon, even though I'd offered to cook. Thanks to my foster mother, I knew my way around a kitchen, even if my skills were a bit limited. I couldn't make anything fancy, but a good home-cooked southern-style meal wasn't a problem. He'd probably get fat with all the fried stuff I knew how to cook.

I eyed his body, appreciating not only his ink, but the strength on full display since he'd only pulled on his underwear. He was definitely a sexy sight. I propped my chin on my fist and admired the view. His back and ass flexed as he shifted, flipping the pancakes, then moving them over to a plate. It made me wonder if I could talk him into cooking like this at least once or twice a week, just so I could admire him.

"Stop staring at my ass unless you want me to bend you over the table," he said.

"You're not even looking at me. Why do you think I'm staring at your... butt?"

He snickered. "You can say ass, angel. Lightning won't strike you dead. As to the other, I can feel you watching me."

"Maybe I just like what I see."

He flashed me a grin over his shoulder. "That a fact? Guess we'd better eat, then, so you can see a more unencumbered view because I'm not cooking with my dick out. That's one place I never want to feel a grease burn."

Yeah, I definitely didn't want that part of him burned either. I was a little too fond of it, and the magical way it made me feel when he was inside me. I tried to stop staring while he finished cooking, then we ate. He grinned when he saw how fast I was shoveling the food into my mouth.

"Easy there, angel. Plenty of time. I told Grizzly I'm on my honeymoon effective today until next week. Unless an emergency crops up, I'm all yours, and we'll be undisturbed."

He'd no sooner said that than someone knocked on the front door. He scowled and got up to go answer it. I hoped whoever was there didn't mind seeing him in his underwear, but that did answer the question about whether or not he didn't want his club to see his scars. He must not have liked the idea of sharing me or letting anyone else see me naked.

When he came back to the kitchen, there was a large gift bag in his hand and he had a comical expression on his face. "It seems the guys got us a gift."

"Like a wedding present?" I asked.

"Uh. Sort of." He turned the bag over and the contents spilled across the table. I saw three different types of vibrators, two types of lubricant, an anal plug, and other things that made me blush. "It seems they wanted to guarantee you'd have a good honeymoon."

"Well, that was... nice of them?" I glanced at him and couldn't hold back my laughter. "The look on your face right now is priceless."

"They even included two packs of batteries. Jesus. It's like they think I can't please you on my own."

That sobered me quickly. "Noah, I think the fact we need to change the sheets because I came so hard is testimony enough to show you don't need any help in the bedroom. But I wouldn't mind trying out some of this stuff. I've never used toys before."

"I kind of figured that since you were a virgin and hadn't ever come before." He picked up one of the packages and ripped it open. After washing the toy off and inserting batteries, he shoved everything to the edge of the table and patted the surface. "Come up here."

I swallowed hard and got up, sitting on the edge of the table. He pushed my legs apart and I leaned back, bracing myself on my elbows. Outlaw teased me with his fingers first.

"Still wet enough I don't think the lube will be needed." He grinned, then eased the toy inside me. It was small and slightly curved, and had a weirdly textured part that settled right over my clit. When he turned it on, I felt my eyes go wide and my lips parted. Before I could even draw a breath, I was coming. "Well, damn. I think I like this one. Come for me again, angel."

And I did. He was relentless, making me come so many times my eyes started to cross and I didn't think I could handle one more orgasm. When he slipped the toy from my body, I nearly collapsed. My legs and arms felt like jelly. Outlaw flipped me over and smacked my ass, making me jerk and squeak in surprise. But it was the cool liquid I felt splashing between my cheeks that had me tensing.

"Easy, angel. I want to see if you like this."

Whatever he'd used, it started to tingle and I smelled mint in the air. He worked me with his finger first, stretching me, then he prepped another toy, a slim but longer vibrator. My heart was hammering in my chest when I realized where he intended to put it. He slid the toy in my ass, easing it in and out a few times, then I felt his cock pushing inside my pussy.

I gasped and my back arched at how full I felt. "Oh, God. Noah, it feels so good."

"It's about to feel better." He turned on the vibrator and started taking me hard and fast. I came. Not once. Not twice. But multiple times. It was like my orgasms just rolled one into the other. I couldn't even catch my breath. When he came inside me, he didn't even slow, just kept going. "Going to fuck you until we both can't stand."

By the time he'd come again, I tingled from head to toe and I didn't think my legs, or any other part of me, worked anymore. He tossed the toy aside and lifted me into his arms, carrying me to our bathroom. I leaned against the counter as he filled the tub, then we got in together. Lounging against his chest, he just held me as we soaked in the hot water.

"Think we need to rest a bit, and probably eat again, but we are going to try every single item in that bag before this honeymoon is over," he said. "I think you came so hard that last time you clenched down so tight I thought you'd break my dick."

I laughed. I couldn't help it. The thought of my pussy being capable of something like that... "That's a mental image that I may never get rid of."

He nipped my shoulder. "Impudent wench. Good thing I love you so much."

I reached behind me and tugged on his beard. "And I love you just as much. Don't ever change, Noah. I love the serious side of you, the funny side, the passionate side... there isn't a single thing about you I don't love."

He tightened his hold on me and his voice became gruffer. "Good because I love everything about you too, and I'm never letting you go. You're mine. Forever."

I liked that. Forever. And even that didn't seem long enough.

Epilogue

Outlaw -- Three Months Later

The clubhouse was rebuilt and back in business. I really didn't want to be here. Elena was making a new recipe she'd found for chicken tacos and some sort of Mexican rice casserole. I'd much rather be home with her than drinking a beer with a bunch of naked women running around. None of them compared to my woman. Grizzly had insisted that everyone show up for at least a half hour so we were all seen. It was our first official night letting the club girls back in and having a full-fledged party. Those of us who wouldn't be partaking of the tits and ass on display had agreed to take the first half hour, then we were bailing, but it was the longest fucking thirty minutes of my life.

"Anyone else rather be home with their wife?" Dingo asked from where he was sprawled in the seat across from me.

"Yep. But orders are orders," I said.

"Fuck orders," said Blades. "Let Griz piss and moan, or fine me. I don't give a rat's ass. China is waiting and I'm out of here."

The large man stood and stomped out of the clubhouse, not stopping to say a word to anyone. Badger waited all of ten seconds before he stood too and left. I figured he had a better shot of not getting chewed out since his woman was the daughter of the Pres. We'd already realized he got certain perks if it kept Adalia happy, and honestly, I didn't care. The two of them had been through hell and deserved whatever happiness they could find.

"And now it's just us," Dingo said, glancing around. "And only a handful of single brothers and some Prospects."

"It's early yet. You know this place won't be filled to the rafters for another hour or two. The later it gets the wilder things will be."

"True enough."

A blonde with hair down to her ass ran her nails down my arm. "You want some company?"

"Nope."

She pouted and didn't take the hint, settling across my lap. I snarled at her, then shoved her ass to the floor. Stupid bitch still didn't get it and tried to reach for my belt.

"I said no. Get the fuck off me," I said.

"I can make you feel good."

I heard a snort and lifted my gaze to find my woman staring at the blonde with contempt. At least she wasn't giving me that look. I decided to just sit back and see what she'd do. If she wanted to claim her territory, I'd let her. Hell, I'd love every second of it.

"Does he even look remotely hard to you? He said he's not interested and if that isn't a big enough clue, let me spell it out for you." Elena reached down, grabbed a handful of the woman's hair, which promptly came off in my wife's hand. "Are you kidding me? Even your hair isn't real?"

I bit my lip so I wouldn't fucking laugh, but Dingo wasn't bothering to hold back. The loud guffaws that escaped him drew some attention from the others. But Elena wasn't nearly done with the woman on the floor. She grabbed another handful of hair, this time yanking to make sure it was attached, then dragged her away from me. I watched in amusement as she kicked the woman on the right ass cheek, leaving a shoe print.

"Take your skank ass elsewhere and leave my husband alone," Elena said. "You want to spread your legs or suck a dick, you find one that isn't claimed." A redhead started heading for Dingo, but Elena bared her teeth at the woman. "That one isn't available either. His woman is pregnant and can't kick your ass right now, but I sure the hell will do it for her."

I reached for my wife and tugged her down onto my lap. My dick took instant notice and started getting hard, which made her angry expression melt and a smile curved her lips. She wiggled a little and I smacked her on the hip. "Behave."

She pointed at the two women who were glaring at her. "Was I supposed to just stand there and do nothing about those two?"

"No, angel. Trust me, I'm happy you claimed me, and I'm sure Meiling will be thrilled you chased that woman off from her man. In fact, why don't I take you home and show you just how much I liked the show?"

She leaned closer. "Thought you had to stay for a while? Grizzly's orders and all that."

"I'm supposed to. Don't feel like it."

"We could go home and celebrate. Seeing as how you're up for it and all." She sank her teeth into her bottom lip, then leaned in closer, her breath a whisper against my ear. "You can give me an encore on how this baby was made."

It took a moment before her words sank in and I stared at her blankly. She looked highly amused at my predicament, but I caught on, eventually. "Baby?"

Elena nodded and took my hand, placing it over her belly. She spoke softly into my ear so no one else would hear. "Seems your swimmers work just fine,

Noah. Took four pregnancy tests and they all say the same thing. You're going to be a daddy."

I let out a loud *whoop* and stood with her in my arms. "You guys hear that? I'm going to be a daddy!"

My brothers cheered, but I didn't care right then. I kissed Elena hard and deep, then carried her out of the clubhouse. A hand slapped my back and I broke from her to look at Dingo. He gave me a nod, then walked off to his bike. I'd ridden mine here too, but no fucking way I was taking it home right now. I got into the SUV I'd recently bought for Elena, buckled her in, then made sure I pushed the driver's seat back before I got in. I'd banged my knees enough times to learn my woman had short legs.

We were halfway home when her stomach growled so loud that I burst out laughing. She narrowed her gaze at me, but her cheeks were pink. I knew that no matter how turned on I was, especially now that I knew she was pregnant, I'd make sure we ate the dinner she'd prepared before we did anything else. I had a kid to think about now, something I'd thought I'd never have. There was a tightness in my chest and throat as I fought not to cry like a damn baby, but this had to be the happiest I'd ever felt.

I pulled into the driveway and before Elena could get out of the car, I reached for her, pulling her into a hug. "Love you, angel. You've made me so fucking happy."

"I love you too, Noah. You're not the only who's happy. I want this baby just as much as you do, and if it's our only one, I'm okay with that. We'll spoil them rotten."

I leaned back and touched her belly again, trying to imagine her heavily pregnant. She was already the most beautiful woman I'd ever seen, but knowing she carried my child, it made her shine even more brightly.

"Come on. I'm hungry and so is your kid," Elena said. "Then you can make me come. Lots of times."

I chuckled and kissed her cheek. "Greedy wench. You know I like to watch you come. I'll make you scream my name all night long if you want, and into the morning."

She stared at me a moment, her gaze locked on mine. "Thank you for saving me, for keeping me. You've shown me what it means to love someone and be loved. I know you think you've got me locked up, but I have more freedom with you than I ever have before. You're the best man I've ever met, Noah, and you're mine. I can hardly believe it sometimes. I will love you until my last breath, and even beyond the grave."

I leaned in and brushed my lips across hers. "Love you, angel. Always."

I'd thought I was broken, but I'd only needed the right woman to put the pieces together. She didn't see scars or darkness when she looked at me. I wanted to be her knight in shining armor, be the one to hold her every night, love her until the day I died, and make her every dream come true. And because the Fates had placed her in my path, that's exactly what I'd do for the rest of my life.

She was mine. I was hers. And together I knew we'd be unstoppable.

The Bad Boys Multiverse

Thank you so much for purchasing Dingo/Outlaw Duet! If Outlaw's name seems familiar and you just couldn't quite place him, you saw quite a bit of him in Wire's book (Dixie Reapers MC). I left him in a bit of a rough spot after that one, so he definitely deserved a happily-ever-after. If you're curious about Carson Benson and his wife, Peaches, you can read more about him and his siblings in the Bryson Corners Box Set by Harley Wylde and Paige Warren.

If you're a new Harley Wylde reader, you'll find my series tend to have crossovers. You met Wire and Lavender from the Dixie Reapers, and the Devil's Boneyard were also mentioned. You can find links to their stories on Harley's page at Changeling Press. I also post sneak peeks, FAQ's, and other tidbits over on my website.

Harley Wylde

Harley Wylde is the International Bestselling Author of the Dixie Reapers MC, Devil's Boneyard MC, and Hades Abyss MC series.

When Harley's writing, her motto is the hotter the better -- off-the-charts sex, commanding men, and the women who can't deny them. If you want men who talk dirty, are sexy as hell, and take what they want, then you've come to the right place. She doesn't shy away from the dangers and nastiness in the world, bringing those realities to the pages of her books, but always gives her characters a happily-ever-after and makes sure the bad guys get what they deserve.

The times Harley isn't writing, she's thinking up naughty things to do to her husband, drinking copious amounts of Starbucks, and reading. She loves to read and devours a book a day, sometimes more. She's also fond of TV shows and movies from the 1980s, as well as paranormal shows from the 1990s to today, even though she'd much rather be reading or writing.

Harley at Changeling: changelingpress.com/harley-wylde-a-196

Changeling Press E-Books

More Sci-Fi, Fantasy, Paranormal, and BDSM adventures available in e-book format for immediate download at ChangelingPress.com -- Werewolves, Vampires, Dragons, Shapeshifters and more -- Erotic Tales from the edge of your imagination.

What are E-Books?

E-books, or electronic books, are books designed to be read in digital format -- on your desktop or laptop computer, notebook, tablet, Smart Phone, or any electronic e-book reader.

Where can I get Changeling Press E-Books?

Changeling Press e-books are available at ChangelingPress.com, Amazon, Apple Books, Barnes & Noble, and Kobo/Walmart.

ChangelingPress.com